To Nigel Crump,

Thank you for the years of friendship, support, kindness and collaboration.

I hope that you enjoy the story and are stimulated by the ideas expressed by the characters.

Warmest wishes,

[signature]

Glasgow, November 2007

By the same author

NEXT IN THE SERIES

The Joseph Secret (October 2007)

Einstein's Violin (in preparation)

NON-FICTION

Carl Nielsen (Phaidon Press, 1997)

MOONLIT MESSIAH

Jack Lawson

FIRST IMPRESSIONS

Moonlit Messiah

First Published Edition 2007

ISBN 978-0-9556372-0-9

www.firstimpressionspublishing.co.uk

First Impressions Publishing Ltd.,
Suite 113, 98 Woodlands Road,
Glasgow G3 6HB

Typeset in Apollo by Palimpsest Book Production Limited,
Grangemouth, Stirlingshire

Printed and bound in Great Britain by Antony Rowe Ltd.,
Chippenham, Wiltshire

The publisher's policy is to use papers which are renewable and recyclable.

For my dad, who first took me to the Holy Land

***

The companion of the saviour was Mary Magdalene.
The Lord loved her more than all the disciples
and used to kiss her on the mouth often.
The rest of the disciples said to Him,
'Why do you love her more than all of us?'

—The Gospel of Philip, reconstructed and translated from the Codex

***

A man who walks into a whore-house
seeks in his heart the love of God.
—St Augustine

Author's Note

This is the novel that disturbed a number of mainstream publishers in 1998. It was the first of its type and the prototype of a successful new genre. Portraying the survival of the Davidic bloodline in a young Frenchwoman, it was the earliest thriller to fictionalise *The Holy Blood and The Holy Grail.*

Five years later there was a high demand for this type of book from publishers but I was inclined to distance myself from the inevitable association with *The Da Vinci Code.* Having now decided to début 'my problem child' I only ask, do not diminish *Moonlit Messiah* by applying any labels or preconceptions. The only way to judge a book is to read it yourself and grasp it in full. Inevitably some of its impact is lost but do not accuse me of formula-writing. *I invented the formula* and a driver cannot jump onto his own bandwagon.

I gratefully acknowledge *The Holy Blood and The Holy Grail* by Baigent, Leigh, and Lincoln – although I do not accept it all.

Acknowledgements

The writer and book critic David V. Barrett read my manuscript at two stages. In him I found a committee of expertise in secret societies, modern religious cults, and in the craft of storytelling.

I would like to thank:

The BBC, for allowing my survey of Bush House in London.
The Israel Museum in Jerusalem for access to the scrolls from The Dead Sea.
Michael P. Germano, author of *The First Christians,* for showing me how to reconstruct the Essenes' solar calendar.

For Song lyrics:
George Harrison, *Beware of Darkness*, 1970 (Harrisongs).
John Lennon, *Imagine*, 1971 (Lenono Music).
By the Bridge at Mirabel, set to music by Joseph Canteloube in *Songs of the Auvergne*.

For Literary quotations:
Eyes that last I saw in tears by T.S. Eliot (Collected Poems, Faber & Faber, 1936, 1963).
God's Secret Agent by Timothy Leary (The League for Spiritual Discovery, Inc., 1968).
The Path of the Inner Life by Venerable Sangharakshita (FWBO Publications, London, 1975).

The Jewish War by Flavius Josephus, trans. G.A. Williamson (Penguin Books, 1959).

For Scriptures in English Translations:

The Jerusalem Bible (DLT, 1966) revised and translated from *La Bible de Jérusalem* edited by Pére Roland de Vaux O.P. (Editions du Cerf, 1961).

The Dead Sea Scrolls in English by Geza Vermes (Penguin, 1962, 4th ed., 1995).

The Message of the Scrolls by Yigael Yadin (Grosset, NY, USA, 1957).

The Gospel of Philip in *The Gnostic Scriptures* translated by B. Layton (SCM Press, 1987).

The Gospel of Thomas, first edition translated by Guillaumont, Puech, Quispel et al. (E.J. Brill/Collins, 1959).

Jack Lawson
July 2007

BOOK ONE

Sarah Kelly

MM

GIRL (12) WALKS ON WATER

LOCH NESS 'A MAGIC POOL IN WHICH A CHILD CAN PADDLE AND AN ELEPHANT CAN SWIM'

- EXCLUSIVE PICTURE SCOOP -

AT FORT AUGUSTUS YESTERDAY AT NOON (Wednesday) a fearless 12-year-old, supervised by Indian Yogi S. Yamakarsi, demonstrated levitation of the body. Substantiating one of the miracles of Christianity, Sarah Kelly walked on water unaided and unclothed. She was watched by more than 200 startled onlookers.

The photos – exclusive to THE EAST HIGHLANDS GAZETTE – were taken by our staff photographer who was returning from an unrelated assignment. He has a signed list of witnesses which include Councillor Norman Logan, Fr. Cormack Ryan, two schoolteachers, and a local businessman Donald MacDonald.

A vivacious and mischievous pupil of the Convent of The Sacred Heart, 16 miles from Inverness, the young miss Kelly was orphaned in 1952 by a car accident in the south of France where she was born in 1947. Two years previously her Scots mother married Pierre of the Languedoc, a decorated Resistance hero and collaborator of Charles de Gaulle.

Sarah claims God speaks to her in French.

Professor Yamakarsi is visiting Aberdeen University from the All-India Hindu University. He is Leader of the UN Meditation and Prayer Group in Geneva, and told our reporter 'Whoever awakens the Anahat Chakra in the heart can walk on air. A lake is a magic pool in which a child can paddle and an elephant can swim. This child is awakened.'

More photos on centre pages. Story continued inside.

Chapter One

The office of Michael Leonard News Ltd occupied the entire top floor of a nineteenth century building with a Victorian elevator that was always slow and usually somewhere else. Dim lighting concealed flaking grey paint on the third-floor landing where two men were standing, reading the newspaper article out loud. The journalist of forty-four faced a novice half his age. The younger man was out of breath having run up the stairs. The newsmen – veteran and trainee – were so stirred that they carelessly discussed their discovery in the open.

Absent-mindedly tapping his top pocket for the spectacles he was wearing Michael Leonard examined the front page of a Scottish newspaper and admitted that on 25 June 1959 *The East Highlands Gazette* had reported the first appearance of Sarah Kelly.

The younger man spoke politely but with enthusiasm, struggling to gain his breath, a job, and recognition.

'Boss, it must be Sélène! It says she was born in France in 1947 so she's not the 1945 girl of your Marseilles informer. I mean, sir, if she was twelve in June 1959, this is 1972, so twelve plus thirteen, this year she will be celebrating her quarter century – won't she? *Just like the actress.* So she can't be the illegitimate daughter of Pierre and his housekeeper, *can she?*'

Michael Leonard stared at the face of the new reporter, deflating his enthusiasm by barking an order.

'Come in to the office and sit down, Peter. Lindy is reconstituting this week's tea bag with boiled water so take a chair, answer the phone, and let me consider your job application along with this preposterous story you bring me from the late 1950s.'

1.1 Peter Bartlett had an appealing, devil-may-care smile, dirty blond hair and piercing blue eyes. He was over-reaching himself when the accident happened.

The typist's chair upturned when the centre of gravity of his body made a perpendicular line outside the castors. Bartlett rose from the floor, pretending that neither his pride nor his bottom hurt. A metal wheel had become hopelessly severed. He looked around the office, visibly despising the broken-down furniture and machinery.

Completely ignoring the mishap Leonard commented that none of the nationals had followed the article. And the girl was not 'starkers' in the photos although the reporter said she was, and unless you believe in miracles *she did not walk on water*.

'So perhaps one must accept that in its haste the newspaper got its "facts" wrong. So perhaps she was not twelve in 1959. And even if Sarah Kelly is one and the same as Helen MacRae,' he concluded rather aggressively, 'these photographs are certainly not Helena Capulé. The modern messiah, as you say, my boy, is not she. *She is not Her*.'

When Michael Leonard became irritated an uncouth Cockney dialect poked through the Oxford English veneer he had acquired during four years in the University's debating society. Thanks to social diversions he scraped a 3rd Class Honours degree in Modern History to reward the Victorian benefactor who had established the fund to educate boys from the working classes of England.

Peter Bartlett spoke properly from his earliest years and in a proud voice announced that he had located the photographer who had worked for *The East Highland Gazette*.

'He is retired and lives a short train ride from Paris. May I please go there, Boss?'

As his secretary entered the room carrying a tray Leonard announced that he would travel by himself and without delay. He explained to Bartlett that he did not expect to verify the story, but *to discover the deception*:

'The elaborate scale of this thing takes it well beyond a mere hoax, dear boy. *There is a purpose.* And the photographer is *in on it*, so perhaps he can point us to the perpetrators – *voluntarily or otherwise*.'

Michael Leonard chuckled and then showed a small brown bottle to the job applicant.

'A truth drug, without taste, odour, colour or many long-term effects. Got it from a friend in . . . Her Majesty's Service.'

He called out, 'Linda, let the tea wait. Kindly fax the 1959 story to our office in Paris. Take the front page and photocopy it lest it gets jammed in the machine.'

Pushing the tray to one side Leonard opened the rest of the newspaper on a large oak table. Peter Bartlett leaned over it. The centre pages carried coarsely-grained photos attributed to one Marcel Marchant who claimed that he had made a list of witnesses.

'Surprisingly conscientious for a man who had been so busy with his camera, don't you think?'

Unsure of the correct answer, Bartlett examined the newspaper in silence. Four dramatic photos captured the comical smile of an appealing but fully-clothed young woman.

'Surprisingly mature for a twelve-year old if my knowledge of women is anything to go by. I'd say she's fourteen to sixteen. It's another discrepancy which must have an explanation, and that gives us another toehold in this conspiracy. Do you see how I work?'

Bartlett grinned. He sat down very straight in the office chair, massaging his backbone. The hard floor was uncarpeted and the office had not seen paint for many years. Michael Leonard-now a self-employed journalist and broadcaster-had been raised as a poor working-class boy by his mother. Recently a book and two TV documentary films on his big story had provided money. He had saved it for the lean years which freelance journalists encounter.

He pointed to the newspaper. Pictured in a long, white, flowing skirt, Sarah Kelly was slim, despite the shameful wickedness of the Scottish wind inflating her blouse. The breeze embellished her with the possibility of pneumatic femininity but exposed stem-like young legs. Her arms were slender and outstretched-balancing her body on a wire and aping Christ on the cross. Her feet were shod in elegant white shoes, like a ballet dancer. Leonard commented on another discrepancy.

'No reporter credited, Peter. Why do you think there was no reporter involved in a front-page story? No time for research? Or no desire for research?'

'She was attractive even as a young girl, boss.'

The journalist gestured his disagreement. There was something very cute in the girl's gawky appearance: delicate limbs, elegant neck, and innocent eyes, but she was not beautiful. And without the wind in her blouse she was probably more anorexic than curvaceous. Perhaps the centrally-parted black hair, large forehead, and wide-open eyes qualified Miss Kelly for the part of the World Saviour. Not that this would have been her real name – any more than the actress was Sélène today. *God knows who she was.*

Taking a green felt pen the journalist updated a white board on the wall. Bartlett was impressed by the events chart that connected names, places, and details of the mystery.

'Notice anything else, young man?' Leonard asked Bartlett who was keen to defend and develop his discovery.

'Well, she is scantily-clothed for a convent girl . . . and unconcerned about the wind undressing her, boss. *But not unclothed!*'

'*Look at her feet*, Peter, especially her shoes, for signs of faking. And any sign of Nessie in the background? *Do you believe in Nessie?*'

'The Loch Ness monster is a hoax, Boss, but I see what you mean, and besides, her shoe-leather seems dry. Perhaps the photos werefaked.'

Perhaps the photos were faked.

Before Leonard could smile knowingly, the office was startled by the telephone. Bells rang out in every room. It was answered by Lindy.

'Sir,' Bartlett offered, 'I could paint the office. I mean, in my own time, over the weekend. Unless you like this grey colour. I guess it helps you concentrate.'

Michael Leonard was reacting strangely: disturbed rather than delighted by the discovery of the old newspaper; gloomy rather than triumphant.

Almost as an aside he mumbled under his breath, 'You've got the job, young man, I can't lose you to my rivals.'

1.2 Leonard introduced his smiling new apprentice to the lunchtime pub, but most of the regular journalists were absent. Despite differences in age, background, and temperament, the two men enthusiastically discussed the story in depth and returned to their office late in the afternoon.

Lindy came into the Board Room and handed over a message.

'Boss, a phone call came in from Gautier. *Très urgent*. He will only speak to you. I'll ring him now, shall I?'

The connection was made.

Leonard picked up the extension phone.

'*Bonjour Monsieur Gautier.* Oh, I see. I see. OK. *Merci beaucoups.*' He replaced the receiver slowly. His brows furrowed.

Lindy and Peter's eyes pleaded for the bad news. Silently, Leonard walked to the events board and wrote a few words. He turned around, looked at his two employees, inhaled breath, and coolly informed them.

In July 1959 the same photos were printed in French newspapers. The waters were captioned as Lake de Berre, Switzerland. The girl was called Hélène de Langue d'Oc.

Chapter Two

In the Languedoc region of France a shimmering heat blurs the distinction between heaven and earth, between the deep blue skies and the verdant mountains. But Michael Leonard was a reporter, not a poet. He made it his business to disclose facts and regarded it as the way of princes, priests, and politicians to make it their business to conceal them.

He stumbled upon the story when he was married to Philippa. In August 1965, seven years before he saw the Scottish newspaper, they had taken a holiday in the south of France. The guidebook described Rennes-le-Château as a picturesque village visited by tourists because of treasures found by its parish priest sometime between 1886 and 1891. Philippa made it clear that she was not interested in such nonsense. Leonard rose early one Saturday morning, pecked his wife on the cheek, and drove there by himself. He used the sun-baked, fading-yellow car, the 'demented sewing machine' as he called the 2CV Citroën belonging to two spoiled, chattering teenagers – Hannah and Lauren Gautier. They were the daughters of his researcher in Paris. When he stayed at their holiday house near the walled city of Carcassonne the car was his.

By the time he ate his lunch alone at the small restaurant in the village Leonard knew that his life had changed. What he saw on his day trip to Rennes-le-Château involved mystery, murder, money, and a secret that clearly disturbed the religious authorities. He knew that he had stumbled upon a story whose value was even greater than the treasure it had yielded. Leonard felt a strange kinship to l'Abbé Saunière, the nineteenth century priest, as he stood enthralled by the decoration of his chapel.

After three quarters of a century the mystery remained unsolved yet the cryptic clues in the art made some sense to the modern, English atheist who stood inside the church entering the mind of the priest who had designed, hand-painted, and paid for a huge quantity of expressive statues and murals.

Leonard realised that, poor in upbringing like himself, Saunière the priest had understood his Golden Rule of investigative journalism: that a money trail points to something bigger than its monetary dimension, something of a powerful secret. Leonard told himself that the artwork contained clues to a secret.

The village was attracting tourists on the absurd notion that the priest wished to point posterity to the treasure he had eagerly taken.

2.1 The journalist smiled as he realised that seven years had softened his anger and he even missed Philippa. From the start they were ill-matched: her upper class behaviour was ingrained, authentic, but stifling. Her parents had disparaged him as their daughter's toy boy and predicted that the chemistry would start to loosen all bonds in about two years. The tag, *a bit of rough,* had made the couple in their early thirties escape to youth – highly desirable in the psychedelic sixties – but when their marriage fell apart the description hurt badly.

Bartlett interrupted his senior's thoughts.

'But you said that Sélène's rôle in the grand hoax was disclosed to you by a Freemason?'

'My informant claimed to be a *Templar* – whose Order is a precursor of the Freemasons; some historians say so. Anyway, he told me that one of four girls they knew to be descended from the holy bloodline was to be chosen in 1975, twenty-five years from the end of the bi-millennium, to reinstate the Templars and to put down what he called *the church of the cross.*'

Bartlett was impressed. His face relaxed in response to Leonard's pride of ownership of such a far-reaching story. Sitting on the desk in the main office and resting his feet on his chair, the young reporter listened to 'the true world history' and 'the Christian cover-up' from his boss who brought him fully up to date. Leonard walked through the archway into a dull and dilapidated room, once a large clerical or cashiers' chamber. It was full of books and files.

He pointed to the events board attached to the wall opposite the window. Like a murder enquiry, the chart connected a series of clues by lines and arrows drawn in black, blue, green, and red inks.

'Source-1, a high-society man whose identity I protect, passionately believes that the Mary who was revered by the disciples was the partner – not the Mother – of Christ. And that Mary Magdalene was the Lord's wife in the normal sense, and that through her the messianic line generated heirs of Jesus – deposed sovereigns. They lived in exile having lost the Davidic authority to the popes. And in the sixth century the great mother was degraded when Gregory announced that the faithful must hold that "the Magdalene had clearly used the ungent to perfume her own flesh in forbidden acts."'

Bartlett protested that he had believed that the New Testament stated that she was a reformed prostitute. Leonard corrected him.

'The gospels appear to point to another Mary who was a fallen or repentant woman and they don't demean procreation – in fact the gospels assert that there were sisters and brothers of Jesus. Matthew 13:55, Mark 6:3. So if we follow these through, we have the survival of the royal bloodline and the motive to deny it. If Jesus *were* in the royal line of David this would have threatened the Church in the years of the Roman Empire. *And it still does.*'

Bartlett shook his head and again Leonard set him right.

'The throne of St Peter was created in the absence of the line of David, which was given sovereignty *in perpetuity*. By God. In the Book of Samuel. Check it, Peter. Read the Scriptures and use it against them. The Church Fathers regarded sex as degrading. Eve was a temptress. The Magdalene was a prostitute. Women are not worthy of dignity. Jesus could not have fathered a child. Male patriarchal church suppresses women. *Welcome to Christianity.* It's the culture. I admit it, myself: I manipulate women.'

Leonard gestured disapproval to Peter to remove his shoes from the charcoal tweed of the office chair.

'You are determined to destroy my office furniture!'

The new employee obeyed immediately and asked if Leonard believed in the 'Marseilles Heresy' common in the villages in the south of France: the story that Mary Magdalene had sailed and settled there after the crucifixion with the child of her union with Jesus.

'Peter, it's the orthodoxy that is incredible; *biology supports the heresy.*'

He paused for Bartlett's smile and then continued, 'I mean virgin birth and all that. Even the *official* Gospels state that Christ loved Mary Magdalene and betray obvious editorial excisions every time her name is mentioned. The Marseilles stories still persist to this day. There is a recent book that says the remains of The Magdalene are entombed there, and that the Temple Treasures were probably hidden and found there. But read this one; its very reliable.'

Leonard searched the shelves and tossed over a well-read paperback which landed on the table with a thud reflecting its substantial dimensions. *Massacre at Montségur,* by Zoé Oldenbourg.

The young reporter read from the book's jacket, '*1208 . . . the Catholic Church's response to the rapid growth of a rival Christian religion in the very heart of Christendom.*'

The two men stared at each other in silence.

'What's new, Peter? Slaughter in the name of God?'

The tension was broken by two of Lindy's mugs of steaming tea and a plate of *Penguin* biscuits. The young reporter arranged them by colours on the table.

'Peter, in 1945 in Nag Hammadi in Upper Egypt, the Gospel of Philip – which had been missing for almost two thousand years – was found to support history's most secret liaison. *Jesus Lives* is a resonant myth which stirs believers. Suppose it was true, literally!'

The raw-recruit acknowledged the upheaval the story might cause and nodded, 'True or not, boss, it could take on a life of its own.'

'Yes, exactly! And I'm convinced it is an elaborate plot. But alas for the conspirators, they made no contract with the woman who has chosen Hollywood, very wisely, as the best place to make a career of acting. Either the 1945 girl or the 1947 girl, if indeed the two are not one-and-the-same person.'

Impulsively, Leonard turned from the enquiry board to face Lindy and Peter.

'I'm going to France to interview your Scottish newspaper photographer, Peter. Not to publicise any 'Second Coming' as the man may hope, but to discover how he found her, and if the lensman – Marcel Marchant – can point me to his leaders.'

Chapter Three

NEW YORK, SEPTEMBER 1972

No-one looked out of place here: young and old, drop-outs and celebrities.

Diverse cultures and creeds clashed in a melting pot of New Age ideals. Millbrook Mansion in Dutchess County, NY, was the world's hippy headquarters, the microcosm of a new order, the beginning of a better world. When the use of psychoactive drugs was prohibited and Timothy Leary was expelled from Harvard University, the mansion was donated by the Mellon-Hitchcocks family into research on mind-expanding drugs. By the end of the 'sixties, it had declined into decadence and decay.

It was one long party.

Professor Leary's assistant, Dr Palmer – a slim, dark-haired man in black, casual clothes – was engaged in conversation with an older, slightly-portly man dressed in a cream three-piece suit, bow tie, and white button-hole. This man had presence.

Sélène, the fledgling Hollywood actress, thought he might be the English actor Robert Hardy but he was older and spoke in a seamless fusion of East Coast American and mid-European. His attention wandered from the conversation and their eyes met.

She smiled and walked away, carrying herself with an eccentric lightness and dignity. She retreated to the opposite corner of the room and remained alone, silent, and mysterious. Then she stared back for too long, absent-mindedly rather than rudely.

Dr Palmer continued speaking until he too noticed the woman. He called her over and introduced her to the Robert Hardy man as the Hollywood actress called Sélène.

'The one who is the current lover of Johnny Lord. You know, the movie director. He's hot and his movies are *very* hot . . .'

The man in the three-piece suit shrugged his shoulders. Palmer put his hand on the shoulder of the cream jacket, and continued despite the slight recoil.

'Robert, she's the subject who supposedly "saw" the first-century sacking of Gaul and the hiding places of the Temple Treasures that checked out.'

After an awkward silence, the man in the cream suit made an exit and left the film star with the pharmacologist.

3.1 The eyes of the twenty seven-year old film star followed the man who walked out of the room. Aged about fifty and around five foot eight, his dirty-blond hair was short and well-styled; like a lawyer's wig, it had been shaped with hair cream. Sélène thought she had seen him on television. He was a government official and gave popular science lectures but she was more interested in literature and history. She felt stifled by the former grandeur of the room, its stale aroma, and the atmosphere of the party. Then she was startled by a voice behind her.

'That's Robert F. Kohen – the guy you just butted. He's *America's oldest teenager.*'

The slim, longhaired intruder laughed, bringing over his drink with his amorous hopes.

'I've been watching the two of you. Kohen lacks technique with women . . . surprising, considering he's a brilliant man. Awkward, like many academics. Lures chicks with lecherous talk but never samples the goods. When he entices women to his home they weep with *rejection*. A lot of faggies get cured here, sometimes after a single trip.'

The intruder was repulsed by the young woman's silent reproach but Sélène exuded pity for him. She looked away and quickly walked into the hall where Kohen suddenly let his drink fall to the ground. She picked up the pieces of broken glass as if it was her duty to tidy up after him. The scene attracted a small audience.

Holding onto the iron balustrade with both hands Kohen gazed down into the hall of the nineteenth century mansion. Talking towards the architectural void he advised her to be careful of the broken pieces. She gave him a strange look and ostentatiously crushed the broken glass in her left palm. The tinkle of falling shards caused a gasp and the small talk fell like a gown to the floor. Robert Kohen turned around to face her.

People watched without reaction as she allowed blood to drip for a few moments to deepen the shock, then outstretched her hands, palms facing front. The actress was portraying the stigmata of Christ but the blood was real.

Paying no attention to the gaping onlookers, she spoke softly to Kohen, ignoring his shock.

'Don't pity me. I can't stand weakness in men. I can control blood flow in myself and even in others. It's a cheap trick. I lower the pressure. Yoga can teach anyone to do it. I wanted to ask about your job as a scientist.'

'I report directly to the President although I did not vote for him.'

Kohen raised his gaze to the growing circle of onlookers, "Why don't you get on with your miserable lives?" and lowering his voice, "There are two societies, two symbolic cultures uneasily sharing the planet," Leary says. You are Sélène, the *friend* of Johnny Lord. What are you doing *here*?'

He pronounced 'friend' and 'here' with contempt.

She denied any feelings of guilt. Said her relationships were her own business. But she considered all these things as she struggled with Kohen's questions.

'Sélène, will you kindly permit me to take the glass pieces from your hand?'

Dr Palmer reappeared, dragging Timothy Leary towards them, but she turned aside and pulled Kohen from them.

'You are a doctor of Philosophy not Medicine, Dr Kohen, so I'm interested in your mind, not your cures. Did you mean, *what am I doing at this party?* Or in America? Or in a world full of the living dead? For on this point, I hope, at least, we agree.'

Kohen waved away his approaching male colleagues, retrieved another pocket-handkerchief and took the hand of the woman, but she pulled back and pursued the debate, oblivious to her injury.

'*I don't fit in here?* Is that what you mean?' She pleaded, 'You think

I am not a moral person? But *you* are against drugs, by reputation, yet you're here? Oh! I haven't made up my mind about my career and I feel quite light-headed. Perhaps I'm not really an actress. Maybe just a high class hooker? Some say so, others just hope it.'

'You are not of this world, Death's Dream Kingdom,' Kohen replied with conviction.

She smiled very broadly and sneered, 'You mean that I am pretending to be something *or someone* that I am not?'

She had posed a riddle and Kohen's eyes drifted towards the ceiling as he answered.

'Actors live charmed lives, able to detach or conceal themselves from whatever is their true nature. Especially females, dear lady, flighty, faithless creatures. Acting is a job for women. *An actress is a little more than a woman; an actor is a little less than a man.* You may be surprised, but I too studied drama. I was born in Hungary, as you may know, and I wanted to be a film director, just like your Johnny Lord. But a certain Adolf Hitler from Austria, just next door to us, wanted to be a dictator. The conditions in Europe were such that he got his way and mine was forfeited.'

Sélène looked at Kohen and then downstairs. She leaned precariously on the banister. The crowd had dispersed.

She whispered, 'But you said I am not of this kingdom and Jesus was the last to say that.'

'T.S. Eliot said that, dear lady.'

He placed his hands on her shoulders, 'And Eliot coined the phrase, *death's dream kingdom*.'

Their eyes met and held. Neither smiled. A long silence almost ended the encounter. Then, extending his arms theatrically, Robert Kohen inhaled a deep breath. All traces of his German accent disappeared; he sounded just like Robert Hardy.

'"Eyes that last I saw in tears
Through division
Here in death's dream kingdom
The golden vision reappears
I see the eyes but not the tears
This is my affliction."'

'Gosh!' she said.

Kohen smiled as she pursed her lips and furrowed her eyebrows. Having bowled her over, he fetched from downstairs two glasses of fruit juice. Upon his return, he repulsed the male suitor who had come back to annoy her.

Sélène repeated the lines perfectly. Now Kohen was impressed. She gulped her drink then their words collided but he allowed her to speak.

'You do not approve of the sacramental use of drugs, Robert, yet you are here? I have found happiness from drugs so I speak from authority. This substance takes its ingestor to the Gates of Heaven. Do you believe me? Or are your ears stopped like the rest of them, Dr Kohen? Do you condemn me with your Holy Bible? Do you see only the mask of the actress? I think not. *You know who I am*. It's the way you look in my eyes.' She held his gaze. He gripped her arm.

'You know who I am,' she challenged him.

'This isn't the place to talk.'

She looked around and became aware of the party. It was timeless and spaced out. Some rooms were brightly lit and animated by music; others offered seclusion and privacy. They were used for the full spectrum of mind-expanding human experiences: frenzied and sober discussion, sexual encounters, and various stages of individual and group hallucinations.

Sélène extended her right hand to the arm of a chief Defence Scientist.

'Dr Kohen, your words were very moving. This American poet describes me well. I feel the tragedy of mankind in its division.'

'T.S. Eliot is English, Sélène, and the poem is *Eyes that last I saw in tears*. I'll buy you Eliot's collected works.'

'I never settled at a school long enough to learn literature. I discovered the Holy Grail by the Holy Grail itself, Dr Robert. I took the substance and I discovered that it was ingested by Jesus. I saw back to Him through my father's generations. As a scientist, you call it Past Lives Hypnotic Regression. What does that tell you about who I am? Does it answer your question?'

She said this with pity rather than contempt and looked to the scientist for a response.

'Sélène, did you seek me out?'

She sulked, and her tone switched to scorn.

'Takes one to know one, Darling. Do you know what I mean? I mean these sad people are like clockwork soldiers: turn them round and they'll march wherever they are pointed. But you are fully alive, aware, in touch with your soul. These people need drugs to artificially connect with their souls. Or soul. The Great Soul. You are the Great Soul, the Wise Man from the east and I am the rebirth. You have seen the star in the skies and yet you deny looking for me, Dr Kohen? Why tell lies?'

3.2 On dope everyone is in his or her own time zone. In Millbrook Mansion, as in Las Vegas, not even meal times regulate the circadian rhythm of the senses. As she surfaced to consciousness Sélène could not feel her limbs. She was aware of danger but not of time. *They had torn her clothes off.* Or were they helping her? Someone had spiked her drink. She could not move. Her lips formed the words, *'God, please forgive them.'* A man pointing a broken beer bottle at her crotch was restrained by five or six men brave enough to act together against the superhuman strength of one. The cries had attracted a crowd and Robert Kohen appeared at the door. His mouth fell open in shock. He ran downstairs, pushing through people in the large ballroom and put his hand on the shoulder of a man with close-set blue eyes and long blond hair.

'I know your cover and I'm a Red-One, so get a car here fast. I need you to get a woman out of that room and to a VIP clinic. She's naked, doped to her eyeballs, surrounded by lecherous men, claims she's the messiah, and pouring blood from her head. Reckon you can handle that?'

A young woman handed her fur coat to Kohen who carried the draped body of the dancer-actress-philosopher downstairs. As she regained her strength she protested and wriggled.

Kohen showed the woman her flowing blood and screamed, 'A friendly doctor. I'm taking you to a friendly *female* doctor. Or else that scar will disfigure your forehead for life – which may be short unless you stop bleeding. Look at yourself in a mirror. *Someone, show her a mirror fast!* Can you hear me, sweetheart? You can't do your Yoga trick after ingesting funny pharmaceuticals.'

'Now you are a psychiatrist,' she said, 'You even look like Sigmund Freud and you sound like him too.'

As police arrived, their cars illuminated the courtyard like a firework display. The swarm mentality melted and sanity was visibly restored to each individual. The blond agent flashed his identity card and thanked the cops for back-up. A larger-than-life NYPD grinned.

'Your lot make a mess and we clean it. What's new, G-man?'

The scientist mopped the woman's brow and bundled her into the agent's car outside the mansion. She called over a police officer, 'You're looking for a man called Leon aged about thirty. He must be caught but tell him I forgive him and to seek God's blessing.'

Addressing her but looking at Kohen the officer shouted, 'She's coming with us or in an ambulance to hospital.'

A man walked from the house party and shook hands with Kohen. He looked and spoke like John Lennon including the granny glasses he made fashionable. In the headlamps his CIA badge was furtively produced; it seemed real enough.

'Don't tell everybody.'

He tightened his grip on Kohen's hand, 'Robert,' he whispered in awe. 'She also dictated every generation from her father back to David, King of the Jews. It was transcribed and it checked out. She accounted for the lost kingdom of Gaul's political misfortunes. Get the facts before you dismiss the theory; it's good science.'

Kohen hesitated, then nodded towards the blond government agent, who ordered the policeman, 'Tell your partner, Dr Kohen here is red-one status and my code is 453-222. The woman comes with us. Forget about the assailant. You have no victim and no crime. Is that clear?'

The policemen looked at each other. Disbelief turned to hesitation. One of them wrote down the incident code and the ID of the under cover agent.

Chapter Four

HOLLYWOOD, CA, 23 APRIL 1973
ATTN: M. LEONARD, MICHAEL LEONARD NEWS LTD LONDON.
IN RESPONSE TO YOUR COMM DATED 04-18-73 YOUR REQUEST FOR AN INTERVIEW WITH SELENE IS DECLINED AS IT IS NOT OUR POLICY TO EXPOSE OUR ARTISTS TO YOUR SORT OF JOURNALISM.
RICARDO C. D'ANALIEZE,
UNITED TALENT, INC.

Before he had seen the refusal the journalist had arrived in California and was admitted to a garden party to interview a fading star hungry for media attention. Leonard went through the motions of speaking to the elderly actor until she appeared on the radar. The younger man slipped his reporter's notebook into the back pocket of his denim trousers and walked from the marquee towards the bottom of the sunlit garden.

Sélène was sitting in the shade of a chestnut tree, daydreaming or tripping alone. He walked a wide circle round the tree to contrive an accidental encounter. To avoid startling her he audibly exhaled cigar smoke. In an East London dialect, like Michael Caine, he made a joke about her being under the Tree at the centre of the Garden of Eden.

She smiled, 'God said, *It is not good that man should be alone.*'

'But you are a woman,' Leonard replied rather foolishly, and they laughed.

She told him that she was alone, waiting under this tree for no-one so he asked what it was that separated her from the crowd.

'The greatest gap in the world is not the Grand Canyon nor the distance between galaxies, but it is the divisions of humanity. Gender, colour, class, creed, and mindsets. Things that make people unique and wonderful. But when people come together in the theatre their minds are united by a shared experience, same with the motion picture. *That is why acting is an art not a craft.*'

He told her how beautiful she was without any makeup and that he wanted more from her lips than words.

She smiled, 'I don't even know your name.'

He moved forward but she recoiled.

She smiled as her eyes fell on his Press badge.

'Michael, I was moved through many convent schools and they all taught me that sex is good only between husband and wife to procreate. Do you believe that? You are English. In France we were more sophisticated, and we do not confuse physical attraction with higher aspects of sexual love, but neither do we condemn it.'

Leonard heard the sounds of the garden party and imagined that people were watching them. He stood in front of her, blocking her view of the guests, and she stared at him. She was sitting on a circular tree seat, her feet drawn into her calves – not on the ground. The huge tree shaded them from the Californian sunshine. Silence. Hesitation. He considered their age difference. *It wasn't the only contrast.* The moderate man and the wild child. The English businessman and the French starlet. The rough guy and the aristocratic dame. The atheist and the one who spoke to God.

'I am Michael Leonard, the English journalist. I wrote to your agency but got no reply. You need better management.'

'I was taught how God created us male and female, but now we are separated so we need one another for completeness. It is a spiritual insight. It does not elevate copulation, but neither does it make free love a sinful thing.'

'What would you like to drink, Sélène?'

At the bar, the fading elderly actor invited him to a film preview about to start in the screening room of the house. Leonard made his excuses and returned to Sélène with two cherry drinks and paper plates with steaming sausages and cool salads. The sun dazzled through the green leaves of the Tree at the Centre of the Garden and illuminated the dark hair of the woman.

Handing over her food he suggested, 'The Bible seems to me a little . . . out of date these days. Should it not be translated, 'not good that man *or woman* be alone?"

Her eyes smiled and she laughed, 'It *does* say that, at least to me, especially in New Testament Greek, which I read, just adequately. But you're caught in a groove which is rational linearity. It's a type-two precedence trap in my own home-brewed philosophy.'

He looked at her sadly because she was not stoned but crazy, especially to believe that the Book of Genesis had been written in Greek, but she continued, 'As I work it out, God's alpha-omega creation uses time as a scaffolding. Time is illusory. An imaginary convention in your maths. Of the genders, it's a delusion. The male does have precedence but soon scientists will discover that male includes the feminine, and the female transcends the masculine elements.'

While Leonard paused to switch from seducer to interviewer he thought she said, 'Do you *like* me?' The word *like* was stressed to sharpen the euphemism.

Perhaps she didn't say it.

'Don't you *feel* my eyes, Michael? Don't you find me attractive?'

He started to look around. He saw nobody watching or listening. The house would have bedrooms. A toilet might be safer. A mansion like this would have large and luxurious bathrooms.

When he moved towards her, she shrank back and his face betrayed anger. *She was on some substance.* His contempt for chemical addiction grew from the years of degradation and misery alcohol had brought to his mother until the day his father choked in his own vomit. Once a proud man who built suspension viaducts, he was found by the police in a gutter under a stone bridge that offered down-and-outs some shelter from the night rain.

He was woken at four in the morning. His mother said it was all right but she was trembling and the boy burst into tears. He was taken to his aunt while his mother was taken by the police. He remembered the funeral and then his mother would not mention her husband by name. She was not unkind but escaped unhappiness by cleaning clothes and communal stone stairs which paid for the education of her son.

Sélène gave him the strangest look, then smiled, 'Michael, I am not drunk on the wine of this world. I am not *of this world.* I am not ugly and, see, I am lonely. No-one wants to understand. I came and I found them all drunk. They are afraid of their depths. I am different but I think it is insanity to learn from them.'

The way her beauty pulsed higher and higher in cycles and then apparently oscillated into the grotesque was unique. She alternated between angel and slut, Madonna and prostitute. Leonard thought about his mother and then Michael Mangham, the school bully; about walking home alone each day, hiding behind the high stone wall, which was shaded by 4pm. His companions at this posh school lived on the clean and pleasant side of the park. By his own reckoning, he did not belong.

Mangham jumped from the wall, always from a different place, sometimes with a couple of friends to add to the menace. This time alone, he asked if Leonard was a Catholic. The boy heard himself say he was 'C of E,' '. . . and High Church . . .' without knowing what that meant.

The enraged bully spat on the face of his quarry. Leonard bravely toppled his assailant, aware that he would come out worse. As the struggle intensified, Mangham tore a button from Leonard's school blazer, ripping the front of the purple garment. Leonard knew his mother had washed other peoples' steps to buy this second-hand jacket. Now, unbearably, there was more damage from the very fighting that she had told him to avoid. Mangham rubbed in the insult by noting that the obese ruffian from the east had a second-hand cap that was two sizes too big.

St John's Preparatory School had wanted a couple of east-enders for political reasons and Leonard had, from a young age, desired to learn the language of Caesar and the charioteers. Latin had appealed to him in all its chiselled carvings, concentrated by its brevity, and cool in its objectivity. He wanted to rise above the squalor of London's suburbs; to read about the Roman Empire; to understand how its soldiers fought valiantly and why its citizens deposed their kings. What did they speak of as they guzzled popcorn in their amphitheatres? And what did they think about as they watched Christians and Gladiators facing lions unfed since they had been captured in Africa?

4.1 Unable to recall his prepared questions, unwilling to focus on the story, and blinded by the sunshine Leonard was separated from the garden party in a sort of bubble. He had seen a woman change by her mood and he had seen a woman swing between two personalities, but Sélène was more frightening. She exuded fathomless lust. He could not face this rejection. The investigator walked away with his *alter ego*, the lover leaving the story behind him.

He risked being turned into a pillar of salt but turned for one more glimpse and immediately he saw it: it was a colourful aura around her head. It might have been the sunshine dazzling her black hair but he had never seen anything like it before. He did not believe in these things. But he believed his eyes.

As he walked away, his prepared questions flooded back into his mind too late. He wanted to know the names of the conspirators. Teachers who took a special interest in her. People who might be guardians of the Grail. And if they were connected to the Templars, how much was known to the Catholic Church which was educating her?

Now he wanted to know if those who possessed the Secret had found her with brain miswired or caused the damage while preparing her?

Chapter Five

NEMOURS, FRANCE, MAY 1973

The newspaper photographer from 1959 had retired to a one-horse village about one hundred kilometres south of Paris and at least one hundred years behind the times.

The houses were quaint and modest but neat and clean. It looked like the day before a village garden competition but Michael Leonard was in no mood to appreciate the scenery. His train was shunted in and out of railway sidings for two hours during which archaic mechanical signals were inspected and manipulated with great fuss. At last he was on the single-track railway upon which the old – but spotlessly clean – train ran in each direction twice a day except for Sundays. Despite the chance to rehearse his interrogation by sharpening his key and decoy questions, the delay had made him irritable. He knew that impatience is a bad frame of mind for creative probing.

The upside of the slow pace of life there was that the black Citroën was waiting at the railway station and the uniformed driver seemed undisturbed by the loss of two hours of his time.

5.1 The photographer was a dapper, grey-bearded man. He was retired without a pension and Leonard was aware of Rule One in investigative journalism: *follow the money*. Marchant explained with a shrug that he went freelance in his middle age and had made just enough to retire on.

Intending to return to this subject obliquely to catch him off-guard, Leonard complimented him on his manicured and well-stocked garden.

Marchant's smile disturbed his interviewer. It was a mocking which said that finally he had lured the journalist here to promote Sélène as the modern messiah.

5.2 Leonard felt himself as a trapped animal being appraised through a pair of thin round glasses. The photographer wore a beret in an affected French style and acted as an absent-minded professor. He was so fastidious that the chaos inside his cottage living room seemed contrived – as if prepared for a film shoot. The timbers were dark, stained, and rough; the walls appeared never to have been decorated. The cottage had a stale smell that Leonard tried to identify. The men went through the motions of civilised courtesy but everything seemed false. Leonard pretended to lower his guard and treat the retired photographer with patience and humour.

He was rewarded when Marchant opened a cupboard door. A small darkroom exuded the pungent odour of photographic chemicals – the source of the smell. Beckoning Leonard into the small room he gesticulated wildly while praising some of his own arty prints and describing how each one had been composed in his lens. After five minutes Leonard asked Marchant how he came to photograph the girl on Loch Ness.

'Ah, *La Petite Fleure de Sion*! Let me see, where was it? Was it the Loch Ness?'

'Perhaps it was *Lake de Berre*, Monsieur Marchant?'

'Was it really?' he exclaimed with a false surprise and repeated the motions of blowing dust from a stack of box files. From a box marked 1959 he produced, like a rabbit from a hat, several black and white prints of Sarah Kelly levitated upon a lake. It was the same girl, he said, but the background scenery was different. It looked like a Mediterranean fishing village, however, one difference in the foreground was immediately striking.

The girl was unclothed.

Leonard made lewd sounds to which Marchant reacted with a grand gesture of his hands and an exaggerated accent.

'We French are broad-minded. The Scots refused to show Eve unclothed.'

'So she posed with and without clothes?' Leonard suggested sarcastically.

Marchant replied instantly, 'No, like a painter, a Kirlian photographer sees nakedness in purity. But it is a different technique. You are unfamiliar in the occult arts, *Mr Lee-onaard*. Kirlian photography is a finer vibration than light so the film coating won't even reproduce her physical body but energy levels which you call *auras*. She took lessons, you know, in meditation from Sri Yamakarsi, a yogic guru, but she was also a disciple of our Brothers of the Western *Rose-Croix*. They were present in spirit on this day, but you cannot see them in the photos. They are invisible to the camera.'

The reporter remembered his own observation of Sélène's aura but reverted to hostile interrogation.

'Oh come, M. Marchant. This is all nonsense. I report facts and you once were employed to photograph them.' Leonard protested, but he detected Marchant's observation of his softening.

The reporter tried to remember the aura he saw faintly in the grainy pictures in the Scottish newspaper.

The photographer smiled.

'May I call you Michael? Clothes are earthly vibrations at one level. Angels of heaven are vibrations of another level even above, or finer you may say, to living bodies. You might not see one of the Brothers standing in this very room unless he wanted to reveal himself.'

It was time to demolish the lies and seek the truth.

'Monsieur Marchant, this comment betrays that you yourself believe that you are of an inner circle. I have come a long distance to warn you that you have been used. *You are being used*, Marcel Marchant, by a very dangerous international conspiracy which you do not understand. I know all about illegal secret societies . . .'

'It is legal, sir,' the photographer protested.

'Never mind the French police. Think how will you be punished for bearing false witness? I refer to the manipulators behind this deception. Are *they* above God's truth? Are you bearing false witness?'

Marchant almost fell into his settee and remained silent like a hurt child so Leonard sharpened his argument.

'You, sir, are duped by a diabolic and deluded outer-circle and you are being used to deceive people on behalf of impostors who wisely stay hidden and speak no evil.'

Marchant recovered his composure and fought back with conviction.

'There is a lower truth, *Monsieur Lee-onard*, the sort of events which newspapers will print. Intriguing facts that we recycle because we are mere reporters. Your truths are transitory – but true – whereas my superiors have always known the truth as the universal, perennial, and influential myth. This is termed occult, sir, but it is not evil. Your shallow and materialist outlook poses the great danger to mankind.'

Marchant stepped towards the reporter and gripped his arm with intensity rather than any threat.

'You are a modern man, sir, and as a former reporter I expect you to believe what is seen by my eyes. You think that a miracle is a deception. However, I, Marcel Marchant, like you, a newspaper man for most of my working life, I swear to you that these remarkable photographs captured the coincidence of both levels of the truth. You have my word on that, I swear it to you before my God in the heavens, and there is also the agreement of the many other witnesses on that occasion.'

He spoke with conviction that put Leonard at a disadvantage. Then he saw two more photos depicting the auras he had seen 'in the flesh' with his own eyes under the tree at the centre of the Garden of Hollywood. It was no optical rainbow refracting colours in order of wavelength, but something else. Leonard tried to conceal his hesitation.

'You want to see miracles?' Marchant continued.

'Mastering gravity to you is an impossible miracle, yet I tell you it is still very common. Air India can fly you to Yamakarsi's Ashram. You call your airship technology; primitives call it magic. Once there you will see, on street corners outside the walls of his mansion, shrivelled old men suspended horizontally one foot above the clay pavement. There *you* will call it magic but the primitives call it yoga. Science changes over the centuries but Western comprehension cannot explain anti-gravity or clairvoyance.'

Marchant observed that Leonard remained silent and receptive.

'Yoga Science is aware that the western female organism is better adapted than the male to preserve what little remains of the ancient wisdom. So they used her, if you want to put it that way. There is your conspiracy!'

Leonard relaxed into an old armchair covered with a tartan throw. Placing his palms behind his head like a pillow he exhaled and protested simply that newspapers were supposed to print facts and let the readers do their own interpretation.

Marchant pleaded gently, as if moving to snare his trapped animal.

'We agree to your lower truth. But believe me, God has sent her. She is divine, can't you see? The girl herself might even deny it. You see, in those days when I set eyes on her She was not wholly on the ordinary level of awareness – what you call self-ish-ness. But now She *is* selfish. Explain that! Now She *is* a worldly woman in America. Now She is in *your* world, a world which plays trivial games and permits harm and suffering. She works each day in the world seeking fortune and fame like you. She thinks of her career and relationships. I do not know why it is so. I think maybe God allows her to make mistakes so Her soul will learn the pain of earthly striving. Then she will arise, by her free will. I will make you a coffee.'

Leonard followed Marchant into his rustic kitchen. The floor was spotless but there were books and photos piled on the pine shelves instead of pots and pans. The reporter drew his finger along the shelves. The lack of any dust re-ignited his suspicions.

He enquired softly, 'Where is she now, Marcel?'

'I don't know. She is not our puppet, as you believe, but we serve Her. Yes, it is just as you think, but I think you misunderstand the conspiracy. We taught Her, yes, but not quite. She and I, we are *both* being "used" and *you* are being used, yes, but you and I in a much more humble way than The Daughter. By Almighty God, in His plan, He may even call another woman in the sovereign line. And if called, She too might not agree to His call. Free will is a gift from a loving Father. In fact, Sélène *has* strayed very far from the path of righteousness. She takes drugs and fornicates with sinners if your earth-fact newspapers are to be believed. And I do believe them, for at their level they tell the truth.'

Leonard pointed his finger to the dark room with the photographs:

'Yet you came to Scotland in 1956, the very year the Prieuré de Sion was re-established.'

Silently Marchant took his own coffee into the sitting room, sat down, clenched his teeth, and defiantly pushed his finger through a print, at the top of her crotch. He rose from the sofa but fell back, as if dizzy, and stared at his offending finger as if it might wither.

Leonard sat intrusively on the antique settee beside him. Marchant frowned at the reporter who took the next step in the mind game. He lit up a cigarette and placed the burning match on the leather armrest.

'I really thought that you were sworn to secrecy, the inner circle and all that; but with your actions you talk *too loudly*, Marcel. Perhaps you are angry with the woman, or your colleagues, or you are feeding me with information?'

Marchant used his ill-fated finger to rub down the scorch mark on the settee, removed his damaged print, and sneered.

'You are no longer a newspaper reporter of mere facts, Michael. Like me you have become a witness of momentous events. So if you write her story she is also part of *your story*.

Chapter Six

After sharing supper, Marchant convinced Leonard that he was telling his misinterpretation of the truth. The interrogator now wanted to probe areas Marchant would not willingly disclose by the application of a small dose of a relaxing substance accompanied by a hypnosis technique used by British Intelligence. It worked well with impressionable people such as patriots, salesmen, or religious bigots. The psychoactive interval was short; Leonard knew he had six minutes before the subject became drowsy and fell asleep.

'You took these photos in Scotland or France?'

'It is the same water all over the world, Monsieur Leonard.'

'Is it the same girl of whom we talk?'

'The girl arrived in Scotland as Sarah Kelly but she was Helen MacRae, not the illegitimate daughter of Pierre of the Languedoc and his Scottish housekeeper, as you may think. That is what they want us to believe. That girl is in hiding in France.'

'Who are *They*, Marcel?'

'—'

'You must tell me the whole truth . . . Are Helen Capulé and Sarah Kelly one and the same? I don't understand.'

The photographer played his prints like ace cards on the armrest of his damaged settee.

'You can see but you cannot understand, Michael. If I said that two girls could be one, and one girl might be two, you could not understand it. Observe and write at your own level, my friend. Look, there she is, naked. Do you think the local men would forget that? Interrogate the surviving witnesses. Seek answers to your own questions. *The conspiracy, as you call it.'*

Marchant shouted, and his argument seemed genuine. The reporter hesitated and then pleaded.

'Speak now, Marcel. *The truth will set you free.'*

'I'll help you. All will be known soon. I played games with you because I wanted to see how much you knew, and how little you *understood.'*

'I am in no mood to play games, Marchant.'

Leonard knew the drug was dissipating, so he probed by guesswork.

'They took her to Scotland to conceal her, and they changed her name? Who were they afraid of? Well, then, *what* were they afraid of?'

'They were afraid of Helena Capulé.'

The answer took Leonard by surprise.

'Helena Capulé,' he repeated the name confidently as if he knew all about her. '*The alternative candidate.*' He managed to make it sound like a statement rather than a question.

'Yes. Also she was descended from the Holy Family. But she went bad on them. Even before . . . before the Aryan wing broke away they caused us trouble, tried to take control of the co-fraternity. To force against the choice dictated by the Vatican. Understand? The faction elected by the Holy See had rejected Helena Capulé, but the east chose Sarah-Hélène de L' anguedoc. That was her real name. Both lineal descendants, but the dispute was sufficiently deep to tear the thing apart.'

The investigator dragged the weary lensman to his bed, left a thank-you note, and closed the door of the cottage behind him in haste to avoid missing the train to Paris.

On the train from Paris to Marseilles Michael Leonard felt that every passenger might be watching him but he was pleased with what he had learned. First, even if Jesus had sired but one child, hundreds, perhaps even thousands, of Davidic demigods could dwell among moderns. Second, the conspiracy was a hotter story if the Vatican had played a part in it. Third, the plot to exploit in the twentieth-century the survival of the House of David's bloodline had split into rival camps – and it is easier to break a stone which has a faultline.

Thanks to his chance discovery in 1965, Leonard knew exactly where the clues of this mystery were to be found.

Chapter Seven

Rehennes took its name from the ancient Celtic tribe of Rhedones. It perches naturally on the foothills of the Pyrenees, on the French side of the border with Spain. Now it is a small village that thrives on tourism. The story of the treasures discovered by its priest caused Rennes-le-Château (its modern name) to join Stonehenge and the Bermuda Triangle as the three most famous centres of mystery and intrigue.

The story began in the last decade of the nineteenth-century. The basic facts are simple; all else is speculation. An otherwise obedient priest resolutely declined to explain to his superiors the source of vast new wealth. He was suspended by the Bishop of Carcassonne but reinstated on direct orders from Rome. He was suspended from the priesthood but refused to move from the village. He died with his secret in Rennes-le-Château on 22 January 1919.

7.1 The memory of the holiday with Philippa had faded after eight years but the place still had its magic. Leonard entered the chapel and discovered a film crew conversing in North American English. He showed them that he worked for the BBC so they welcomed him instead of asking him to leave.

Left to his own devices he examined the statue of Jesus and the Baptist. It was John who carried the banner which read *Agnus Dei*. Leonard broke out in a cold sweat having identified a Templar motif. The unspoken heresy was that Jesus has taken the disciples and the leadership from John.

The investigator, feeling some guilt at the half truth of his BBC credentials, examined the statue carefully. He took notes of details on the sides and obverse which was not shown in the photographic reproductions.

Sarcastically, Leonard crossed himself as he lowered his head and left the building. He walked along the narrow path into the sunshine. The Canadians were shouting goodbye.

He found Peter Bartlett, kneeling beside a gravestone, copying the inscription:

'This one is a cipher, Mr Leonard, and it won't be too difficult for me to decode it. I don't mind telling you that I'm excited by this.'

'Call me Michael. I have much to tell you, young man.'

7.2 They walked to the town square. After lunch they enquired about the period of German Occupation. The villagers were friendly but cautious.

An old man called Maurice knew all about Christmas 1944 and had learned to speak English in the Resistance. His friend – code named Lyle – had informed London by wireless about the German search for treasures. It was true. The landscape here was undisturbed, vast, and haunting. It was just the sort of place that art might be hidden. For three days Maurice took the journalists to explore hidden caves and disused mines until they had to return to London.

'When we get home I can access War Department files which are still Classified,' Leonard told Bartlett.

7.3 Before Leonard's contacts in Whitehall were able to oblige, London's public libraries yielded some books and articles about Nazi treasure hunting.

During the excavations of 1944 in Rennes-le-Château many villagers had sided with the Germans. Some were persuaded by incentives; others by the promise of the restored sovereignty of Gaul – separated from the North under the Third Reich.

Leonard believed that it was not the religious nor the monetary-artistic worth of the lost treasures which had attracted the Nazis but the power of the relics to re-instate the deposed rulers of Gaul. In support of this, he noted that the German archaeologists were not reporting to curators of art or antiquities. Like the priest who discovered the treasure in the nineteenth-century, and like Michael Leonard, Berlin was aware of the political significance. It concerned Gaul's King Dagobert II and his usurped sovereignty.

Working through the night in the third-floor office, Bartlett suggested over a Chinese home-delivery sweet-and-sour chicken that there had to be more to it than that. *Reinstating Gaul as a Grail kingdom was the Nazis' plan, to be sure, but long after the War, nobody could be serious about breaking up modern France. Were the conspirators anti-republicans, anti-communists, neo-fascist, or pious extremists? What was the connection to the girl who walked on water? And where was She now?*

Leonard poured the spicy sauce over his fried rice. His assistant confessed that he felt 'nervous' about working on these files at 10pm in the dark and undisturbed depths of London.

'Why should the conspirators, if they are so powerful, allow us to expose them?'

Leonard sidestepped the question rather than admit their motives might not be in conflict.

'After fourteen months of trodding through chapels, secret meetings in art galleries, and choking with dust in basement libraries,' he declared.

'The time has come for me to ask the woman for information. If she agrees to an interview, I will make sure her feet are on the ground, and dry ground.'

Chapter Eight

LAKE DE BERRE, SWITZERLAND, July 1974

Leonard's second encounter with the actress also took place in the open air but the Swiss lake captioned in the French newspapers fifteen years earlier was his suggestion.

This made it cooler than California but he felt stifled. After more than a year the sight of Sélène rekindled his passion even before he was certain that the figure in the distance was hers.

He was shocked to discover, as he approached the waterfall, following her directions, that his legs weakened like jelly. He was early and he allowed his mind to drift into erotic daydreams.

Happily, she was on time; perhaps she cared. But his heart pounded with a sense of frustration: *she was unreachable like the moon; he was not in control; the French were always one jump ahead. Like Marchant, she too was playing with him.*

On the northwest bank of Lake de Berre there was an open meadow and a golf course. The lake fed a spectacular waterfall. Below the bridge, the water disgorged into a narrow, rocky river and disappeared into a forest. The meeting place was the footbridge over a deep ravine.

She stared at him and then looked away. She was fidgeting with the fingers of her right hand. She was equally ill at ease, but for a different reason. Leonard had imposed a condition. She must come to meet him sober and undrugged.

'Fresh air and orange juice are potent conducers of highs,' she had answered. 'And the rendezvous you agreed is a place of power.'

Magnetic. It certainly had a resonance in this investigation.

On this early morning the bright sun was shaded by the trees to the south and east, yet Michael Leonard was sweating. He walked across the log footbridge almost one hundred feet above the narrow but turbulent river. He got close to her but with the torrent of water it was hard to hear what she was shouting. He laughed that they were both nervous and that he was the one who needed a drink. She smiled, then admitted, yes, she had contrived a 'non-chemical oceanic feeling' by asking to meet in the National Park near Lake de Berre on which she had once walked.

So, she was making this claim.

Leonard conceded that the numinous feeling of the place was majestic.

'I am your majesty,' she responded. *Another claim.*

Over the roar of cascading waters he shouted to her that she was under great stress and her drugs had been a temporary shelter. She agreed, yes, she was facing a terrible choice, living out a personal drama. Acting made many people lose their own identities. She felt vulnerable. Hollywood had cast her in parts for her body, not her mind. She pleaded with exaggerated distress to engage him, *what was she to do? Only he could advise her. She could trust no-one else.*

'So, your affair with Johnny Lord and your Hollywood career are over?' he shouted over the waterfall.

'Why do you want to know?' she asked, meaning, *who is asking these questions, personal admirer or professional journalist?*

'You have been set up,' the whole man replied calmly, 'What else do you want me to say? Together, we can expose the conspirators.'

This stirred Sélène. Her face became enraged and close to tears. Her crystal clear voice was raised, now audible against the roar of the waters.

'Listen, Michael, to the words which pour through the stones because they have been passed over and erased by the Pharisees and scribes. Yet these words will never be recalled. 'I am the Daughter of Israel, ravished every hour from my youth. Behold, I am Understanding and Science and the Spirit dwelleth in me. I am in the House of Stone, which is in the shade of heavy clouds, yet its rains wash me at night and I glow in the morning sun. My feet are swifter than the winds and my hands are gentler than the rays of moon. My yoke is gentle; I am deflowered and yet still a virgin. I am a harlot for those that will ravish me and innocent with such that will know me not. I am loved by all, but a lover to few. I walk on waters but am walked over."

She shed a tear.

Leonard interrupted her ravings and shouted over the noise of the falling waters.

'You are crying because *they* want – and *you want* – to re-enact a biblical drama on the stage of the modern world, but, my dear lady, religion is well past its sell-by date. Superstition, hypocrisy and . . . *lies*. Let's go where we can talk and I will help you.'

He had provoked her whole body and soul close to detonating violence.

'But Michael, I read everything you write. You don't deny my descent from the Holy Family and in the newspapers you boast that you are very close to finding the Secret Genealogy.'

'But I haven't been able to see the alleged document.'

'But you know it exists! And what it is!' She shook his substantial frame with a gentleness that comically demonstrated her anger, 'And yet you say I am deluded and I need a psychiatrist.'

'I only said you had a chemical addiction . . .'

Leonard hesitated. He desired to know her in the Biblical sense. He also wanted to write the authorised story. *So why enrage her?* His head thought, *another impossible romance.* His heart said that gaining her trust would make her need him. His conscience replied that this girl needed help.

He looked away to avoid her eyes.

Scissors cut paper, paper wraps stone, stone breaks scissors. *I am a suitor, a journalist, a decent person. I want her in my bed. I want to expose the conspiracy. I want to save the saviour.*

Instinctively, the journalist asked her directly if she was still in contact with the Guardians of the World. She looked at him with pleading or puzzled eyes. She wasn't angry, so he carefully framed the next question.

'Would it help if I meet them?'

She sealed his lips gently, sweetly, with her index finger.

An antique-style copper bracelet engraved with the Davidic star swept down her smooth olive forearm which gently stroked his cheek.

Through her white sleeve the erotic Mediterranean sun cast the silhouette of her body like an x-ray. She was wearing no bra. Stone broke scissors.

8.1 With his right thumb and first finger the suitor encircled her third finger and said, 'We are hot,' and she kissed him deeply.

'Yes, Michael, it is decreed that we shall marry.'

He broke out in a sweat as the hormones released triggers through his body. No woman had placed her lips on the mouth of a man as she did, and the skeptic found himself closer to heaven than the angels. She really was divine. She embraced his top lip, and he kissed her lower lip. Her mouth became tender; he did not know how to react. He thought with his head. She caressed his lips one at a time, side to side. She told him in French that his lips were alive like a ripe fruit on the tree. She played with her tongue and licked his teeth, swearing that no man had held her as securely as he did.

Leonard mentioned the film stars and directors with whom she had been linked. She protested in a sharp, child-like voice, with some French phrases.

'I told you that the actors lose their minds. Unlike you, the princes of Hollywood cannot cry, and they crave success because they are compensators, power-freaks, and controllers. They don't love, and can't love people. They play with us. They are the children of celluloid marriages, celebrities who pose in public but in private turn away from intimacy. Darling, these people all, I repeat, *all*, use drugs and perversions to gain sexual satisfaction, but fortunately I was brought up very strictly in convents.'

She looked to him for approval but he was reliving all those newspaper stories. Every month she had been linked to a new man of power. Her voice became husky and very angry – full of resentment and violence. She changed character. She laughed.

'So what if the newspapers call me a bad girl? Would it help if I told the truth, that I was boring? In truth I love your strength and honesty and your confidence makes me feel secure and feminine. So what if I boosted a few male egos. I didn't dare tell your fellow reporters that Johnny and I *never slept together*. I promise that is the truth, Michael.

I had my own room. The stud is like a frightened schoolboy with me. Believe me, Hollywood is all dreams and illusions. They soon believe it is real. But you seek truth. You are respected in journalism and that is why I trust you. You are naïve and direct, and so am I. We are so alike.'

She has said it all. There is no line between acting and living. Four people were present at a meeting of two. As the actress reasoned and the little girl pleaded, Leonard switched from suitor to journalist who recalled a detail from his notes.

According to the Italian convent school, Sarah Kelly had been left-handed, a sign of the diabolic they believed! But 'Sélène' had used her *right hand* which had gently sealed his lips. He panicked as his hypothesis collapsed for Hélène and the Capulé girl. *So, they were two distinct persons.* Adding to his confusion, was Helen MacRae a cover for Sarah St Clair. Why force their little actress to switch nationality? And especially this one, who speaks of truth, such a magnificent manipulator of lies. In her mind game she perceived herself to be a virgin despite her well-known liaisons with half the grandees of Tinseltown. And Leonard was asked to be the first and finest prince who has tasted her lips.

She didn't learn to kiss men so exquisitely at convent school.

Once again Sarah – or Helen – sensed his suspicions.

'What about Senator Weidfeld?' he asked sarcastically.

'Not my type,' she answered too quickly. 'Listen, I will tell you something,' she declared, having stopped her passionate kissing.

Adopting a slightly American dialect her words tumbled out.

'I gave a reading before an invited audience in USA. At *Harvard University*. AMR – Ancestral Memory Regression – admittedly drug-induced. PLH (Past Lives Hypnosis) is now well-respected.'

'By whom?' he enquired.

She had to shout to make herself heard over the noise of the waterfall behind them. Each time he signed to her to move away from the edge, she refused to move. She kept her arms around the rustic log fence which protected people from falling over the bridge into the deep, narrow gorge.

'Senator Weidfeld broke my fingers but I'm a quick healer, Michael. *PLH rewrites history and explodes science,*' she protested, 'and do you know what I saw under Ancestral Memory Regression? No, you do not, because only *I* am able to transcend the biosphere. You have the greater brain, Michael Leonard, but it is stuck firmly in the selfish needs of your present, practical, and personal predicament. *Isn't that poetic?* So I will tell you that I impressed some very clever researchers like you when I retrieved an episode from the unchronicled childhood of Jesus Christ.'

She waited for his reaction.

He said nothing.

In frustration she clenched her fist tightly and crashed it down on the rough edge of the wooden fence. She drew blood but ignored it. Leonard played the power game. He turned and walked away. She followed him along the path of small rough stones to a set of stairs descending to the river. It was quieter and more shaded by bright green bushes.

He told her that he was reading a book about the pre-Gospel Infancy stories.

'*I knew it*. Because soul mates are telepathic,' she explained.

He shook his head. He never believed in such things.

She continued, tugging his arm, 'Michael, I was able to tell them that one day the child Ye-ho-shua (she pronounced the name with great respect) and his companions were playing on a rooftop, and one of them fell to his death. The others ran away, and the Son of Man, left *by Himself*, was accused of pushing the boy to his death. *The Son* went to the dead boy and asked, "Zeinunus, Zeinunus, who threw you from the rooftop?" and the dead boy spoke the name of the friend who had done it.

'Then, one of the Harvard professors enthusiastically declared that this was recounted by a terribly ancient, obscure Arabic legend . . .'

'*There you are, then*,' Leonard declared in defence of reason, '*you see? It was not paranormal powers.*'

'No, no, Michael, I had not, *could not possibly* have . . . known . . . of it,' she stammered betraying her disappointment.

He scolded her like a pupil slow to learn.

'Listen and I'll spell it out, darling. *They . . . have . . . set . . . you . . . up!* They hypnotised the story into your mind. And I will prove it. I'll prove it. *To you first*. I promise. Not to my readers or viewers. Because I love you. I want you, Sarah or Helen, princess or plain citizen, just as you are, whoever you are, an ordinary person. Not deluded. Not deified.

I want you to be who you are. Don't become anything for anyone. There is no such thing as the Second Coming. Even if you, or many survivors are descended from the Messiah's family, so what? *It won't change the world.'*

She smiled.

'Michael, will you really take me as I am? *Whatever I am?'* she demanded, 'Give me your unconditional promise. Then suppose I really come from the ancient Family of David, the world's sovereign monarchy in perpetuity? Could you handle that? No, Michael of modest family, I think you could not! *You could prove it and sell your books on it, but you couldn't accept it.'*

Placing her hand on his shoulder, and adopting a slightly French accent, she pitied him. 'You can sell the story to others, but you cannot consider that it may be the truth.'

He looked her in the eye. He could not admit that she had found inconsistent behaviour in him. Worse still, she had also shown him that his mind had been confused by the Catholic Church. He didn't really believe in the virginity of Mary so *why recoil against believing in the offspring of Jesus?* And he didn't really accept that Jesus was divine, *so why believe that he was celibate?*

Michael Leonard stopped in his tracks, closed his eyes, and repeated four times, *'Oh, my God!'*

Still licking her injured hand, Sélène asked what troubled him.

He was smiling.

'Mary Magdalene of high birth! The legends of the Languedoc say that after she escaped from Judea with the child in her womb, she was rejected by many of the Judeans living in Gaul because she was a foreigner. *A black princess whom Jesus took as his partner.'*

Sélène looked up to him, wondering where all the scholarship was leading.

'Sarah Kelly was a false name given to you by your guardians to conceal your identity. *It wasn't your real name, was it?'*

She shook her head.

'Well, listen, Sarah Kelly. The Queen of Sheba in dynastic alliance conceived the offspring of Solomon. Then she returned to Ethiopia where, centuries later, the Ark of the Covenant was taken and concealed with many replicas of the ultimate relic. The real thing disappeared from the Temple of their Judaean ancestors who were now defeated and scattered.'

She pleaded for him to make this relevant. She did not have long to wait.

He smiled at her.

'Egyptian was spoken in first-century Ethiopia and *Sara Kali* means Black Princess. *Aren't you pleased?*'

She was so pleased that tears of joy broke through her laughter.

Chapter Nine

THE PLAZA, LOS ANGELES, JULY 1973

The Graduation Ball of the American Academy of Dramatic Arts is the place to be seen. From 8pm until midnight once a year posing polarises the ether. Fun and flirting are not unknown but some serious encounters take place under the chandeliers of the Great Ballroom in the city's finest hotel.

Two months after her first meeting with Michael Leonard, Sélène had graduated with a diploma.

Senator Spencer Weidfeld was on the lips of many as the most eligible of the unmarried men. As handsome and energetic as Jack Kennedy he had obvious prospects and he was coming to this year's event.

Recruited by the Republicans at the President's Yale reunion party, Weidfeld was initiated into the Skull and Bones, connected to powerful men, and rose like a meteor on the Committee on Foreign Relations. After five years, the Party's media consultants begged him to clean his image and prepare for high office. Join a church. Find a good woman. Have 2.4 children.

Whoever married him might become America's First Lady in years to come. The people behind the scenes who watched over a young actress from France were experts in dynastic alliances.

9.1 Aged twenty-eight in 1973 more than twenty years had lapsed since Sarah Kelly had seen her parents and left her native country. She spoke

English with lapses into French, Scottish and American accents. Like Weidfeld, she was a Catholic, and with her reputation, the description lapsed could be applied with certainty. This gave him comfort.

He admired her black velvet evening dress, which exposed acres of bared shoulders and unblemished skin. He stroked her naked back with his eyes. He stood behind her and ostentatiously inhaled the fragrance of her shiny black hair. As he savoured her, she turned round and stared momentarily. He met her eyes, wide open, brown, and very innocent. A girl who looked so much like an angel could only be a slut. *'The press reflects its own prurience,'* he uttered to himself.

She turned away from his gaze.

Suddenly she was speaking to his friend, Carole-Anne. *Was she asking his name?* He heard but could not translate. Too many words wee in French; but they were whispered furtively.

Grasping the situation, Senator Harvey Karman grabbed Weidfeld's shoulder in a panic.

'Jesus H. Christ, man, *don't even think about her?'*

'I can handle it, thanks, Harvey.'

Weidfeld extended his hand in what looked like a friendly handshake.

It drew tears of pain from Karman's eyes. The ring on his left hand bit into the bone of his finger.

Weidfeld turned to Sélène. She displayed effervescence then cool indifference like a child resisting the need to grow up. *She just had to be in therapy. Emotionally damaged and capable of exploitation by the formula of flattery, presents, and persistence.* Sélène's waifish, cute looks were in vogue and appearing in the colour magazines in America and Europe. It was the look of the angel-next-door, the short-dark-haired girl in a black dress. Plain – but indecent. Twiggy had made the emaciated figure fashionable, if not irresistible, to the modern macho. A portrait of Sélène had won an award on the New York graphic arts scene but in the flesh she had presence. In his mind he undressed her.

For the second time she looked round and met his stare which she held too long. She flushed visibly at her clumsy error.

She could be taken very easily from Johnny Lord, her movie director boyfriend.

Sensing the situation, Carole-Anne introduced them.

'Spencer, darling, this is a very close friend of mine, Sélène, who is a graduate of the Academy. She combines the nobility of Grace Kelly with the purity of Audrey Hepburn.'

Sélène raised her demure downcast eyes and pouted.

'Mr Weidfeld, please don't listen to her nonsense. I hear great things are expected of *you*.'

The band was playing Smokey Robinson's *The Tears of a Clown*.

The newspaper which broke the story quoted a political friend who had turned against the young Senator.

According to the gossip columns Weidfeld said he had a good nose and had liked her body fluids. (The actual quote was much more vulgar). Weidfeld's lawyers turned these words into a $2m lawsuit: 'My client said he liked classy women because they wore expensive perfume which did not obstruct nature.'

Chapter Ten

INVERNESS, AUGUST 1974

Michael Leonard visited the Convent school in Scotland twelve years after the girl they called Sarah Kelly was forced to leave. Her third expulsion made it a recurring event in search of an explanation. He interviewed a former schools inspector in Edinburgh, as the Scottish Education Department was independent from the English Ministry of Education and Science. In this way, he acquired a list of the teachers who served in 1958-59.

The girl had been sent down from two previous convent schools (first in Paris, France, and then Sora, a village in the south of Italy). But the Edinburgh file merely described her as being *a spirited girl*.

Discrepancies pointed Leonard to a cover-up. In Paris, the Scottish pupil sent back to Scotland had been named Helen MacRae. A deceased mother's last known address and that of her next-of-kin were entered on the report. The mother's home in Aberdeen led to a false trail commencing with an unrelated MacRae family which had resided there between 1926-1945.

The other address in Lanarkshire near Glasgow had greater significance to Leonard's investigation. And from the file he discovered that the young Miss MacRae was sent with church funding to The Margaret Alan Private School which was close to Inverness. She had attended it for two months until she attained fifteen – the minimum leaving age under the law of Scotland.

In June 1965 she left for America convinced that, having been born in 1945 and reached grade three when she was orphaned in France, she was, in fact, aged seventeen.

10.1 In the school village near Inverness Leonard found a retired schoolteacher – a lively old woman called Jessie. A few drams of the local firewater loosened her tongue. Her companion, a police constable, spoke about the girl as having being reported missing from the school on several occasions.

Nobody here knew the girl as anything other than Helen MacRae.

Leonard found eight of her school chums lcally, in each case using an approach appropriate to their characters – from a friendly chat to an official interrogation. They all said that Helen spoke perfect English although she was French by birth. He asked if anyone thought it odd at the time that the orphaned child used a Scottish mother's maiden surname. Blank stares and shrugged shoulders expressed inability or unwillingness to answer. She was lots of fun, they all said – a wild child – fearless – attention seeking – the life and soul of the party. But she also had depressions that would last for days. Some said these began when she was scolded. Despite her rebellious nature she craved the respect of her elders. Helen was a high-achiever, taller than her classmates and athletic, but her brazen arrogance meant that none of her friends resented her superiority.

Leonard harvested a bewildering variety of responses about the behaviour that resulted in the expulsions. Helen did the things a teenager out of control did. She smoked, escaped dormitory to town, and at the tender age of fifteen had 'a real boyfriend.'

Got laid? Her friends said this was not unusual for Inverness even at the time. *But this was not why she got expelled.*

No, it was not her sexual prowess, they all agreed. Leonard had to surrender his salacious story, yet nobody would betray the real explanation.

Leonard retreated to his Bed and Breakfast. The home cooking of local produce was delicious and le lay fully clothed on top of his bed half-asleep, kept awake by his overactive brain.

What could have been so bad? A young mother of three who had befriended Helen had asserted, *They refused to believe in her.* When Leonard tested this on the other witnesses the reaction was a knowing silence rather than denial. Her school friends insisted that there was no messianic delusions until after she went to the USA. Leonard showed them the newspaper of 1959. According to her girlfriends, the day she walked on water was known to everyone, but one had said that it paled to insignificance beside *The Other Thing.*

10.2 The secrecy tantalised Leonard in its unanimity, spontaneity, and water-tight security. Not one brick could be dislodged from the wall of silence. Tongues were stilled and the recollections of local doctors and police were impenetrable. Bribery could not break the professional ethic. Was it a superior native culture, or had these people an inbred will to conceal something of a heretical nature? Leonard became aware of the strong religious mindset in the north of Scotland across varied sects of tightly-knit communities. When, from 1207, the secrets of the Templars were exposed and exterminated by popes and kings, the continental Europeans saw Scotland as the safe haven for their relocation and revival.

Leonard visited the senior child psychiatrist in Inverness. Without an appointment, he turned up at the cottage clinic. After the last patient had gone the journalist was offered tea and the textbook explanations of delinquency including the trauma of losing both parents at the age of five.

Was she not seven?

The healer turned the pages of his file and repeated that in 1952 the child would have been aged five. Leonard scratched his head and challenged the doctor who declined to deny that the convent had threatened him against an allegation that sexual abuse had taken place while the girl was in its care. Then he claimed that he never had adequate proof. The interview went well: the psychiatrist did not object to Leonard's pressure, and appeared to say what he knew.

In those days no-one talked about sex, far less sexual abuse.

Leonard returned to the modest home of one of her school friends he believed to be the weakest link. Hers was a modest, council-owned home and he employed flattery, persistence, and cheque book journalism but she did not want her name in the audit trail. As a last resort Leonard used his truth drug.

She started to talk in the broad Scots accent peculiar to the far north. 'The nuns drilled into us the fear that boys know their own evil thoughts and are ashamed of themselves. They used to say that Our Lady blushes each time one of her girls uncrosses her legs. We were said to be immoral but Sarah was regarded as more than immoral, but evil. No, *possessed* was the word they used. She challenged the nuns because she was totally immune to punishment, pain, or corrective instruction. As a parent, I can relate to the nuns.'

Leonard drove back to Fiona to test his emerging discoveries on another of the school-friends. She kept him standing outside the timber and glass porch of the higher class home; she kept claiming her husband was away and could not let him in. The house was the top level of a red sandstone baronial house with a well-kept huge lawn. Fiona was articulate but cautious, and could not be fed with the drug.

Motivated by boredom and loneliness, she talked for the first time about her friend. In response to punishment Sarah had demonstrated her teachers' lack of control over her by gouging wounds or carving initials on her hands or feet. Fiona attributed her friend's self-inflicted physical pain as a numbing pleasure to atone feelings of guilt. In the early days of this problem the nuns had seen this as diabolic. Villagers had called it witchcraft. Even in those days the locals talked briefly, in hushed tones, and never to outsiders.

The real suffering which tortured Sarah, according to Fiona, was the absence of love and respect from her foster-parents and teachers. For this reason, Sarah strived to come first in every class – lessons and sports – except one subject. Religious Instruction attracted Sarah's contempt: she told them she knew that the trinity and virginity doctrines were nonsense.

Fiona confirmed that Leonard's central questions were posed even in those days, twelve years ago. Her teachers wanted to know *who was telling her such things?* According to Fiona, 'Sarah just knew all things.'

At this crucial point the interviewer had to leave.

10.3 Leonard had been granted a twenty-minutes audience with Monsignor Salandini in a building attached to the Cathedral of Inverness. The journalist opened the interview by asking what the Convent knew about the previous identity of their pupil. The clergyman said she was

French-born and used two British-sounding names. Asked to explain this, Salandini enquired about the purpose of the interview. Asked to explain the expulsions, he stated that decisions to remove pupils from convents, including his, are reluctantly taken in order to restore order. He did not deny that three serial expulsions would constitute a pattern of events pointing to a root problem. He would not talk further about that pupil and answered questions with unhelpful brevity. He denied that the problem was sexual immorality. Leonard suggested it must be the reason because there was enough of this on file for the visiting prelate to hide the truth and divert the interview from 'The Great Secret.'

As the allocated minutes expired Salandini's fingers drummed on his polished desk surface. The interview was being timed out.

Silence. The rain had stopped and the afternoon was bright. Through the leaded glass the sky was clear and the leaves glowed in many fluorescent shades. Leonard asked if they could walk outside in the fresh air. He was told it was permissable with the authorities so long as they did not walk on the grass. The message was so clear that Leonard smiled to himself.

Don't walk on the grass.

He broke the silence by remarking that the outdoors smelled so fresh. He allowed time for the unspoken meaning of this to offend Salandini.

Your office stinks, pal.

He asked the Monsignor if he could disclose the reason for expelling Helen MacRae which was even more terrible than her sexual immorality.

The six-foot tall Italian prelate of the pope said he *could* do, but he would not. Silence. Impasse but Leonard felt victorious. He thanked the clergyman in order to annoy him and walked out of the garden with a feeling of satisfaction. He had confirmed that there was something worth the effort and waiting to be discovered.

10.4 If one shop cannot supply the goods you try its rival. There was also the Church of Scotland. When 'Helen' was in Inverness, the reformed national church was split in a heated debate which had narrowly voted to set up a Committee for Psychic Studies. While Leonard searched for the events that three convents were unable to handle he found a *Glasgow Herald* story of a Scottish minister who specialised in exorcisms. He had advised the newspaper that poltergeists and telekinesis (extra-sensory disturbance of objects) 'are by no means unknown in the houses of troubled and energetic children of the age group 12-14, especially females in Scotland. But this subject is discussed by medical scientists with great reticence.' Within the last six months the Protestant Minister had personally assisted in eight cases of 'haunted houses' in Glasgow that involved police, social services and housing authorities to sort out real troubles. For several weeks Leonard drew blanks. Possibly because of the great Celtic divide between Protestant and Catholics Helen MacRae or Sarah Kelly were not on the files of the *Psychic Research Committee*. And because her visions were heretical and offensive to her own side of this great divide, the Convent brought in modern psychiatry.

Obtaining clinical records was cheap. In a narrow lane behind the library in Inverness Leonard bought a sealed envelope and handed over fifty pounds in cash to the boyfriend of a medical secretary. To the hesitant informer Leonard defended cheque-book journalism by saying that a free society depends on an open press. The surly youth watched Leonard open the envelope. Instead of an unprocessed film there were six prints. Leonard asked for the negatives, but the youth smiled, returned Leonard's miniature 'spy-camera,' and walked away saying, 'You did not say you were the only customer. The photos aren't legally yours, are they?'

Leonard made new negatives and enlarged the photos to reveal almost illegible documents. The diagnosis of the illness of Helen MacRae, and the explanation of her claims was a delusion of grandeur – a Freudian syndrome called The Family Romance. 'In this condition a child believes his or her ancestors were aristocratic and that their anonymity or mediocrity will pass when fate restores their true status.'

Helen (also known as Sarah) was officially labelled crazy. *How very convenient for the authorities.*

10.5 Nobody stopped Michael Leonard from walking off the street into the girls' dormitory of the Convent of the Sacred Heart outside Inverness. On the third floor he found a white-tiled corridor leading to a courtyard built around a light well. He found Room 35 whose door he pushed open to reveal a whitewashed cubicle. It measured about ten feet by twelve with unpainted window frame and a carved crucifix, nailed above a plain iron bed.

A soft Irish lilt emerged from behind the door.

'Mr Leonard, I presume?' An elderly woman removed her glasses and put aside a book she was reading.

He was taken by surprise; managed to mumble a few words.

'Your door was open, sorry . . . you must be Sister Margaret, but . . . ?'

'*How do I know you?* You've traced everyone else, so I figured it wouldn't take you too long to find *me*. And I will be the one to tell you what you have set out to discover, if you will be kind enough not to attribute it to me. Sit on the bed. We only get one seat in these rooms. Can't imagine why.'

Margaret told Leonard that she was the only Sister who had some influence for good over Sarah – possibly even kept the child from tumbling into the bottomless pit – by talking to her, often and at length.

About what, Leonard asked.

'About The Kingdom of Heaven, about the love of Jesus for little children, about her *anima christiana*. You see, she constantly denied her Christian identity. Once, for two days I defied my colleagues and joined Sarah – her real name was Helen MacRae, incidentally – in the detention room, sharing her hunger, force-feeding her on the Gospel of John. For a long time Helen stopped her ears and she screamed that she was Jewish, *'And so was Rabbi Lord Jesus, our Prince and our King – and his* wife *Mary Magdalene, and John the Baptist, and even John who wrote the pornography you name the Fourth Gospel. But perhaps you don't want to hear the truth. But I have seen things you will never see, yet you try to teach* me."

Leonard nodded and Margaret continued.

'Eventually Helen became calm and the mysterious words of John's Gospel soothed and coaxed her into eating food and reaching a compromise with her teachers. She was so arrogant and strong-willed. No, that doesn't begin to describe it. She blackmailed us with injuring herself so that the sisters would get into trouble.'

Leonard's attention was transferred to the movement of someone in the gardens outside the small window, *like a prison window but with an ecclesiastical mind-arch instead of bars*. The man in a long coat was looking towards this window. Leonard's attention was distracted when he heard the nun's astounding confession.

'She destroyed my faith but restored it in most of the others.'

He turned slowly to face her in astonishment.

'Mr Leonard, Helen saw things we can't see. When she blasphemed, she said words that I wrote but have taken ten years to comprehend, but even at the time, they etched into my memory, word for word. *'It's okay,'* she said, *'you can forget God and live, but without LOVE you are a vacuum and a vessel of pollution and sin and prone to disease. Only in love you discover truth and beauty and all the enchantment of the world and its sources of power. And then you let God in by whatever name."*

'Someone simply fed her this line,' Leonard prompted.

'Yes, I know that, and a lot of fifteen-year-olds *are* serious-minded but *she* understood these words, whereas my ears were closed and I was forty seven.'

Leonard sat back on the bed but kept the eye contact.

'You want to tell me something, Margaret, but you are holding back. Why? Jesus said that the truth will set you free, and all things will be made manifest. So what comes before this truth that you should stop it?'

While Margaret reflected on this, the journalist invited her to a high tea.

10.6 The reporter walked with the nun to the village tea shop. So she was willing to be seen with him but she would not disclose The Great Secret without recounting the full story. The Northern sunshine teased them through the branches of tall leafless trees that lined a stone-walled, damp, narrow country road. The cars splashed dirty spray as they walked along a muddy pavement. In the tea room they ordered a pot for two and a selection of cakes.

'So this is cheque book journalism.' Margaret laughed nervously.

'It's time for me to put up or shut up? She once told me that St Augustine had said that a man who frequented a whore house was seeking in his heart the love of God. She didn't say that to defend her own morality but to show me that she was sophisticated.'

Margaret stared at the reporter in earnest, hoping for something to avoid the moment of truth but Leonard's silence invited her to offer more.

She continued, 'As you said, someone fed her all this, but she took it to heart, Mr Leonard. It was her deep understanding of the problem.'

'What problem, Margaret, was she a prostitute?'

The nun was shocked at the suggestion and denied it absolutely. At his prompting, she admitted that perhaps, in theory, like other convents a small number of the ordained priests and even the nuns . . .'

She became agitated and waved her hands.

'Were friendly with the prettier girls?' Leonard suggested as he poured her tea, added her milk and sugar and stirred it.

'It's not what you think, Michael.'

She sipped her tea slowly.

When she was relaxed, Leonard unzipped a slim, black leather case and handed her the Inverness newspaper story from 1959, and a *Glasgow Herald* story of 'psycho-active' teenagers in Scotland. She nodded a sad little agreement when he asked her to describe the supernatural events in the convents.

'It was terrible. Her hands displayed the stigmata of Christ. We brought her food to her room. T'ings got so bad,' she whispered in her soft Irish lilt, 'that at one time all our images of the Virgin Mary were removed or covered up by order of the authorities. Can you imagine that? Even the life-size statue in the chapel was boxed inside a casing to restore tranquillity.'

Leonard looked at Margaret in pity as he took in her words.

'Not only the girls but the sisters became hysterical when the graven images were seen to move. Plaster statues shed tears and collapsed and one day a huge oil painting of Mary Magdalene called out when Sarah was walking past, *My Daughter.*'

Chapter Eleven

BETHANIA, JUDÆA, 33CE

At last. After four days he was on his way.

Martha hurried to the village to meet him. Panting with exhaustion and flushed with rage, she spoke to him, softly but in anger.

'Yashi, had you been here your brother-in-law would not have died.'

Two townsmen from the Essene brotherhood nodded their heads in agreement. The one who had sponsored the ritual initiation of her brother pleaded, 'Yashi, we know that God grants whatsoever you ask of Him. I beg you to come with us.'

There was nobody else they could call upon because the Pharisees had expelled all the Essenes and Therapeutae from Judea as sorcerers in the ways of the Egyptians. Yashi turned to Martha and said softly, but with his casual pride, 'Your brother . . . will rise. Whoever has faith in Me shall live in eternity. The Son has authority over time itself.'

They looked at each other in amazement. Already they had smelled the decomposing body of Lazarus although it had been left in the coolest place. The village rabbis who loved Lazarus were already asking the sisters to justify the delay in the burial.

One of the sisters of the Essenes from the Holy City pleaded, 'We know that you believe in the resurrection of bodies which will take place.'

Miriam was more anxious. 'Yashi, our brother was poisoned by an error of dosage and it was not God's will, but your Essene friends here who might be found guilty . . . of murder . . .' At this word the perpetrator recoiled, and Miriam wept, 'So you must ask The Almighty One who can do so, awaken Lazarus if his time has not come.'

Given the opportunity to save his lover's brother, not even a Messiah could resist. Therefore, contrary to the policy against gratuitous signs and miracles, Jesus pointed to the flask of the Therapeutae.

'Take Me to him.'

Two men and two women – all four rejoicing with joy – pulled Jesus by the hand, hopping and skipping energetically.

'Off we go, off we go. To the cave in the hills, it is there we go.'

The one who had administered the extract of Fly-Agaric to Lazarus found new strength when he saw the priests were still at the cave. They all helped to roll away the stone and withdrew, fearing the stench after four days. Jesus shook one of the men to reproach him for his lack of faith.

Always the preacher, he was making this an issue of faith!

He entered the cave with the flask shouting, 'Heavenly Father, I know that you hear me but I shout for the sake of the people that they might believe.'

Some hours passed by. People gossiped and prayed. Outside the cave the small group became a large crowd of people from The City of David and they waited patiently, exchanging and embellishing unfounded rumours, wailing, swaying, chanting holy songs, listening to the echoes of prayers and the entreaties from within the cave.

Nothing happened until well after dusk which, everyone agreed, seemed very long in coming and they were very hungry.

Suddenly they heard a deep resonant voice, 'LOOSE HIM. LET HIM GO,' and Lazarus came out, shaking away the linen bandages. The people screamed and wailed, rending their clothes in thanksgiving. Word was sent to the villages. In Jerusalem, the news arrived just before nightfall. Crowds gathered by the empty tomb and people danced until the morning. Lazarus was a righteous man and well-known. Jesus was placed on shoulders and asked to speak.

Traders from the City began to arrive selling food and drink. The Morning Service of the Synagogue was performed here in open air (although the farmers from the valley said they had already recited prayers). Jesus was persuaded to lead, which offended the village rabbis. Among the crowd, grim faces discussed how the nation might be saved from the collapse of God's authority in the hands of the Romans.

When Jesus returned to Jerusalem, the Council had Him arrested and charged with multiple breaches of the Law of Moses. But the witnesses were inconsistent and the Law was argued to invert itself to absurdity. The Galilean sect – popular even with some Judeans – risked a serious confrontation with the High Priests. Every issue now exposed their weakness and if things got out of hand the next dispute could cause their overthrow. Therefore it was decided that without delay the Council should inform the Roman Prefect of their detention of a man who said he was King.

Five years had passed since Pontius Pilatus had been chosen by Rome to integrate the Jews who populated one of the smallest but most troublesome nation-states in the empire. East of the Mediterranean, South of Syria and West of Babylon, these people refused the harmonisation of sound central government. They threatened the peace and prosperity which would result from a single European currency and an administration funded by moderate taxation.

The Nazarite was like many of the sun-crazed preachers of the desert but Herod was known to be a little touchy about his recent elevation to royalty. Sovereign bloodlines take two or three generations to mature.

Nevertheless there would be a fair trial.

In less than five minutes the prisoner was condemned to death by crucifixion despite the view of Pilatus that, in this district, the torture and death in public was a waste of the costly imported wood beams – if not counter productive.

Pilatus pursued a taunting debate with his prisoner, recognising his intelligence and respecting the courage of his supporters. Worshippers of an invisible and single god apparently deriving from the legends of El Shaddai.

'Are you their king, Jew-boy?' he managed to utter in basic Aramaic.

'Are these words yours, Prefect, or have others told them to you?' Jesus replied in perfect Greek, sparing his inquisitor further linguistic humiliation.

'If you can work miracles, Jew-boy, why don't you save yourself? Or at least make some sort of a case to me! You are obviously an educated fool. The courts dispense imperial justice even in these remote parts. Don't you want to live? Answer me. Perhaps you are only the prince of Galilee?'

Pilatus asked this with sarcasm. 'It would then be a territorial dispute with the Herodians.'

The sycophants laughed nervously.

One of the enemies of Jesus, seeing the scheme of Pilatus, intervened, 'We have no king but Caesar,' but Jesus answered the governor, 'This is not my kingdom. I have come to bring the truth.'

Pilatus bellowed sarcastically, ' Oh!! Truth?? And what is truth?'

His words bounced off the stone walls of the chamber and, finding no response, began a journey into eternity. There was a long interval in which nobody knew what was going to happen to Jesus.

Least of all Pilatus.

If the Prefect's question was cynical it might mean that he preferred Greek reason to Hebrew theology. Or perhaps the governor was displaying an uncharacteristic regret that truth plays such a minor part in power politics.

One of the mob came forward and placed in front of the prisoner a wooden board on which the black ink ran, still wet and lethal, ***Jesus the Nazarite, King of the Jews.*** *His fate was sealed.*

'SCOURGE HIM AND CRUCIFY HIM.'

The Pilatus of legend washed his hands and blamed the Jews.

The Pilatus of history returned to an inner room where a man was waiting. A friend of the prisoner. The Prefect knew Joseph of Arimathea was one of the pious men, but he was also well-connected, reliable, and often very useful. And so the elder of the Jewish Community was granted a short private meeting.

The centurions assumed that money had changed hands for they were ordered to carry out all the executions before the Passover but permit the 'king' to be given stimulation salts on a saturated sponge. They were ordered not to break this prisoner's bones, but to hand his expired body to the sons of Joseph as soon as he appeared to have died. They would be given something for the trouble, although the governor said that he himself had taken no money. 'Do it now, before nightfall.'

Gaius Cassius was the one to lance the side of Jesus but dropped his spear in the shock of partial blindness healed. He was dragged away proclaiming that he 'saw it all.' His friends were laughing.

The body was handed over.

All Pilatus had asked from Joseph was the assurance that nothing more would be heard of 'King Y'shua'.

It may be hard to believe, but the assurance was given in good faith.

Chapter Twelve

New York City, 09-28-1974

Dear Mr Leonard,

I sat with Dr R.F. Kohen in Brasserie Angelique on the evening of July 23, 1974. Dr Kohen was Chairman of Project Psi Group 2, co-ordinating various defence applications of paranormal human and animal powers. We met a vice-president of a pharmaceutical corporation in connection with a program to develop humane alternatives to weapons of mass destruction. Later, Kohen turned to me and asserted that these things are a pack of lies exploiting fears and superstitions in leaders on both sides of the Iron Curtain.

I was shocked. He smiled and I knew he was feeding me company disinformation. He then said to me, 'I'll show you how it works, Harvey. My girlfriend is in New York, and she is coming here by my will power. Right to this address although she doesn't know I'm here. If she arrives, observe her surprise, and don't play gooseberry.'

I thought he was talking crap but I did not say so. Twenty minutes later I looked up and saw the famous film actress Sélène – I knew he admired her. She was standing by our table with a surprised look in her eyes, almost scared to see Dr Kohen sitting there. I also felt really spooked by his powers so I did as he told me and I left them alone.

Yours very sincerely,

Harvey M. Rosenberg PhD

12.1 In the early 1970s *Brasserie Angelique* near Central Park was redecorated in the style of *fin de siècle* and priced to deter the casual stalkers of its rich and famous patrons. The elegant tables and chairs were painted white and upholstered in violet. The Chagall stained glass windows were modern and expensive.

Kohen exploited Séléne's surprise to deepen a long kiss on her lips. Thus the embrace no longer seemed spontaneous and she became angry. He denied all knowledge of her existence in New York. She reminded him that he held the Essene belief that all things were predestined because they were known by God from the beginning of time.

'Sit down, Séléne, the beginning has not yet happened. All civilisations fear time, but time fears the pyramids – time machines which link the future and the past, the living and the dead. This is Harvey Rosenberg, my colleague. Being seen with such a famous Hollywood actress will raise my stock and I hope my minders have cameras with them today.'

'Minders?' she inquired.

Rosenberg volunteered, 'You can't imagine that a Defence Department Chief is allowed to walk streets of New York unprotected? Even his informal comments are a risk to our national security. He rates two bodyguards with Red-One access to Service back-up. Aha, nice to meet you, Séléne, I guess I'd better go. *A sort of prior commitment.*'

Kohen said condescendingly, 'And what would Séléne like this evening? A glass of her preferred French red wine?'

'You are asking, do you not, if I'm on drugs?' she replied, 'But you are nervous of *minders*. Who are they? Robert, is it . . . ? I'm sorry. I ask too much. What do these squiggles mean? Is it modern art?'

With an elegant silver ball point pen Kohen was sketching something on the white table top. 'Don't worry, the table is only a painted reproduction. Look, Séléne! If you fail to understand time you will waste your life – but you are not from the herd that drinks from the poison well of oblivion.'

Rosenberg returned, claiming that he had left his umbrella.

Kohen glanced angrily at Rosenberg, then beyond him, and behind his own shoulder. He half-heartedly waved goodbye to Rosenberg and only then he pointed the actress to his inked drawing on the table top.

He explained, 'The observer on planet earth is you. At the Festival of Lights you get a gift of a powerful telescope and so you can see this calendar in a house on a street on this distant quasar. There, our galactic alien celebrates Passover. But for you it is Lights. Light is fast but not instantaneous.'

Rosenberg stared at the drawing for its meaning and for its being etched directly as graffiti onto the table.

Kohen seemed aware only of the Sélène and explained to her, 'Then on earth, your Passover comes and you get out your telescope and observe the calendar on the same quasar is still last Passover. Now, we might understand a delay caused by the speed of light, but is Sara puzzled because she has not perceived my insight of unequal delays? Simple! Now, see what has happened – because the implications are scary to the betting world and to the dealers in stocks. *I have here a time machine.* The same image has been bent unequally, forming two light paths as in this ellipse round the galaxy. I do it all by smoke and mirrors. Like the Creator Himself.'

Kohen looked up, 'Harvey, it was nice of you to come back yet again, but I apologise, I am busy.' He turned to Sélène for her response.

'Robert, my Catholic convent school taught me only enough science to know that there are two things that you have not invented, and the other one is a perpetual motion machine. Free energy is impossible.' Then she whispered, 'And I'm afraid so is a time machine.'

Kohen hesitated again and watched his colleague walk away. Then he turned to Sélène and pointed to his drawing. 'This is the most secret invention in the world. I have Archimedes' lever and I can move the globe. You don't believe me; it's because you don't understand.'

Kohen waited in silence until Rosenberg sulked and left without further delay. In the elegant wine bar, the panels of glass and suspended mirrors reflected shadows and lights menacingly.

'Did you know I was going to come here?' she enquired nervously.

'I caused you to come here.'

Now that he and Sélène were alone his lips were sealed. A kinetic mirror assembly bathed them in cycles of darkness and light. She looked around without identifying any people who might have been spies.

Kohen, clearly ill at ease, spoke quietly, 'Einstein made the greatest leap of scientific *imagination* this century, but I have made the leap in *technology*. Because politicians made his work into a bomb I won't trust them with my time machine and they know it. They can't force me but they watch me.'

Suspended in disbelief, Sélène stared at him silently, blankly.

A girl came. The waitress. Pencil-slim figure, sallow complexion, *definitely not a spy*. Sélène ordered, 'a *Cointreau et limonade*.'

'You know my poison, Miss Angelique,' Kohen barked at the dyed-hair female with one earring, and then he said, 'As usual you have your white make-up. Very gothic.'

She responded, 'Yes, Dr Robert, a little of what we like does us no harm, so I shall personally make your favourite drink for you *con amore*.'

He nodded to her then turned to his guest. 'Sara – for you will be called that – she thinks that she wears *a little* make-up. They accept Einstein as proved by maths and by observation, but Aryans still invent things based on the Newtonian mind-set like composers who ignore Schoenberg's 12-tone row. Jew-haters are blinded by envy and by Christian mythology.'

Sélène stared in shock at Kohen. He avoided her gaze and mutilated his sketch. He was foiling the CIA by redrawing his invention.

When the glass was placed before him the scientist recited rapidly under his breath, 'Blessed art thou oh Lord who has created the fruit of the vine,' then Sélène lifted his glass and casually let it drop to the floor.

In astonishment Kohen looked up from it to examine her face.

'You hypocrite, Robert, to thank your God but condemn the woman who brought the wine for you, *con amore*, a mere gentile you think, but a creature in Her image into which She breathed Her Spirit. Okay, sorry about the gender grammar, but it's not my fault. You should pity a sylph who lives in this urban hell to serve ungrateful guests like you. Can't you see she is an angel lost in a city of wolves? I can feel that her sexuality was crushed in this over-populated hell. *Of all people, Robert,* why don't you feel it? You see the tears but not the eyes, it is your affliction.'

She was stirred but he remained cool.

'The first time we met, Sélène, you helped me with a broken wine-glass? Now you smash mine. Coincidence fascinates me. The fact that we meet here by chance, and then *this*. What does your convent science education in causality and determinism say about that?'

She looked at him with a mixture of respect, contempt, pity, and anger.

Kohen demanded the bill and apologised for the breakage. 'Damage seems to happen when you're around, sweetheart.' The waitress awaited payment.

Theatrically, the actress proclaimed, 'Oh, I shall take care not to be so clumsy, darling.'

Kohen did not smile. His unruffled behaviour took another unpredictable swerve when he paid cash and used the credit card voucher to write, 'HOSTILE WATCHERS. DO AS I SAY.' He flashed this message to her, inhaled deeply and asked, 'Do you feel like taking a walk, *darling*?'

In a low voice he explained, 'I don't know if you follow domestic politics, but this Watergate thing is going to bury me along with Nixon's government. The turmoil will ease my own predicament. My offence is that I've spent a lot of funds on 'my special project,' humane weapons, but for our allies, my own people – the Children of Israel. The only democracy in the MidEast.

'The 'Children Imitating Adults' have closed in on me, but timed properly – and time is something I understand, ha-ha – I will make an agreement acceptable on all sides. I know too much for any another outcome. *I just need to get the timing right.*'

He said this last bit very loudly.

Her eyes widened; her mouth opened, 'Thank you for the explanation, Robert.' Then she realised that it was not meant for her, but still she saw no spies.

He cautioned her, 'By meeting me in this way you'll get into CIA files but, of course, you are there already. Anyone visiting Millbrook gets on CIA files. They see peaceniks and spiritual seekers as subversives.'

'Don't you . . . ?'

He waved his arm, and changed the subject.

'So, my dear Sélène, what brings you to New York?'

She told him about the Charity Film Première Gala opening.

'I star in the new Johnny Lord film.'

No response. She felt uneasy. Kohen was not listening to her. He waved to the waitress with his gold credit card, 'Call me a cab, please,' and to Sélène 'Call me old-fashioned but the waitress is flat. I despise gender-benders. I'm taking you to my sister. A real woman.'

'I give up trying to make you human, Robert. You hurt me.'

They travelled by cab in silence to the home of Caroline Kohen.

'You know more than she does about my political problems, Sélène. I prefer not to worry her. And don't *you* worry about me. I am a few jumps ahead of them. Don't believe everything you will read in the newspapers when it happens.'

'I suppose you've read the future headlines!'

The taxi drove into a well-lit residential district of New York. It was raining heavily but visibility was good.

'There's Caroline's building. I must assume my minders have followed me. Half of them pay me to develop telepathic spying and the other half put old-style goofs on my tail. Let's play their game. Give this to the driver. Run, don't walk, through that alley, enter a black steel gate marked 254 in white paint by keying in the sacred number, treble-6, followed by my secret number of Gematriya, 515, and I'll meet you.'

12.2 Sélène ran along a service lane full of garbage. She felt afraid but the steel gate led to a tunnel and a doorway made of fine white marble. A uniformed janitor met her in the lobby and Kohen was already there. She felt uneasy. *How had he driven to the back, or through the lower level, then walked to the lobby in such a short time?* She had suffered no blackout or lapse of time. Without exchanging a word Kohen summoned the elevator. He smiled. He did not look at her. He did not need to see her discomfort.

12.3 The apartment was on the third floor. It displayed wealth and taste.

So did Caroline Kohen. She was elegant and well-groomed with blonde-streaked hair. She shone like the Hollywood stars of the recently bygone era. If she had escaped occupied Hungary with her brother in 1944 then she had aged very well. Sélène fought the idea that time manipulation might have been involved and continued to admire the older woman. With a little make-up she looked so refined and calm. Her classic figure was created by a bra under a soft cashmere knitted robe in blue, the colour of the mallow flowers of her silver brooch and the Wedgewood theme of her Drawing Room.

An elderly seated guest rose to his feet, introduced himself shyly as Alfred Koenig and added, 'My field is the study of the written word and the evolution of the alphabets.' He was a small man with Semitic features but a perfect English accent, kind eyes, and a receding hairline.

His presence launched Kohen into a recital. He rendered the words in his amateur theatrical style.

'It is Thou, oh Lord, who created breath for the tongue
and Thou knowest its words;
Thou didst establish the fruit of the lips
before ever they were.
Thou dost set words to measure
and the flow of breath from the lips to metre.

'It's from the *Hodayot*, Sara, the Hymns of the Essene Bible, the *Megillot Qumran,* or, as the gentiles call them, The Dead Sea Scrolls. Caroline's friend Alfred Koenig is a specialist in diachronic linguistics, the structural changes which take place in written language. We are collaborating on a secret project. And he is also writing one on something the Newtonians have overlooked about predestination.'

'Would you like some coffee?' Caroline asked.

Before Sélène could reply she was stopped.

'I'm writing on the evolution of language,' Koenig told her with enthusiasm, 'through which one can gain an insight into causality, predestination, and the perception of time itself. There is a single source from which all language originated, and to which I believe all tongues will converge.'

Ignoring the others, Robert spoke to Sélène.

'I assume that you can see my theory of time and causation originated in the poem of the *Hodayot*? Why do we moderns dismiss the ancient peoples as primitive beings? At least two thousand years ago they identified the paradox of predestination and they recognised the moral responsibility of the individual for his or her own actions. That's hardly uncivilised. It's amazing . . .'

'You are slipping back into the old paradigm,' she suggested.

Ignoring the parallel conversation, Koenig continued his own dialogue to Sélène.

'All tongues have started to converge in the Information Age as the world converges. American English, the domination of McDonalds and Mickey Mouse are the signs.'

Kohen waited for a respectable gap and continued to Sara, 'Most people – even Timothy Leary – incline to one or the other but cannot handle both. I mean, he thinks that your ancestral memory is purely chemical, but simple arithmetic is against him. No human has enough brain cells. Imagine if I could prove *scientifically* the existence of the collective unconscious and of past and future in an eternal present.'

'Our book will be ready in three years,' Koenig promised.

'This book is unrelated to the project I have just been talking about, dear Sara,' Kohen continued. 'Within three years I shall be the most famous man in the world. While scholars try to reconstruct Biblical events, I will restore *the original* Bible from its texts that have been excised across the centuries.'

Caroline poured the coffee without making any comments.

Chapter Thirteen

GOLGOTHA, JUDÆA: 14 Nisan, 3793 (33AD)

The Saviour accepted his fate.

The dark-skinned woman with braided red curls from Magadala supported the mother who fell and wept at the foot of a wooden beam in an avenue of many others. She was trampled upon by people who were shouting abuse at her eldest son. Until now Mary refused to accept the Magdalene as her daughter-in-law but the African woman had proved her love and loyalty for Jesus. Although she said she was descended from Solomon through the Queen of Sheba, a dynastic marriage to the first-born of David's line would provoke an uprising at this time. And a marriage to a foreign woman was unacceptable to the family.

Jesus would never do anything in a customary manner.

Today he would pay the ultimate price of non-conformity.

Clinging together, the two women saw very little through the jeering and gaping crowds; the grief of the two mourners merged as their bodies intertwined. They were deafened by the noise but felt each stroke of the leaded whip the soldiers inflicted on the man they loved. So gentle, yet so strong, his will hardened as his flesh was painfully softened.

It could not really be happening.

The priests had followed their deposed prince outside the walls of the city where execution and burials were permitted. Already there stood long rows of wooden beams, most of them occupied in various stages of the lingering surrender of breath; they were the last prisoners to die before the festival. Everything went to plan. To satisfy the Sanhedrin the guards agreed this one too would be finished by nightfall, the beginning of the Passover.

Martha, who considered herself his sister-in-law, arrived.

She shook herself free from the others and squeezed through three of Jesus' brothers – Joses, Simon, and Judas. Martha screamed, 'Yehosh'ua, you are not the rightful king of the Jews,' then she was pushed aside by a Roman guard who warned her in a friendly way to keep her mouth shut. The metal on the back of his hand tore her lips apart. The brothers of Jesus considered self-sacrifice but instead dragged the woman away. Two witnesses prematurely signed the death document as the wooden cross bore the agony of the man pulled skywards by two ropes from the ground. Mary, the mother, tugged at the ropes to attract His attention but it seemed that He was already outside his body.

The Magdalene, who loved him more than anyone, never lost her composure. She smiled through her tears and comforted the mother of Y'shua,

'Listen to me. Your eldest son is very happy today, Mother of my very own name, I am with child. He made me promise to keep it for this moment to tell you the good news. He said we must flee from our land which will be destroyed by the will of God. The plans have been made and Yashi knows that our future is saved. You must help me in the province of Gaul where he ordered us to live until our land is free and our people worthy of the truth.'

The mother of the Lord wiped her tears aside and listened to the plan.

'Mother, you would not let us marry, but under the Law of Moses, where parents are unmarried, not of forbidden relationships, and in all ways free to marry, you know our child is legitimate. In the ancient rite I anointed my Lord and by the will of God it will be the male first-born of Yashi who will carry forth the blood of our common ancestor, David, safe and in hiding, overseas.'

Chapter Fourteen

PARIS, OCTOBER 1976

Watergate was a turning point in American politics. Investigative journalists became part of the democratic machine; probing reporters became respectable even in Europe.

In the Versailles annex of the Bibliothèque Nationale Michael Leonard walked through shelves D12-14 to meet his own 'Deep Throat' – a sinister, mumbling, and clumsy man in his fifties with heavy spectacles. He greeted Leonard with the password, the quotation from Lewis Carroll.

'It's a poor sort of memory that only works backwards.'

At the previous meeting he had offered no information about himself but dropped hints to retain Leonard's interest. Patience was not his prominent virtue; persistence was. The journalist felt sure his informer was waiting for authority to divulge something momentous. They arranged to meet next time in the Louvre. There they could walk and talk.

On the third meeting, after he had discussed pre-Raphaelite art, the informant told Leonard that he was a naturalised American (as his accent clearly betrayed) and the CIA 'had something on the celebrity scientist, Dr Robert F. Kohen who was something of a showman.'

They sat down outside a pavement café. DT sipped his drink and Leonard resisted a smile when the elusive man who spoke for a secret organisation could not stop himself talking.

'The American Right is an unstable and unstoppable combination of government and anti-government, anti-communism, capitalism, pioneerism, extra-terrestrials, and of course, religion. Protestants tend to identify with God's chosen people. Some support the Jews and others say the conspiracy *is* the Jews.'

Aware of the drug's short window of influence Leonard steered him back on the rails and listened.

'A certain element within a secret society – let's just call it that – had the child's mother killed in 1952 to avoid genetic tests which modern science now makes possible, but both parents died. During the Occupation of France patriots changed social registers to conceal from the Nazis two bloodlines, Merovingian and Jewish. You see, the mother of the chosen girl was Jewish by their reckoning but not according to civil records, her family having converted two centuries previously.'

Leonard observed that they were walking past an oil painting of a mounted knight wearing a white tunic with a red cross pattée. He stopped and waited until the American appreciated the coincidence. The two men admired the painting in silence.

The American spoke quietly.

'Their copy of the Davidic Genealogy was out of date and complex – like a neural network of a leaf – even in the 12th century. Before 1952 this element believed that the Scottish housekeeper was the candidate's biological mother with whom Pierre of the Languedoc had, well, *lain* as the Bible puts it, with his wife's approval from her sick bed.'

Leonard wondered if the spokesman of the secret society was genuine, and was he talking so much because he was mad, or nervous, or releasing energy which had been silenced for too long? They walked back into the main hall of the Gallery and into the coffee room where the man seemed more comfortable.

'The brotherhood split down the middle, one side proposing an Aryan messiah – Helena Capulé who, they believed was descended from the Holy Family. Lefebvre's knowledge of this saved him from excommunication, just as it has protected all who come to possess the secret. It is the Holy Grail. Literally, the power of powers. The ultimate *puissance* over this world and that beyond, over present and future.'

The American took his coffee to a table. After paying Leonard followed him. They sat down and finished their refreshments in silence.

The journalist mumbled the phrase, 'An American in Paris,' then asked if he lived here.

'Sure do.'

Leonard knew that his truth drug was expiring but the American seemed more anxious to talk.

'De Gaulle gave strict orders to disband the Committees for Public Safety. But listen carefully, newspaperman. The French police, who monitor secret societies, knew that one network persisted. It had changed its name but what was its goal? Former Resistance agents now spying on their French compatriots made regular reports. These reached Winston Churchill's office, and after two decades it was from British Intelligence that the CIA got this information about the political agenda of The Priory of Sion.'

The men left the café and Leonard was ready to return to his hotel when he was taken by surprise.

'If you tail me you'll discover soon enough I return to the Embassy and you may surmise that I am not a commercial attaché. I have told you what you need to know; now I will tell you what I want to say.'

Instinctively they walked through the gallery until the American stopped and inspected a painting.

'I think we have studied this fine impressionist canvas closely enough, Mr Leonard. If anyone is watching us . . . Let's move on. Robert Kohen uses – at the highest levels of government and of academe – sensitive military secrets as a lever as well as the powerful secret of the Holy Grail. He uses high technology to obtain anything he wants. He uses his gay connections, the Jewish mafia, his anti-Communist credentials, his genius, his escape from Occupation, and his American patriotism. Kohen is the major, repeat *major* threat, way out of control, but he cannot be retired. He has the ultimate insurance. *The joke is that it was the CIA who let Kohen in on the secret the Holy Family.'*

Chapter Fifteen

WASHINGTON, DC, MARCH 1977

Michael Leonard booked a transatlantic flight to attend in person the Senate sub-committee Hearing on the Watergate affair. A local reporter mentioned a Hearing literally just down the corridor in a smaller Committee Room.

Dr Robert F. Kohen, a Pentagon Defence Scientist, was accused of wrongful appropriation of intellectual property. Leonard showed his Press ID and found all but two of the Press seats unoccupied. He chose the front row because of the hushed tones. The Hearing had started early.

Sitting relaxed at a table draped with a red cloth a smartly dressed, portly man with blond hair and a bow tie looked his interrogator straight in the eye and listened carefully.

'Dr Kohen, you escaped to USA in November 1944 from Eastern Europe?'

'I came out of Hungary in November 1944. I was flown here in May 1945.'

'Were you in hiding over that summer?'

'My work is classified under Project Paperclip.'

'What was this?'

'Patriotic work stemming directly from the War in Europe.'

The attorney turned to the Chair, then the stenographer, and finally to the camera.

'For the benefit of the American public who have not heard about Project Paperclip I will refer the Hearing to the publication of the *List of Nazi War Criminals Residing in the United States of America.* Our Office of Strategic Services, which became the CIA in 1947, arranged at least six hundred leading scientists to leave the employment of Adolph Hitler and work for Uncle Sam.'

Kohen's attorney shot to his feet and loudly filed an objection. His client had lost most of his family, been a victim of Nazi torture, found refuge in USA, and assisted the safety and defence of our nation even before he left the danger zone. The Deputy Attorney General had praised Dr Kohen's contribution since 1944 to American technology as 'immense.'

The lawyers, called to the bench, were locked in exchanges, then the scientist was asked how the Nazis had killed his family but spared him since his captivity. Leonard missed the drift but heard the question ending, '. . . in when?'

'November 1943.'

Kohen, upon request, repeated his answer audibly.

'So clearly you were of some use to the Nazis for some six months?'

The Deputy Attorney General was pompous and radiant, having grasped in the heat of debate a line of inquiry that was capable of upsetting a predictable outcome.

'Would you like me to repeat the question, Dr Kohen? I accept that you assisted the United States but I am suggesting to you that all Jews who survived after round-up were of some use to the Nazis.'

For the first time Kohen was discomforted.

'I provided information about people who could assist the Allies after the War. I also smuggled documents fully informing and pleading with the Allies to destroy the gas ovens and railway lines.'

In a heated exchange the Chairman ruled this evidence as inadmissible and he agreed that it may be relevant to know if Dr Kohen had assisted the Nazis at the same time as helping the Allies and earning his ticket to USA.

Kohen was furious.

'They killed my people, raped my country, extinguished my family, my sisters fled to stay with righteous gentiles, and my life was destroyed. By this time, the Nazis were exposed and losing the war. *Is it likely that I sided with them?'*

There was a heated exchange in which the lawyers were summoned to the bench once again. An adjournment was refused. The Deputy Attorney General representing the Pentagon appeared to triumph.

He turned on his heels and faced Dr Kohen.

'I am now asking you for the last time to inform the Hearing how you helped the Nazis in order to delay for at least six months your own transportation and murder along with ten thousand Jews *per day* at that time.'

The room was very silent, Kohen moved back from the microphone and breathed deeply under extreme duress.

Although the room was still quiet Leonard strained to hear the words.

Unable to hold back tears, the Scientist, a man of hard resolve and dignity replied, almost inaudibly.

'They used me . . . *as a woman* . . . a young Jew with blond hair was a fascination to their perversions.'

Kohen's attorney stated that he wished to submit evidence at this point which had not been cleared by the Pentagon. The Pentagon's attorney raised an objection. The lawyers conferred with the Chairman and the Hearing was adjourned.

Within an hour the case against Kohen was lowered to the charge of misuse of funds. He resigned office with no pension and a fine of $100,000.

15.1 Outside the Pentagon, Kohen appeared at a triumphant encounter with the media. His lawyer announced that his client had turned his sights upwards to Heaven and renounced his career regarding even non-destructive weapons research as inhuman. He had private funds to reconstitute in New York and Jerusalem The Essene Community of the Dead Sea Scrolls dedicated to peace and prayer.

A young reporter asked if this sect was positioned with Zionist, Orthodox, Progressive, or Liberal wings of Judaism. Dr Kohen took the microphone.

'The Essenes began three hundred years before the Christian Era to oppose the corrupt priesthood and the reforming rabbis in a quest to return to the covenant with God to live wholly in line with the Law of Moses.

'I have become afraid that I will die without seeing nine tenths of the

Dead Sea Scrolls. As a personal campaign, I am going to force the authorities to publish the full find of which has been wilfully withheld since 1947 by the Dominican Order of the Catholic Church and since 1967 by collusion and in secret pact with the Government of Israel. I have seen evidence of a fifth Gospel suppressed by collusion of Rome and Jerusalem.'

15.2 While one retired public servant presented himself as a born-again Jew a rising American politician was posing with Billy Graham and the evangelical lobby to whom he promised, if elected, America's return to family values, moral cleaning up, and fiscal propriety.

In March 1977 Spencer Weidfeld was announcing policies as if he were a President-elect. In television encounters he thought faster and talked louder than anyone else. His coaches drilled into him his ABC: Conceive, Believe, Achieve. He had a fine smile and the clean look of confident, youthful idealism. He had risen from poverty from the days of his father's immigration and he carried working people. But as a conservative he reassured his elders. He was the perfect politician – all things to all men, and by careful design a threat to nobody. The only question was when the long election would end.

Weidfeld's campaign office had agreed with the power brokers that Reagan should serve a further term and then be permitted to lose – in all likelihood – the following administration to the Democrats. In anticipation of not being called to run for President until 1985, he was advised to gain experience, friends, funds, and be cautious in financial dealings and sexual liaisons.

Leonard read in the Press that his actress had broken a four-year relationship with the film director Jonny Lord. Some feature writers now linked her with the presidential candidate.

Chapter Sixteen

LONDON, MAY 1977

English Victorian banks with high ceilings and marble pillars have a calculated, calming effect and Leonard was risking a lot of his hard-earned cash. At the end of April he had transferred £2,500 to the Operating Account of Committee 122 for Public Safety at Banque Crédit Lyonnais in Genève. In return he met a spokesman for the Committee at the Temple of the Rite of Philalethes.

'Your money is in a deposit which will be returned if you act in good faith exactly as our agreement. We will introduce you to the Grand Auteur, three Commandeurs, two Chevaliers and one Ecuyer. Do you understand?'

'Of the *Prieuré de Sion*?' Leonard asked the spokesman.

The bespectacled English gentleman in pin-striped, three-piece suit seemed to x-ray the journalist before inviting him to enter a small chamber from the main vestibule. It appeared Masonic: a chess board floor, stained glass windows, and Hebrew letters distinguishing the stone building from any church Leonard had been in.

'If you take my advice you should also forget about that foolish book you spoke about.' A new voice echoed from a large hall, a distinctive English accent which Leonard thought must originate from Bristol.

Dressed in a camel business suit, the second man had referred to the sensational book *Les Dessous d'une Ambition Politique* written by a Swiss journalist first setting out a conspiracy of world domination.

'Look, sir,' the second man shook Leonard's hand, and motioned him into the large chamber, 'The Prieuré's history is almost entirely fictional. It is a decoy, a popular game played for the spectators who are permitted to approach by constructed routes and outer walls. It is all part of the story but you will be speaking to the real conspirators. *The hidden regulators and controllers of world affairs.* We are affiliated to the timeless and truly universal church, 'The Church of the Fish."

Leonard's frown was cut short.

'Ah, but you will say that it was defeated by the male and materialistic church of the cross and disappeared from history, but history is bunk. You cannot destroy the vine by pruning the blossom that appears above the ground. Now, I will be brief. You will be asked to travel to Marseilles and wait for the *rendezvous* arrangements. You must be prepared to take an oath to Almighty God that no Christian man should fear. If you are unhappy, your money will be restored to you in full.'

Michael Leonard proudly described himself as a lapsed member of the Church of England, presumably a division of the 'male and material Church of the Cross.'

How asked how far the 'Church of the Fish' went back and was corrected.

'It is not antiquity but *authenticity* which confers validity.'

'So that's why you had to buy an old bank?'

In the silence Leonard helped himself to a brochure and began to read about the Church of the Fish. Instead of the gentile-pagan festival of Christmas, it still celebrates Childermas on December 28th. It commemorates the birth of the Messiah and the continuing significance of the secular authorities' continuing desire to slay Him. It honours the innocent boys, victims of Herod – the Roman who usurped the Jewish throne and thus feared for his own demise.'

The man in the camel suit handed Leonard a street map of Paris and contact information written on a sheet of paper. The man in the pin-striped suit showed him out onto the street, and the huge wooden doors were closed with a resonant thud.

16.1 Arriving early at Heathrow, Leonard had time to argue against transfer to a later flight with Air France because they had double-booked his seat. He lost the argument.

At Paris (Charles de Gaulle) Leonard collected a hired Renault to drive to Marseilles to interview the Church of the Fish. But despite missing the early flight there was a detour to a remote and disused warehouse.

The researcher in Paris had found a man who admitted an involvement in an automobile accident of 1952 to abduct a French girl from her parents. Although the local detective was capable, Leonard wanted to participate in the interrogation. The French team had found a vacant industrial warehouse to question the ruffian. If things went badly, he would find himself buried there with little ceremony, the interrogator had said. Leonard drove up in a grey Renault and shook hands with his man in Paris before handing him an envelope.

'Thank you for waiting. My flight was delayed. I hope you were not serious about . . .'

The large French detective, who had sounded almost effeminate on the phone, looked every bit the executioner. He turned on Leonard, his paymaster, with contempt.

'Cease guy, Mr Leonard, killed her parents, her boy brother, and you seenk it ees English gentleman game?'

Leonard responded by offering a small bottle, his truth drug.

The interrogator spat a laugh and turned away.

In a disused boardroom, the contract killer was tied by one foot to a heavy table. His trouser leg had been torn away. Lying on the floor André Albain boasted that he came from the upper strata of society, but after losing the family business manufacturing electrical parts, taking to drink, and leaving his wife and children, he became well-known to the French police. He did one contract per year, had never been caught, and he intended to keep it that way. Nothing would make him talk; it was a matter of client confidentiality.

Hours later he found himself unable to leave without divulging the information. Albain was threatened, drugged, and hauled down two flights of concrete stairs to an empty warehouse. Leonard had to remind himself that the poor fellow was a professional contract killer. When he realised that he was approaching his own last minutes of living he began to empty the content of his memory.

In this particular contract, the targets – mother and father – were married, the tortured assassin claimed, *but not to each other*!

And there were two children in the car, both illegitimate children of the adult male in the front seat.

'I killed them also,' he said before he became delirious as a result of a wrong dosage. Gautier commented that every physiology is different but asked Leonard why Albain had invented two victims plus children?

'*Why confess to a worse crime? There were no children involved in the accident*.'

Leonard retreated to an adjacent room and read his notes. He realised that it was dark outside and saw that the time was 2am; no wonder sleep deprivation was kicking in.

As paymaster, Leonard was drawing the line defining the treatment of the villain. There still seemed a real possibility that he may end up buried here. He returned to the warehouse where tanks of some liquid were being poured over the victim. The interrogator ignored or failed to hear Leonard's orders to stop. Everyone was shouting.

Anger and fatigue escalated the violence until Albain named the instigators of his 1952 contract as highly-placed Churchmen connected to the state. Leonard smiled. He imparted to the French interrogator information concerning the brotherhood to prime the subject. This yielded details about the conspiracy which, the assassin alleged, involved François Mitterrand.

'This is the reason I won't ever get arrested and you will never get accurate information from the French authorities.'

The interrogator informed Leonard that the subject was losing consciousness, time was short, and he did not believe what was emerging.

'This is what the bastard told me, M. Leonard, but although you have paid much for this information, I'm telling you it is all fabrication. I've had a lot of experience with altered mental states by various means, and this bastard has been sent as a decoy. He knows nothing. That is the best way I can help you. For some reason he blames Mitterrand. Perhaps he wants to waste your time. Perhaps he threatens you with his bluff of high placed protection. Is he safer left here permanently?'

Leonard grasped his moral dilemma, rose from his chair and walked to the door. As he left the room he beckoned Gautier then turned to the interrogator.

'When I have paid a dog I don't do the barking.'

16.2 The connection to Mitterrand was spurious but worth checking. Leonard's bedside telephone rang back just as he was about to leave the hotel for dinner alone. His colleague in London, scrutinising declassified British Intelligence files, had identified a former French Resistance man – a senior agent known by the improbable nickname of Lenny Leonard. He had worked closely with the Committees for Public Safety in the occupied territories and liaised with John Logan, a British Intelligence officer now living in France.

One entry in the Paris telephone directory seemed most likely. In a broad Scots accent the man was desperate to ask Lenny's old buddy to do all he could to help their mutual friend in decline and distress. No point in wasting time and a hired car. While in Paris this lead could be followed.Leonard's namesake lived in a cheap suburb in a permanent state of inebriation, on an inadequate war pension, repeating that France was a country unworthy of heroes. The journalist carried a bottle of wine up three flights of stairs. From Lenny's war stories it was almost impossible to work out who had engaged and discharged him from active service and who had spoken to him concerning the job of 1952.

The more Lenny imbibed, the more confusion emerged: he believed that other people he called friends were slowly killing him with alcohol. It seemed paranoid delusion until the journalist tested an alternative explanation. Agents in possession of secret information were rendered harmless not only by an assassin but by mind games, career destruction . . . why not alcohol poisoning?

Leonard's sympathy with this man was genuine. He was alive. He could talk. But his neural network had been rendered safe by alcohol prescribed by people with something to conceal.

In France herbal, holistic, and homeopathic treatments were common and Leonard paid for him to come off alcohol for two weeks to gain relief from his gout. It made the journalist who had paid for the torture of Albain feel a little more comfortable with himself. The return to London was postponed.

16.3 One morning Leonard returned with medication which was more wholesome than hallucinogenic. In gratitude Lenny introduced a friend – a small man he named only by the initials, JML. The man called himself Leon but this name and his accent were unconvincing. He sat quietly in a settee in a corner of the room reading a book illuminated by a window. In a strong French accented English Leon made a promise of help.

'I am trying to obtain photos for you to see the registry files as they were before 1952 concerning two girls you are interested in. Helena and Sarah-Hélène. And if the conditions are right, I can introduce you to a man of high office . . .'

'In the Alpha Church?'

'I will not say, at present.'

'Like you, then, he is a Mason?'

'Leon' glanced up from his corner settee.

'You did not respond to me; you are not of the brotherhood. But he is a *Hermetic* Mason, Monsieur Leonard.'

'Then he is aligned against the Church?'

'He is of high rank in the Church, M. Leonard,' he smiled.

'The Catholic Church?'

'The true and universal church, but not quite the same as the Vatican hierarchy, M. Leonard, do you understand me?'

'No. Of course I don't understand.'

'Precisely! You cannot tell the truth because if you understood then you would be close to the terrible truth. Two messiahs, M. Leonard, and two Churches in one body. Male and female. The Church conceals this truth for a clear reason. The second messiah will be female and she is born. The word is out; and like Herod, the Church is afraid . . .'

'Which Church, my friend, for you say that there are two.'

Lenny gripped the journalist and gently sat him down. 'My friend here is Jean-Michell LeBlanc. Tell me that you know of this famous writer on sacred structures from Stonhenge to the Pyramids. He is a high authority in the church *and* a Hermetic Mason. My English is not so good enough and your French is disgraceful. *He* can tell you everything.'

Leonard silenced his own laughter or protestations. If these two men felt safe they would disclose more.

Leon, Logan, or LeBlanc walked from the corner of the room to sit beside Leonard. In perfect English, he spoke.

'Listen to me, Monsieur Leonard. Father Saunière understood the problem quickly enough, but he had good reason. The Holy Church condemns women because they compare them to an ideal of Our Lady, the Mother of God. They enforce their purity and subservience. It's the problem of society, a psychological crisis. Gender suppression has its equivalent in Islamic society with equally unhealthy results. In the west it is the male Church which wages war on the female planet. The Roman Church of *Sol Invictus* continually does wrong because it *is* wrong. It is the devil. Saunière said so.'

Leonard watched the former Resistance fighter pour himself a drink in breach of their agreement but replied to the man with no name but three aliases.

'What is the priest got to do with our problem?'

Swinging comfortably into a Scottish accent the enthusiasm was infectious. Even Lenny returned from the kitchen and listened.

'Mitterrand personally knew France's leading medium, a woman who informed him of the girl with the great soul, the oversoul. It sounds rather foolish to say she had two souls, like a two-headed monster. In the old days they spoke of casting out unclean spirits, now it's neural disorders, but the brain is like a telephone exchange or a wireless set which can receive more than one personality. I know it sounds crazy.'

He had described Sélène so well. Leonard admitted that her mood swings were two personalities in one head. Until now he had assumed that in her drug-induced Ancestor-Memory Regression performances she had merely fed back information as we do to pass school examinations.

As he drove back to his hotel Leonard wondered, *suppose people CAN see the past, and suppose she WAS a medium. Was it connected through her genes? Was the past haunting the present?*

Chapter Seventeen

MASSILIA, 720 AUC (33CE)
Moreover, the people of Jerusalem, in accordance with a certain oracle that was vouchsafed by way of revelation to approved men, had been commanded to depart from the Holy City before the war. . .

'More Judeans fleeing from the war but these ones are rich, Marcellus.' The forty-five year old North African imported labourer used imperial names acquired with the purchase of freedom.

'Board that boat, brother, and speak to the man clad in purple. Tell him we can take his family to the city and find him clean rooms for the night in a safe house owned by Jewish citizens. Say that I can send a boy ahead of them to the inn to prepare hot kosher food.'

The cart owner's brother came back with a piece of imperial coinage.

'The Master Joseph – for that is his name – thanks us for our kindness. He has been met by his family here but the women have six caskets of great weight and he asks to hire your cart and we are both needed to help them to their destination.'

'Oh well, business is business, brother. I think that we should wait for a full hour. We have been adequately recompensed for that. Most unlike a Jew from Palestina. You'll get your share when I can get this coin changed, my friend, I promise you that.'

The cart owner examined the bronze *sestertius* freshly struck at the imperial mint at Lugdunum. The portrait of Tiberius frowned back at its new owner.

The hour passed slowly as the two freed slaves watched cargoes being loaded and off-loaded. Sailors were being recruited and others paid off. New owners of jingling coins set out for taverns which loosened their tongues and made them of interest to loose women. Merchants jostled, argued, and exchanged contracts. Overseers directed the organised chaos of freight. There were two other ships due to arrive that same week because the Romans had restored Massilia as a trading centre rivalling even the Carthaginians. It was also a distinguished centre of Greek learning.

About seven hundred years AUC (after the founding of Rome) Massilia had fallen from grace having supported Pompey against Caesar. The people had been permitted to retain the city charter in recognition of its support of Rome in the Punic Wars. However, Rome had stripped her of the towns and trading posts she had established along the coast. In the interval, the port had doubled in scale.

The cart owner was disturbed from his nap by a Palestinian who tried Greek and then struggled in the Celtic dialect. They found a translator who took his payment in advance from the foreigner.

'Master Joseph requests that you will provide transportation for the rest of the day to take four women of his family about three or four hours ride from here to the north west while the rest of his party will go into the city. He has heard about your good reputation and trusts you with his wife and her sister and two children. I will travel with you to show you the way. Please request your brother to help load, and at our destination to unload. You know what women are like. They always bring too much luggage.'

Soon two small carts were fully-loaded and creaking with the high-born, dark-skinned women and their children. The cart-owner felt the plight of the Judean women and children. Some settled here but others travelled beyond Gaul. Why did they travel further north or west? The free citizens of Massilia – even former slaves and new immigrants – had benefited from Roman rule. They prospered and considered themselves protected rather than occupied or dominated; they were unlike the ungrateful and rebellious Judeans.

The Judeans who had fled here brought with them their nightmares of the slaughter. Not only of their poorly-trained swordsmen cut down by imperial soldiers, but strife between their own leaders and parties. They had one god but many causes. This gave the Romans the means and the right to introduce government to their land. The elders of Massilia hoped they would not bring their bitter feuds and Roman retribution to these parts although a few followers of their god *Chrestus* had already arrived to make converts. And trouble.

Some Massilians said their city was already too cosmopolitan, tolerant, and complacent to the Jews who were probably too tribal to submit to *pax Romana*. The Galileans had successfully broken the careers of two of the best procurators who went out to prove their worth. Mind you, Jews were people of learning, good masters to slaves, kind to animals, and honest traders. Their leaders paid tribute, refusing only to gaze upon the emperor's image or accept the state religion. But the peace had been uneasy ever since the death of their great king, *Herodes Magnus*. Word was spreading that *Chrestus* was no god, but a philosopher-prince who had prevented his people rising up against the empire. Some Judeans proclaimed that he had saved their nation. Others were leaving it in droves.

But here it looked sad. At the port there were tearful partings when two women and two children climbed onto the cart. The cart-owner was paid half in advance and instructed to set off behind a sturdy and ornate carriage. He had noticed this one before as very tidy and well-kept. On one occasion at the harbour he had even spoken to the driver. The owners were second-generation immigrant Judeans who owned a farm settlement which was rapidly becoming a small village about three hours to the west of this port. No doubt this was today's destination.

This knowledge had not fully reassured the nervous cart-owner who wanted to avoid trouble. Granted the clients were of good character but some of the chests were too heavy to be clothes or pots. There must be metal, coin, and treasure. It would explain why this rich Joseph fellow had made careful inquiries before engaging him. But there was also food and drink packed in a commodious trunk with a curved top in the Eastern style. There was enough fresh food for three meals for all eleven travellers although no more than two stops should be required including the return journey. It was generous of a good Jew, the cart owner thought, for him to provide for the return journey to Massilia when they would have no further use for their servants. The Master Joseph had even asked about, and augmented, the feed for the donkeys.

The brother of Marcellus returned with the reassurance of the governor's port supervisor of taxes, but the cart owner, fearful of some clandestine business, kept alert, looking for soldiers, recommending a quieter route avoiding the towns lest he got mixed up with smuggling. It was obvious that these women hid their faces and wished to travel anonymously, beyond the empire and far away from the authorities.

Presumably it was the Romans they feared for thankfully there were, as far as he knew, none of the Jewish authorities in these parts. The messianic gentiles who lived here in hiding kept themselves strictly apart from the settled Jews.

Today's fugitives were high class, peaceful, and orthodox Jews, but even if the imperial port supervisor was silent there was something sinister. The cart owner, having worked fourteen years for a family of Jews in Mauretania, pretended he knew nothing of the language of his passengers. In this way he learned that the heavily pregnant slave-woman with the curly hair the adults called Ruth was 'Aunt Miriam' to the small children who giggled when they were nudged in response to their carelessness.

Chapter Eighteen

Immersed in deep discussion in the college cloisters of Oxford University the nineteen-year old Michael Leonard was one of six conscientious young students. He felt good that these eager and refined men had befriended him. Always the outsider, he was a historian but they were theology students – training for the ministry at home or abroad. Their spoken words were resonant in the vaulted chambers.

The young Michael Leonard listened in detached silence and learned the subtleties of New Testament Greek. It was a language with many words for love to contrast lust, brotherhood, and charity; and it had separate words for fish to mean wildlife in the lakes and food on the table.

18.1 PARIS, MAY 1977

Sitting, waiting in the resonant chamber of a temple, Michael Leonard thought about the former Resistance men's theory of memory ingrained in the soul of the survivor in the sovereign line.

Looking around him he remembered his early discovery about the authentic language of the gospels. Instead of a cross, the giant fish, the original symbol of the church, was his first sight when the blindfold was removed. It was done with the gentleness of a trained nurse. She was a dark-haired and chubby matron. She left the room. Two male escorts, thick-set and muscular, sat down on either side of the journalist in front of a long table. He felt like a man on trial, and perhaps he was. As he had guessed from its acoustics he was in a small cathedral. But instead of a cross, there was the alpha symbol of the Fish.

The table – carved from solid oak – was covered by a blue cloth with gold-embroidered occult symbols. The room was cool but he was sweating. It wasn't the money that worried him because the contact had reassured Leonard that the package before him contained his 'deposit' in American dollars for a full refund if he was not happy with the outcome of the meeting. He also stated that the secret society regretted that others had set out to mislead him.

Leonard asked what was the committee and were they a part of this church? He was asked to be silent.

Two men and three women sat down at a more modern, lighter, table. It was made from oak but it was not hand-carved from solid timber. Leonard lowered his eyes as one of them recited a short blessing. Then one of them asked him to read from a card, *An Oath of Blessing to the Universal and Unincorporated Church of God* and overleaf a *Statement of Honour in all Dealings with the Assembly and with its Brothers and Sisters Worldwide.*

Leonard read aloud the two paragraphs, which were no more than an undertaking to avoid blasphemy or dishonesty. His money was removed from the table. One of the women thanked him for coming and asked if he wanted anything. To test her sincerity he requested a glass of cool lager, and this, she said, he would receive after an interval. He began to feel relaxed. He sensed a floral fragrance. Time was in suspension. *Could be a the truth drug, but he hadn't taken anything. The request for a beer was possibly foolish.*

A soft male voice with a Scots accent did not resonate in the domed cathedral. It was Leon.

Authoritative but friendly he explained, 'For many, many years people have been on the edge of a truth which the Church of the Dead Christ has feared to divulge. Beyond the doctrinal debates are the cosmic issues. *Why has God abandoned humanity? Who has misled us? In what form does Satan manifest? Where is the Church in all this? Why did The Holy See turn from seeking the Kingdom of Heaven to the conquest of earthly sovereignty?'*

The journalist hoped that he had not paid for a sermon.

'As you found, Mr Leonard, eighty-four years ago a secret came into the possession of some priests at Rennes-le-Château in France but they were silenced. Here, simply stated, is the discovery for which many people search and speculate. You should study in depth the village itself which is now reduced in its circumstances. Even before men gave it a series of succeeding names throughout its long history, it was significant because it was an intersection of energy lines, a place of power. Even now you can feel its numinous energy. I don't like to bore people but, like you, history is my favourite subject. Rennes is now but a tourist trap and a place for pilgrims long abandoned by the brothers.'

Leonard recalled his first visit to the village with his wife as the Scotsman continued his speech.

'Father Saunière, you see, had been sent to dig for treasure, harmlessly – or so the authorities believed – to a chapel which they considered insignificant. But the past is eternal, Mr Leonard, and the chapel of Mary Magdalene had been built on the site where, in 671 of the year of our Lord, King Dagobert II married Giselle de Razès, a niece to the king of the Visigoths. It was a major dynastic alliance arranged by St. Wilfred in pursuance of the *assimilation* – but one might more accurately say, *destruction* – of the Celtic Church into Rome's hegemony. This conspiracy which you chronicle is the prototype of the unhappiness of modern humanity. You see, *the past is eternal*.'

'Leon' paused for a sip of water. No-one had introduced him. No-one whispered a word. Leonard's eyes remained fixed on the spokesman. He smiled. Already they shared a secret.

'If you were disturbed by the alteration of a civil register of Sarah-Hélène of the Languedoc then you will be shocked to learn how people have altered the records of history. Satan's method is to break the spirit of Man, to reduce it to a slave mentality. It makes the world divided and ruled by men of cunning, not by the guidance of the Spirit.'

Leonard was served with an ice-cold beer but he ignored it.

'Who seeks to divide and rule? Who altered the girl's entry in the ledger?' he asked Leon.

'The entries in the French ledger may offend your English sense of clerical accuracy, Mr Leonard, but this is a small cog in the greatest deception of history. On the royal genealogies in France there once appeared Dagobert I and III but none in between. Now that the common people can read and count to three, *voila*, he reappears. Reinstated when the reason for his removal is safely forgotten.'

'May I know the reason for his removal?'

'We will show you.'

Leon sat down. During the interval Leonard sipped his drink and licked his lips. Velvet red curtains opened to reveal a white screen about eight feet in width. The lights dimmed. He heard an old-fashioned projector start up, and saw its beam. Leonard pushed aside his beer as soon as the film began: it was a pictorial catalogue of the evil of the world – cinematic clips cutting to mushroom clouds, priests blessing soldiers, crusades, burnings at the stake, holocausts, torture, rape, gruesome interrogations, and scenes of the Americans in south east Asia.

To his surprise he found that he was swearing under his breath, *Jesus, God,* and weeping along with the others. *This was their truth drug* and he was very attentive when the film ended. The lights were switched on. One of the women at the table spoke. Then she stood up and faced him. Aged between forty and fifty she wore a yellow-green cardigan. Leon lightly supported her lower arm or hand.

She claimed that in his capacity of reporter to the people, Leonard was the first of the 'common ranks of humanity' to learn *the true secret concerning the hidden controllers of the world. The great secret to which the treasures of Rennes-le-Château merely pointed. The secret which stirred Saunière and his colleagues. The reason for the Crusades, the Inquisition, and the Reformation. The reason for war, the atom bomb, and for all evil.*

'The worldly Church is not evil, but *corrupt*, M. Leonard, which with your knowledge of Latin, you will know simply means broken. *Religion* means bound together, the opposite of corrupt – not the opposite of *evil*. The allies fought evil, but not corruption. The church fulminates against sin, which is natural, but the purpose of the church is not to oppose evil but to bind heaven to earth in the name of Jesus.'

Leonard listened to the woman but looked at the committee seated along the oak table. Leon was looking up to the woman standing beside him. She was looking at the journalist.

'If you feel like an outsider, Mr Leonard, it is a taste of the isolation Jesus felt as a maverick genius, if that phrase is strong enough even to hint at what he was. He loved his enemies, ate with gentiles, and forgave sinners.'

She paused and as her words echoed in the chamber, she resumed.

'And then he married Mariam; perhaps she was a distant descendent of Solomon and Sheba but a black foreigner and not a Jewess. And we know that he enjoyed making love to her. The rewriting of his life story began even before he died.'

Leonard interjected angrily, 'How do you know all this?'

'We have the lost gospels. The ones the church *withdrew from circulation.*'

Her response was immediate and confident.

There was silence, and Leonard's mood was so strange that he heard himself offering a foolish confession that he too loved sex and women loved it also. The woman just looked at him in astonishment and he felt her stare. He had to regain their confidence, and he knew exactly how he to do it. He quoted from one of the Gnostic gospels, '*Every woman who makes herself male will enter the Kingdom of Heaven.*'

The churchwoman continued the quote, '*When you make the two one, and the inner as the outer, and when you make the male and the female into a single one, so that the male will not be male and the female will not be female, when you make eyes in the place of the eyes, and hands in the place of hands, and feet in the place of feet, and an image in the place of an image, then shall you enter the Kingdom*. These are the words of the Lord in the secret tradition.'

The others answered in unison, 'Amen, these are the words according to *The Gospel of the Lord's Twin.*'

A man stood up and the woman gave way and sat down.

'I am Mattias. I am Spanish and I apologise for my poor English. Today you speak with the Church of the Fish, which does not exist according to history, for long ago our gospels were destroyed and we were all put to the sword by Church of the Crucifixion – the church which bears the symbol of the suffering man they claim was not man. The church which has cast earth from the heavens is governed by men who have rewritten history. And woman whom they subordinate has evolved to be less corrupt. So the Second Coming of the earth saviour is woman incarnate. I pray to Her God she can repair the planet for we are about to face a terrible danger created by technology. They have no respect for God, for mankind, nor for our home, this wonderful planet.'

The man sat down, and I noticed that the women on both sides looked at him with some scorn and he lowered his head in shame. Tenderly, but also erotically, they embraced him. There was a warmth and bonding within these people, but Leonard felt that they were cranks and spoke up.

'What if you are simply another Christian sect – let me see, number 2,201? Oh, sorry, you all claim you are the original.'

The committee conferred in whispers.

The first woman began to speak, informally from her seated position.

'She is in our world, now, and *you* are fortunate because you don't have to *believe* for you have seen her. If you recognise Jesus after he dies then you expect another man in white robes and sandals. Again, God offers humans the Kingdom of Heaven, Mr Leonard. Look carefully at her and you will see why she troubles the grey men who check and strengthen the seals and locks of the their vaults. They know the game is up. The people have seen the joke. When the earth moves, this time their castles will fall. This time the saviour wears trainers, not sandals.'

Chapter Nineteen

MILLBROOK MANSION, NY, MAY 1977

Under a clear blue sky, pink apple blossoms formed a heavenly canopy in the orchard forming part of the colonial style mansion, now serving as the headquarters of the hippy movement.

She felt relaxed thanks to the carefully dosed substance rather than the present company or the task that lay ahead of her. The unadorned fingers of Sarah-Hélène of the Languedoc slipped from the grip of Dr Jeremy Jesus-Leviticus, Director of Research of the League for Spiritual Discovery (LSD).

The acronym explained why the project which began at Harvard University had been forced to move elsewhere.

Underfoot, twigs snapped as the man led the woman from the stone path to the wild grass. It seemed to Sarah-Hélène like another planet. She had been taught in Yogic tradition to expel a deep sigh to expel her worldly cares and stress. She placed her hands around a tree trunk and relaxed her body weight. She breathed in pure, fresh air.

Jeremy Palmer followed her closely; too closely, she thought. It was time to make a start but he was lingering where nobody could see them and she was losing inhibitions. Women crave pleasure, but also motherhood and partnership. At her spiritual level of attainment she could offer cosmic awareness by sacred sex. She knew that it was no sacrament in which this lustful man foolishly sought sex at this moment, and she shed a tear of pity.

Regarding a wrist-watch as an assault on his freedom, Dr Jeremy

Palmer (as he was called until recently) suggested that ten minutes had elapsed since the woman had ingested the substance. He broke the silence.

'Give it ten minutes more. You know, Sélène, I believe today the world is entirely captured. The jungle is a zoo and there is not a square inch on God's earth unspoiled by some political regime. They use satellites to photograph us here in Millbrook.'

'I thought you denied the existence of God, Jeremy?'

'You have a terrible hang-up with narrow Christian concepts. Whatever you seek, you will find God, but not the jealous creator-god who issues forth retribution and alters destinies in response to your prayers. At the level of the cell, God is not the DNA, but the DNA code. Did you know that the tree that you hug has DNA of the same chemical origin as HS?'

She let go the tree and enquired the meaning of HS.

'Homo Sapiens – whose racial memory courses through *our DNA*. Yet we deny the tree species any rights because they lack the will to organise anything but themselves. They are apolitical.'

'Oh Jeremy, this stuff is so beautiful. We're swimming in a swirling sea teeming with life and all the forms of the life are one and the same. You talk of trees but I *am* the trees; they're my limbs and my antennae.'

'If I . . . make love to you now, it would . . .'

She turned away and began to sob, 'You also believe that I am easy to have? I offer you much greater depth but you choose the most shallow.'

He turned offensive and sounded like Woody Allen.

'You only moralise things because the Catholics got to you. You said you saw sex as a sacred act of melting the minds from the ego trapped within the body towards the higher echelons of . . . freedom from time.'

'Or sex is lust which traps the ego even more into the body, and tell me, which is it with you now?'

Sarah-Hélène let go of the tree and ran away from Palmer into the building. She knew her way through the washrooms, the main vestibule, and into the former drawing room that served as a lecture theatre.

Robert Kohen accompanied her to her seat at the centre of the raised dais and introduced the séance with a speech. Something went wrong with the cameras then the sound and Kohen was asked to begin again his introduction. The impatience of the audience of around two hundred surfaced with an allegation from a heckler, 'Sorcery contravenes our religion, Dr Kohen.'

Kohen replied that this revealed the woman's ignorance and in a display of power he asked her to leave the room. It seemed rehearsed. She was probably planted and the stunt – typical of Kohen – rendered the audience susceptible and attentive.

'For the benefit of any other ill-informed persons, we are demonstrating *Regression Hypnotism*, a simple practice. This is as far removed from my own scientific invention of *Radio Archaeology* as is a bicycle to a space ship. I have no association with spiritualism, despite that imbecile who has departed so hastily from us to continue with her shallow existence on this planet.'

Kohen pointed to the audience and accepted a cautious question.

'What about drug-induced hypnotism, Dr Kohen? Is that scientific?'

'Hypnotism is on the fringes of orthodox medicine. Interrogation of a subject who has ingested drugs is at present unlawful in the USA despite our political campaign. Unless, of course, you are the CIA.'

There was a flicker of laughter from the minority who thought this was a joke.

Dr Kohen ascended the dais and pronounced in his best Oxford English, 'In the *scientific discipline* of Radio Archaeology we call our subjects *intermediaries*. Our sensitives tap into the *inosphere*, not on tables.'

Having drawn some nervous laughter from the audience Dr Kohen continued, 'And with great respect to the pharmacologists, many of whom I respect as good friends, I have shown that consciousness is *not* chemical. The memory is *not* transmitted in the genes. DNA is merely the apparatus affording access to the message.'

Kohen walked to Sélène and swung his pocket watch like a pendulum before her eyes because he was a showman. Under his breath he spoke a few words to send his subject into a trance. At his command to relapse as far back in her ancestors as she could, information tumbled out of her mouth in a stream of strange tongues and modern Eurospeak: French, Spanish, and some new words with Latin roots.

Kohen's face turned from puzzle to joy and he announced that she was talking fluently in the langue d'Oc, the ancient tongue of the Mediterranean region on the French side of the Pyrenees. A heckler challenged Kohen, 'How do you *know* it is so fluent? Are you now a medieval linguist?'

19.1 The lights are dimmed. The lecture theatre is dark and silent. No-one pays any attention to the interruption, least of all Sarah-Hélène, who acts exquisitely. She sounds perfectly ordinary. No groans, no dramatised hesitations of the trance. She calls Kohen *'papa'* without emotion, and suddenly switches to French like a frightened child aware of distressing events around her. She stumbles and begins to weep then her language reverts to American English. She covers her eyes and she reacts in shock.

'It is my family and it is the port of Marseilles a long, long, time ago. The soldiers return from the Holy Land. Is that possible? Yes, it is the horror of the Crusades. Yes. Madness and confusion in the family of Ibrahim. The world is in pain and I see their red crosses on black tunics. It is so vivid and real. But they speak old French. But they . . . no, I feel . . . we are weeping because . . . I do not understand. It makes no sense.'

'Go on, go on!' Kohen interjects.

'I have touch with two personalities in different times. It is not *painful* Robert but it is not comfortable. They are weeping, but it is because their soldiers have killed the enemy and the others cheer. Was it the enemy? I don't know. We feel . . . sympathy for . . . the infidels . . . but these are our enemy? It is *more than two personalities.'*

Kohen interjects loudly.

'Who was the enemy, Sara? Tell me, who was the enemy?'

She starts to breath loudly and as she struggles to speak Kohen guides her forcefully. He tightens his grip on her. She wakes up from a trance and he shouts, *'Don't try to work it out now with your own brain, just tell me honestly, quickly, exactly what did you see?'*

She is fully awake.

'*We* were the enemy, Robert. But I really don't understand it. We were cheering for our troops but we felt . . . *hostile to them?* That's how I'd put it. No, I simply don't understand.'

Kohen is very excited; apparently this had not been rehearsed.

He pleads, *'Please don't try to understand. Just tell us more. This is so very important and only you can tell us.'*

She grabs him and says, 'That's not it. You see, we pretended to be with the Crusaders who were fighting . . . the infidels . . . no, it was us. We were spies. *Were we?* Yes, so that's why they were fighting *us. The French soldiers were really our enemies.* Yes, that's why we were afraid. That's why we were crying.'

Kohen lowers his voice to exclude the audience.

'Please go on, Sara. In seconds you will forget it just like a dream, if it isn't already too late now. They can't hear us; tell me.'

'Robert, you know it. It is *our* people. They . . . *rather we* . . . slaughtered our own people. Oh, I feel the pain . . . I feel so sad. We are turned against ourselves.'

'I wanted you to say it. I don't want to put words in your mouth. Don't you understand scientific integrity, woman? Who were the Christian soldiers killing?'

The room full of people is dark and silent.

She breathes loudly.

'Paléstinas, followers of the Prophet, and ones they called heretics . . . and Judeans. *Judeans,* Robert. But I don't understand. Then my family are Jews. The Docas were Palestinians naturalised by the bishops and barons of northern France. Then it is just as you said, *I am a Jewess.*'

Turning to the audience, Kohen closes the session.

'I thank you, Sara, for this interesting experiment which caused you pain because it offends your sweet, innocent, but misguided unconsciousness of race. You need to love and be loved by everyone somewhat uncritically. Because you are insecure you must discover who you are. You did well to recognise Marseilles harbour seven centuries ago. It was destroyed in the war just before you were born so you have only seen it rebuilt and beyond recognition, yet you correctly identified it.'

'Yes, I did,' says Sarah-Hélène, in amazement.

The recording ends and the cassette is rewound. Leonard had to hire a special machine which played the American videotape.

Chapter Twenty

In August 1977 Robert Kohen applied for a licence to operate a radio station. In USA many are owned by religious organisations. Kohen emerged from the secrecy of his defence career into the brightly lit public arena and into the scrutiny of Michael Leonard.

The American public admired Robert Kohen's charisma, science lectures, and his youthful escape from Fascist Europe. He described his career as a contribution to western defence – that American families might sleep safe. He claimed that during the 1970s he had persuaded the military-industrial men of the wisdom of his new 'soft weapons program.' His recommended policy was to develop systems of combat acceptable to a pink future. Humane weapons made cold military sense by avoiding the destruction of places they would soon occupy and rebuild. According to Kohen, Nixon's men scoffed, but when the president fell Kohen jumped ship. The Defence scientist renounced the arts of warfare and became a pacifist.

Inspired by the Dead Sea Scrolls Dr Kohen founded The Modern Order of Essenes, a celibate order of Jewish males registered in Jerusalem as a kibbutz and in New York as a charity. He preached disarmament to the Jewish settlers defending the borders against Syria and Jordan. He began to preach, 'Love your enemies,' which he had previously denounced as *Christian morality*. In America, he joined the efforts to limit arms along with the Soviets, and in Israel he joined *Peace Now* – a movement advocating settlement with the Arabs by restoring to them captured territories.

A White House spokesman coined the term 'Kohenfusion.' President Ford regretted 'the loss of a gifted scientist from the defence program,' but pointed out that humane weapons projects had started in the early 1950s BK, *Before Kohen*.

Robert Kohen had left Ford and the White House behind; he was playing with much more powerful weapons. After the Israeli 'Six Day War' in 1967 re-united the Holy City, the Scrolls had reverted to Jewish patrimony as spoils of war. Among those who became interested in the message of the Dead Sea Scrolls was his friend, Sarah-Hélène.

Chapter Twenty-One

Reporting for work at 8.30am in their London office, Peter Bartlett had only one sip of his Monday morning tea before the boss arrived rather agitated.

On the table was a twelve-year old press cutting. *The Catholic Herald,* 27 August 1965.

Leonard caressed it with his eyes, thanked Lindy for his tea, but turned to his young assistant with a smile of approval.

'You've done it again. How did you find this one?'

With a well-earned pride, Bartlett explained that his girlfriend was a librarian and when she wasn't busy she laboriously sifted through dusty bundles of newspapers in the hope of finding something relating to the story.

Leonard widened his eyes in disbelief and turned to the article. There wasn't much to it. Except that it concerned a Father James Ryan, who taught the Holy Scriptures to Sarah Kelly. He had been transferred from a girls' school in Inverness to a boys' school in Nottingham.

Michael Leonard pointed to his new recruit, 'I can see the nun standing before me right now and hinting to me. I've paid seventeen quid for a day's parking and valetting of the Jag, but *I'm* going to drive it away to see Father Ryan's female pupil of 1961. You, Peter, must go to Inverness and confront 'Margaret' today.'

Sarah-Hélène agreed to meet the journalist. She admitted that she knew Father Ryan and Leonard put pressure on her to describe his weakness – *alcohol, gambling, heresy*?

She shrugged her shoulders, 'Judge not, lest ye be judged.'

'Well,' said Leonard, 'I'll ask you biblically, did your teacher James Ryan who you knew, *know you* in the Biblical sense? Did he *like* young girls?'

She raised her face upwards but it did not conceal her difficulty in holding back tears. She hesitated and then admitted, 'For his behaving like a man I was kicked out, Michael, but he was kept employed. No-one was fair to me, but I lied to save him, so maybe it was my fault.'

'*You lied for him?*' Leonard was flabbergasted.

'He was so kind. I dissolved into his beautiful kisses. I think I must have gone warm and red with embarrassment and happiness at the time. But the terrible guilt feelings came later. They tortured me. I had lied. And he had loved other girls. I had many confused thoughts but I knew my inner woman had done wrong. I had degraded myself and I had liked it, so the woman inside cut skin from the palms of the harlot outside so the pain took away the outer woman's conscience and my guilt flowed like the blood and it was another way for me to enter into the world, not be separate from it and I needed him. Do you understand, Michael?'

He told her that he did not.

'Try to understand: I was a rebel and I always hated the school, but self-mutilation was to avoid sex, make my body ugly, maybe make the priest feel guilty, or expose him without telling on him. I don't know why I gouged my palms. What I did with my hands that made me feel dirty so I cut them, but the nuns went hysterical about the stigmata. Constant bleeding which I could make flow or stop. When they found me they dragged me, not to the nurse, but to Mother Superior. She looked at me and her mouth fell open, 'Mother of God, it's a miracle. I never thought I would live to see this.'

Sélène smiled at Leonard.

'The three of them continued to visit me when I was at my new school, brought me presents, always stared at the palms of my hand and worshipped me, so I kept it up. *I could work miracles.*'

BOOK TWO

Sélène

MM

Chapter Twenty-Two

NEW YORK, AUGUST 1977

'GOOD MORNING USA! THIS IS RADIO QUMRAN, THE VOICE OF THE JEWISH PEOPLE RESTORED TO NATIONHOOD. Listen to the words which seep through the stones because they have been excised by the nameless ones who want to rebury the Dead Sea Scrolls. The word sent forth can never be recalled. In our year 5708 which is 1947 of the Christian calendar, God restored his nation and also the lost scriptures. Hear ye the call of the Messiah for it is clear to those who will listen.

"I am the Daughter of Israel, ravished every hour from my youth. Behold, I am Understanding and Science. The spirit dwelleth in me. I am in the shadow of the House of Stone which is in the shade of heavy clouds. Yet I am washed by its rains at night and I glow as the morning dew. My feet are swifter than the winds and my hands are gentler than the rays of sun. My yoke is gentle yet I am deflowered and yet still a virgin. I am a harlot for those that will ravish me and innocent with such that will know me not, for lo, I am loved by all, but a lover to few. I walk on the waters but am walked upon."'

The voice-over was Sélène and the media interest in the French actress was guaranteed by another 'manifestation.'

Since 4th November 1975, RADIO WXQR had broadcast New Age atmospheric music, 'global sounds of the seas, the skies, and the drifting motion of the continental plates.'

These stress busters were illegally transmitted outside the station's licensed hours. Strange noises focused and faded like a giant searchlight from outer space. The sounds were usually gentle whooshing, rain, tides, birdsong, and calls of dolphins. People tuned in as they believed it gave their houses a natural calm for free. As the weeks passed American listeners became increasingly curious and the growing audiences boosted advertising revenues.

A case of illegal transmission was filed against the station and its owner, Robert F. Kohen.

Meantime a grotesque and disembodied deep voice was being syndicated from coast to coast and discussed by everyone. Indistinct syllables formed words which were barely discernible. It was like someone trying to get through in a confused jumble of archaic and modern European tongues.

The story took on a life of its own and Leonard flew to report on it because of the connection to the woman. His stories were published in Britain. He wanted to know more and submitted the taped broadcasts to an audio laboratory. The owner of Sonus Forensic Audio Labs in Los Angeles proposed an explanation. He told Leonard about a controversy around claims being made by a man called Rupert Sheldrake.

In December the three men took part in an American prime time TV show. Scientists condemned the theories as beyond the paradigm, so a series of repeatable experiments had been set up worldwide to have Sheldrake's principle statistically proven. Leonard was reluctant to support weird theories tainted with New Age irrationalism but he urged his readers to accept scientific proof of a theorem without an explanation: *things in the air are learned by people and even animals.*

As the months progressed, and (crucially) as more people listened in to WXQR, the same incoherent, deep-voice utterances *apparently* had become discernible: three linked clauses were first written down by a fifteen-year-old schoolboy from Kentucky. On 22 March 1978 he mailed the answer to a monthly science-fantasy magazine to win his prize.

THEY SHALL SEEK . . . (indistinct) . . . THE RIGHTEOUS TEACHER . . . (indistinct) . . . PRIEST AT THE END OF TIME

A few days before the boy's answer was published, increasing numbers of people *independently* began to discern the cryptic message. At first it was assumed that the sounds were becoming clearer but comparisons of the earliest taped recordings showed them to be identical to the latest, and the weird theory was proclaimed to explain the phenomenon.

'Sheldrake's Principle of Formative Causation' stated that increasing perception can be shown to occur telepathically as if minds are linked to form a great network.

Despite its challenge to scientific determinism Leonard was prepared to state on television that, 'Mr Sheldrake's theory was supported by rigorous experiments with no connection to the modern messiah or radio broadcasts.'

The three phrases originated from The Dead Sea Scrolls and for this reason someone nicknamed the station *Radio Qumran*. Kohen was accused of being the instigator of a small hoax rather than the perpetrator of an elaborate plot rooted in Europe as Leonard began to suspect.

Some kind of an electronic device was the explanation suggested in Leonard's first article exclusively for an American newspaper. On the same day, Kohen stated that the voice was the invention he termed 'Radio Archaeology.' He also invited – no, challenged – the Englishman to send in engineers to inspect the electronic device. Leonard could not refuse. On Easter Monday his engineering team of three visited the premises of 'Radio Qumran' with flight cases full of electronic equipment.

22.1 The receiver of the signal from space, which the journalist called 'The Jesus Dish,' was nothing more than a standard make of apparatus mounted on the tower of WXQR. It was examined by a radio technician who confirmed and copied the signal source as a commercial satellite transponder. But this failed to explain the phenomenon because the orbiting craft was not getting its signal from planet earth, the only known source of intelligence! Moreover when the transmitter went interactive it responded in human conversation and Dr Kohen was thought to have completely outwitted his critics, but it was still assumed generally that it *was* a hoax.

A $50,000 prize was offered by *Scientific American* for the solution but Leonard predicted that it would never be won because the US military was unable to confirm or deny suggestions concerning its Star Wars Program.

Phrases deciphered by radio listeners and forensic audio experts from the Qumran broadcasts began to fall from the heavens, crystallising to form a clear winter pattern on the glass. Like snowflakes, fragments of Dead Sea Scraps were falling by radio to the planet while a clique of translators based in Jerusalem outrageously withheld the texts and parchments in embargo year after year.

The Dead Sea Scrolls were highly sensitive. They were Biblical texts which had not been touched by religious censors nor corrupted by the errors of copyists. The discovery of these books had made its mark on the public psyche. Collisions with the 'received' Scriptures would not slip by without being noticed. Therefore many people alleged that the delay amounting to decades in publishing the Scrolls was suspicious. Robert Kohen was a leader in the campaign.

At the heart of the matter were the Scrolls' messianic prophecies, and now the most sensitive phrases were publicly broadcast across the USA.

HE DIED BEFORE HIS TIME . . . FROM NINE PARTS OF LIGHT . . . BUT SHE SHALL BE BLESSED ABOVE ALL WOMEN . . . SHE SHALL BE NAMED AFTER THE WIFE OF ABRAHAM

Chapter Twenty-Three

NEW YORK, AUGUST 1977

Sélène, or Sara as Kohen insisted, refused to give any comment or indication of her reaction but she turned down all film contracts she had previously strived to attract.

In a stretched limo the thirty-year-old film star rehearsed lines for a real life confrontation. The wrong words would incite the hero's ferocious violence. Going over her lines she trembled and doubled the dose on the assurance that the substance wasn't addictive.

One, I am leaving you because I think that's what you really want (*so you're leaving me)*. Two, I still love you (*boost his ego*). Three, no publicity, it would destroy my career (*joke; read, your career*). Four, I don't want your money. *Return to me enough of mine to live in France for three months until I start a job.* Five, no kiss and tell, no careless talk to my friends, no return to acting, performing, modelling or anything. I'll never trouble you. I'll leave USA today. *That is the deal.* Would he buy it? Would he set her free?

23.1 Senator Spencer Weidfeld's concièrge helped her out of the limo and took her by the escalator to the penthouse love nest – *isn't that what it's called?* She felt eyes. They could see her, the neighbours and she knew their minds were disapproving. The gatekeeper left after telling her she must wait for Mr Weidfeld; she knew that it was his style to anticipate enemy action.

She closed herself in her bedroom. She looked at the telephone but knew it was best not to call her best friend. *At the turning points of your life you are alone in this world.*

The evening came and went and the Senator did not arrive. The coke had built up her confidence and clarity. And allowed it to subside. His minder had come and gone but gave no clues about his master's whereabouts.

Weidfeld arrived 'home' at 4am. She was asleep. A hammerblow shook her door which she unlocked before he beat it down. She was terrified. He was high – elated by an evening of alcohol, socialising, and power-broking. He had returned with a drinking partner, a Scottish 'chap' he introduced as his new lover, Lanark Hughes. Sélène smiled. Weidfeld had no traces of humour or homosexuality, but he knew instinctively how to confuse the enemy.

Invasively, the confrontation took place in her bedroom.

He wasn't at all upset about what had happened to their so-called relationship.

'What relationship? Women are whores.'

According to the newspapers she screwed everyone. He sneered: 'One more screw and I'll let you go. No, no, not me, my friend here.'

Weidfeld felt the blow to his face. He hadn't seen it coming. She had never hurt a fly but now she made up for it.

Hughes, the friend, was frozen to the spot. No-one provoked Spencer Weidfeld. There must have been something sharp in her hand. It drew blood from the senator's right cheek but hurt her more than it hurt him. He was shocked. Her rage transmuted into love and she wept as she soothed him. Hughes followed them into the en-suite bathroom finished in white marble with pastel-grey. As she mopped the blood from his face he calmly shattered the disinfectant bottle and pushed it into her right hand.

He shouted to his friend to observe that the creature is abnormal. Then he undressed her, at first slowly, then tearing her clothes in a frenzy. Her eyes pled for mercy and the gulps for air intoxicated her with the smell of the spilled disinfectant. Hughes stammered and tried to leave the private bathroom, but was ordered, 'Stay, or I'll fire you. She likes pain or it's your turn.'

Weidfeld pushed her across the room into the shower. Instinctively, Hughes jumped out of the way. Her head hit the tap and began to bleed; he showed her the blood on his hand. He stepped on her hand, calmly exclaiming, 'Same fingers, broken for the third time now. Maybe you'll learn I'm bad for you, wilful whore. At this stage Hughes was whining and pleading with him to leave her alone. He was firmly pushed aside.

Weidfeld turned the shower on to full cold, and dragged Hughes to the living room. He lay down on the settee. He called Sélène back from the front door (which, she discovered, was locked). She entered the room after knocking on the door, and crawled to the corner to protect herself behind a drinks cabinet. Weidfeld got up and exposed her by toppling over the cabinet. The grin on his face widened. He turned to Hughes and calmly stated, 'Your turn. You'll want another drink first, but sorry. None left. All smashed. What's the matter? You said you liked classy whores. Don't you like mine? *Do it!*'

Do it! It was just another order. Weidfeld dragged the trembling, bleeding female human from the corner to his colleague's feet. He lowered Hughes' trousers, 'What's this, my God, my God, dear boy, no reaction at all. She's supposed to be – no *she is* – one of the most beautiful babes in the USofA. We'll call you 'limp cock' in Party Headquarters and throughout the media from now on. *Unless you do it, I would guess it's the end of your career in politics. I suppose you could work for a supermarket.*'

Weidfeld waited and laughed. Hughes threw up over the settee and carpet.

'So that's what it is like to live in fear. Fascinating! The woman is more a man than you.'

The telephone rang. For a moment everyone froze. Except Weidfeld, who answered it calmly, 'What noises? *Do you know who I am?* We'll ask for help when we need it.'

The Presidential candidate replaced the receiver and his grin turned into laughter.

'Cover yourself, woman, have you no decency? I thought you were well brought up in a convent. And get me a drink from somewhere, and clear up this mess. Hurry. You badly need a drink, Limp Cock. Baby, get him a drink. My new media man's passed out. He can't take it. Get up, woman, and walk! He don't know how bleeding is nothing you can't control. He doesn't know nothing. No-one else will give him any job.'

Sélène was able to get up. In the main bathroom she washed herself and took a white dressing robe before appearing back in the blood-stained garment. She pointed to the smashed drinks cabinet and the sticky alcoholic pool of broken glass. Why should she fix him a drink from this? What could he do – she asked – hit her again?

She lit a cigarette and stared at him.

Weidfeld stared back at her, then turned to Hughes, 'I told you, women are stronger than men. Bear that in mind while we recruit staff. Let's get out of here, Limp Cock. Call a cab and tell Randall we'll stay over. I'm taking a shower before we leave.'

23.2 Hughes, momentarily left alone with her, whimpered, 'Miss Sélène, I'm so very sorry. I'll phone you tomorrow to make sure you're okay. You'll get everything you need, the very best attention and money.'

She sat down on the settee. 'Is that a man speaking, or is it a press officer?'

'It's best this way.' He brought over her cigarette when she pointed to it.

Inhaling deeply, she whispered, 'It's my last cigarette. My body is my temple. I've seen the light. Tell Spencer when he is sober there is nothing to forgive but plenty to repent, and I shall always love him very much. I know his head imprisons demented demons; they are fallen angels of fear and hate. But he is destined to lead his nation if he will heed the warning. But I must deliver it to him personally.'

Weidfeld had re-entered the room, 'What fucking warning, darling?'

His question was delivered with aggressive sarcasm. She replied softly.

'"Soubs l'opposite climat Babylonique . . ."'

'Oh, no, not this, again,' He sighed and explained to his friend that it was quotes from Nostradamus.

Sarah-Hélène also turned to Hughes and reverted to English.

'"In the land of the opposite climate, Babylon,
There will be great bloodshed,
By land and sea and air the sky will pour tribulations,
Sects, famine, kingdoms, plagues, confusion."'

'Mr Hughes, if Spencer is to lead his nation, he should remember how I showed him Michel de Nostradame's correct predictions of Hungary, and of Hitler coming, and Israel, and submarines and warplanes. And in the sixteenth century he predicted these things from the sky. Spencer admits to me that President Carter is preparing a Rapid Defence Force and so he knows that there will be a war and God will punish Iraq.'

Weidfeld complained to Hughes about her attempts to convert him to her belief in the occult. He believed it was all nonsense. Hughes nodded in agreement but admitted he knew nothing about the Pentagon's Gulf policies, nor its massive funding of Project Psi and other military exploitations of the occult sciences.

Much closer to the oak-lined office of Lanark Hughes in Campaign Headquarters, the erstwhile actor, Ronald Reagan, was employing an astrologer to align the favourable timings for the Republican Party to sweep to power in the next election.

Chapter Twenty-Four

MASSILIA, 70CE

The grandson, four years after he first read the Law in synagogue, was restless.

'Why do we wait and hide like dogs? Tell Mother she must proclaim me openly as the king and I shall raise an army and march against the Kittiim.'

'You talk bravely like a man, but not wisely like your grandfather. May his soul rest in peace. You are alive, my boy, only because of his wisdom which is the truest courage of men and because we women fled from the madness where our own people were more dangerous than any of the Kittiim whom you despise and I fear.'

Miriam still used the old term for the Romans, avoiding the need to distinguish the hostile races within the empire.

'I beg you to be true to your solemn oath in word and in deed, or your mother and sisters will surely perish. I do not matter. I am an old woman and my days are fulfilled when the Lord wills it, but our whole community is put at risk by one careless word from your lips. Is that what you want, Daniel?'

'No Grandmother.'

'Even a careless word at the prayer-meeting. You know that many of the cult of your grandfather, the most peace-loving man who lived, blame him for the downfall of Judea? We must have faith in God that when He wills it these times will pass, and you must obey the will of your earthly father who has gone to heaven. We are here for his sake and for the sake of our Father in heaven.'

'Amen, Grandmother.'

'I won't hug you because you don't like it. I know you are a good boy, and the safety of us all rests well in your hands. You are standing in for your grandfather. He was the bravest man in all the land. I think it every day.'

Miriam had received a letter from Simeon, the grandson who headed the household of the late Joseph of Arimathea. He warned her about the messianic gentiles who were now openly in dispute with the messianic Jews. Neither would support the defence of the Holy Land which they saw as futile.

'If you want to survive in this world, neither of these sects are your friends,' he wrote, saying that he himself had been excluded recently. 'You will live in safety only by making them believe that his line has perished.'

Miriam nevertheless resolved to keep her appointment with the Bishop of Rome. She would tell him that his authority was a denial of the Holy Family and contrary to the will of God.

24.1 A Records Officer in Marseilles Police confirmed to Michael Leonard that access to the files of 1952 was not possible. They were missing, probably just misplaced. However, he had discussed the incident with a colleague who had higher authority. According to the records there was no evidence of foul play. The case was closed. There was no liaison of an adulterous nature involving either of the deceased persons. And there were no children involved in the accident. The victims had been a childless couple.

Leonard's face was well-known so he used an investigator who drove to the area where Sarah-Hélène had been orphaned. He said he was retiring back home after a career in Paris. He spoke with a local dialect and soon began to extract some information.

None of the villagers remembered 'the car accident.'

With a high-level government intrigue, files can be lost, facts denied, and officials evasive, but how can the inhabitants of a small town be silenced?

That worried Michael Leonard a great deal.

24.2 HOLLYWOOD, CA, AUGUST 1977

Cathy Douglas-Diller accompanied Séléne to Johnny Lord's attorneys. It was only to sign some papers to end their relationship, but now they wanted her to adopt a son the film director had by a Latin-American woman who was dying in a drugs clinic. The five-year-old boy was quiet and pleasing. The lawyer said a substantial allowance would be provided.

Sélène said she would not consider it and asked them to close all her accounts and affairs in USA, as she was about to leave the country.

She told her friend that she wanted things to be done quickly, cleanly, anonymously.

'I just want to have enough to live on modestly for a short time.'

The lawyers asked for her forwarding address. She gave none; she had none. Was she going to return to live in France? She said she did not know.

Suddenly she asked her lawyer if she had not inherited land in France from her parents. The lawyers said that they would make enquiries.

'Please take your fees and put all my remaining money in a Swiss bank account and I shall contact you when I need it. I just don't think I can be a mother for the boy. I've never even met him.'

The women left the building having signed a portfolio of documents.

'Cathy, in two days plus eight hours I will be on an plane. I don't know what I am looking for, but I have reason to know it's written in the Dead Sea Scrolls.'

Her friend pointed it out. Exactly six years after she came to America seeking a part in the movie *Jesus Christ, Superstar,* Sélène was flying alone and on an impulse to Jerusalem.

The former actress called Sélène made no response.

Chapter Twenty-Five

JUDEAN DESERT, 70CE

There was no door to close behind the Teacher of Righteousness as he entered the scriptorium. Its crudely repaired wall was a reminder that the fortified building had been constructed on a site afflicted by earth tremors and subsidence.

The Womens' Committee for Defence of the Villages of Galilee had gathered in the large room once used to copy books. All fell silent in respect for The Teacher. Each day he grew visibly more old and disheartened. Each day defeat by the Empire drew closer. The community saw itself as the pure Israel, the real Israel, and the seed which would survive to produce the future generations. They called themselves the Sons of Light because they alone were Israel untainted by the aliens' way of life and worship. The Holy Ones lived by each word of the Law. They despised the sacrifices of animals of the wicked Priests of nearby Jerusalem and the legalistic interpretations of the Scribes.

The Teacher was ninety-one years old. In darker moments he would admit that everything had gone wrong. The young men were leaving the villages and training for war, replacing their compatriots who had already fallen. The nation faced destruction.

The women were shocked by his skeletal and wrinkled head with thinning wisps of white hair, and by his talk about the end of days. Things had not been as bad for as long as anyone could remember.

'Learned Teacher, we have pleaded with you to pronounce on the status of women in this Community for our supervisors and the village rabbis differ from place to place on our status. We implore you to write a manual . . .'

The women sat on the plaster bench built around the walls of the scriptorium where so many books had been copied; on one occasion, ten at a time.

The Teacher's nephew helped the old man to his chair which had been carved from a large stone; found in Jerusalem, it was said by the Therapeutae to have come from Egypt. The young man sat at the head of the stone table and spoke.

'The Teacher has been at prayer since early in the morning. Perhaps he has more important things to do before repeating again how you women can best serve the Lord God, blessed be the Holy Name.'

'Blessed be the Holy Name,' all repeated with conviction.

The Teacher laughed in his squeak which became higher in pitch with each passing month. He climbed onto the seat of his stone chair and proclaimed.

'AhaHaHa, it is the end of days and too late to write books. We have hidden all our books already. AhaHaHa, we have not enough caves to hide them all. You know that we found very old bones and pots of some people who actually lived in the caves in the days before our buildings, but we do not know who they are. But there is no time to write more books. The important thing is this. All those people, both men and women, who have lived a good life will live again. The others will end in Sheol. That is what matters, for our days here are drawing to a close.

'By His mercy and great goodness, He hath strengthened the spirit of man in the face of evil, and He has purified the erring spirit of a multitude of sins! Yea, the wickedness of Jerusalem has brought down upon us the wrath of the Lord. They think that Blessed-be-He sees not into their hearts. There are some of the Kittiim who lead more blameless lives in comparison to our own sons. Yea, the Sons of Darkness will prevail upon these lands and our days here are numbered so do not concern yourselves with Rules for the women in the Community.

'Truly, women are blessed, for it has been written that God will raise a princess who will blossom like a beautiful flower longer than the one baptised by Johanon who was sent to warn the nation . . . Yes, yes, you are in anguish, so speak, child, speak on behalf of your gender.'

'How long must we wait, Teacher?'

'For the sinner the years last long. But we use the rightful calendar of

the sun ordained by God, not the measure that the wicked ones use in the Holy City. Eternity is divided properly by the nine hours of our days, and our holy days divide the seasons, seven days per week, and the seasons divide the years by the stars. Do you not know that the years take not a moment to pass for the faithful? For what is time to the Nameless One? It is a wisp of desert wind. A moment is a crossroads of fate, and yet a thousand years can change not one thing. For every thought that would be formed in a man's mind, and every word that would be uttered in his mouth was fully known to Almighty God before the first moment of creation. So answer your own question, what is time? It is the reason I warned the indolent many times that they have no time to hesitate. And you see, now there is no time for the writing of books. Rejoice! Your labour is done. They are all written!'

The Teacher's nephew, brother of the last but one leader of the brothers in Jericho, turned to the women.

'General Vespasian has come to conquer the land of Abraham, and they will most certainly defile it in their way. James the Righteous and Peter have both been murdered and the Kittiim set loose the crazed Saul of Tarsus to turn the feeble-minded from the Law. He now works for them and calls himself Paul, as he once worked for the messianic sect, and before them did he not work for the wicked priests? Hah, lest he should confuse us with a third name yet he still misleads those who believe they can have eternal life outside the Law because he preaches with the energies of ten men possessed by unclean spirits.'

The Teacher interjected, 'Nephew, there is much light within Saul. Blame his converts, for they are weak. Is it not written that 'The false teacher causes terrible darkness for the many?' Am I going too fast for your writing?'

The old man reverted to his dictation of books despite his observation that, at the end of time, books were for storage and not multiplication.

'Women are to wear decent clothes and to conduct themselves modestly, without expensive garments, braided hair, gold, or jewellery. Their adornment is pleasing to me if it is good works. I do not give permission for a woman to teach or tell a man what to do. A woman ought not to speak first because it is written that Adam was formed first and woman by his

side; and the woman was led astray and led him astray and fell into sin. But she will be saved if she lives a blameless life, in constant faith and love and holiness!'

In the pause, the whispers of the women ceased. The midday heat became oppressive and the air in the small room was stale. But The Teacher looked upwards, as if the ceiling was invisible. Everyone waited for his words. With eyes closed he breathed deeply. His voice dropped in tone; then it became more slow and clear.

'And yet I can see, at the end of time she will come forth and be named after the wife of Abraham and be raised above all men and blossom longer than the son of man! For she will bring peace and . . . oh!'

Nobody dared to speak for several minutes in case anything more was forthcoming. The Master continued, and his nephew wrote down, 'Oh.'

'Oh! How beautiful the look of her face and how fine is the hair on her head, how fair indeed are her eyes and how pleasing her nose and all the radiance of her face. How beautiful her breasts and how lovely all her whiteness. Her arms goodly to look upon, and her hands how perfect. How fair are her palms and how long and fine the fingers of her hands. Her legs how beautiful and how without blemish her thighs. And all maidens and all brides that go beneath the wedding canopy are not more fair than she. She will be known as the one who can walk on straw.'

The Teacher was dead within one week. His nephew ordered the caves to be sealed and everybody to disperse to the four corners of the world; to travel light; and to worship in secret. Men cried out loud on the day families dispersed. The nephew of the Teacher refused to assume the hereditary title.

'It is all over,' he said, 'It is finished.' He hesitated and then proclaimed.

'But in case we might come back, our treasures will be hidden in as many places that number two multiplied by itself six times so that, in the end, when we are raised again and we are lost, they will point us to the beginning.'

Two legions of the Kittiim arrived on the third week. Their General Vespasian had heard the rumours about the powers of the water. He had three non-swimmers bound and thrown into the sea. To his astonishment, the bewitched Waters of the Kumra valley supported them. They did not drown. The General felt uneasy. He had arrested people who said that their saviour had walked on water.

BOOK THREE

Jerusalem,
The Eternal City

MM

Chapter Twenty-Six

JERUSALEM, SEPTEMBER 1977

Even for non-practising Jews a visit to Israel can seem like a return to the homeland. It catches people off guard and the sense of *déjà vu* provokes a wide range of explanations.

As her plane touched the ground the passengers applauded. It was a herd instinct, the moment of relief from danger, but Sara was preoccupied with her own thoughts. Upon leaving the plane, the heat oppressed her. At the bottom of the steps, she felt giddy and stopped to rest. In Jerusalem she recorded events in a new diary.

> *I could not see for weeping. Gripped by a heavy sensation of homecoming I walked on tiptoes down the steps and placed my palms on the concrete of Lod Airport. My tears kissed the ground and were stolen by the sun. There I sat for what seemed like an eternity. Like the Tower of Pisa, I was leaning on my left palm. My long skirt covered my legs gathered into my buttocks which were burned by the stones. And yet it was pure. I have come from the toxic fumes of Europe and American turmoil to purity and liberation and to my homeland.*

The woman sat until she had cooled her small patch of the Holy Land. She felt dizzy and paralysed by the arid heat but she felt obliged to move. Her strength returned, but only slowly. She had not lost consciousness yet an uncertain time had elapsed.

My thoughts were so detached from reality that I measured time by the passing of 300 passengers who had disembarked. I saw a man who was a doctor and even he walked by. Full of his thoughts and plans. No question of asking, 'Are you all right, my dear?'

I felt at home, but I was still alone.

She stared up at the Boeing 747, blinked her eyes, and with much relief saw that it was not named *Enola Gay*. The illusion gone, reality returned. She blinked again to check that it had reverted permanently from 1940s US military colours to the modern blue and white of the Israeli passenger carrier. She kept her eye fixed on the plane but accepted that the old world was slipping away.

Her past and her future were neither in Europe nor in USA.

The vision was a gateway to Heaven and I felt a destiny I was starting to act out. There was no script but it was predestined. It was different to the goal-orientated routine that people call life and choice. I had freewill. I could go anywhere and be happy, return to France, or Scotland. Or I could stay here and be crucified.

As she crossed the runway the heat was oppressive and the noise overwhelming. She felt she was still being watched. By the ones who killed her parents. By the Church. By the CIA. By two former lovers, both rich and manipulative men. Let them watch – she would never repeat the mistakes: submit to the male mindset, seek love through power, and engage the control freaks. She tried to find some reason for the years of her manipulation: reciting lines, performing, singing, dancing, waitressing, trusting men, looking for love, psychedelic escapism, and finding life so empty that she would be caged in a luxury apartment with nothing in return but subsistence.

She needed a cigarette so much that it was painful to think that she had declined a duty-free pack of two hundred for a few dollars of loose change.

The woman wondered, why had she sought out men like Lord and Weidfeld? In California a therapist suggested that, as a gentle soul, she sought completion in her opposite male. A counsellor told her she must break free from this relationship pattern. These ideas kept circulating in her head until she wrote her own explanation in her diary, determined to recover in a third continent without resorting to psychiatry or relationship therapists.

Lions eat people. People who are alive are not eaten. In relationships we repeat patterns. I have learned to be spiritually alive so I shall not be eaten.

She then wrote down the words of her hero, 'Cappy,' Captain Alfred Hubbard, the first American to see LSD as a mind-expanding and transcendental drug.

'Most people are walking in their sleep. Turn them around, start them in the opposite direction and they wouldn't even know the difference.'

For the first time in my life, at the ripe age of 30, I knew that I was in control. I did not see a quaint, rickety flying machine from the past, nor a ghoulish ghost of a pilot with bomber jacket returning to our time like an angel of death. I saw our own modern Israeli aircraft, a brand new wide-bodied passenger jet, but then it was painted ENOLA GAY. I heard the voice of the Emperor resonating within, 'We Japanese are a divine nation on earth'.

I understood, after Hiroshima and Nagasaki, the Emperor lost his divinity when his voice was heard for the first time on radio, as if he had finally admitted to his people that he was not from Heaven. But from his voice, I knew that he was wrong in his confession, and his new claim which he made to survive in the modern age was the lie. From Robert's work I could understand my vision. Thanks to him, spending evenings forcing his science down my unwilling throat, I knew I was not crazy but finely tuned into the great Radio, the Inosphere as he named it. I understood. But I was very glad when it left me after an interval of short time. I was not alone, or so it seemed. I saw no-one but knew that I was not alone. I had already started to suspect what was happening. I was not tuned into it. I WAS IT.

26.1 Airport-survival mentality gathered her senses and pushed her forward with the crowd walking towards International Arrivals. She was searched for drugs. She felt humiliated and felt it was personal, but none were found. Not even cigarettes.

She emerged from the airport into the powerful sun, dragging two heavy suitcases towards a line of taxis. It was sixty-three kilometres to Jerusalem but time was not a problem to Sélène. She observed that, like USA, people here pushed themselves forward to hire the best taxis, or the biggest, or newest ones. They avoided a battered old Opel for the newer Mercedes cars. She was surprised to see German cars but soon learned that Israel was full of War Reparations – money and contacts.

As a lone traveller with two suitcases Sélène had no need of the commodious and faster Mercedes cars. She helped the elderly driver of the battered old Opel to load her cases but the old fellow would not have a woman aid him.

She smiled, 'How much to Jerusalem, sir?'

It was three something, or thirty something. She didn't understand Hebrew but he seemed trustworthy and at least he had fixed the fare. Tourists are ripped off in such circumstances but he spoke only Hebrew and a some Slavic or European language which she couldn't understand. 'THREE MIGGIES,' were his only words. He grinned as he held up three fingers. She smiled back, wondering how much was a miggy. Ten US dollars? Or Israeli pounds? They were in the Holy City before she realised that the radio in his car and loudspeakers on the streets were blaring the news about three miggies.

Three Arab pilots had been shot down in the very latest Russian-built MIG-23 fighters.

Like everyone else, the driver was very happy.

They were not his sons.

She tried to conceal her feelings behind the Italian shades but tears fell as she thought of three mothers, three families, three wives or sweethearts (or maybe both), and three circles of sisters and brothers; currents of misery which would diminish humanity forever.

She had come here to save her people. She had come here to be crucified.

The driver saw she was distressed.

'You miss your boyfriend, young lady?'

In silence the driver concentrated on the roads.

He had a few more words of English but none in response to her French.

'American? Pretty girl. You will meet my boy? Thirty, in the army. Not married. Swell kid. He likes Coca-Cola.'

She tried to explain in French, English, and Italian that she had not been born in America but the language barrier never silenced a loquacious old taxi driver. Dodging the oncoming traffic he showed her a photo. Apparently he operated the car with this son who read American comics all day and he painted the doors of their old taxi with the cartoon. *So this taxi was very famous.* Something about a mule.

'That's what they call us. The mule. So, you arrived in the City of David in The Mule, like Jesus Christ.'

He laughed.

She sat motionless, stunned by this information. She did not smile. *Robert Kohen could not have set this up.*

After a long interval of silence, the driver apologised for the offence.

'I was thinking you are Jewish.'

'I was educated in Convent schools in Europe,' she replied almost inaudibly.

At the Hotel Capitolina she watched the money the driver slowly counted from her hand. He said goodbye and collected another passenger in a hurry. Everyone here was in a hurry. Nobody came forward to help the young woman with two heavy suitcases and she was too busy struggling with a new currency to notice the rusting taxi until it drove off. Then she observed the cartoon character which was painted on its door.

She was exhausted and wanted to lie down in her air-conditioned bedroom. But the clerk was sure, everyone was so sure here, *they had no reservation*. The travel agent in New York telephoned back to say he had no trace of any payment made by the client.

She paid the hotel for a second time but she was unable to suppress her giggling.

The man at the Reception desk had no idea what amused her. Riding into Jerusalem in The Mule and now, no room at the inn!

Had she taken Johnny Lord's child, she would have been taken to the stables with a son she had not conceived.

26.2 JERUSALEM, 77CE

The Righteous Teacher had been gathered to his ancestors before he could see the destruction of the nation. His seventy-two year old nephew had two further tasks before he could claim the Sleep of the Elect which endures until the resurrection at the End of Time.

By the mercy of God, the first part of the priest's final task on earth was now set in motion. And providentially, Simon ben-Yoseph of Arimathea was at home. He immediately recognised the old man and asked why the new Teacher had risked a dangerous journey on foot to Jerusalem.

'I am not The Teacher. There is no longer any office and there is no community. Roman soldiers are not troubled by a weary old man, Simon, and you know of the fate of our swordsmen. They lost our sacred scrolls, their lives, and the people's gold.'

Simon frowned. 'Your order of words implies the scrolls are more important than the lives of our swordsmen, including my cousin and your own nephew.'

'Only the Almighty counts lives, Simon, and it is His time that we spend in this rotting domain. I do not ask you this for myself, but for our people, I must prevail upon you alone to do something even if it risks your life.'

'Then I will do it if I can.'

'To honour the memory of your dear father, may his soul rest in peace . . .'

'I will never equal him, but, tzadik, saintly man, tell me what I can do.'

'I came here alone and I ask you also to work alone because no group is safe from the enemies of our people. The treasury is of small consequence. It serves us now by diverting our enemies, but it will reveal to our generations to come and to our friends after their resurrection the locations of the register. The list of the treasure is more important than the treasure. I'll explain this riddle, Simon ben-Yoseph.

'The copper scrolls contain the decipherment key of all past generations of the royal line and the priestly line, for it is as we prophesised, The Temple of Herod will be destroyed even before the last of his craftsmen finish it. Use all your cunning to find the hands into which the scrolls of encrypted copper fell. You must recover them and place them in hiding with our books.'

26.3 JERUSALEM, SEPTEMBER 1977

The tourist strained to hear the words of the official guide.

About one thousand years before Jesus walked its streets, the vainly named 'City of Peace' was taken by the Habiru tribes temporarily united by David.

It was nothing more than a small settlement on the eastern hill, flanked on two sides by deep valleys. Philistines and Canaanites, who had developed the use of iron and chariotry, controlled the valleys that flowed into the mountains. The city's impression of military strength was an illusion which probably contributed to its fate for it was destroyed and re-occupied more than any other city in the world. It is not a fortress and its walls form a boundary not a barrier. By bringing the Ark of the Covenant within its walls David made it the symbol of a religious aspiration which gave it another illusory strength.

Sara judged the holy city with the eyes of yet another claimant. She knew what was around each corner and tried to attract peoples' attention with her spooky powers; instead, it turned people against her.

She recognised a plant from her childhood home in France when she saw it spreading uncontrollably along the ancient citadel. A man with a skull cap and a prayer shawl deflated her by closing the discussion in front of a circle of new friends.

'Madam, by profession I am a botanist. The plant is *Hyoscyamus Aureus.* And the authorities are unanimous that Golden Henbane does not grow on the other side of the Mediterranean.'

After challenging her claims of *déjà vu,* one of a circle of new friends reminded Sara that she had been here in 1971 with the film crew of *Jesus Christ, Superstar.* She was seeking the part of Mary Magdalene.

'Moreover there is the frequency with which every corner of the Holy City is photographed and documented throughout the world of its three religions. And the way you preach no-one will thank you to start a fourth!'

For several days the claimant queen explored her land in Sélène's familiar Italian shades; she even wore a white blouse and khaki pants with the Chanel leather belt which boasted her Gallic pride. Not surprisingly, the starlet was recognised and photos were snapped by tourists. She bought a cheap camera but her first film was spoiled by the door springing open and the second film was lost or stolen with the camera.

Its bereft owner continued to visit the remaining tourist attractions unencumbered by gadgets. She visited the Israel Museum where she observed a taxi dropping off a husband and wife, apparently Americans, who joined a group forming round the diminutive figure of a young female tourist guide. The battle-weary Opel drove away. It was still painted with *The Mule*. Unlike a 747 named and painted *Enola Gay*, the taxi was solid and familiar to the locals who knew the name of the cartoon.

Determined to tour the city alone, Sélène left behind the tourist parties disgorging from buses at the museum gates. She noticed that her precious wrist-watch had gone but the sun was at its warmest around midday. The timepiece left a mark on her wrist so she was sure she had worn it this morning. It might be sold to a tourist or more likely to a dealer in the Old City but the thief was an angel of the Lord, having suspended her in the timeless cycle which is Jerusalem. She thought of the lunch she had accepted with an Israeli soldier. But she observed a building which had a white dome roof modelled like a giant clay lid from a first-century scroll jar. Apparently this building housed the Dead Sea Scrolls. Like the trickle of visitors along the path, she felt drawn into the Shrine of the Book.

It's a Jewish pyramid, joked one of the tourists.

She recognised the female tourist guide she had seen near *The Mule*: why did this five-foot girl carry an oversized holstered gun? Probably grew up in a frontier kibbutz. Dressed in a military khaki with shorts and wrap-around sunglasses she looked something between cute and comical.

'The Jewish people,' the official guide explained in French, slowly and inaccurately, 'hid the Dead Sea Scrolls in the year seventy of the Common Era, when our land was captured by the Romans. *The Scrolls were hidden until the time when the Messiah would come.*' Sélène walked through the crowd closer to the guide who was reciting her lines.

'They believed the righteous would rise from their graves, but the others would be judged harshly. We returned in 1947, or more accurately, a few of us lived here continuously under many occupiers, but we actually began to return in numbers in the late nineteenth-century. It is significant that the UN recognised our nationhood in 1947 on the very day the Scrolls were purchased for the State of Israel. *Let us move on.*'

Fascinated by the tour guide as much as her commentary, Sélène met her eyes and joined the group. Without a pause the Sabra switched to fluent English.

'The dedication of this land for holy purpose is stated in the Bible, and much to our relief the Scrolls have served to confirm the stability of our medieval Bible texts for the preceding one thousand years. This supports the great care and accuracy taken by our scribes through the centuries of copying by hand. *Please follow me.*'

'So had the Scrolls contained nothing new?' Sélène asked the guide in French.

The guide blushed, aware of her linguistic slip which no-one had interrupted.

'Mademoiselle, the scrolls contain minor deviations of spelling and points of interest to Biblical scholars only. You can buy a book on the subject at low cost in the souvenir shop. Professor Yadin is the most reliable.'

'Merci beaucoups,' Sélène grinned.

If Robert were here he would have taken hold of the young tourist guide's arm and said to her with a firm voice, 'What about the books and passages cut from the Hebrew Bible in the First-Century? If they amount to nothing, why do the authorities conceal these things? Why do they wish them reburied?' And to Sara he would have said, 'Do not speak. Heed the voices of the Scrolls. Listen, but do not speak.'

She walked directly into the museum. The tall backlit scroll mounted behind the glass held tourists gaping for a few seconds, after which they quickly followed their guide to the next exhibit.

'How symbolic of peoples' trust and conformity,' she uttered under her breath and she did not move on. She was captivated by the scroll and by a small white placard quoting from them, 'You came here . . .'

She believed that it spoke not about her repatriation but of her birth into the world. The backlighting shone through the Isaiah Scroll and she tried to understand its squiggles.

I felt a deep love for Isaiah and his love for his Maker and his Maker's love for his creatures, blind though they were. I understood everything that had fired his eloquence and the enormity of his message was changing my life. He was a seer and the first who sensed the coming of the saviour of mankind. How could these scrolls, so much closer to Isaiah himself, not stir us deeply even now? But the visitors just walked on to the next display. They heard nothing. But I heard things. Am I crazy? I think not!

An American-English-speaking guide who followed with the next party seemed not to notice the bi-lingual woman who joined his group. Or in her mind *they* joined *her*, but they moved on, leaving her still under the spell of the museum's most complete Isaiah Scroll. She walked round the glass case wondering if this was the real thing or a facsimile. On this subject she wrote some words in her journals, betraying something of the French respect for religious relics and her aristocratic perspective of the unworthiness of the masses.

After German-speaking tourists entered the chamber and passed her by, the guard began to increase his surveillance of the woman who was founding her own sect.

I wonder why are we drawn to the Dead Sea Scrolls? Should they influence our lives today? Why were they found in the year I was born? And of the Jewish nation reborn. Were they waiting for the second messiah? God in His great Wisdom (oh thanks be to God) had the awareness of my needs and sent me here and seeing how perplexed I was when I left the Shrine. He sent me a Remarkable Sign.

She walked to the counter and exchanged eight Israeli pounds for a copy of Professor Yadin's book, *The Message of the Scrolls*. She started to read it in front of the Scrolls themselves and when the armed guard approached her she asked if the exhibits were facsimiles.

'Nobody can say for sure, Miss. *You are* Sélène, *the American soft-porn film-star?'*

She smiled, 'Porn is from Biblical Greek and in its true meaning cannot be softened.'

She read aloud from a page her thumb had found in Yadin's book.

'"*He has driven me from my country like a bird from its nest. And all my friends and acquaintances were thrust afar from me. And they thought I was like a lost vessel and they, the interpreters of lies and prophets of guile, they formed against me plots of Belial. Wanting me to barter Thy law which thou hast engraved on my heart, for the flatteries which they address to Thy people.*"'

'Yes, I am the star of David. Watch over this building well, dear guard. It is a gateway to the great knowledge that I have come home.'

He asked for her autograph. She looked at him with surprise.

'I can give you the life of the spirit and yet you ask only for my autograph.'

While he considered this, her thumb continued to select passages of Yadin's paperback. The author was a celebrated hero in Israel. In the 1940s as a soldier in the War of Independence, then a politician, and then following the footsteps of his father (who had identified and purchased these Scrolls for Israel), Yigael Yadin became his country's leading archaeologist. His popular book became her first step to understanding the Dead Sea Scrolls and her mythical view of Judaism.

She set off for her hotel – where she intended to read the book and write up her diary. She became aware of how the scrolls began to haunt her. It would be a huge task to acquire enough knowledge to challenge the experts, but somehow she must learn *the message of the scrolls*. She could not depend on anyone to do it for her. Even the longest journey begins with a first step, but perhaps those loved by God might hope to get whisked up on a Golden Chariot.

Chapter Twenty-Seven

Outside the Shrine of the Book, Sara saw a man in front of a professional camera (the type that does not spring open). Saul Bercott, Dean of the American Institute of Ancient Oriental Civilizations, was being photographed to publicise his book on the Essenes.

Bercott observed the European woman who stood in the oppressive heat waiting until the end of the photographic session. Before long they were locked in an endless stream of questions and answers about the Dead Sea Scrolls.

In the professor's view, the issue of consistency – or changes from the medieval copies of the Old Testament – while highly significant, was used by the theologians to conceal the main issue: complete works excluded from the selection which formed the Bible. The unorthodox books revealed what happened *between* Parts One and Two of the Bible – the vital years between Old and New Covenants – which still splits Jews and Christians between each other and between themselves.

'The Scrolls are surviving witnesses which the Roman army missed. The others were dispersed . . . or *died*.'

He softened the last word to spare her feelings but she knew her history. He offered his sunhat to protect her head and continued.

'It was in these years that rabbis usurped the rule of the high priests, and the followers of Paul usurped the leadership of James. That's what the public don't know. They've lived their lives to rules built upon historical accident and power broking.'

'Then I'm not *the public*, Professor. Are there dangerous revelations?'

'You must ask the International Scrolls Committee because after thirty years only that handful of men know the list of texts awaiting publication,' Bercott answered.

'Except Robert Kohen? He claims to know more,' she suggested tentatively.

The professor smiled.

She persevered, 'You . . . think that he is meddling in your field?'

'He has written two essays connecting the Scrolls to his own expertise, *The Predestination Philosophy of the Essenes*, discussing his scary theory of time and the human concept of eternity. And in connection with the Scroll Sect's use of 'light' meaning enlightenment – which is actually from the Iranian prophet Zarathrustra, incidentally – Dr Kohen discusses his career as a Defence Scientist, something of a euphemism, I'm afraid, for a weapons builder.'

'I hate weapons.'

'Well, it was his discussion of the flash before the nuclear mushroom and the sacred symbolism of the mushroom. He linked it to the archetype of God as destroyer as well as Creator. *Lux fiat!* Some Japanese students denounced him for saying that the Americans were modern gods entitled to destroy their divine empire. It was a strange controversy in the early fifties, five or six years after the Bomb. It is forgotten. He won't talk about it now.'

The professor complained of the heat but she did not notice it.

'Was Dr Kohen involved with the Manhattan Project?'

He took her arm and walked towards the shade of trees.

'Oh no, he came into the H-bomb project, long after the end of the War when there was no excuse about having to beat Hitler. By then we were at war with the Russians, and remember that they had occupied his country. You know his origins? Now the fellow really has *seen the light*, if you'll forgive my pun, oh dear, a very bad one. Now that he is a pacifist, his colleagues do not verify his description of his so-called Defence job. You'll remember his trial for misappropriation of funds was really for misleading his superiors. Kohen is economical with the truth. Let me buy you coffee. Then I'll reclaim my hat and make it for a 3pm lecture.'

* * *

They sat down under the shade of a canopy outside a tourist coffee shop. She wondered if her lunch date had forgiven her.

'Professor, I've come to study the Scrolls. I met Robert in the States. I wonder, is there anything you know against Dr Kohen's ideas?'

'Well, he's crazy to expect the rabbis to surrender power without a struggle. And the Israeli government needs the Religious Parties' support in the Knesset. For Knesset read Sanhedrin and you might be forgiven for thinking that nothing's changed in two thousand years. It's like a time warp.'

It's like a time warp. She repeated these words slowly, then decided.

'I'll decline that coffee. I have a lot of thinking to do, and I need to do it by myself.'

'So, you don't have time for a coffee but you might want to attend a lecture on the Dead Sea Scrolls?'

27.1 They shook hands in the sunshine outside the Shrine of the Book, the scholar with his distinguished white moustache and the French film star wearing her white tee shirt and dark glasses. They had been drawn together by the Scrolls, but now they returned to their own genders, ages, rôles, and separate worlds. Separated, she thought, like the ages of Jerusalem in which Jews fought Romans and Jews fight Arabs. He took his hat. She felt isolation as pain. She put her arms around Bercott and deeply kissed his lips. He apologised; he had to be at the Hebrew University for a lecture in under an hour. She grasped his arm, but he avoided her eyes. She let go. She already knew that he was here to deliver the lecture of 3.00pm. A few years ago, she would have despised a man who was gentle and kind. Now she sensed the real power of a man like Bercott.

She watched his white suit disappear into the horizon, and to distract her mind she opened *The Message of the Scrolls*. With a pen that now leaked, she blotted ink on the absorbent pages and underlined Yadin's translation before copying the words into her diary dated 21 September 1977.

I thank Thee, Oh Lord,
For Thou has delivered my soul from the pit
And from Sheol Abaddon
Thou hast brought me up again to the top of the world.

27.2 JERUSALEM, THE ETERNAL CITY

Sarah-Hélène de Saint Clair from the Languedoc woke up on Thursday morning in an exalted state of mind: in search of past roots and future orientation. Instead of seeking pain to extinguish guilt she felt a sensation of being in control. She felt no urge to overcome isolation by friendship or relationship and asked her journal, *Is this what normal people feel? So my head is not mis-wired? The therapists need only take us home so we can face our demons.*

She visited the next dot on the tourist map.

Yad Vashem is the Israeli museum which commemorates six million Jews who perished during the outbreak of European mass amnesia – the psychopathic projection of hatred onto other races. But Sarah-Hélène no longer identified herself as European; she felt no guilt for what had happened. Indeed she understood the isolation in which the mind of the person loses itself and attaches to something outside itself, however evil or mechanical.

Belonging to all religions and none, and coming from no country in particular, she walked through the unadorned stone corridors of the Holocaust Building. Was it really so cold or was she chilled by so many photos and documents which portrayed terror? *Her parents' generation had emerged battered, bruised, and bloody from the cracks of civilisation, but they were not broken by war. They healed themselves through their children, and maybe through Sarah-Hélène, the woman of peace.*

Photos of atrocities: piled corpses, ruined buildings, and rows of cemeteries for the privileged few. Perhaps the dead were the fortunate ones? Only the survivors were forced to see the failure of reason. White cards starkly declared in Hebrew and English totally unacceptable facts and statistics. And the women. And the children. And the old people. Why were they the saddest? Because they were innocent. Because they were unfulfilled. Boys who would never adore a woman. Girls who would not live to bear their children.

Tape recordings replayed the chaos of the 1940s: sirens, voices, and violins which had been silenced for over three decades. Personal artefacts which had survived to protest their owner's deaths with unbearable eloquence. A diary which stopped on 22 September 1944. A ladies' watch, its leather strap having perished, had stopped at five minutes past seven

– morning or evening, who knows? And what had happened by this fateful hour? Nobody could say, but Sarah-Hélène (on drugs no more potent than fresh air and orange juice) stretched her atavistic powers and saw.

In a ladies' makeup box, a hairbrush with vanity mirror – silver with inset ivory and blue enamel. Sarah-Hélène held the mirror to her face, 'saw' the owner's eyes, and fled the building in panic and distress.

27.3 She emerged from the dark decade 1936-45 into the cleansing, blinding sunshine of Jerusalem in 1977 and found herself walking in the gardens of the museum. She walked through 'The Forest of Six Million Trees.' For a long time her mind burned with the engraved image of the girl with the silver-handled hairbrush. She was silent, and she smiled, but tears could not be held back.

She knew herself *to be* the 1944 girl with the innocent eyes and dark, intense brows. At last she accepted – if not understood – the idea of more than one soul being perceived within a single body. For the mirror eerily reflected the girl's foolish thought. *Had she only been blonde*. Sélène's heart pounded in terror at her dissolving identity. *No man is an island;* the separation between souls is like the seven seas; *isolation is delusion*. For Sélène brushing her own long black hair each morning would become part of 'the final solution.' It was scary; now she was losing control to grief and it felt like falling down a well. *Isolation is survival*. She understood the human tragedy. She sat in a remote corner of the memorial gardens and retrieved her diary. She searched her bag and her hand emerged stained with black ink. In frustration she ran towards the museum, abandoning some of her cosmetics and personal possessions. She stopped a group of tourists and persuaded one of them to give her a pen.

She returned to the far corner of the garden, curled up between a tree and stones, and stuffed her possessions back into her ink-stained bag; pausing to look into her vanity mirror for a few seconds. Taking up the good pen, she looked towards the sky then back to her diary and cursed when a tear splashed onto a new page. She headed it YAD VASHEM, SEPTEMBER 29, 1977 and neatly used the ink to make a thumb print.

If my head is misled, I must think again. How many evil people did it take to establish a war? None, just group madness. The women did not kill. My parent's generation did nothing to cause the war.

She looked up and 'saw' a unicorn, a non-existent creature which dissolved into a rainbow, a non-existent promise. Behind it was a group of children, playing; unaware of what this place said, but drawing her back to reality.

I am in the House of Stone which is in the Shade of heavy clouds yet I am washed by its rains at night and I glow in the morning sun.

Below that she drew a tree and wrote,

'Branches, Buddha, DNA, UNO, roots, the tree of enlightenment.' Now I see it but I cannot explain it: DNA-Tree, family-tree, United Nations. I understand the madness. It is caused by our own pain. I see it in myself. I see it in all others. We feel alone.

She copied from the Thanksgiving Hymns in Yadin's book about the Dead Sea Scrolls.

But I am of dust and ashes,
What can I plan unless Thou hast wished it?
And what can I devise without Thy desire? . . .
And how can I be wise unless Thou hast created me!
How could I talk unless Thou hast opened my mouth?
And how may I answer unless Thou hast made me wise?

She closed her diary and packed her bag. A few moments later she was walking past a theatre announcing Professor Bercott's lecture on a poster.

'IN PROGRESS' was written over it by hand.

Had she not come here to learn about the lost Scrolls?

Like an uninvited guest she walked through corridors until she encountered some early leavers. The lecture was coming to an end. At the back of the theatre she sat near a pillar. The four-hundred seat hall was filled to capacity and there was tension in the air, far from boredom. Bercott was winding up his talk with a quotation. It made her panic because she felt that she owned the words.

> *Religion means binding together, of individuals and ideals, of heaven and earth, but the old religions of Jerusalem are sick, sectarian, and schismatic. They dissolve into oceans of selfishness. The Essenes' cult died long ago, for despite its strength and influence it was inflexible and dogmatic. Like then, cousins and brothers fight each other; it is not only between Muslims, Christians and Jews, but white Jew against black, Shi'ite against Sunni, and Greek Christians against Catholic Christians. Understand conlict. Much that we can learn from the Essenes is from their mistakes. Their separateness.*

She heard the applause and watched other people leave in protest. She thought about congratulating Bercott but decided to take the evening off. She left the hall quickly.

Outside she met some Australian back-packers, two Danes, some born-again Jesus-freaks and they were fascinated to learn of her acid days in the legendary Haight Ashbury. *She really was there?*

As the sun set she walked with two girls and their boyfriends. After clubbing, the party returned to the YWCA where they laughed and drank Coco-Cola until they crashed out.

27.4 On Day-2 of her enlightenment Sélène slept until noon and woke up alone. She paid for two more days but stayed in her room; she thought and wrote her diary.

On Day-4 she collected her belongings and checked out with two suitcases and a scribbled address which she had almost lost.

She commented that the architecture was plain compared to the exalted reason for its existence.

'Government buildings are designed by geometers for people to work without aesthetic sensibilities.' One of her Danish friends appeared from nowhere. She shook hands and walked into the building.

'Take a seat, Miss.' That's all they said.

The iron painted-cream windows of this office were shaded from the sun but she was sweating from excitement.

'Come this way.' *At last.*

Her heart skipped a beat as she entered the partitioned office.

She sat down and decided there was no better way than to declare it without delay.

27.5 *'I want you to know that I am Jewish.'*

She paused but the civil servant with the scull cap betrayed no reaction. She defended her claim.

'I once read in a book that you don't recognise the forced conversions of Jews provided the heart is unconverted to the religion they force upon you. Does this apply to my ancestors?'

The clerk with the skull cap said she could bring it up in her interview.

The Immigration form was completed in the hand of a friendly woman whose name was Olga Orlinski. She had immigrated to Israel in 1952. She came from Bulgaria. A small woman with white, freckled complexion and red hair, she said she had turned fifty this year.

They laughed when Olga said that Sara looked Mediterranean and more Jewish.

'People, ask if I am Japanese!' she replied.

'I suppose you could be. I'd better ask the police to check you very carefully,' Olga smiled, and then invited the applicant to come home and meet her family.

To Sara this came as no surprise as the year 1952 was a portentous sign. The death of her parents. Now Olga Orlinski was adopting her.

The family lived in a small flat in Tel Aviv. They talked about nothing else but Sara's new name and her settling in Israel. They began to teach her some songs and words of Modern Hebrew. It was far from the Hebrew of the Dead Sea Scrolls.

The letter was addressed to Sarah-Hélène, requesting an appointment which devastated her. The immigration department was unable to process this application because her identity could not be confirmed by her native records.

Surprisingly, Mrs Orlinski not only believed Sélène's explanation about the false information in the French national records but took it as supportive evidence of her Jewish and aristocratic roots.

Enthusiastically she exclaimed, 'In 1945 the French Resistance were protecting your Jewish family from the Nazis.'

As Sara was Jewish, Olga Orlinski agreed, then she should live in this country and could stay with her family until the authorities were satisfied and then she would settle in a kibbutz.

'The world has only tolerated Jews during convenient intervals, my dear. We must be strong and self-sufficient. What makes you think that Churchill or the Pope or the Americans owe us our protection? You are a clever and caring young woman, the type of person we need to build this state. Here we take care of ourselves.'

Mr Orlinski owned a white Peugeot 504 taxi. He disagreed with his wife's 'ghetto mentality,' and boasted that during the holocaust, like Sweden, and Denmark, their country had taken care of *all* her citizens, Jews and non-Jews.

'The Germans knew where to place their camps of concentration and extermination and there were none in Bulgaria. Not one. A handful of Jews died there. Five or six, and that was too many, but that is all.'

They talked all night, first about the European war and then about the recent political upheavals in Israel. Labour had been ousted after twenty-nine years and Begin had been elected. This had stunned both foreign and domestic opinion because of his aggressive stance to the Arabs. The Orlinskis explained that the black Jews from North Africa and the Middle East felt themselves to be an 'oppressed majority' within Israel. They had voted to end domination from white political intellectuals who saw Israel as a Mediterranean partner of the European nations.

27.6 The Israeli Defence Forces invaded south Lebanon, a campaign one newspaper called 'our Vietnam.' The name stuck because of the domestic political fissures which were exposed. Israel was now divided externally from all Arab neighbours and internally into hawks and doves, left and right, religious and secular.

While waiting for her papers and placement the new arrival soon realised how much this had disillusioned her. She had perceived Jerusalem as some kind of romantic dream, a haven of refuge, a protective womb, but now it had turned out to be the faultline of human division and conflict.

What she had glimpsed in the taxi, in the Holocaust Museum, and in Jerusalem's buildings built upon layers of ruins began to unravel the City of Peace. She described it as 'her vision of cyclical violence.' Jewish leaders had vowed that they would never again leave their people homeless and exposed to hostility. *But the victims have become the perpetrators.* She admitted to Olga that even Robert Kohen had divided Israelis for and against pacifist views. Here, each citizen had his or her own solution for the Arab Problem, The War, The Economy, and The Religious Problem.

One evening Mr Orlinski happened to mention that he had driven a Swedish inspector of the International Atomic Agency to his hotel. *They are watching Iraq.* These were the words Sara knew that she had overheard for a reason and she copied them into her diary. Somehow she doubted that Orlinsky was an ordinary taxi driver. American policy concerning Iran and Iraq was added to her extra-curricular education until her studies of Biblical Archaeology began.

As the weeks turned to months 'Optimistic Olga' always said things would work out, but Sara's application to stay generated delay. In the French registers there was a clear identity – but not the one she had claimed. Questions were raised. *How did she obtain legal entry to USA?* She could not answer this. *Please attend an interview.* This was all communicated with courtesy, which was unusual in this country, although in such sensitive matters this was hardly surprising.

27.7 'This meeting is being taped by consent of Helen MacRae, formerly Sarah-Hélène de Sainte Clair under French records, and according to Ministry procedures. You were known in the United Kingdom as Sarah Kelly? Is that what I should call you now?'

'Will you please call me Sara, S-A-R-A, which I have adopted legally?'

'Fine, I was just going to ask you about your signature. *Sélène?* That is a fifth name, but I realise it is a stage name. Informal. That gives us no problem. It is quite straightforward as an element of naturalisation which I hope we shall quickly be able to initiate. Just another official form, I'm afraid. Before I discuss the way we view the problem of foreign documents containing a discrepancy, we have been a little more thorough than usual. You weren't exactly a model pupil at your schools?'

'The nuns weren't model teachers. They force-fed gospels to me. I rebelled. You see, I never believed in their religion.'

'You attracted a lot of attention. Was it the death of your parents which caused you to become . . . *disturbed*?'

'I think that it was the circumstances. It didn't seem like an accident. Even at the time I knew that I was always being watched and manipulated. Moved about. Isolated. Why was my brother taken away and not allowed to see me? Then they denied his existence and messed with my head. It is hardly surprising that I became disturbed and the psychiatrist chose to believe that I was crazy rather than admit that the authorities had dealt with me harshly.'

She began to sob. The official continued, ignoring the tears.

'Why should that be so? Why should the authorities treat you harshly?'

'After the war France had many wounds of dissension to heal, sir. The Nazis had treated my father with respect. That was wrongly interpreted by ordinary people. The girls at school treated me differently. The nuns treated me differently. I was not like them. The Nazis wanted to use my father to invite them to govern legitimately.'

'Are you claiming that you are not Catholic or you are not of the common stock?'

'My great-grandfather owned lands and was a powerful figure. My father was gentle, maybe a weak man. He was not a man of action. But he was aristocratic and the Nazis suspected his descent in their search for French nobles who would support their unlawful government to split France and govern the occupied part as a new country. From there, they would attack the north. I have already explained that this is why the patriots of France had social registers altered and new identity papers were issued to protect the identities . . .'

'I understand.'

'. . . of the aristocrats and thus to enable them to side with the Resistance.'

'Did your father?'

'To the best of my knowledge, I doubt it very much. He was refined, as I recall, but not a man of action.'

'Thank you for your honesty. I realise that you were aged five when you lost your parents, but was your family religious in any way?'

'Actually, I was seven, and my paternal grandfather had been ardently Catholic. My father was . . . I know not what. My mother, who was Scottish I think, had no beliefs.'

'You mentioned . . .'

'. . . I don't know why I was sent to a convent. My uncle George was to blame. He didn't want me to live with him. I hated him . . . I . . . I don't know why I call him uncle.'

'There was a child psychiatrist to whom you were sent. Was this after the episode of you walking on water in 1959? Who put you up to this? Was this one of the games in which you constantly craved attention?'

Cold, damp Scotland seemed a world apart from this immigration office in Jerusalem. The pity which the applicant felt for Sarah Kelly's disturbed childhood extinguished the anger in the thirty-year old survivor.

Perhaps they were not one and the same person?

Avoiding the questioner's gaze Sara declared, 'It has been my misfortune to be sent to psychiatrists so perhaps you can say that I've been tested as sane more often than you, sir.'

The interviewer hesitated and sat back in his chair.

While he made some notes she overheard from the corridor phrases from other applicants in a variety of languages. How tasteless was the entire row of cubicles in which the hopes of humans were tossed and turned. It was like a very poor school.

The interviewer looked up. He was a small man in his early fifties; his receding hair was not covered by a scull cap. Civil servants wore more casual clothes here, and this man had an open shirt. His voice was soft but firm. His English was fluent but betrayed none of his origins.

'The label a French child psychiatrist affixed to you translates roughly as *delusional*. Did you know about another newspaper article appearing in 1962 in Britain? It concerns a female patient aged 15 who causes Collateral Hysteria in the presence of images of the Virgin Mary, and the cause is cited as a classic example of Freud's syndrome of the Family Romance. Did Dr Begrich explain his diagnosis to you?'

'He questioned me a lot. You see, I don't *feel* that I'm crazy, but perhaps crazy people don't. Sometimes I feel the world is *crazy*. I think that we all have some degree of neuroses, paranoia, etc, but until you commit a crime or hurt yourself everyone leaves you alone.'

'Unless you seek attention.'

'Yes. But I have never committed a crime. I've never hurt anyone.'

'But attention seeking. This you have done before?'

'Yes.'

'And now you come to Jerusalem, and you make very astonishing claims about yourself. Agreed? *About your identity.*'

'Yes,' she sighed, 'I see your point, but if I am just a crazy girl, why make the same mistake as the Roman authorities did before you?'

The Inquisitor smiled.

'Since you raise this point. By coming to Jerusalem Jesus was killed. Why should *you* repeat the same mistake?'

'I actually don't remember walking on water.'

She said it without emotion but her opponent was clearly angered.

'Young lady, are you joking, or are you serious? For the record, I note she makes no response. Miss Saint Clair, or Miss MacRae, or Miss Kelly, look, I have something further here. Something you yourself wrote. You say that you were told it was a secret that your parents never had sex. Is that correct? Did you make this absurd claim? It seems strange that America's New Age high priestess of libertine sexuality, if I may say so, should endorse the Catholic teaching of sex as sinful, don't you think?'

She hesitated, started to frame an answer twice, and then said, 'Look, I think that the interview should relate not to my morals and beliefs, but to my Jewish blood. Isn't it a simple matter of one-eighth bloodline, yes or no? And forced conversions are ignored? So I need to prove a single great-grandparent, which my papers do show. Will your law courts uphold the error of your present stand that I also have to conform to your approved religious and moral beliefs?'

The man took more notes and Sara watched another interview passing meltdown in which a man and wife got up to leave, shaking their fists.

She wondered if they would try to block her return to her homeland, and to the Davidic throne. If Almighty God had decreed the perpetual sovereignty of the holy bloodline, then a mere civil servant, a clerk, a pen-pusher – indeed the Prime Minister of Israel – could not keep her out. She smiled but held silence.

The interviewer turned to her and said, 'Well? If your parents did not have sex, as we have here as your claim, then your own evidence contradicts itself, does it not?'

Chapter Twenty-Eight

During 1977 Jews were being purchased from persecution in the Soviet Union which needed hard currency to finance the Cold War. The government of Israel negotiated a *per capita* price in US Dollars. The money was raised from the Diaspora but the American diplomats were sworn to secrecy.

Sarah-Hélène's case had been delayed in this deluge of immigration. She had been plunged into the racial and religious politics of Israel where they were most emotionally charged. The authorities wanted strict proof of her Jewish origin while they were admitting hundreds of Russians of dubious descent, people who simply wanted to escape from economic gloom.

Sara's American lawyers had not remitted any money and she had to postpone matriculation at The Hebrew University by one year. She was not permitted to seek employment or housing but Mrs Orlinski remained optimistic. She urged her new daughter to join a language and naturalisation programme. She suggested a rabbinical college which assured conversion to Judaism within twenty-four months.

'*Why should I apply for conversion?* I am Jewish already, Olga, and besides, I possess authority far above theirs.' The two women laughed at the joke but they were nervous about the forthcoming interview at the Immigration Office. Sara brought a packed lunch and a heavy paperback.

28.1 The waiting room was uncomfortably warm, noisy, and overcrowded. Men had stared at Sara before, but this felt uncomfortable. Finally, the swarthy man's wife shouted at her.

'Are you one of us? My husband says you are Japanese.'

Sara smiled.

The fat woman in a brightly coloured shawl spoke in a French dialect. The woman, a north African, scorned her husband for leering at Sara. He was also neglecting their three children whose patience had long ago expired in this crowded waiting room. The woman held their fourth child – an infant. Her husband was unshaven, chain-smoking, and insolent; his eyes feasted on the starlet.

At first Sara was unsure if she was being addressed but the man was staring into her face, waiting for an answer to his wife's question.

'You know that they call us *schwartzers* here?' In a husky voice the man explained, '*Niggers*. We sweep their streets. That's if we get a job at all. They think we're stupid. No, they think we're *dirty*.'

Sara, of olive complexion, flushed and considered who was meant by 'us' and 'them'. The man with no name put her right.

'*The government likes these Soviet immigrants because they are white voters.*'

Sara looked over to the other side of the room. She played with the dark-skinned children and calmed them down. Soon they were soothed.

Their mother would take much longer. '*Schwartzer* is a Yiddish word,' she spat, 'which nearly became the language here although there were always more of *us* than *them*. But *we* speak Ladino. Do you know how rich is that language? How beautiful it is? Do you know what I'm talking about? No-one even suggested *our* language for the new state. *Know why?*'

Sara shook her head in shame. The woman spoke some phrases in Ladino expecting to confuse Sara, but to the surprise of both women there was understanding. They smiled. The husband was so impressed that he extinguished his cigarette and his aggression.

'So you speak Spanish? Where did you come from? What is your name?' His tone betrayed suspicion.

Sara gave her newly adopted name and admitted that it was not Spanish she could speak, but she was from the Languedoc region. 'Many years ago we were allied with Spain. Our district was conquered by the whites from the north of France. We too spoke a noble tongue, the langue d'Oc, which is closer to Spanish than to French! You see? The tyrants made a world of oppression and anxiety. They are white-skinned but they shut out the light.'

The woman seemed pleased, 'Well, the white Jews from Europe, America, and Russia are called the Ashkenazim, right? They founded this country by their astute politics and we thank them. But this is a Jewish state, *not Ashkenazi*. Right? At least it was the last time I looked. And all Jews by the Law of Return of 1970 may settle here. *And it is a democracy, right*? But more of *us* came here, from Turkey, Iran, Iraq, Yemen, and Morocco. Like us. That's why they're filling the place up with lots of white Jews from Russia. It's to outvote us.'

The husband added, 'She means the government. *Us* are the Jews from North Africa, whose ancestors were expelled from Spain. Ladino is from old Spanish just as Yiddish was the language derived from German.'

The woman explained, her words tumbling out in anger, 'But was *ours* even considered as the language of Israel? Of course not! We are clean but they sprayed us in the camps, here. Yet it was Germans and Poles who came from European camps full of lice and disease – not their fault, you see, nevertheless *they* were dirty but *we* were sprayed. Do you understand what I'm saying? Then tell me *why*. Go on, tell me.'

'Because,' Sara spelled it out, 'we . . . are . . . BLACK.'

'That's right. We are like the Arabs. They took in the Ethiopians but made them 'convert' to Judaism. Why did they do that? Tell me. Tell me. Go on. *Because they were black*.'

'No, my dear friend,' said Sara, 'I think that this time you are wrong. You see, they are doing it to me. Don't let them get to you. I try not to but it's hard. I thought they would . . . accept . . . me here.'

Finally, *Helen MacRae* was called. She reddened, and then became more upset when the clerk made a pointed remark about her waiting with the ordinary people. In this state of mind, before she was seated, the meeting was compressed into a sentence.

'To avoid beating about the bush, Miss MacRae, if you convert to Judaism you will be an Israeli citizen within two years.'

28.2 Mr and Mrs Orlinski, who stood as Sara's religious sponsors for conversion, were not observant Jews so the Rabbinical College obliged them to attend synagogue weekly with their children. Each Saturday morning they walked dutifully – as a family with the new 'sister' – down the narrow streets of the Tel Aviv suburb. Their smart dress betrayed their destination as one of the city's synagogues. The children walked furtively, almost hiding their faces in shame. As Sara was proud she did not understand this until they crossed the main road and were mocked as *froumers* by other children.

'In Israel,' explained Mr Orlinski, 'there are no shades of grey. It is a secular state. The majority sees religious people as friends of the fanatics, the ultra-religious people who give it all a bad name. Jews who will not even speak Modern Hebrew because they see it as a desecration of the ancient language of their prayers. Their prominence exaggerates their numbers. They are portrayed at prayer at the Wailing Wall. They throw stones at cars which drive on the Sabbath and, like our enemies, they will not utter the name of the country which shelters them. 'The Jewish State cannot exist by God's will,' they say, 'until the Messiah comes. It is written in the Torah."

Mr Orlinski was getting heated and continued.

'I despise the pious ones. They wouldn't recognise the messiah if they bumped in to him on the street. And where does it say so in the Torah, Sara? You tell me. You are a biblical scholar.'

But she was silent.

Chapter Twenty-Nine

JUDEA, ISRAEL, MAY 1978

In the Spring of 1978 Sara moved to a communal settlement which ran language and naturalisation programmes. David Borokovitch was an archaeologist, a fruit picker, and a candidate for the Governing Committee of Kibbutz Kalia but everyone knew him as DD (meaning Dr Dave or Disco Dave). He was relaxed and respected. He looked and moved like a Hebrew Prophet. He introduced himself and told Sara that an immigration officer had been asking questions about her. DD informed Sara the official was back again and pointed the man out. She confronted him.

If the immigration department didn't believe her, she told the civil servant in anger, then she would see them in Court. He explained that he was, in fact, from a department of the police and asked her for an interview.

Mrs Orlinski was telephoned. She advised caution, so Sara postponed the encounter and had the man followed by a girlfriend until a genuine police detective picked up the trail. After a few days, she learned that her suspicions were well-founded: the interrogator was a journalist. The Israeli police were not worried; after all, she was a famous actress romantically linked with a man who was tipped to run for the White House. They did not even mention the matter of her bloodline.

She told them she had joined the commune in the Judean Wilderness to escape journalists and to find her ancestors.

After the harvest she volunteered to help the team which worked on the northwest banks of the Dead Sea. The dig was what two thousand years of decay had left of an earlier commune – the Community of the Dead Sea Scrolls.

This employment provided her with a subsistence of one hundred Israeli pounds per day plus seventy for food and beer money. However, the greater reward to newly arrived Jews was the vital connection between modern life and their ancient heritage. America, Sara had seen, was a melting pot of disorientated minorities with hatred and violence. Two thousand years of roots in the Scrolls might unite the nation when the war against the Arabs came to an end. Working in the scorching heat of the desert Sara felt she was becoming indistinguishable from the second-generation of the girls; they were nicknamed Sabras after the home-grown pears which are hard on the outside but soft in the centre.

Sara, who was beginning to understand why the land had this effect on people, spent her evenings after work with 'Disco Dave.' He was happy to satisfy her thirst for knowledge. The part-time lecturer could not hope that anything romantic would develop with such a beautiful woman but they were both passionate about discos, dancing, and Dead Sea Scrolls.

They spent many cool evenings walking around the caves and the excavations.

Aware that she was converting to Judaism he concealed his anti-religious sentiments which were well-known throughout the commune. In his opinion, the Jews were more reluctant than the Christians to face the implications of the Dead Sea Scrolls.

'Which do you like best, dancing or digging?' she laughed.

'What about you?'

She thought about it and then said, 'Well, the whole body understands dancing, but the Scrolls, they too have a spooky power. They drive people into frenzy. Everyone wants to re-bury them.'

'You've just noticed?'

'I once thought my crazy scientist friend, Robert, was paranoid. What do we Jews want to hide?'

Disco Dave lit his pipe and sat on a rock. Even late in the evening it was hot and humid. She waited for a considered response. Together they admired the view of the desert and the Dead Sea in the background.

She had a crazy thought about trying to walk on it. He pushed three matches into the sand. The three ends formed the points of a triangle.

'We – the modern Israelis – live and feel the power of destiny. The world respects us as an ancient nation. As for the Scrolls, they are housed in architectural splendour, right? You've been in the Shrine of the Book?'

She nodded. He continued with sarcasm.

'It's the modern Temple – *outer show concealing inner blindness*. Two thousand years ago our predecessors buried the Scrolls when the nation was conquered. And in our lifetime our founding Prime Minister purchased them while the UN voted to recognise us as a revived nation. The scrolls were discovered by the Arabs, Sara, but not during all nineteen hundred years of our dispersion. No, it was when we came back to this land.'

He buried the matches kicking the sand with his foot.

'I respect the Scrolls and I'm not religious but I see nobody religious who wants to contemplate their true message. And yet these Scrolls scream out against the very same mentality of servility to God but intolerance to Man.'

He tried to hold her hand but she rejected his advance.

'What is the inner message of the Scrolls, Dave?'

'Love thy neighbour. It's the message of all religions.'

Sara's smile turned into shock.

'What!!?? They sure do make you scholars crazy, Dave. You choose to ignore texts that fulminate damnation and curses against non-believers, the high priests in Jerusalem as the spouters of lies, enemies, collaborators, gentiles, even their own converts and a poor novice who transgresses the law by the merest smidgeon. And the Scroll Community planned a terrible war against all foreigners. It excluded from salvation the entire outside world as children of darkness. It set horrendous punishments against their own brothers who erred, like spitting, or garments carelessly loosening to reveal their thighs. There is much divine casting into the Pit. There is the denunciation of women as beguilers and seducers. Defilement by mere contact with non-sectarian Jews especially those who defiled themselves by trading with gentiles. And what about the little arsenal they owned?'

He was shocked by her rage but she was not finished.

'Doubtless you'll also impose humanist teachings on Jesus? Anyway, why don't Jews accept Jesus? He taught love thy neighbour. The church was *a Jewish sect* destroyed along with the Essenes and the Ebionites. All religions are power politics. Hell, you make me mad! Why was I forced to convert? Same reason my ancestors were forced the other way. Religion's all domination, control, power, and politics. Why can't we just love Jesus? I'm Jewish but I want to love Jesus. What's wrong with that? He didn't believe in Christianity. You're right, the history of religion shows it isn't even worth criticising. It destroys itself. Like this.'

She ripped her necklace to pieces. The beads flew in all directions. She had also torn the neck of her sweat-shirt. She wriggled from David who tried to ground her but he avoided gripping her tightly as he was aroused by her bared flesh. He shouted that he would not hurt her. She shouted back.

'Religion is nothing more than mind control and yet I still want to convert. *Because I don't want to be an outsider.* I need to be accepted. I've never been accepted for what I am.'

They were both sitting on the sand but still. Emotionally she was stirred and she broke down.

'But I love Jesus too. He was the most wonderful man who ever walked on this planet and we are in his land. Why don't people just do as he says? It's God's message. It's perfect. But you will think that makes me Christian, *but I'm not*. And I'm not confused. The world has nearly won. I won't let it win, Dave. I'm a nice person and I won't let it make me mad. Don't walk away from me. I need to talk. Please don't leave me. Do you like me? I know you like me. Make love to me, Dave. I like you too.'

He looked at her in pity.

'Now I understand why you slept around with your hippy commune friends. You're an outsider who can't take isolation. I need to get back inside now. Will you be okay? Sara?'

Nobody saw her come back that night. She slept outside and returned to the building as the sun rose. She was very hungry. At breakfast everyone looked at her except DD. In a single sentence she admitted to a girlfriend that she had a problem controlling her mood swings after a disturbed upbringing.

* * *

After that day Dave's eyes met Sara's pleading gaze at meals and at the Saturday evening dances but he looked away. Three weeks later Dave was elected to the Governing Committee. At the end of the summer Sara was advised that the vote would go against her if she intended to apply for membership of Kibbutz Kalia.

Chapter Thirty

JERUSALEM, SEPTEMBER 1978

In the summer of 1978 all horizontal surfaces in Sara's bedroom in Kibbutz Kalia were covered by open and closed books on Hebrew language and culture, Jewish status, and the meaning of the Dead Sea Scrolls. In September she was accepted by the Hebrew University for a three-year degree course in Archaeology and Biblical Studies.

This was where the first Dead Sea Scrolls had been brought thirty years previously when the War of Independence might have made the nation still-born. Eleven years had elapsed since the Six Day War of 1967 when East Jerusalem was captured and additional parchments had been discovered by the Israeli Antiquities Department. It was believed that many more would emerge to provide twenty years of work for qualified specialists. Biblical scholarship seemed like a good career move and Sara rented a one-bedroom, ground-level flat in a rebuilt and affordable suburb south of Jerusalem's Old City. Her two suitcases were bulging with books on Biblical Hebrew, History, and Archaeology.

A law to have all the Qumran texts published after decades of delays was debated in the Knesset. Many people suspected a conspiracy. The English scholar Geza Vermes dubbed the thirty-year delay as the 'academic scandal per excellence' and Robert Kohen headed the American campaign. His radio station was broadcasting excerpts and inspirational messages from 'The Jewish Bible' in order to attract the world's attention. It was said that two hundred specialists would be needed to reconstruct thousands of fragments into two thousand works, according to some estimates of the material piling up from eleven caves.

With the money from her American lawyers Sara purchased her Jerusalem house. 'The family wealth,' she joked, 'possibly came from this city in the first place!'

Michael Leonard had no sense of humour but he had reason to boast of his own security: he had signed a contract with the BBC to make a documentary but he needed Sara's help. He arrived in Jerusalem without warning and apologised for the phoney 'civil servant' or 'police department' researcher he had sent to Kibbutz Kalia to find her.

'Tricks of my trade,' he explained on her doorstep.

She let him in and a second man followed. Her eyes demanded an explanation but Leonard was full of his plans.

'I offered the BBC a sequel to the film I made on the Treasures of the Second Temple,' he said proudly. 'So they asked me to make *The Messianic Conspiracy*. The contract was signed, and here I am, myself, in person. With Timothy, *the producer.'*

Sara nodded and shook hands with Timothy, *the producer*.

The three of them sat down in her small living room with a stone floor, low ceiling, and bare whitewashed walls.

'There is no such thing as bad publicity,' Timothy exclaimed.

'Exactly what is it that you wish to know?' Sara asked coolly.

Leonard missed a beat; he must have seen that this was not the same woman as Sélène, the wild child he had fallen for. This was a calmer, wiser woman. She dressed and carried herself differently. She was a middle class property owner in the living room of her own house.

'I wish to know exactly the same as you,' he replied. '*The truth*.'

'Everyone wants to know their own truth.'

Her tone carried the clear possibility that she might not co-operate. Timothy looked at Leonard who sat forward in the settee and pleaded with Sara.

'The truth concerning your parents and the car accident, or murder, near Toulouse about which the French police will not speak. And why the civil register concerning your family is false. And why the French police do not enforce their disclosure requirements on a certain secret society. And why a Templar society, which does not officially exist, has an interest in you. Yet they are watched by western police who also watch you.'

She displayed a flicker of interest. *Timothy looked respectable but Leonard did the talking. What did the BBC man think about her living room? He seemed very posh and proper. The room was basic 1950s plus tasteless eastern and ethnic ornaments.*

Leonard was saying, 'I want to know about the treasures that surfaced in the south of France in the nineteenth-century. And why the Germans searched for them. I know that they deceived your father, pretending they were an agency wanting to restore the Temple Treasures to Palestine. What was your father's knowledge of the treasures? Did he inadvertently help the Nazis? He was no collaborator but was he killed by French patriots or under this pretext?'

She remained silent.

'We should try to defeat the conspirators by sharing what we know. We should work together. You, me, and Tim will bring in the huge resources and prestige of the BBC.'

Tim was on his feet, inspecting her shelves. When she asked if he was rude of if it was a strategy to irritate her, he put back one of her books and nodded. Sara hesitated but in response to Leonard's momentous questions she was curious as he had hoped. She was fidgeting. She said that until recently she had wanted to forget all the problems of her past as they weighed heavily but she would offer a deal.

She turned away and thought it through as her eyes moistened.

'I shall disclose to you things that I know, piece by piece in exchange for your information, judging its worth and your good faith. You should start to deal the cards because you have come to me and I am on my guard by your previous confession of trickery. Agreed, *Mr Leonard*?'

'Agreed,' he said abruptly and it seemed that the deal marked the end of his amorous ambitions.

'Then it is agreed, Mr Leonard! And I consent to your memo tape recording. What have you learned about the treasures of Rennes-le-Château? *Were* they the Temple Treasures which slipped through the hands of the Romans? *Where are they?* Can you as a historian confirm my genetic memory glimpses? Will you call me crazy to say that my family was descended from King David and Michal, the daughter of Saul; and from Jesus, the King who never reigned?'

'Please call me Michael and my BBC colleague here is Timothy. Please be kind enough to let me call you by your beautiful new and resonant Hebrew name, *Sara*. And as we have a long evening ahead of us may I ask you for tea? We English can't work without tea, and made in a pot.'

Sara scowled. She rose slowly and suspiciously. As she left the room she apologised for hesitation but she watched the men from behind the door and threw a pen into the kitchen to make it seem that she was there, making tea.

She saw Timothy whisper to his colleague in anger, 'You're wasting time.'

'Don't tell me how to handle her, Timmy, I've done well so far,' he said with a smile, 'She was right to suspect me.' He held up a small pharmaceutical bottle.

'Wee Eengleish cannot work witoot teee . . . I suppose you're now thinking up some information to trade with her. What do you have, Mike?'

'Chemistry, of two types, Timmy. For the first type to work you will distract her while I pop it in her tea. For the second type, after fifteen minutes you must *leave me alone with her*. Allow me to regain her confidence. I have the power.'

While Tim was trying to swallow this Leonard looked around, inspecting disordered piles of books stacked on a stone floor. One of the indigenous giant insects crawled round from behind a stack of books to watch them and Timothy jerked forward to frighten or batter it.

Leonard stopped him, 'Not advisable, Tim. It's an Israeli citizen. While she's out the room, I have something better to do.'

'You're being paid by the Beeb, Micky. You're a company man now. You can't prospect on your own just when we are about to extract gold.'

Sara crept to the kitchen and filled the kettle. The men could hear it.

The living room was plain and the chairs basic, reminding Leonard of the post-War utility-furniture he had known in Britain. The book case was a sort of Scandinavian G-plan – teak veneer shelves on black ladder rungs. This modern state still had a war economy. Apparently Sara had gone native and abandoned her Hollywood opulence.

Inspecting the shelves, he observed a mixture of books on archaeology and erotic sex.

She called out to Leonard from the kitchen across the hall, 'The interesting books belong to the last owner. French women make love from instinct and experience.'

The men looked at each other and smiled until Sara brought a tray.

Tea was served from exquisite china and a silver tea set.

'And a French lady who can make tea to English standards!' Leonard spoke as he watched Timmy inspecting her belongings. He rudely leafed through her magazines even after she poured three cups and should have sat down. She kept glancing towards him. He had successfully diverted her attention.

'Timothy, you're being anti-social,' Leonard said, after he had spiked her tea. Tim pretended to resent the comment and reduced the room to a company of two. She closed the main door behind him.

30.1 They watched Timothy walk down the narrow street of terraced modern houses. Leonard started to explain his method of investigation to Sara.

'Everything has costs, so to find facts I follow cash trails as a link to most events.'

'I'm listening,' she said as she served tea.

'The treasure of Rennes-le-Château started as the object of my research. Then it pointed me to the Marseilles Heresy, the legend of Mary Magdalene, to the Priory of Sion, and then it pointed to you.'

To allow his truth drug time to loosen her tongue he played for time.

'The disciples were jealous that Rabbi Jesus loved his woman as much as the Law. The early church denounced women in general and selected gospels in which Mary Magdalene's rôle was reduced. She came to the crucifixion and was the first to see him when he defied death but her past was blackened. Why?'

Sara shrugged her shoulders and listened to the Englishman. She occupied the entire settee and comfortably raised her feet from the floor.

'The Heresy says that Jesus sent his wife (or partner) to the safety of Marseilles, bearing his child. The royal line was now safe and in hiding. It suited everyone to believe that really she was just a loose woman.'

Hoping the truth drug would be entering its first phase, rendering the ingestor loquacious, Leonard tried to become silent to let her do the talking.

'Would you like more tea?' she offered, 'I mean, how was my father involved in all of this? Did he know it? Was he murdered? Did he do anything wrong?'

There was an emotional edge in her voice and Leonard realised he was probing in deep waters. For him it was an intellectual game plus an income but for her it was her life.

'What are your questions?' She demanded, 'Tell me what you want to know.'

He began to beat about the bush and eventually admitted that he had lost track of his questions.

She reacted by laughing, 'I admire professionalism, Mr Leonard, but you might have harmed me. You took tea from *my cup* so let's swop and we'll both go with the flow. It works best when the interrogator ingests and joins in. I'm fussy, though. I lived in California and was spoiled by a plentiful supply of the famous orange pills. It wasn't the purity of the early batches that made them the best but the fact that they were the last substance they made for love, not for profit, and not in fear. Do you understand? After that the government made it go wrong so that criminals became the suppliers and the suppliers became criminals.'

Leonard made no response. She exchanged cups and continued to lecture him.

'Love is the drug. If you will look below the surface – which merely reflects the image of your world – you will see what I have seen. The Holy Grail. It is the treasure. *The contents and not the cup.* The love of money is the root of evil, Michael. The authorities created the monster in their own godammed image. We will share the cup, Michael, and I hope it brings you luck. Poison made with love will nourish. Just think about the pure food of the gods and see how I can dream without sleeping and hallucinate without drugs.'

Leonard spoke while her dose began to take effect.

'I'm a freelance, Sara. My contract with the BBC is just to make another film. But I have invested thirteen years in this story – money, persistence, and initiative – because it is commercially valuable. I grew up in poverty. Your story is a property. Intellectual property that belongs to me until I sell it in books and films. But it is sensational and earth shaking. There is one thing that I had not planned to disclose to anyone but I must do so. In time I shall substantiate my conspiracy theory with full details. But now, I want you to sign a confidentiality agreement. Then I will tell you a secret.'

Leonard dictated and she wrote the letter with some of her own modifications.

Sunday 24th September 1978

Dear Mr Leonard,

Concerning what you are going to disclose to me today concerning my family, whether verified or challenged, it will not be divulged by me in any way, or to any person, until 24 months have elapsed from this date.

Solemnly signed,

Sélène.

'That's still my legal signature,' she laughed.

Leonard was satisfied with the letter. It was written in a large, pretty, calligraphic script and he said it really looked like a charter.

'And what is a charter but an exclusive right conferred by royalty?' she asked.

He folded it carefully and placed it in his inner pocket, asking, 'Sara, who is Paul?'

'Take off your clothes, Michael. We're not going to have sex, but we are going to be totally open. Like Jesus and the Magdalene. They were like one soul in two bodies.'

'Sara, we're keeping our clothes on. Now, *who is Paul?'*

'My elder brother!' She said it as if he should have known already.

'But there is no 'Paul' in the birth ledgers.'

'The nuns and my foster-parents denied him.'

She awaited a response. She expected Leonard to condemn her vivid imagination but instead he told her that in this conspiracy the French authorities had even dropped a king out of history – Dagobert II.

She smiled a little smile, shrugged her shoulders and convinced him that she had no idea how king 'D-2' was related to the subject in hand. She simply repeated that *They* (the Mother Superior, nuns, foster-parents, and psychiatrists) had all told her that Paul was a male character who had entered her mind because she was lonely and unchaste.

'Mother Superior permitted me to entertain him as a myth but only for six months. I tried her exercises to control my mind but the memories flooded back. It isn't like a dream, nor is it an ancestral glimpse which is a more vivid experience but less 'real'. Paul was a gentle person with light brown hair and a hooked nose! He looked like an owl. In 1965, family friends told me that he ran away from an orphanage and joined some hippies or Buddhists somewhere in the north of France. Often I planned to run away to find him.'

'Who told you he joined the Buddhists?'

'A family who lived near us. I think that Father was upset. I think that my grandfather was Jewish but concealed it to protect us because the Nazis never left our region; they just went underground. Michael, you would tell me if you heard anything about Paul? It's above the deal.'

'Yes, darling.' The term of endearment just slipped out. He asked her to name the family but she was searching her handbag then produced a photograph.

Leonard guessed, 'Paul? *That's Paul?*'

He restrained excitement until its truth was verified but its value was sensational. *If his theory was valid and Paul was her elder brother it made him the M-word.*

Sara was unrestrained in her excitement.

'Look, see. This photo is the most precious thing that I possess. Mama, Papa, Paul *et petite moi* in our garden in the house near Toulouse. It was summer 1951. No-one else knows about this picture. I left it in France with a friend and did not have it in Italy. I retrieved it after I left Scotland and flew to America. It keeps me sane. *No-one believes me.* Now, tell me if you know anything about Paul.'

He snatched her photo and prepared to rip it in two. She went crazy and knocked over the table with her leap over the settee to save the fading picture.

She grasped it tightly. He looked at her.

'I had to test you. I'm sorry, so sorry, I'm sorry. I tested you.'

She collapsed into his arms. He now knew that *she believed* that the photo was genuine. She breathed deeply and he could feel her heart throbbing. It seemed to resonate through his body. He let her go. By instinct they had mutual trust but she broke free; the one who had suggested taking off clothes. She was angry.

He was staring away, not at her.

'In answer to your question, Sara, I didn't know that Paul even existed. We must find him. We must go to France. But if they killed your parents they are still dangerous . . . *and we are dangerous to them*. And Paul may be . . . dead.'

She spoke over him.

'But who are *They*? And what do we threaten? What extremists would stop the truth? The Pope? The French government? The Israelis?'

Leonard looked around her apartment as he explained that the Israelis and the Vatican both perceived a threat from this thing. Then he said he could not disclose his discoveries in a room that might be bugged. He asked, 'More tea, please.'

She shook her head so he had to stop stalling; besides the tea was cold.

'You *must* tell me,' she pleaded. 'Tell me. The creatures are the only bugs in this room, I think.' But her hesitation disclosed her doubts.

'Okay, I will tell you what you need to know.'

He turned on the radio and TV and led her outside her house.

'The Pope is a sovereign without much tax or territory. Must annoy him like hell. He rules because he says the authority of Jesus was handed down to the apostles through Peter but the early church was headed by the Lord's brother James, nicknamed 'The Righteous.' It says so in Paul's Letters which were composed at least twenty years before any of the Gospels started to rewrite history.'

'So the people who killed my parents were the Vatican?'

He hesitated then said, 'Wait. We're coming to that. The descendents of the family of Jesus kept emerging from the woodwork throughout the fourth to tenth centuries. My big breakthrough came from the war files in Berlin. The survival of the line of David was accepted by some of Europe's modern rulers. Hitler thought they were now Aryans, by the way. And in 1804 Napoleon had been crowned as emperor and to his coronation robes were attached the golden bees, symbols of the Merovingians. Sara, people in top circles of today's authorities, *are* aware of a genealogy, and that is the thing I must find. Where would it be?'

'In the Vatican? Locked up with seven seals?'

'That's exactly what I think. In the Vatican but known to very few people. Unless they found one or more genealogy with the Dead Sea Scrolls. Think about it! When the Romans invaded Judea less than one thousand years had elapsed since King David founded his eternal dynasty. The priests would hide the secret of sovereignty while collaborating with the Romans. The genealogy document also may have been part of Saunière's Temple Treasures, or the treasures merely pointed to the genealogy. So, answer your own question: what is the one thing which would persuade the Vatican that a genealogy really existed?'

'If it saw the genealogy. *Or if it possessed it?'*

'Crown Princess Sara, you are not so crazy after all. Why did the Pope organise the Crusades? Why did the monarchs agree to it? Why did the Vatican do nothing to oppose Hitler? Was it because the Church was blackmailed? Anyone who gets close to this secret has a bargaining counter to manipulate Rome. Saunière, Lefebvre, and even Hitler.'

She thought about it.

'This is my theory, Sara. In 1945, the Nazis threatened to exploit the secret by asking your father, a modest, unassuming man, to become sovereign of the new kingdom of Gaul, to 'save' northern France from Communism and republicanism. The secret is unlimited power. Now, Sara, you are not certain that you were born in 1947?'

She interrupted, 'The War ended in 1945. Michael, listen, please! Who killed my parents in 1952, and what happened to Paul? I was aged seven then, not five as per my French birth certificate. I was persuaded otherwise, but I know by the school classes I had attended. I remembered but I never let on. 'I'm no daft,' that's how they say it in Scotland. But Paul was three classes my elder and so he would assume any . . . *royalty*, would he not? *He is the modern messiah*. Please tell me if you know if he is dead. Oh, if only Paul were still alive!! I long to see him. Things are beginning to make sense. Oh, Michael, *you will help me!'*

Sara's expression switched from anguish to wide grin.

'Just imagine if you could get the Royal Genealogy in time for my Hearing for Israeli citizenship I could upgrade it to a claim for the throne.'

Michael ignored the joke in case she was serious. They agreed to meet the following day. He kissed her goodbye; it was 50% formal and 50% sexual. As he closed the door of her Living Room he left her sitting on her calves on the settee.

Chapter Thirty-One

Michael saw himself out, carefully closing the door to the street of the terraced-house cluttered with the possessions of past and present female owners. From the warm atmosphere of a Jerusalem night he glanced inside to check that she was safe.

As he walked down the road he wondered in what sense, if any, she really was the princess of this strange and foreign city; and how long would she remain silent on her settee, like an Indian yogi contemplating her royalty. *Or was she thinking of him?*

He looked round and realised that she was calling out from her front door. 'Michael,' she whispered, 'Paul is mixed up with the violence.'

Leonard walked back. He stood outside her door. Flying insects – attracted by the lights of the house – were irritating him.

'How do you know that?'

She said that she had not seen or heard of Paul since 1952, but she *sensed* violence.

Leonard observed his colleague running towards them and ordered Sara to go back inside.

The BBC producer didn't ask Leonard about his progress. He had his own drama. He blurted out that someone was tailing him. And more. He had snatched an infrared camera as proof.

'I gave chase to the agent and he dropped it, Mike. A French military camera, with *"infra-rouge"* night-time film. I hid it in case we get captured. Had you left me the car keys I would have driven away and I now suggest that we both do so without delay. It proves you're right;

we're on to something but I suggest we return for the film tomorrow morning. I'm being watched. The Frenchman got away ten minutes ago. Someone is trying to radio him. Have I persuaded you to get the hell out of here without delay?'

Leonard paused to consider if Sara was in danger. The camera and the film were a welcome lead to confirm that the watchers were more than Tim's imagination. *But suppose they were watching* ***Sara****?* She always spoke of being watched.

'Don't you think we should go, Mike? Right now?'

'Okay. Let's go.'

Early the following morning the film producer returned alone to collect the film he had buried near a mailbox. Leonard had asked him to deliver flowers to Sara and to see that she was safe. But outside her house Tim was arrested by Israeli police on charges of assault and theft of the camera. When Leonard arrived to help him at the police station he was detained for interrogation. The contents of his pockets were listed but the pharmaceutical bottle was taken for analysis. When he asked for British Consular access a young Israeli policewoman smiled.

'Your behaviour is equally unacceptable to the British authorities, so don't expect much help.'

31.1 As Leonard woke up in a small cell he drank the strong black coffee although it was cold. He banged on the door but nobody came. He cursed under his breath until he was diverted by a bulge in his pocket. It was his truth drug; or rather the bottle, now empty. To keep his mind active he habitually reviewed and revised his research each morning upon waking. He began to realise that he found himself doubting the conspiracy he had consolidated in his mind only hours earlier.

Without warning the door of his cell opened and he was dragged to a room with nothing but a table and two chairs.

The female interrogator spoke softly without any trace of violence or threat. *What is your proof of Sara's claim? If it is true it proves there is no conspiracy. If not then you have no story. You are collecting hundreds of conflicting claims by lunatic fringes and rejecting the majority of pieces of jigsaw which do not make a design you have preconceived. You are watched by surveillance agents in every country because you really believe you can burgle, bribe, and drug people with impunity. You are on an ego trip because you recycle worthless trash and make lots of money. As a consequence of your actions our country is positioned into confrontation with our Christian allies.*

Leonard agreed with her. He was so relaxed. Within twenty minutes or so – it was hard to measure time – the interview ended suddenly; he was back in his cell.

Significantly, the next session took place shortly after lunch. Again he recognised the effects of his own substance. 'You bastards,' he exclaimed under his breath, as he recalled the spy film in which the captured agent gouges his palm with a rusty nail to resist the delirium of a truth drug. 'I am telling you nothing so what are you going to do about it?'

'We can feed you a higher dose of your truth drug, Mr Leonard, but already it makes you sleepy.'

Prison breakfast the following day was a large cup of strong coffee, some biscuits, and cheese.

A senior Israeli officer came to apologise for any inconvenience. He wore plain cloths, rimmed glasses, and looked like an English professor. Speaking quietly in fluent but accented English he said that he once read a story about a Man from Mars who read every book written by earthmen. He was especially annoyed with William Shakespeare whose plays deceived men with distortions of history. The Martian demolished the theatre and exposed everything behind the stage. 'See, Earthmen, it is all lies. Now you can be free.'

Leonard stared at the man and asked about the relevance of this. The interrogator explained, 'The conspiracy *is* the conspiracy, and you are its mouthpiece, Mr Leonard. Don't you understand? It is *your* interpretation of evidence which *you* set out to find.'

Suppose the fantastic deception had been conceived to **protect** *the Capulet Family and Sara's family was being built up only to prepare for the guardians of the secret to pull the plug and discredit the whole cult? And Leonard had the bad fortune to be in the wrong place at the right time.*

'I am the spokesman?'

'The Interrogator asked, *'So now you understand you have been used?"*

Seems like the conspiracy is to make the world believe that it is all false. They are going to turn it inside out and make itself absurd? To protect what?

'To protect a secret that you will never be allowed to get close to, Mr Leonard!'

Leonard's thinking was becoming confused when he vomited and passed out. Two uniformed officers arrived and roughly hauled him to a small cell where he fell into a delicious erotic dream so vivid that it was more than real.

Our bodies were intertwined and as the climax came we merged. I wore a crown of thorns, blood trickled, a rusty nail gouged into my palms. As our brains merged I was Christ and Sara was the Magdalene but she was black and looked like the Queen of Sheba. I thought with her mind, I saw her dreaming, I understood her wisdom.

Leonard woke up with a shock. He felt the strong presence of Sara. Suddenly he knew why the conspiracy was confused: it had split into more than one group which opposed the other. He smiled. A stone with a flaw can be split. The immediate problem was release from the Israeli jail. The BBC and Her Britannic Majesty would soon see to that.

Chapter Thirty-Two

JERUSALEM, 15 SEPTEMBER 1978

Under Israeli law no building is permitted to change the horizon of the Holy City.

Sara's house was on a narrow street of modern terraced houses on two levels. Many are occupied by staff of the Hebrew University as the young students cannot afford to rent here. The neighbours distanced her after she had joked that the family money she used to buy hers may have originated from Jerusalem when the Jews were dispersed in the failed uprising against the Romans in the year seventy.

Nineteen hundred and eight years later a mirror-black limousine – so stretched that it seemed to cover the entire length of her house – stirred the imaginations of her neighbours. Curtains rustled with furtive curiosity for twenty minutes until Sara walked down the pavement with groceries. She panicked, knowing that the car belonged to a government.

A uniformed driver sat inside the car, his shirt and tie loosened. She let go her brown bag and quickened her pace towards the man in smart civilian clothes who stood beside her front door.

They met each other's gaze and twice their words collided.

('Mrs Weidfeld, Madam? You are she?'

('It's Spencer, something's wrong? He's . . .'

The memories flooded back. In their small talk he made a politician's promise they would marry, but he had simply played a game with her mind, had he not? He had never meant it, and surely he could not have told the authorities that they were married? *Were they married?* People said drugs would waste your brain.

('May I speak with you in private?

('Yes, yes, something is wrong. He's hurt, no, he's dead?'

She asked the man to state his business.

'Mr Weidfeld and, his, er, a casual lady friend of his were murdered last night. At least their bodies were discovered last night. In his Hollywood home. A 'frenzy-envy murder.' My identity card. I am from the United States Embassy. May I talk with you?'

Sara inspected his card, unlocked her door and demanded, 'Oh, yes, I see, Mr Gardner, but will you kindly wait outside?'

She seized the initiative and ran into her house. Fearing that she was being kidnapped she double-locked the front door, and in shock she threw up while she switched on the television and radio. Then she telephoned a friend to check the news about the murder. She dialled from memory. Before the number rang out the TV came to life and a bulletin carried the news.

IN A GRUESOME RITUAL MULTIPLE MURDER REMINISCENT OF THOSE ARISING FROM THE DRUG-AND-SEX-CRAZED ORGIES OF THE SIXTIES THE BODIES OF FILM DIRECTOR JONNY LORD AND HIS LATEST PROTÉGÉE 21-YEAR-OLD FILM ACTRESS LAURA SHANNON LEE WERE FOUND DISMEMBERED ALONG WITH STRICKEN SERVANTS AND FRIENDS IN THEIR SECLUDED AND GUARDED NEIGHBOURHOOD COMMUNITY . . .

Sara pulled the plug of her TV set, which still left Israel Radio-1 playing music in the background. It was Smokey Robinson's *The Tears of a Clown. This was their song. It was Spencer who had died; but what happened to Jonny? He died too?*

Disorientated and in tears her forearm swept off the table her old-fashioned radio – the French, cream and blue, bakelite 220 volt apparatus with its glowing valves. It fell to the tiled floor and its power cable and plug followed like a tail. She watched it smash to pieces. In delayed motion. Time was in suspension. It was an instinctive, satisfying act like the rending of clothes. She sat down and, her worst rage released, she wept loudly knowing there was no-one to hear. Then she remembered the black car. She cried for the marriage she had wanted so much and for the distance between herself and his soulless body. Now dead, if she could believe the news. Or was it Jonny? If both, then it was organised crime, she thought. Why, at this moment, significant only for her, should the radio in Israel broadcast the one song which carried the memories of how good she had felt in those days; to be in love with someone so . . . marvellous. But in reality, that person and that marriage had both been exposed by time to be illusory. Perhaps the whole world was illusory. It made no sense. She had lost her mind. *Was it doing drugs? The aim is to survive.*

She smiled at the glass pieces of the radio apparatus on the floor and cut her palms and arms to make amends to the radio. She wanted to cry more, think more, be left in peace, but the limo was still there. Mr Gardner stood outside her house like a frozen statue and a driver waited at the wheel of the car.

The radio, now in pieces, had confused her. She turned on the alarm-clock radio by her bed which was tuned to the BBC World Service. The detached monotonous voice of an English newscaster announced the assassination. *She was right.*

Spencer Weidfeld had been killed at 12.31pm EST. She covered her eyes. Both men had died and she was the connection.

The authorities knew it too. As the terrifying thought sunk in, it empowered her. It was not spooky; it was a conspiracy.

Through the window she saw Gardner was waiting at her door. She knew he was genuine; but the world was false. Despite his imposing authority he was gentle. She let him in. He asked questions like a detective. Had she any idea of who might do it? She said nothing; he had failed to clarify his question. – *Had he any enemies?* She laughed. Powerful men have enemies. *Had he been in touch with her?* – 'No.' True; she had not heard from either man. – *Would she fly to USA for the State funeral?* – 'Yes.' So he was talking about one man. – *Would she please accept the hospitality and sympathies of* ***the new President*** *who had been sworn in?* – T-h-e *n-e-w* p-r-e-s-i-d-e-n-t? *Had Spencer been President of USA? What year was this?* The confusion with time induced a panic attack and she felt unable to refuse his demands. Unable to think or talk.

She was asked to join Mr Gardner in a US military flight to Washington; all arranged for her. *The limousine had been sent to collect the First Lady.* She ignored the remark. Gardner produced FBI and extradition documents to *compel* her to return to USA. She asked the American diplomat if she was a suspect.

'Off the record, no Ma'am. Strictly off the record, may I level with you? We have a little bit of flexing muscles here, ma'am. The mystery began with a short phone call from Mr Weidfeld himself.'

Did he mean that Spencer was alive or had he called before he died? What else could America do to her? She phoned a lawyer who verified that there was no obligation on her to travel to USA *at this point in time,* nor to answer any questions.

Sara telephoned her neighbour to say she was going to America *at this point in time,* 'Please look after my house, and leave the glass on the kitchen floor.'

She looked at Gardner: he had not grasped the significance of the phrase. Suddenly she understood: if she was crazy, it was the opinion of others. If her mind connected two time zones, it was a gift, a natural occurrence, not a delusion. *But if Spencer was president and she was the First Lady,* it was a parallel universe which may be proven in Einstein's theory according to her new mentor, Robert Kohen, but she did not believe it. *The broken glass destroyed the radio and anchored her in the present.* For this reason she liked pain. The will power lowered her blood pressure and kept her in this world.

The chauffeur attended to the cuts on her arm. He said that there were ingrained particles which the MO would attend to but she was not listening. A few moments later she was a passenger in the air-conditioned cabin of the black limo. Like a torpedo the car sped through the warm air to a military airport near Tel Aviv. From there, she was told, she would be escorted to Capitol Hill.

'The new President wishes to speak with you.'

'Mr Gardner, I can picture the day we took a picnic in the trunk of his red sports car. Spencer looked so handsome. I was wearing a white blouse, precariously windswept, and a fetching black gymslip. The Politician and the Film star. Our black hair. My shades. We turned heads.'

He did not reply.

Now it was a stranger in the back seat of a black limousine used only for VIPs: it was Anthony Gardner of the United States Embassy who rode with Sara in the commodious rear of the car and in the front was a paid driver. It was a dream, surely it could not be for real.

Delirious, she began to sweat. *This is for real, it is not drugs, and we are in a world, here and now, which I have to save.*

A soldier was picked up on route making four people in the car. He was speaking on a crackling radio when he was not listening to it. She listened to the jargon exchanged in flat tones: '126, BE THERE IN TWELVE MINUTES, ROADS QUIET, AIRFORCE 2C ETA 30 MINUTES, three-zero. NO MENACING CIRCUMSTANCES. Confirm, FORMER VICE-PRESIDENT HAS LEFT FOR WASHINGTON TO TAKE OATH . . . Acknowledge, HE WISHES TO SEE MRS WEIDFELD ASAP.'

Mrs Weidfeld! Sara whispered to herself. It is a name which had been suspended in time, *Who is Mrs Weidfeld? For she, I think died long ago. I was she, the real she, was I not?*

'Ma'am?'

'I mean the death of the First Lady happened a long time ago, Mr Gardner! For he married, what was her name? And don't say, Mrs Weidfeld.'

She doubted if Gardner understood anything about parallel universes and disturbed time zones.

'After you came and told me, I saw my radio fall in slow motion, suspending time, heightening tragedy, not despite, but *because* it was only a material thing. It has memories. The radio is myself. My soul is in it. I am a receiver, Tony. An old-fashioned French thing with a good tone. And I too am in pieces. I have fallen. A radio is the reverse of what you think. Ask any technician. It tunes out the *unwanted* stations. *La poste de radio* was from a house in France. Paul owned it and I brought it to Israel. I'm sorry, how can you understand all this? The soul of Paul was inside the radio. My problem is that I receive many signals at the same time. And time itself is confused. Let's just call me crazy.'

He looked at her but could find no words.

'Mr Gardner, please may I call you Tony? And will you call me Sara?'

'Please call me Tony, Mrs Weidfeld.'

'No, no, no! Not that. I am Sara. Legally and morally. Mrs Weidfeld died long ago, if she existed in our reality, and I can be whom I please. My problem. I am a radio that tunes more than one station at a time, in other words, you might call me a defective sensitive. Schizophrenic in the popular sense.'

She laughed. 'In his red Mercedes SL we listened to a well-worn cassette of Mike Oldfield's "Tubular Bells". Some Mozart tapes were still shrink-wrapped and priced. Would I marry him? Could I trust such a careless poseur? More to the point, could I stop myself? I feel bad because I left America. And now he's dead.'

'With respect, Ma'am, it isn't your fault.'

The limo took a strange turning and came to rest at a concealed gate to the military airport. It seemed very high with plenty of wire and led to a second check point but there was no trouble in clearing the separate Israeli and American security booths.

'They don't even trust us to take care of ourselves, here,' the Army driver complained.

In the American Base her wounds were cleaned. Coffee and canapés were served in fine china and silver until USAF-2 had arrived and refuelled. She sipped her coffee and wondered aloud what would have happened had she stayed with Spencer.

Tony Gardner was shocked.

'Stayed with him? After what he did to you?'

'It was only done to my body, not to me.'

'He tortured you, you said so yourself,' he protested.

'My body invites sin as wealth provokes theft. In my twenties I was an idol who desired to be worshipped. At school they called me an attention-seeker.'

She took two tablets from a pillbox. Gardner became alarmed and other military personnel were alerted but their courtesy made them hesitate.

'They aren't prohibited drugs, if that is what concerns you. Spencer and I were photographed clinging together at the glittering première of 'Herbie Goes to Monte Carlo' – a movie which seemed good at the time but what it was all about I cannot recall. The champagne was intoxicating and I felt very good. He had ordered a carnation for his evening jacket and a corsage which he sweetly placed in my hair. The Spider had booked a hotel. The Fly had no other plans.'

Gardner mumbled something about men in power. She ignored it.

'As we slept together for the first time his media men were already at work. We were linked romantically forever. By texts and photos electronically networked to the world's news agencies in time for their morning papers. I was tricked but I didn't care. I dreamed that night in the most beautiful suite of New York City's finest hotel. I had grown up in dormitories sleeping six to twenty-four girls with clay figures of Jesus bleeding each night a slow death for our sins.'

32.1 In the VIP Suite of the airbase Sara recognised the American Ambassador to Israel and his wife. Pompously they avoided her. If only she could make them understand who she was and how much she believed in the prospective President and in the Program of Purity. *A Thousand Days* she had set for them to put the world to right – three years from the day of his election.

The Ambassador might have found himself under her program to embrace the world, not exploit it. Now he was on a flight to Washington sneering at her from his seat several rows in front. With his wife. They were eating and drinking, engaging the flight attendant fully with many requests. Tony sat beside Sara. She wept.

'Why do they despise me?'

She sat in silence, refused any food, and sat upright in contemplation until she fell asleep.

Chapter Thirty-Three

Michael Leonard linked the deaths of the politician and the movie director and had flown from London to New York, the east coast being the quicker and cheaper of two options. Unable to contact her at her home in Jerusalem, he worried until the media reported that she was in Washington. Once again, Sélène was news and he traced her with the assistance of journalists. She was staying at a four-star hotel.

They met in the lobby. She hugged him and asked if they could go somewhere quiet and private.

'Are you hungry?' he asked.

She hadn't eaten for two days. And she knew of a great place to eat.

'I like Japanese food; do you? But I need ten minutes to get ready. Let's meet back here, okay?'

Leonard had a copy of *The New York Times*. Weidfeld's death was the big story. Jonny Lord was page five. The two events were not linked. Leonard saw the connection but not the explanation.

He looked up and saw the face but not the woman. He blinked his eyes then burst out laughing.

'Well, I am a trained actress,' she said.

He linked hands with 'the Japanese woman' and they set off together to find the oriental restaurant.

'Where did you get the dress?'

She smiled. She said nothing until they were in a restaurant.

* * *

It was a small Italian restaurant. Sara agreed that the Japanese might suspect a motive for her disguise.

'Japan is special to me. It is in my blood.'

'When you left school and you went to America . . . ?' Leonard asked Sara. 'Was it to escape the people who were controlling you?'

'I danced in *Hair* and in *Superstar* I was Mary Magdalene's understudy in Paris and Copenhagen. That's why I went to America and should have gotten the film part. Wanted it. Needed it. It was mine but I was too late. I got other work, though. By the time of my 21st party I had an Equity card for two years. But by the time of my 21st party I was already 23.'

'Huh?'

'Place not thy faith in newspapers or French social registers which give my birth in August 1947. But when my parents were killed I was in my third class, so people were lying when they told me that I was five in 1952. When the earthlings nuked Hiroshima my Father in Heaven knew I'd have to go there to sort things out. Anyway, I was part of the scene. So what if my twenty-first was two years late? Who else can say that Mick Jagger was at their party? And that Paul and Ringo must have had bags under their eyes working in the Abbey Road studio the morning after the party?

'Anyway, that's where I was. And my gang of four were: me and Susie, George, and Bruce Wayne. It was his idea, as most things were, because Bruce was always right. He was born to be right. You couldn't argue with him. We called him Bruce MacWayne because he was a big guy who talked like a Scottish cowboy; he was Scottish but he had been to America twice. And thus he felt more American than the Americans. He said, 'Look man, there's going to be a rock festival like nothing before. It's going to change the world. Three days of love and peace. And we should be there. Why not?"

'And what can I say about Woodstock that hasn't already been said?' Her eyes moistened. 'It was three days of love and peace. The greatest be-in yet. The apogee of acid culture. Half a million kids converged from the four corners of the galaxy. On the first day the food ran out, the well dried, the clinic closed, the toilets overflowed, the farm was turned into a mud bath – and we didn't even realise that we were in trouble. Leary boasted that we were the third biggest city in New York State.

The cops were scared. They waited for panic and rioting. They sent for the National Guard. But everyone stayed cool. On days three to four they shared the food and looked after anyone who needed help, and then they headed home.

'Well, not everyone. The four of us headed to Haight-Ashbury, the centre of the new scene, and that was our new home. We found Nirvana, man, and Bruce was right again. We certainly weren't going to go back to l'Europe. A year later *he was back*. He was a good-hearted guy but got into trouble for working without a green card, driving drunk, not paying utilities bills, and possessing two crumbled half-smoked roaches. I heard about it second-hand. Susie had forgotten about her sweetheart and, for her free love meant group sex, orgies, dependence and soon she was getting stoned to hide the degradation from herself. I had to cut loose from them 'cause I saw that the beautiful people despised themselves. It was more inferno than Nirvana. Egos weren't dissolving but rotting. After six months I was unsettled and had spent all my American money so I became a waitress. George became a sound technician with a rock group. Anyway, it's all in the past. *I like everything on this menu but I'm not hungry.*'

The waiter came for the third time but still she had not decided. Leonard ordered a Minestrone, 'You can't go wrong with that in Italian restaurants worldwide.'

She skipped the starter, 'I'm talking too much. Besides, Michael, I feel a bit foolish in my Japanese disguise in an Italian restaurant. By the time I left Haight-Ashbury it was not safe to walk at night. Flower power had withered. The Aquarian commune had become a rotten metropolis. The free clinic had collapsed, bad drugs were now sold for profit by organised crime, and the kids resorted to anything to raise cash. Nixon had the cunning to undermine us by his lies and tricks. Left to our own devices it might have worked but Nixon would not take that risk.

'The journalists peddled his myth. They found a few pockets of decadence and established it as the reality. The idealists moved out as the rough elements were attracted in. Perhaps the media were honest to the truth as they saw it. Lies become truth. Place not thy faith in journalists.'

Leonard smiled nervously taking care not to stop her flow; for him it was a cash flow.

'I hadn't wanted to be a hippy. I wanted to be famous and I had set my sights on the film that was being made of *Jesus Christ, Superstar*. I wanted the part I had understudied on stage in Denmark.'

'You were infatuated with the rôle of Mary Magdalene?'

Sara smiled, 'Game, set, and match to Michael Leonard the journalist who can prove that charm school made the actress, and evening classes turned me into the modern messiah. *Because the lie becomes the truth. Life imitates art.*'

The waiter interrupted the flow by serving his guests with theatrical style and ceremony. Humans create meaning and adorn the plain truth.

Like Sara, Leonard only played with his food, 'I'm sorry this is not a very romantic evening but I want to know everything about you.'

'It's my fault for talking too much,' she said. 'I don't feel hungry. You eat and we will meet later at the hotel, OK?'

She got up to go. He stopped her.

'I'll pay the bill and I'll drive you home. Can we have dinner tomorrow, same time, same place?'

'Can't make it tomorrow, darling. *Meeting another man.* But don't worry, he prefers boys and he's old enough to be my dad.' She knew that Leonard would identify his rival suitor.

33.1 The Nemo is an unlisted, exclusive hotel for people who can pay for the highest standards of hospitality, security and privacy in New York City. Its tariff is as secret as its existence and location. If you need to ask the price you cannot afford it.

A few minutes after 8pm Sara entered The Nemo and saw Robert Kohen in the lobby. It was opulent with archways leading into six secluded meeting areas. Each one was furnished with a Persian table and leather settees. Doric pillars were softened by climbing plants. He accompanied her into one of these areas and they sat down on opposite sides of the table.

'Sara, you are very gracious to meet me in these circumstances. You have my sympathies and my wish to you of a long life. Here is coffee with non-dairy creamer and one round of kosher salt-beef sandwiches. The best in New York.'

Kohen called over a waitress carrying his tray. '*Put them down right here, my dear, I'm really hungry.*'

Turning to Sara, 'Of course, you don't eat meat, so I ordered a veggie platter for you. Not to beat about the bush, I want you to do a broadcast from my studio with the Faraday Cage. It isn't channelling. It is *technology*, controllable at will.'

He studied her face for a reaction. She betrayed nothing. She felt uncomfortable on the hard leather Chesterfield, squeezed close to the ornate bronze coffee table. Kohen moved to her settee. She sat still as if wooden.

She whispered, 'More radio experiments, Robert! Now what do you have in mind?'

'Sara, I have already permitted more than eighty experts to investigate my so-called time machine.'

She was frowning, so he paused to answer her objection. 'I only invented a new type of sensitive aerial. I can't even patent it. The idea seems simple to me – it just came to me in my bath and followed directly from Albert Einstein. A radio receives a wide band but tunes to a selected frequency; that much is well known. It is tuned to the present because the electrical and the magnetic elements are precisely aligned. A gap of one nanosecond corresponds to 93.45 years in atomic clock time, not calendar nor astronomical time. The trick is to introduce such a fine gap. I am only a servant of the Lord, like you, so I cannot make it go forward. And I must not change the past but how can I deny His will? Listen, it is not I who wants you to try Radio Archaeology, Sara, *I already know that it works*. Even with ordinary people, and we all know that you are not ordinary. You have a biological antenna.'

'If I do have such a gift, Robert, then why did I learn of my former lover's death by the television?'

'I have told you, if our brains allowed everything to enter from the overmind we would be swamped like a radio set untuned. Bedlam. Every signal would engulf us and we could not survive. A hundred million years of evolution have favoured the short-sighted and the narrow-minded. That is why we need you in this world. That is your sacrifice. It is why we must love you and protect you. You are in great danger.'

'Robert, I'm confused more than you imagine and I wonder if my brain is in decline after taking too many substances?'

'Em, well . . . Technically, my dear, you are simply aware of the infinite and your filters are weak. Call it brain damage, yes. That is why you need someone to take care of you. Someone more than a newspaper reporter who is an atheist who needs to check up on you all the time.'

Sara was shocked: 'Is he following me?'

'*Eat your sandwich. Pour me a coffee.* Sara, once all humans were psychic but for the last forty centuries clairvoyance has been weak and unpredictable. Now I am making scientific advances almost every day. Secretly funded because of the media fools like your current boyfriend who sells sensations and dubs my equipment a time machine. It is a wholly new thing I call Organic Technology. Transducing brainwaves into radio waves. The mistake we've made is to confuse brain and psyche. Drugs act on the brain, suggestions on the psyche.'

'Robert, you're gripping my arm very tightly. Besides, I'm hungry.'

'It isn't strange that I'm excited by my work – the combination of modern science and ancient wisdom, the realisation that technology is no less miraculous and no less sacred simply because it must be rediscovered or contrived. Mathematical, digital, plastic, man-made – call it what you will – it is all 'natural.' I look at the galaxies a billion light years away and I marvel at the telescope as much as the universe. And I behold the observer as much as the sight. Because you are a woman, and very beautiful, I love you.'

'Robert, I need to go now.' She was very scared, but he gently gripped her arm and her curiosity.

'Cosmic time has no direction, Sara. That is the key to humanity's philosophical paradox – an error. Causality is choice; destiny is preordained. How can I explain the apparent contradiction? Take Einstein's maths in which time is not only relative to the observer in value but it is relative in direction. I will unlock the mysteries of the universe. I'm getting closer every day. Do you believe in me? I believe in you. The millennium is an exciting age to live in, but I am not asking you to help me in a scientific enquiry.'

'Robert, please can I go now? I don't want to scare you, but I think I just want to die or kill myself.'

This time he reacted with shock. He paused and then spoke softly, 'Who will save the saviour?'

He grasped her arms and said, 'The time has come for Sara, and for the world to encounter the one who wrote the last scriptural books and hid them by the Dead Sea 2,000 years ago.'

'Robert, people spy on me but what really scares me is that . . .'

'What?'

'. . . that you can destabilise my sense of roots in the present. That you have invented a time machine and you are trying it out.'

Robert Kohen showed her a legal document.

RADIO CONNECTICUT INC, ARTISTS ROYALTIES AGREEMENT.

He placed it before Sara for her signature.

'Robert, your radio archaeology goes back in time. I mean, the one who wrote and concealed the Dead Sea Scrolls died 2,000 years ago. No-one will believe you.'

He handed her a pen. 'Well, you are a critical and intelligent woman so let us see if you will believe what you will hear. I have heard it. It is a miracle, it is science, it is providence, and it is your duty. It is the fate of mankind and it is a commercial broadcast with value.'

Chapter Thirty-Four

CONNECTICUT, SEPTEMBER 1978

RCI, better known as 'Jewish Radio,' was housed in a 1950s section-built concrete building painted in a gloss finish between pink and beige. A white plaque engraved in blue bore the Star of David and read, *WXQR, Radio Connecticut, Inc, 1012 Central Square Avenue. Licensed Proprietor Robert F. Kohen.*

Inside, lowered acoustic ceilings and bleached oak panels on the walls had been installed to soften the concrete starkness. These were the walls which journalists said concealed secret apparatus. Sara used her hands as a metal detector but felt no response.

Kohen smiled as he walked her along a corridor like a hotel, knocked on a door numbered 5, then handed her over to a studio team. He became absorbed in the general administration of incoming calls, signing outgoing letters, and talking to staff.

Sara was introduced to Amanda – an enthusiastic and friendly young woman who clung to her and softened a stream of demands from an overburdened director, a neurotic sound engineer, and an egotistical anchorman. A motley team, male and female, small and large, they were diversely dressed but synchronised like trained monkeys; the men were wearing skullcaps. Only Amanda displayed human warmth or awareness of Sara as a person. The men ignored her. From a sealed bag Sara was handed a pair of white headphones with furry earmuffs which Amanda adjusted to cover the groomed hair of the celebrity guest. Sara experienced something new: a feeling that she hoped was not a lesbian experience.

I recalled that the name Amanda meant lovable. The encounter was momentary and fleeting, but very tactile and aromatic. At this point I had been used and abused by men and I only craved the loving touch of other humans.

Immediately, Sara was chilled by an eerie atmosphere. Through the headphones she heard the New Age sounds which WXQR had broadcast since 1974. It was totally unlike her spontaneous visions or drug-induced readings.

There was a clear solid voice coming through the headphones. The sounds at first were frightening: disembodied, spacious, unearthly, not like the in-the-head tunes you normally get from headphones. An old man cackled in a high pitch and gasped for intakes of breath. I threw off the headphones in fear but the engineers had patched the sounds into the studio monitors which made it more oppressive. The station piped its on-air broadcast through its offices and this one caused consternation. An audience was forming around the Studio 5 window. Suddenly we all jumped out of our skins in fright, especially me! The voice was very loud and clear. Without gender, like a high-pitched distant old man. He shouted at me.

'The Spouter of Lies and the Wicked Priest have perished but see, I do not taste death. I heard the Word of the Lord spoken to Moses and I did write six books and *my* language lives. The Word sent forth can never be recalled. Hear ye now, all knowers of righteousness, consider the works of Almighty God, for he has a dispute with all flesh! In the days of Noah he destroyed their evil by water and now men will cast lots to destroy their own evil by fire. Speak to me, Sara if you can save the world, you can do so only by extinguishing the evil.'

She spoke nervously, 'I – I don't know who you are, Father, so please tell me.'

'I am The Teacher of Righteousness,' the loudspeakers boomed, **'Founder of the Assembly of the Holy Ones you call the Sect of the**

Dead Sea Scrolls. It is I, the anointed prophet-priest of the Lord that speaketh up to your Holiness.'

'I'm scared of this. I am a nice person. I didn't do anything wrong. I didn't hurt anyone. Who are you? If you are a hoax I fear people will laugh at me. How can you speak from the past – it is impossible.'

'Through your radio machines, it is Eleazar ben Zadok the Alexandrian, in the line of Aaron, and I do not bear false witness.'

The disembodied voice complied with Sara's request to become calm.

'Those who want proof will find that my identity and even my words can be proven for I spoke and modern man has found in the writing of my scribes what I prophesied: *your* coming, your name, and your description as the anointed one to save the people of the second era of creation. Look in the library of the Dead Sea Scrolls.'

Sara sat still in front of the sound desk and listened.

'Daughter of the Royal House of David from the Tribe of Judah, you are the one chosen, but you cannot by your own impurity be the world's saviour, messiah, redeemer, ruler, and elected as the one to whom authority is given by the Lord God of Hosts, the Holy One above the world and Time itself. Father, Son, and Holy Line.'

Sara was trembling. She put on the headphones but the voice continued.

'You have fornicated and deviated but is it not written? 'The sceptre shall not depart from the tribe of Judah. When Israel is in the ascendancy there shall not fail to be a descendant of David upon the throne. For to David and his seed was granted the Covenant of sovereignty over all his people for everlasting generations.' I command you to find the Davidic genealogy, Sara, and proclaim the truth! My people rejected the Son. On you the glory is merely reflected and you are but a woman, so I shall call you 'the Moonlit Messiah'.'

For a few seconds the loudspeakers overloaded and people looked at each other in shock. Sara looked around for reassurance but no-one was there. *The trained monkeys had become human beings. Amanda was on the floor in tears. Sara was unable to move; her muscles were frozen.* The strange sounds animated the loudspeakers again. They boomed so that the very walls seemed to radiate the sound.

Robert Kohen burst into the studio. He was white and his state of shock seemed deep and genuine. He stood at the door and looked at Sara as if he needed her permission to approach her.

He looked up to the wall-mounted speaker cabinets just as the disembodied voice began again.

'Sara, listen! Dictatorship has failed; democracy has failed. Restore the Dynasty of David, King of Israel, sovereign of the world of the righteous gentile. The genealogy of the messianic line is in two parts, both of which you must find. The cipher is inscribed on copper scrolls and the generations are concealed in the Holy Scriptures copied by the scribes who are aware of the words but not of the message for they are preserved letter-perfect by the cipher.'

Robert Kohen prompted Sara, 'He said you were chosen but you cannot be the messiah.'

The voice boomed out, 'Sara, you are seven of nine parts from the House of Light, imperfect soul, I do not anoint you as 'Daughter of Israel.' You are not a messiah in your generation because you will take a life in anger. You cannot lead but you may point *all* people to righteous ways; you are above all earthly kings; you are queen over kings, and by the grace of God we are below you.'

Sara protested, '*I cannot take a life in anger.*'

'I have spoken. The future is not yours to see, only the past. Past events cast long shadows. Who lifts the sword will die by it, so *you will be killed within a short time.* You may ask of me three questions which I shall answer. So, Sara, shall you now ask your last question as the first?'

Kohen prompted Sara, 'Ask a question to test his interactive response. It is essential to authenticate him. Ask him where to find the genealogy.'

Without hesitation Sara asked, 'What must I do, Father?'

The response came immediately, 'The prophet Micah wrote, 'What is good has been explained to you, oh man. This is what God asks of you, only this: to act justly, to love tenderly, and to walk humbly with your God."

Kohen prompted Sara: 'That was not a response specific to your question. Test his interactive ability by seeking a direct answer.'

Sara ignored him and spoke into the microphone.

'For that guidance I thank you, Father Eleazar, and I know that you are true. My second question burns. As a writer of the Holy Scriptures, you must tell the people, if the Word of the Lord is found in the heart or in books.'

There was silence for four or five seconds.

'If you read books, keep open your powers of observation and keep your thoughts going. Heads really work, HaHaHa. All two hundred thousand volumes of the famous Library of Alexandria were burned in the year 640 of your era. And thus modern man lost much ancient wisdom. But the Caliph Omar who burned these books was no fool. He was a man of action who captured the great city of learning but he was no fool. He reasoned like this: IF THESE BOOKS AGREE WITH THE BOOKS OF GOD, THEY ARE USELESS AND NEED NOT BE PRESERVED. IF THEY DO NOT AGREE, THEY ARE PERNICIOUS AND OUGHT TO BE DESTROYED.

'Now, what would you do, Daughter, ruling the world? Tell me the truth. You destroyed your little radio in anger!

Sara was shocked. *'How did you know that?'*

'Your answer, please! If you ruled the earth planet will you destroy books?'

'No, no, I would never permit work to be destroyed unless I lost my temper, for a book is the product of the spirit, and of the eye, and of the hand.'

'Ah, yes, Sara, a book if rough will hurt the reader, and if smooth will reflect him. As for myself, I am weary of books. They have drained my spirit, blinded my eye, and stilled my hand.'

'Master, where you are you have risen; please, my genuine first and last question . . . ?'

'Ask, but you know that you will regret it. The Scriptures warn against reading the future, but in this they admit the possibility. The future belongs to God, not man.'

Sara hesitated.

'I will regret the answer, so already you know the question? Should I not ask?'

'The choice is yours!'

Sara's grip on the microphone was so tight that the plastic holder snapped. She turned to Kohen. 'I just have to ask.'

Kohen held Sara but she did not pay attention to him. The lights fused and the emergency lighting made the whole building safe if not bright. The bang apparently took out the audio equipment. It seemed that the Teacher had gone, but Sara shouted.

'Paul, my brother, he is the first-born male. He should be the messiah *but where is he*? He is gentle like my father but angry.'

The sound emerged from the stark silence of the walls, quiet, low in tone like a rumble but inaudible. Then the lighting resumed and the building came to life.

Through the speakers The Righteous Teacher boomed, 'Your brother is he who does the will of God. May Almighty God be with you!'

The engineer called out, the voltage is peaking over 140, man, the limiters are switching before we are cut.

'Please – please, don't cheat me, oh Teacher,' her voice was faded out, 'Oh please, tell me where is Paul. Oh please. Why is he not . . . ?'

THIS PROGRAMME ON WXQR IS SPONSORED BY COCA-COLA . . .

34.1 Robert told Amanda that the phones in the office were jammed and needed everyone to answer them. She left the studio. The engineers followed her.

This left Robert and Sara. He was white as a ghost. He stared at her. Former actor and former actress stared at each other in disbelief.

Kohen turned and shouted, 'Amanda, never mind the phones. We'll sort it out later. Please do two things in this order, make sure the broadcast schedule continues, and get me a PAB. Sorry, Sara, jargon for program as broadcast, a tape required by the licensing authorities. Even with it, they're going to shut me down now they have the excuse.'

Amanda put out a call for the studio director. After a pause, Kohen walked over to Sara who was clinging to her chair which was in the corner, 'I'm being selfish. Are *you* feeling okay? You spoke well, even had you been prepared you could not have spoken more truth.'

Her eyes glistened as she nodded and put her arm around Kohen.

Amanda came back into the room and handed Sara a mug of tea.

'Terry's bringing a coffee for you sir.'

Chapter Thirty-Five

NEW YORK, SEPTEMBER 1978

Michael Leonard was in New York to launch his book *The Aquarius Conspiracy*. He was accused of being a part of the conspiracy he was reporting and reacted by accusing his rivals as hunting in packs. They alleged that he was the mouthpiece of guardians of the Secret, perhaps unwittingly; or that he was driven to construct a conspiracy by the facts and evidence which fitted it.

Leonard was aware that the thing was much too elaborate to be a hoax and indeed had conflicting layers and elements; not the least of which was emerging as former Defence scientist, Robert F. Kohen. To address this problem the English journalist hardened his resolve to explain and expose the radio stunt. He hired a well-established firm of investigators called Ellis, Bell & Teloppe to inspect the premises of WXQR at 1012 Central Avenue, Connecticut.

Two days after the broadcast from first-century Judea, he stood side by side with Sara at the televised Mass for Senator Spencer Weidfeld. *At least it clarified which parallel universe she was in today!*

The funeral intensified her morbid anticipation of her own impending assassination and in the chapel she told Leonard that she would set up her own Secret Service to gather intelligence and maintain an armed personal guard. She was opposed to weapons but she cited the comment in the broadcast by the Teacher, *'You'll most likely get yourself killed within a short time.'*

Leonard scoffed and reasoned with her premonitions and predictions. She was called to the lectern where she praised the new pope who had been elected one month ago. 'Truly God's choice for the Age of Aquarius, and he is a good man. I feel so happy about working with him.'

From that day, Leonard realised that Sara believed in herself.

35.1 But she was human. Sara and Michael slept together at her New York hotel and rose late the next morning. He was the one to pick up the newspaper outside their door.

On September 28th 1978, the newly elected Pope John Paul I was found dead in the early hours of the morning. Among Catholic and other investigative journalists there was shock with the inconsistencies of Vatican statements and the speed with which all evidence had been destroyed. The bedroom had been vacated and the bodyguard had not been in his place as the Holy Father had given him the night off.

Sara asked Leonard if there were real grounds for suspecting a violent death; he told her everything he knew, which was not very much.

'The Smiling Pope is dead,' she said, with tears pouring down her cheeks, and I know why he spared the bodyguard. Albino is no more. *God's choice has been taken by the hand of a man.* I don't understand it at all. Michael, the Church will slip back. She is in the grip of Satan. I see it but I too must drink from the poison well, who else will do it?'

After a respectful pause, Leonard said he was hungry and since breakfast was prepaid, it was a pity to waste it.

'By the way, are you aware that I am saying that I too will surrender my life?'

Sara looked at him and asked if he wanted to eat to live or live to eat. She said she had something more nourishing than food. She took him by the arm and they went down to the lobby.

She called a taxi to take them to a public library. In the car she explained that the archaic southern French tongue is not as moribund as the English written by Chaucer.

'The langue d'Oc is still spoken by a few older people in the region in which I was born.'

'I see,' Leonard shrugged his shoulders. 'And where does this take us?'

They entered the magnificent nineteenth century library and crossed the black and white chequered marble floor.

Despite Leonard's denunciation of clairvoyants and crystal ball gazers, she sat him down in the reading room and showed him *Nostradamus: Prophecies and Predictions*. In a few seconds she found Quatrain X:12 which she whispered.

'Esleu en Pape, d'esleu sera mocqué
Subit soudain esmeu prompt et timide,
Par trop bon doulz à mourir provocqué,
Crainte estainte la nuit de sa mort guide.'

She pointed to the translation of the 16th-Century prophecy for him.

'Elected as Pope, he will be mocked by the chosen ones.
Suddenly and unexpectedly removed, prompt and timid,
Caused to die through too much goodness and kindness,
He will fear for the guard killed on the night of his death.'

Leonard made a cynical comment, asking if she had not interpreted the prophecy after the event to which she replied, 'You forget that to me Nostradame was a local! I read him long ago as a child and I remembered this quote. Now I have looked it up and committed it to memory. No-one has brain-washed me.'

The journalist drummed his fingers on the reading desk.

'Listen, Michael, and I shall tell you what is remarkable. Many people know that the Church of Christ has gone very wrong but they do not know why. The church is an earthly body, dear Michael, not a spiritual thing, and it is subject to disease of its members, what used to be called possession by unclean spirits, you know? The good and the bad cells struggle to survive when they are in darkness.'

'If it is the truth, then why don't *you* say it openly?' he asked, 'I mean now you have the authority.'

'My mouth cannot pronounce it. I cannot create divisions.'

'I thought we had a common cause in truth.'

'There are surface truths, Michael – you see what the public wants and you sell it back to them – and there are essence truths. Like the priest Saunière, I too cannot speak but I can show you.'

She held her cupped hands like an antenna around his cheeks, but at least six inches away.

He fell to the ground and screamed. Two librarians ran over to help him. Readers were annoyed by the disturbance. Sara was firm.

'Michael, I am very sorry if I caused you pain.'

'Ah! Ah! You did that on purpose, didn't you? That was a party-piece, a sign or something? To impress me?'

His legs recovered their strength. Sara helped him up and he recovered his dignity and sanity. A curator appeared from nowhere and suggested that they should leave the book on the desk and leave the premises without delay. Sara took the arm of her startled companion and marched him out.

'Now think about what you saw. You *felt* it, Michael, did you not? A dream fades like a bad memory but a vision persists forever because it is a higher reality impressing on you. The knight crusader wore the cross of the Church. Did you see Christ, or did you see the Devil, at work?'

'I saw the devil, or the Church, Sara. And I neither read nor heard the words but, *Et in Arcadia Ego* . . . What does it mean? Why are you making me say these things? I don't believe in the devil.'

'And you don't believe in researching history except from books. You know nothing of the mind which is trained to access the memories of the past. You have seen it now, but you will still call it black arts and superstition because someone brainwashed *you*.'

'I know more Latin grammar than you, sweetheart, and the phrase is incomplete.'

With great feeling Sara turned and proclaimed, 'To me the phrase is anything but lacking. It's deep; shall we not call it fathomless?'

Outside the library Leonard walked away from Sara. He was angry. His head was aching and he was troubled by what Father Saunière had seen – Europe's own Crusade in the lands of Father Saunière – and now Leonard himself had seen it. Or imagined it. He now felt strongly bonded to the priest, seeing him like a brother and a real person with real reasons for his strange behaviour. Bérenger Saunière was no longer a character from history. *But Leonard still could not understand the words indelibly etched on his brain which now echoed in his head:* the motto of the mysterious and archaic Prieuré de Sion.

Et in Arcadia Ego . . .

And in Arcadia I am . . . *what?* Arcadia, the land of innocence. It was the key to the mystery but still made no sense to Leonard even after his brain implanted movie.

Rather than ask, the know-all Leonard determined to use his old-fashioned history books to research the events of the thirteenth century.

He looked round and confirmed that Sara was walking briskly away from him. She was right, though: the vision persisted in his memory unlike a dream which faded quickly.

Chapter Thirty-Six

ET IN ARCADIA EGO . . .

The Occupied Territories of Toulouse, AD1216

Cotorino, the little shepherdess, felt very hot.

The mountain no longer shaded her because the sun had climbed to the highest part of the sky.

She ate a piece of sweetened bread her mother had placed in the pocket of the coarse-woven blue frock which was the usual dress for a girl of her young age and low rank. Antoine, her brother, was an apprentice carpenter. As a boy he was given the larger half of the loaf but Mother had specially baked the holiday bread sweeter than normal for the girl's fourteenth birthday.

Cotorino could not see Antoine in the workshop, yet she ate exactly when he was eating his allocated portion. Her sheep were safe so she sat on a rock, eating the bread, and all she had to do was watch and count them. She counted them in the big numbers they used in the north.

Cotorino had felt emboldened by the importance of her advanced age. Her mother said that the teachings of the north were wrong.

Cotorino felt she had made a sin. She had felt sorrow for the flock of the sheep in her care because the grass had shrivelled in the heat. She had not taken them round the mountain, as she normally did, but across the river which was forbidden. But no-one would know except the Lord Jesus who saw down from heaven and also into peoples' hearts. She was just big enough to carry the sheep one-by-one over the wooden bridge, the big ones first, and the small ones when her energy ebbed.

Only the good ones would get the fresh pastures. Of her own strength and sureness of foot she was quite certain. But she knew the danger of two flocks separated on each bank but only one shepherdess. Not even the Lord Jesus could be everywhere at one time and surely he would not find out.

There was nothing to worry about. While the sheep had the fresh grass on the other side of the river Cotorino had done another wrong thing. She took off her frock and felt pride in the midday sun as she ate bread and ran her fingers over her new breasts. As she caressed and examined her body, her mind glowed with pride and ecstasy before she put back the frock whose roughness she hardly noticed.

At first she suspected that it was more guilt – '*the disease of the north*' as her mother called it – that made her feel uneasy, but then she *knew* that she must run home without delay. She knew it would take her many, many steps. She forgot about the safety of the sheep. The good ones were still on the other side. Now they were separated. They too felt the terror and were running wild. The bad sheep followed her. She wept with the thought of the good sheep that might be lost. Then she knew that what she felt was much, much darker. It was death. Death in the idyllic pastures. First her father, and Antoine, and the others. She listened carefully but could hear nothing. She pressed her ear to the ground. She looked but she saw nothing. She breathed deeply. No tears fell. She just knew that it had come. The war from the north had reached them.

So, it was true. The Lord Jesus was not the saviour. How foolish had she been to trust him.

Cotorino ran across the bridge. It was against all instincts, which were to guard her animals, but her intelligence guided her that sheep were of no use to a dead family. It was her own fault for doing too many wrong things in one day. Crossing the river. Admiring her body. Especially for thinking about her loved one, and imagining that they would make children. She had seen the village in which they would live, the place he would work, and where they would worship. She believed she had known these things from the beginning, also for all of her brothers and sisters. Vision-making was now secret; in the north it was a witchcraft and punishable by burning at the stake.

She ran as fast as her stained legs would go, until the smoke rising from the village could be smelled (but not seen) through her tears. She screamed. Fell to the grass. Ear to the ground. Riders! It *was* the war from the north. The Lords of the Church of Jesus had burnt down other villages. But her father had said it would not happen here.

Cotorino knew that if she was lucky she would have a quick death, then join the Lady Marie Magadala in Heaven. Or would it be in Hell with eternal Damnation as the Church taught was the wages for her sins? She ran. She fell.

Now she choked in the black smoke that smelled of flesh. She rose from the ground and yelled in defiance. Her eyes were dry. She would fight them. Her legs carried her until they expired. Now she saw black knights, crusaders with the red cross of the evil Jesus, doing His work, ridding the world of sinners, witches, and heretics. She was all three – disobedient, magician, and non-believer – and she must die.

She thought that the black one was Simon de Montford himself, because he was everywhere at once, because she deserved the top man, because she knew of no-one else by name, and because he was riding across the fields towards her, and to her alone.

She knelt on the ground and accepted death in Arcadie.

His sword, hanging from his body, grew more threatening.

Greater.

He grasped the sword and it glistened in the sunlight.

Closer. Greater. Bigger.

She was transfixed by the horse's steady gallop. Prayed that God would bless, mummy, daddy, all her brothers, sisters, gran . . .

She knelt, now very afraid, and stared at the lone horseman.

She saw only the animal, its training prevailing over its nature, an instrument of war.

Closer. And Time slowed.

She sneezed, but vomit emerged. Unconsciously she evacuated her bowels. Foolishly, she had eaten a little grass. Closer still. Time froze. The vision became eternity. Et in Arcadia ego; in death's dream kingdom.

Still kneeling, preparing for the better fate, she tied her long black hair above her head exposing her neck, welcoming the oblivion of a sweet quick death.

* * *

The sword lowers on the rider's side and a smiling girl delivers her words of defiance, 'Jesus is not our God, sir Knight. Our Lord Johanan knew suffering and was put to death like us. Your Jesus was not born of a virgin but by a man entering a woman. And your pope is the Antichrist. He will burn in Hell.'

Eternal present: the mounted knight approaches ever closer. Fifty two years made one week, seven weeks in one day, twenty four hours in a minute, sixty minutes in one second. Time inverted. Her life seen in the moment before . . . what?

When she was twelve a village oven had been built and her Mother, being the best baker in the village, got to use it three times a week and even sold some loaves. Others she gave away, which annoyed Cotorino's father. Until she was ten, Cotorino had gone to lessons and even been taught by the pastor. At the classes she would see her lover and smile. Shortly before then, in the years 1210-11 of Our Lord, many people had died of the fever. The village was closed off and Cotorino had seen much death. Her infant brother Josefo had died despite all prayers. She saw her mother crying, and cooking, and had watched the making of the next child to come. She knew she would do this with her lover when she will be eighteen. In the proper churches in the north they said this is a sin. But the animals do it without being blamed.

The sword is very close, dangling. Like the phallus of the rider, menacing like the grim reaper. She feels very little fear herself but the soul of the battle-hardened, charging horse is in anguish.

When she was very small Cotorino hid under the tables in these very fields to steal food at the Feast Days. If caught, she would be scolded with a big stick or a slap. She ate the food herself and did not share it. She watched *la pastoura als camps,* the shepherdess in the fields. She felt proud. It was her big sister and one day she would have this job when she became fourteen. Already she wanted to dress up in the blue hessian frock of the shepherdess, but mother wanted her to wear the red ribbons and pretty frock.

Perhaps it was when she was only five or six, but Cotorino saw herself in a rage striking her smaller sister, Morgoridoto, and feels the pain rebound. It is her first vision.

Her first memory: aged two, Cotorino nearly drowns in this river. For many minutes the water carries her out while her mother screams. But Cotorino feels no fear. The air under the frock keeps her floating while mother finds a branch which Cotorino catches and gently pulls herself back, cheating death. Almost choked by mother's tight arms. Drowned by mother's tears. Cotorino is spared by the Lord who placed the branch here, for there are no trees growing by this river.

Closer. Now the rider blocks the sun's light.

For hundreds of years after her death, people will lament this day in the forbidden tongue, the langue d'Oc. Long after Cotorino is forgotten, the story is concealed in music and proclaimed by the troubadours. On the worst day of the slaughter of a war to restore orthodoxy to the region sixty thousand people are cut down; men, women, and children; Cathars and Catholics. De Montford's general issued the infamous order, 'Erase the heresy. Kill them all! God will recognise His own.'

The knights were awarded lands, confiscated property, and forgiveness for their sins. The written history of the region omitted this chapter; echoes survived by word of mouth. In the troubadors' poem, the truth was concealed. The bridge acquired a name, the girl was given to wash herself, her composure was turned into tears, and the horseman now has two colleagues. The sheep were forgotten. For three hundred years minstrels sang at royal courts until the meaning was lost.

Jou l'pount d'o Mirabel
Cotorino lobabo,
Benguèrou o possa
Três cobolhès d'ormado,
Jou l'pount d'o Mirabel
Cotorino plourabo.

At the Mirabel bridge
Catherine was washing,
There came by
Three horsemen from the army,
At the Mirabel bridge
Catherine was crying.

And even in Arcadia death is becoming and I am death.

Chapter Thirty-Seven

NEW YORK, OCTOBER 1978

After the broadcast of The Righteous Teacher, Robert Kohen was interrogated by many radio and TV presenters persuading him to confess and describe the hoax. Michael Leonard was unable to speak to the former Pentagon Chief Scientist but was told that Dr Kohen had already arranged to visit the BBC in London.

People whom Leonard recognised from the Church of the Fish flew from Europe. They advised Sara to cancel interviews because she too would be asked to explain things. An office sprung up in Geneva. Calling itself The Messianic Organisation it announced that Sara would retreat for forty days of contemplation and preparation for her rôle. A 'Sara is Saviour' movement was started by her former hippy friends in California and promoted by some New Age people who owned advertising companies.

'So, from now on I'll have to communicate through your PR?' Michael Leonard asked.

Sara kissed him. Electricity flowed from her lips and he became aroused. She whispered, 'Communication between us is more personal.'

They were hiding out in a fashionable loft apartment owned by Sara's friends. Worried that he had lost her, Leonard needed very little encouragement to have sex with her midway between breakfast and lunch. The love nest was deliciously secret and they were there to ignore interruptions. All phone calls were captured on tape for the owners of the house. No doubt Leonard's media friends were searching for him.

On a huge rug in the middle of a former warehouse he held her tight and began to peel off her clothes. He asked if she was fertile and if she wanted to have his child. So gently that it was ambiguous she appeared to nod without enthusiasm.

He was testing her delusion. If her child was to be the successor to King David could Michael Leonard be the father?

She was exquisite, and her kissing was deep. Then she stopped, as sweetly as possible, letting him down gently, giving him pleasure, and placing her fingers over his lips when he tried to talk. She told him to use a French Letter. 'That's what the nuns used to call it,' she laughed.

So Leonard accepted that he would not father the son of God. What would the critics and rival journalists think if the Englishman ceased to be a mere reporter but a member of the Holy Bloodline?

What Sara knew about heightening tension and pleasure was unlikely to have been on the convent curriculum and Leonard soon forgot about his story.

After they made love, they lay together for some time.

She got up from the bed. 'Forgot we were doing it in someone's home.'

They had ignored two callers at the door and two phone messages.

37.1 Leonard went out for groceries, agreeing that she could no longer walk in public, even disguised.

'Sara, I'll contact the Israeli Embassy in New York to ascertain their decision in the new circumstances. I'll tell him that you want to continue with your studies, conversion, and status-litigation. *But you aren't claiming their throne.*'

'Michael, you are my Guardian Angel.'

He folded his shopping bag and as the doors of the elevator closed, he called back. 'Yes, I'm becoming your baggage carrier, majesty.' By the ground floor he realised that her conversion to Judaism would rule out her marriage to a gentile.

37.2 She was waiting at the door when he returned with some groceries and a delicatessen hot lunch, authentic New York style. Something was troubling her.

'Michael, I was just wondering. Are we going to look for Paul?'

'Yes, that fits in with my plans,' he answered firmly.

'Mine too, for if we find him, then surely he would be the messiah?'

'It would suit me, but I'm not an expert on messianic succession.'

'But you make films and write books about it, Michael.'

He thought for a bit. Biting into a bagel Leonard spoke.

'That doesn't make me an expert. Look, honey, I leave the Holy Bloodline research to my people in London and Paris and I can rely on the investigators here to sort out Dr Kohen and WXQR. The radio hoax is a technical matter and these people are American high-power motivated by results pros.'

He saw her face and then promised.

'But I will handle Paul myself, not just another story, but as your brother. I will find him for my lover. I will fly to Marseilles. After two thousand years the Dead Sea Scrolls won't go away and the hoax will create a diversion for the other journalists. They will drink from a common well that I have poisoned with even more lies and confusions.' He smiled.

Sara's face expressed contempt until he explained that he needed to buy time while he pursued Paul.

When she expressed her delight and her desire to accompany him, he replied, 'Okay, but give me three days by myself. I'll get a lot more done.'

'Listen, Michael!'

He turned round and listened to her.

She proclaimed, *'It is no hoax.'*

37.3 When Leonard arrived in Marseilles, he entered into a joint venture with an investor to clear the loan on his London house which had been risked to fund the investigation. He accepted $40,000 for half royalties for three years from the story of Sara's secret brother. To make fast progress on the Rennes mystery while he was searching for Paul, Leonard hired researchers but informed them no more than they needed to know; others were fed with false information.

He was in a game with powerful manipulators, like Kohen, the Holy Bloodline guardians split into rival camps; perhaps even the Church and government agencies with unlimited resources. But he worried more about the other journalists scooping 'his' story.

He used his time to make a public deposit of faked documents, construct decoys, and secure defences. Sara would come to Marseilles depending on him for messages, daily necessities, and focussed entirely on finding Paul.

Leonard had announced nothing of his liaison so once again he had to divert the other journalists who he met foraging in Marseilles – attracted like the Magi to the birthplace of the modern messiah. They believed that Leonard was there for the same reason. They could not imagine that he was one step ahead of them, pursuing a man who, if anyone, was the true surviving messiah – male primogeniture permitting.

37.4 The night before meeting Sara at the airport, Leonard drank English beer in a French pub with an entourage of European journalists. They told him that two or three photographers were arriving at Sara's 'homecoming' which had been leaked to the Press. Leonard feigned surprise but he knew he was still ahead of the pack.

'You're doing well, Mike. Crazy story, this messiah thing,' said the hack through a haze of smoke and alcohol. 'Of course it'll all blow over. Problem is that we need new photos. She doesn't look like the young cool film star she once was, and the funeral material from New York is recognisable. Course you've been on this story much longer than us. You got lucky. *Can I get you another drink?* As for the broadcast, Kohen is setting up the woman, obviously. And why should she complain? Isn't it transparent? A put up job. Actresses love to prove they are deep. But being a messiah is a bit too much. Mind you we all get something out of it. We get a story. The public gets its glamour and gossip.'

'And the Church will get its come-uppance and the oppressed will get their sigh.' Leonard answered with sarcasm. 'You know, there is nothing to beat a *genuine* English pub. In England.'

'But you don't *believe* in it, do you, Mike?'

He wasn't going to allow anyone to devalue his story.

'Depends what you mean by "messiah". A lot of blood and ink have been spilled to define the term, so it's a good bit clearer now. At least it's clear to me. A messiah isn't a bad thing, you know. It gives us a leader. And suppose we actually locate the genealogy and the reason it has been concealed. It makes her an ordinary person, *but* . . . a modern messiah.'

The Scotsman nearly choked on his beer. 'A messiah is just an ordinary person?'

'Just like you and me! Except, to the best of my knowledge, you and I lack the one thing which exists for Sara. A tree.'

'A tree?'

'A family tree. Breeding. Genealogy. Ancestors who seem to scare the hell out of the Establishment. And not just the Church of Rome. But Hitler, Napoleon, and other European monarchs, too. *If that drink is still on offer, I'll have one.* The whole conspiracy theory is wrapped in an enigma. If she's a fake, George, then who is behind a funded and futile fabrication? And if she's authentic, then who is supporting a conspiracy to conceal her claims and reduce her influence?'

Another round of drinks was served and an inebriated Scot counted small coins with a barman who was more familiar with French Francs.

'Yes, yes, of course, Mike. Your genealogy! You've got to believe in it because it's your story. I saw your TV documentary on it, *The Priest and the Painter* or something. It's a good story, Mike, but – you don't really believe it? You can confide in me. It's just personal curiosity.'

His eyes pleaded to Michael Leonard for the truth, and his Scottish accent exuded an earthy decency. Leonard nodded his head slowly and spoke with conviction.

'Every fibre in my body knows Sarah-Hélène of the Languedoc is genuine. Because the legends in these lands have resisted all attempts in history to suppress them. The effect of the genealogy and the secret known by the church can be traced through history, therefore it exists. It explains the family of Jesus posing a threat to Constantine in the fourth-century; it explains the royal blood in the veins of European monarchs; the Crusaders' claim over Jerusalem; and it explains many Vatican policies otherwise puzzling. It is the great unrecorded history, but like a hidden artery it is always there, in the background.

'And now the same can be said of the missing Gospel from the Dead Sea Scrolls collection. The bearer of the blood of the family of Christ. It is the Holy Grail. The power to rule the world. It is such a shock.

Contrary to all the teachers of the Church who said Jesus couldn't have been a real man. Now it seems he could fire on all six cylinders. Significant, I believe, that here in Marseilles where his child was allegedly born and raised that the people are the last of all in the world to reject my story. You may have noticed that here they aren't saying, 'Oh, that's just Pierre's little girl.' Amazing, don't you think? I'm going to ask Sara about that when I meet her tomorrow.'

The newspaper reporter laughed at Leonard, 'You're going to *see her*?'

'Unbelievers can't see the truth when it's right under their noses.'

37.5 Before he set off to meet Sara, Michael Leonard had another encounter. He had first met Ernest Mayorkas in Jerusalem. He was a well-spoken, multi-lingual, stocky, Swiss Jew whose short hair was going grey. Leonard had believed that they had spent a pleasant evening together by chance until their paths crossed for a second time, now in a hotel lobby in Marseilles. He was still jovial and still struggling with the same pipe.

Leonard called out, 'You should try a better brand of tobacco, my friend!' Mayorkas faked surprise and then admitted his interest in Leonard's knowledge of the treasures of Rennes-le-Château. Either he was pleasant, as he appeared, or he aimed to disarm with charm. They sat down at the hotel's bar.

Leonard kept things cool but friendly.

'So, my friend, we meet again. Are you Mossad or CIA?'

The laughter of Mayorkas was deep and from the belly.

He was too rich, too individualistic. Not a Company Man, so Leonard guessed.

'OK, you're a fortune hunter. Antiquities dealer? Ah, you seek the treasures? *An Israeli arms-dealer?* A Swiss banker. You're too clever to be a journalist, and far too rich. How many guesses do I get?'

He laughed deeper, 'You're getting very close, my friend.'

'You're a Government art-hunter of some sort?'

'Yes, yes, very close. We have never really taken the Temple Treasures very seriously until now.'

'We?'

He handed over a visiting card identifying himself as Consultant to the Israeli Antiquities Department.

'I told you that you were close so I comment unofficially, but helpfully, on your recent contact with our Immigration people concerning Sara's status. Civil Servants prefer uneventful lives free from mistakes and blame. On that basis they'll delay difficult decisions until Ministers or Secretaries ask them to pop upstairs for a few moments. Whatever he is playing at – and we do not know – Prime Minister Begin is very interested in the Copper Scroll from the Dead Sea. And as you know it is kept in Amman. He has suddenly changed everything for Sara. He has also brokered a deal with the rabbinic colleges so Sara will be recognised a Jewess on her terms. She will be a citizen but we would appreciate your co-operation.'

Leonard smiled. His caution turned to excitement. Once again, a government takes this conspiracy seriously. He hardly listened to the words of Mayorkas.

'Of course, my government isn't worried about her claiming sovereignty of Jerusalem. The Arabs are doing the same and Europe sent armies for centuries. If she wants to play religious politics in our country she'll find herself at home. We're a modern, democratic republic committed to consumerism within a war economy, but all of this combined with the highest *per capita* population of religious crazies from A to Zee. If she wants to play extremist religion she's in the right place.'

While Mayorkas lit his pipe Leonard asked.

'So why give her the rope? *To hang herself?'*

'Because we give the Vatican another reason for wishing they had opened direct diplomatic relations with us. I guess of all people they know that the mythic content rather than veracity is what moves hearts and minds. Michael, they haven't been this worried since Martin Luther, believe me. Eight copies of the Genealogy document you seek were found between 1947-1956. *Eight copies.* Now there's some inside information for you.'

Leonard tried to conceal his excitement but his beer was untouched.

'How did you manage to keep *that* secret?'

Mayorkas unfolded a sheet of paper taken from his pocket.

'Eighty percent or more of the Dead Seas Scrolls were bought on the black market. They are found by Arabs or Bedouin and sold in a game of cat and mouse. The State tried to pay the top prices but the effect was to encourage more middlemen and more delay. Secondly, old scrolls fade into illegibility and crumble into dust. Thirdly, we are overwhelmed with fakes and forgeries which can be sophisticated alterations to genuine articles. Hard to be sure about anything. Fourthly, we did not realise until now that the Copper Scroll was a cipher for a scroll we already possess in photographic plates. In return for your help I have another suggestion . . .'

Mayorkas was talking but Leonard was engrossed in the document in his hand. It was a receipt in Italian dated *l'undici settembre 1958* in which the Holy See acknowledged items 1 – 6. These were described as vellum scrolls, and items 7 and 8, which Leonard's knowledge of Latin indicated as two inscribed cylinders of copper. Each of the eight entries was described only as *genealogia*.

'Jesus!' Leonard exclaimed.

'Yes,' replied Mayorkas as he gently relieved Leonard of the facsimile and shook his head in response to the anticipated request for a copy. He locked it in his brief case from which he produced and pointed to a map of France.

'Let's adjourn to my bedroom, Mr Majorkas, where there is privacy. I'm staying here, as you probably know.'

They sat down beside a small desk. The map was unfolded. The light was poor. Leonard followed the speaker's pointing finger.

'If I were looking for the brother of Sarah-Hélène, I would send someone to this village, Mike. He might pose as an English holidaymaker with a wife and a small child. He has a modest hired car. Make it something French. He has taken the wrong road. He will be their guest. It is a traditional village. Make it late in the day so that they will be inclined to let him stay with him overnight. He will befriend them. Gain their trust. This man here was a university professor.'

Mayorkas flashed a photo of a man in his late sixties.

'His wife is now dead but his daughter was in the same class at school and knew your girlfriend well. She was called Helen MacRae in France from 1952 until she was moved in August 1958 from Italy to Scotland then her guardians renamed her Sarah Kelly; Sarah with a letter H. The prof has an amateur ciné film of the two girls at play together *circa* 1950.

Her first screen test, you might say. I've seen it myself. The Professor may be a victim or perpetrator of your conspiracy. You will have to judge for yourself. He claims that as a child, Sarah-Hélene spontaneously, went into trances, and spoke tongues which he identified as the old language of the region. And the professor says she poured out the quatrains of Nostradamus in torrents, which he thought was very strange for a young girl. Probably she was taught it, or it is a psychic phenomenon, I don't know which. I didn't used to believe in such things. But on the train from Zurich a few months ago I met a fortune-teller, and I don't know why I spoke to him. He told me things I did not know about myself. I had never seen him before. How could he do it? He asked for no money. What were his motives? To deceive me? Intelligence is used for two purposes, Michael, to inform your own side and disorientate the other. I thought maybe the fortune-teller was on the train to disorientate me, so I had him arrested. He was either genuine or very well-prepared.'

Leonard handed over his card and excused himself for a prior engagement.

Chapter Thirty-Eight

MARSEILLES INTERNATIONAL AIRPORT, October 8, 1978

The PanAm flight from New York was delayed by one hour.

Airports blur the truth. It meant at least one hour. Michael Leonard drifted to the newspaper stand where his attention was captured by a headline. The Conference on the Turin Shroud had been presented with a scientific paper. Various international newspapers reported the discovery of pollen proving that the cloth had originated from, or once had been in, Jerusalem. Leonard became aware of stares from the staff who felt that his browsing was unlikely to lead to a purchase. They were wrong. On the book shelves he found some copies of *Le Trésor Maudit* by Gérard de Sède and a book on The Dead Sea Scrolls. He filed the cashier's receipt in his wallet.

As Leonard killed time in International Arrivals, he examined his motives. He considered his previous income as a slender means to the unmasking of the puppeteers. He persuaded himself that he was merely pretending to be duped by them, but who was 'them?' Now that the Israelis had emerged as part of the puzzle, he realised that the jigsaw had too many pieces which did not fit comfortably.

Were the Israelis conspirators or investigators?

In his mind, Leonard tore up his Publisher's Proposal for a sequel. His first book, *The Aquarius Conspiracy,* was based on a false premise. *How to keep faith with his readers without admitting his mistake?* If the genealogy was authentic and troubled its possessors then the true conspiracy was in their silence and secrecy. The premise of his book was that Sara was false. *But was she?*

From the lounge he watched her American plane land seventy five minutes late. A lot of journalists and photographers waited for Sara.

A skeletal Gothic grunge girl caught Leonard's eyes; but she gauged the situation and looked away. She had spiky green and red hair. Under his breath he laughed and swore profanities as he had to glance again at her long-green stockings. She seemed so thin. And how had she made her skin so white? Her genius was the bizarre behaviour. Aware that the journalists were expecting a woman trying to conceal herself this one was drawing attention to herself. Asking the crowd in a Cockney accent, mocking his, if they could spare a copper for a drink.

Leonard watched her enter the ladies toilet and waited for a long time. Presumably she was removing her disguise – but why should she do so? And *how* did she do it without her suitcase? Four women left the toilet then Leonard crossed two illegal boundaries; into Overseas Arrivals, and into the ladies toilet. A voice emerged from a cubicle. It's door flew wide open.

'Thought you'd never fetch me,' the androgenous pale-faced female said in Sara's husky voice as she kissed his cheek, 'Did *you* inform the newspapers I was coming?'

'Why are you hiding?'

'Michael, I was warned that they will arrest me at the airport so I must avoid the Passport Control and I must leave my suitcase in the airport.'

Although this was really her homecoming she told him that touching the soil had not caused the same emotions she had experienced in Israel and this 747 wide-body jet did not metamorphose into a World War II fighter bomber.

'Eh, darling, save your autobiography until later,' Leonard interrupted, 'I am not enjoying being in the ladies toilet of International Arrivals Marseilles and I wonder if you could disclose the next step in your plan.'

'It is relatively easy to smuggle drugs through this airport by escaping through that cleaner's office, there,' she assured him.

He followed her. She pointed to a frosted glass window which she swung open and Leonard followed her onto the runway. He wondered whether it was ordained or fortuitous that they were met by a passenger bus and they merged with passengers leaving a flight.

On the bus she acted like his twenty-year-old daughter or secretary. To her it was a joke. He acted the part until she embraced him extremely passionately. Leonard felt awkward. She was queen of the world but he chastised her. She dressed like a woman refusing to grow up. She clung to him and embraced his mouth.

'Don't worry, this is France,' she said. 'The home of French kissing.'

'It's just that we don't want to attract attention.' He whispered but he was perspiring.

He drove her to the hotel and they waited for her suitcase, which she had complained had been lost. Before it arrived she borrowed Leonard's money and bought new clothes. To avoid the journalists they moved to another hotel.

By the evening Sara said she felt relaxed and happy to be back in the south of France away from the pressures that formed USA or Israel. She said she loved thinking in French which she called a civilised language, restoring genders to words, reliving memories of her past. Above all, she longed to see Paul and she told Leonard that they would find him.

He suggested they might meet an actor who got the part. *The best way to predict the future is to control it.*

She stared at him. He reassured her ambiguously that they were both seeking the truth.

'But you still don't believe me; so you do not love me.'

He changed the subject. As he drove her to a restaurant he asked her about her ability to speak the ancient language. She replied with great sadness that she could no longer speak it.

'Try it,' he urged, 'Just to please me.'

'Later,' she promised.

When they reached the city and discussed dinner she was in a strange mood which he suspected was chemically induced. Perhaps she *had* smuggled something through the airport; if so he admired her nerve.

'Din moun pois lous omès bous aïmoun è soun fidèls!'

Before he could ask her to translate, her face was flushed with tears.

'What does it mean?' Leonard asked.

She sobbed, 'You might understand . . . the words . . . but not the meaning. It is a sacred language. Does not translate into a lower tongue.'

'Say it slowly and let me write it, please.' Then he ordered harshly, '*Say it*.'

'Take me home, now, Michael.'

'We'll only go to the restaurant when you recover your composure. You'll be okay in a few minutes. Now write it down and tell me what it means.'

'Take me home.'

Leonard slammed on the brakes and made a U-turn, forcing drivers to avoid him.

'Michael, it means . . . like Jesus said, no-one gets to . . . Heaven . . . without first becoming as a little child. We moderns are in a cinema and we are content to watch the screen but we sit in darkness.'

'No, sweetie, I think it means, 'In my . . . something . . . men . . . something . . . faithful'.'

'You do not participate, you dream, Michael. You are sophisticated but you don't comprehend thoughts. You process words. You crucify Christ every day. *You are part of the conspiracy*. He neglected the poor. Said they would always be with us. Well, I have decided that as I am different I must . . . *participate*. Do you understand? I want you to understand. Every day I change a bit and I am the prototype for humanity. Perhaps you think that I sound conceited? Yet I ate from the Tree of Knowledge of Good and Evil. Do you know what that means? It means the opposite of psychopathy. It means conscience and compassion.'

38.1 After a dinner she described as the best food she had eaten since leaving France they took a taxi. Leonard was drunk but reminded her that they were here to find Paul. He asked if her mood was *drugs or what?*

Post-WXQR, she said, she was *in the world but not of it*.

'I am blind to the machinations of man and you must be my guide through the minefield you must call the real world.'

38.2 When they arrived back at the hotel she went to bed with a headache. Leonard had a letter from a local historian who had waited until 10pm and then left some books on the churches and statues of Marie Magdalene in this region.

The concierge had handed Leonard a second message. His London office had received urgent information, a letter from a viewer who had seen the TV film. The writer knew that a certain library had a copy of the genealogy of the House of David updated to 1939, thus excluding only Sarah-Hélène. The institution was unaware of the document in its own possession, yet it was accessible to the public. *Please reply by advertisement in The Times.*

'No mention of a brother, sweetie,' Leonard pointed out, 'and no contact information either. What's the difference between a tease and a crank?'

Leonard returned to London and placed a classified advert requesting further proof: 'Journalist seeks genealogist to assist his inquiries. Please state terms.'

The single response sent to the Times Box Number was a post-card on which was typed.

> 'Paul was the son of Pierre Plantard and Mathilde Stefanie MacRae, born December 27, 1942, 04.12am, Narbonne. Messiah. Nine parts from the House of Light.'

Leonard turned the card and read the handwriting in a light blue-grey ink:

> *Be patient. I will call you. Yours sincerely, Jacques Pascal.*

The investigator was so excited that he punched the air.

Leonard woke the next day, depressed, wondering why he had felt so sure that the response to his ad was genuine. Perhaps the conspirators were providing him with saleable material for public consumption but diverting him from something real, and bigger.

By phone Sara insisted that, whoever Paul was until 1952, and wherever he was now, her brother had really existed until the French government said – or pretended – otherwise. There was a click and the phone line became distorted and feint. Leonard could not think of anything to mislead whoever listened in the background because he could not work out their identity or motivation.

38.3 Ten days later Leonard returned to Marseilles. He drove Sara to the house of Henri Duval, his researcher in Paris. She watched him filing press cuttings about François Mitterrand, Freemasons, and secret societies, before she saw a school photograph with the face of an effeminate boy aged around fifteen circled in ink. She stared at it. *They were testing her. It was Paul.*

Leonard observed Sara's response. She just looked at it for a long time until his attention turned to a large brown envelope.

Drinking coffee in the balcony of his study overlooking a river, Henri showed them a clue which seemed much less exciting. Leonard flicked through *Les Prophéties de la Mer Morte* – a pamphlet written about the prophecies of the Dead Sea Scrolls. The facts seemed common knowledge. The Essenes had established a community in the remote desert on the northwest edge of the Dead Sea where they had written and stored scriptural books. After two thousand years the land – subsequently named Qumran by nomads – was nothing but an arid archaeological site in the Judean Wilderness.

Underlined in pencil, the pamphlet continued, 'However in the time of the Book of Joshua it was settled and thus, it must have had a name. It was probably the place rendered variously in different translations of the Bible as Irmelach, or *the City of the Salt Lake*.'

Leonard read aloud to Sara.

'"Whose modern successors," declares this French pamphlet, "have always maintained with scrupulous care all records of places, peoples, and generations of the world". D'you gettit, honey?'

Much to his surprise, she grasped the significance of the Salt Lake City.

'*The Mormons*. The Church of Latter Day Saints. To save all souls in the world they maintain vast ledgers of the world population as alternatives to the governments' and possibly more accurate.'

Sara could not let go of the school photo of her brother. She did not break down.

'Look, Mike, that is a teacher. An Asian, and Paul became a Buddhist. I recognise the place. It is the Buddhist centre near St. Sulpice, the Catholic seminary. There was a healthy rivalry between us. We called each other 'the enemy'. This is about 1957. Let's go there, Mike.'

Michael Leonard started to learn all he could about French Buddhists. He impressed Sara with their saying, 'Those who know do not speak; those who speak do not know.'

With Sara and Henri, Leonard spent two days visiting Buddhist centres but they contributed no information. Their philosophy of personal identity was anonymity, equality, and the acceptance of things. Why should they allow him to trouble one of their monks about his past life?

A slim man dressed in orange said, 'You ask where he is, Mr Leonard, but we wonder *who* he is. The soul has its centre nowhere and everywhere. I accept that he was at this school if you say so.'

Leonard turned to Sara and joked offensively, 'He probably got expelled like you, Babe.'

She turned away from Leonard and pleaded in fluent French.

'Master, please help me. I have no reason to enquire who he is. He is, in this life, my blood brother. He is descended from the sovereign house of David of the Judeans. We think that people of lower enlightenment abducted him and are concealing his identity from him for selfish reasons. I believe that he is ill-at-ease now.'

The Buddhist monk formed a rooftop with his fingers and asked Sara to contact him again.

Michael Leonard had another path to follow. Once again, his work was on the other side of the Atlantic. She travelled with him.

Chapter Thirty-Nine

SALT LAKE CITY, UTAH, NOVEMBER 1978

Sara and Michael were met at the airport by Carsten Wolff and Edgar Larsen of The Church of Jesus Christ of Latter Day Saints. Their leaders had agreed to open their global register of births and deaths. Leonard, who never believed in free lunches, asked them about their view on the Second Coming. They admitted that they were keen to see Sara.

They couldn't take their eyes off her.

Larsen, a tall blond Scandinavian man, was clearly overawed and nervous for ten minutes. Even Wolff, a brooding, intellectual German, spoke too much to conceal his nervous excitement. He was excessively courteous, smothering Sara by anticipating her smallest needs. He addressed her as 'Your Holiness' and she did not bat an eyelid. Larsen adhered to his church's policy and showed respect but no acceptance of her rank.

The Mormon clerks told Leonard that their demographic records were compiled with scrupulous care and could be relied upon. They recorded the souls of all men and women who lived, however briefly, because each one needed salvation. Each person was ticked off after accepting Jesus in this life or after his or her demise.

Without digressing to challenge posthumous conversion, Leonard discussed the problem of the forged French records before 1945 and promised that he would credit the source of any genealogical information they provided. Sara followed him into a room decorated with flowers. She was served soft drinks – not chilled tins but a delicious home brew with real fruit adorned around a silver jug. The Mormons were excellent hosts, courteous and attentive. The chief clerk answered everything Leonard asked.

From 1939-45 the Church's record-keeping was stepped up to meet the chaos of millions of refugees, missing soldiers, and displaced persons – not to mention the tragic scale of death and disappearance. The Mormon registrars claimed that they had access to wartime and post-war charitable and government agencies in respect of many occupied European nations, including the south of France. Then Michael and Sara were invited to noon prayers; clearly their visit was on a strict timetable. At 1pm a collegial luncheon took place in the main Dining Hall and Sara was the object of curiosity and veneration. Leonard asked if the Church had discussed her status but no clear response was given.

After lunch, in a reading room, the Mormons handed Leonard a file which said that the French documents had been altered *more than once*. The Church registrars had conducted their own research. They found that 'Sara' must have been conceived no later than 20 November 1944 as the war had separated her parents. In anticipation of the German occupation her identity was switched to the daughter of her uncle, Pierre Plantard, and Lisa MacRae. A birth in Scotland was probably invented to explain later clerical documentation which emerged as false. The family and a few others knew the truth. Sara shook her head vigorously especially when they produced the entries of her *cousin*, Paul, born in August 31, 1942.

Sara said to the clerk, calmly but firmly, 'The conspirators saw you coming. They have sown more weeds in this field.'

The disappointment in the integrity of their records was palpable but they were prepared to admit that perhaps they had been misinformed. They discussed it with a numbers of clerks. The presence of Sara was causing rapid rethinking behind the scenes and on the hoof. People were coming and going from the reading room; the those round the table were being replaced.

Leonard announced, 'Gentlemen, we all get fooled. I can show you that the Grail societies are aided and abetted by the highest people in the west including inner circles of the French Government who are responsible for deluding this woman and the world. They control the international police through Masonic networks. Do you really believe that Dr Kohen's radio fraud adds to the Holy Scriptures?'

'Why do you still debase her claim, Mr Leonard?' One of the Mormons suggested, 'Surely it is your opinion, after much research – and we respect your diligence – that the Holy Family *did* come to Marseilles and survived to this day. You have stated you have evidence that the Genealogy exists although you have not seen it. But now you imply that the conspiracy is setting up Sara – not in *concealing* her. From this morning, do you now think that she is *not* of the family which constitutes the subject of your research?'

'No,' Leonard replied immediately, 'I see so much manipulation in the shady background that it makes me very cautious for there is a serious agenda. This is my interpretation. If Sara is of the line, so be it. But the messiah status is today invalid, past its sell-by date. *Monarchies disappear permanently.*'

He paused for his insight to be absorbed but the interval invited an equally impassioned response.

'Unless one trusts the Bible, Mr Leonard,' a male voice behind stated firmly. 'The Judeans wanted a sovereign. One Samuel chapter eight. When Saul was deposed, David was anointed and God promised that his seed would reign in eternity; Genesis 49:10; 2 Samuel 22:51; 1 Chronicles 17:14; Psalms of David, sample the eighteenth; Isaiah 9:6; Micah fourth chapter . . .'

Leonard nodded agreement without enthusiasm and suggested, 'So you think that she may be accepted as the Queen of Israel and the Head of the Church of Rome?'

Larsen pointed out that Jesus wasn't accepted either.

There was a long silence.

Sara said, 'The ocean refuses no river. Anyone may speak.'

Larsen said to Sara, 'Thank you, but I don't even know how to address you with proper respect.'

She said '*Sara!* I've had three names already. I'm not changing again!'

This cleared the atmosphere with laughter which somehow made Larsen's next statement credible.

'Am I the only one who can see your aura? I have never before seen anything so beautiful.'

The Mormons strained and peered to see it but Leonard remained silent; he knew that he had seen it himself once before. Edgar was sweating profusely and his face was red. He described the colours of the aura in detail. Most present agreed with Wolff's contention (as if they were qualified physicists) that it might be an objective truth because Edgar's sight might have a physical sensitivity compared with 'normal'. Apparently human colour vision was still evolving rapidly. Our ancestors were relatively colour blind. *Perhaps Larsen was a mutant!* They laughed.

They summoned others and Polaroid photographs were taken. The rainbow aura showed up in several photos but the Mormons declined to give any prints to Leonard.

They were still discussing the Church ruling on the status of Sara as she and Michael were leaving their compound on a helicopter.

Chapter Forty

MARSEILLES, NOVEMBER 1978

Flying back to France, Michael Leonard woke up with a start. The female flight attendant offered him a choice of tea or coffee. Drowsily he foolishly replied *either* and waved her on.

Ivor S. Kaplan! The signature had appeared on a banker's cheque dated 1952 from The Prieuré de Sion to Leumi Bank Jerusalem to purchase Dead Sea Scrolls from T'amirah tribesmen. Today Mr Kaplan was the designated Secretary-General of the Sanhedrin to be restored one day by Robert Kohen's Essenes.

Leonard spent an hour reading and summarising information he had received from the Mormons. He thought about a copywriter to flesh it out into a saleable story or a chapter of a future book.

Leonard's plane landed on time in Marseilles. After meeting Sara for lunch they returned to his hotel bedroom. He started to tell her about Ivor Kaplan but there was a hand-written note on the table. A telephone message from his London office. Sara was struggling to understand why the lock on the door 172 was not opened by the key number 172. He read the message out to her: *"Boss, I am close to a man who looks like he is Paul. He is reported to be visiting Los Angeles for five days. Gone to lunch with a cutie. Pray that she loves me. Peter."*

Wide-eyed, Sara watched as Leonard grabbed the bedside telephone.

'Hello, it's me, Lindy, where's Pete? *Out to lunch?* Oh, London's an hour behind us? Find him quickly. So now we're at the whim of some girl who has sent our Peter off into the land of romantic dreams. He *must* phone me within thirty minutes. *See to it.'*

He slammed down the phone.

'Michael Leonard, you're an impatient man with so little perspective on life,' said Sara.

'I love you too, sweetheart. Do you want to lose track of Paul? The little guy only gets off with it because he has a golden touch and a lot of luck. Listen, if Paul is visiting LA for a few days, it means that we have no time to lose if Bartlett is right. Back to America. If you are messiah, honey, can we please rent a Concorde?'

'Mike, we shall find Paul regardless, because it is written.'

'We seem to have lost Peter.'

At 4:50pm came the knock on the door of Room 172 which Leonard opened.

'*Peter!* Where the hell have you been?'

'Heathrow airport and on a plane to Marseilles to meet you. And not alone. *Meet Estelle.* We met in London but she lives here. She can help us. If it's okay with you, boss, I'll pay for her ticket. Even if I've really found your brother, Miss Sara. *Hi!* Pardon me, how do you do? I'm really pleased to meet you for the first time. This is Estelle, she's French. You French are just gorgeous girls! Estelle, meet Sara.'

'Peter, *about Paul.*' Leonard barked out furiously yet it still sounded so biblical.

'Yes boss, I know. I'm over the moon. I nearly decided to become a Buddhist but my conceit is . . .'

'Peter, I've told you before I'm freelance. I'm paying for your time. Now get to the point.'

'Yes, sir, boss. I happened to go back to visit *Les Amis des Boudhisme de l'Ouest* and spoke to a Danish monk called Rasmussen who has created the exhibit for this year's *World Faiths Conference* in LA. He speaks good English and he knew a monk who quit in 1971 and reverted to calling himself Paul. Then he was thirty, the age the Buddha was enlightened. Paul got unenlightened. Paul trained in St Sulpice. Mr Rasmussen is good, boss, I checked him out. We're on a fresh trail. Paul's in LA. I'll put my month's salary on it.'

Estelle smiled lovingly and squeezed the hand of her grinning hero.

Michael looked at Sara to exchange glances but tears were racing down both sides of her nose. Bartlett sat on the bed and continued more quietly, 'I checked with the tourist office, boss. In LA there *is* a conference running for four days and today is the second day. How many tickets to LA do you want me to book?'

'If you can leave Estelle at home in France for a few days and come with us, three tickets, Peter, on the first flight. You can phone the BBC's travel agents in Paris, put it onto their account. I want to speak to Sara privately then we'll meet you in the lobby with our cases packed.'

Peter flew out the door, but returned after a few seconds.

'Return tickets?'

Sara instructed him to purchase four return tickets on full-schedule fare, 'just in case we need to change our plans. I'll pay for them all, Michael. And Estelle wants to come. *You can accompany us, cherie.*'

Michael looked at Sara with astonishment, 'Did you find the Temple Treasures?'

Sara smiled knowingly but without uttering a word of denial.

Despite the time difference Leonard rang a friend in Los Angeles to confirm the existence of the Symposium; then he telephoned the Dawson Conference Center. A recording announced that this symposium was held each year and was aimed (Leonard switched on the loudspeaker) *'to showcase the world's religions to the New Age. Admittance is $4, children under ten, up to two per adult, free. Closes this year on Tuesday evening at 7pm. Dates to be announced for next year. Attendance up on 1977 by 16%.'*

Sara packed the suitcases just in time for collection by the porter who received the last of Leonard's French coinage.

40.1 The flight seemed to drag but Sara was very excited. An elderly purple-haired American lady recognised her.

'Gee, you're the Daughter of Israel. I've been reading the first instalment of your authorised biography in *The Post.*'

Sara gasped at the idea of an authorised biography. She glanced at Michael. He shrugged his shoulders and quipped, 'I'm too late then?'

Leonard suggested that Sara would cause chaos in a conference of people who were spiritual seekers. He persuaded her to let him seek Paul unhindered by the sensation they would attract if she insisted on making an appearance. She said *'yes'* but her tone said no.

She returned from the toilet groomed but she sat beside Peter Bartlett. Estelle sat beside Leonard who reacted very little to her cultivation of the boyfriend's boss. He felt uncomfortable. He looked at everyone and everyone looked at him. Was it Estelle? Who was she? Could she be trusted? And Who *was he* now? Journalist or messianic consort? Up there in the sky, the closest to God that he would get! Suppose the Mormon fellow was right and he just couldn't see the halo? What else was he missing?

As they prepared to land Leonard overheard Sara who was telling Peter how to win the love of Estelle. *Whose side was she on?*

'Peter,' his boss interrupted, 'a word in your shell. You're here to work; you're not on a holiday with Estelle. You must find Paul. I must accompany Sara around the show if she *insists* on attending it.'

He responded with a detached 'Yes, Boss,' but turned back to listen to Sara.

If we find Paul, Leonard thought, Sara might 'only' be the messiah's sister. Or cousin. *Perhaps then we could marry.'*

To win the love of Estelle, Sara was telling Peter, he must appear before her with an equally beautiful female as a threat to her, and keep the company of handsome male companions to establish his status. 'Make her feel special. And pay no attention to any other female. Speak of no other woman in your past. Be very sensitive to the way her moods change. Touch her at the right times only and just as she likes it.'

As a mere Englishman Michael listened carefully to the art of seduction and feared for his own prospects. But she was speaking just loudly enough to enable him to hear every word.

Chapter Forty-One

LOS ANGELES, NOVEMBER 1978

Using Sara's credit card Leonard reserved four single rooms at a hotel close to the 1978 Convention of World Faiths. On the coach Peter Bartlett turned to his employer. 'Chief, we need to fill the gap of Sara's time in Haight-Ashbury and for sure many New Agers will be found here. You need to speculate to accumulate. I want to marry Estelle. I want to earn serious cash. You give me a budget and I'll find hippies to sing. You said one day we would be in partnership. I like Sara and she's really nice to me. But she's a professional messiah and I'm a professional reporter.'

'I'm impressed, young man. What is your plan?'

'We have a fight, Chief, and you fire me when Sara discovers that I'm digging up her past. Of course I'm still working for you, but free-lance. I'm sure we can come to terms.'

41.1 Just as Michael Leonard had feared, the appearance of 'Stella Invicta' at the 1978 Convention of World Faiths created a sensation that impeded the pursuit of her brother. The Dawson Convention Center was an old building. On the outside it was a combination of redbrick and red sandstone with ornate windows and iron gates. Inside the main hall was a large expanse over a plain concrete floor with a glazed suspension roof.

Thanks to the broadcasts Americans flew to Los Angeles and others set out to drive to see the 'Modern Messiah.'

They arrived in cars and coaches despite the warning that the roads around the Dawson Center had been cordoned. For some reason Sara attracted hooligans who wanted to cause trouble. The local police promised to send for the National Guard if Sara and Michael felt threatened.

The crowds escalated. By the time the main doors were closed at noon he stood bravely by the side of his lady. He was ordering various people around although all that was being protected was his self-esteem. He pointed out that if one loose cannon desired disaster the decorative doors would be unhinged and they would be engulfed in rage. High-moral ground Christians incited ruffians who threw stones. One side mocked her as 'The Moonlit Messiah' as the other screamed, 'The Whore of Babylon' until at 2:00pm they were silenced and dispersed, not by civil forces, but by New Age bikers. Sara, Michael, and the others now felt safe enough to emerge from the building.

Two of the bikers somehow came from the back doors and told Sara that they had arranged a Press Conference on the Second Coming at a hotel five minutes drive away. The Hotel California was mobbed. Three bikers whisked off their saviour who dragged Michael through a laundry to a waiting truck. She assured Michael, 'It's OK,' as leather-clad hippies concealed them in laundry baskets and they escaped from the besieged hotel to the side entrance of another building.

Walking through employee corridors into the lobby, Michael, Sara, and her secretary were asked to wait for an hour in an opulent bedroom suite. Sara was protected and treated like royalty. When the time passed the bikers escorted her to the ballroom and the waiting Press. As she walked to the top table one of them immediately asked her if she used Jesus as a rôle model. She swept her outstretched arms from her hips to form a cross; from one hand her bracelet dangled; her breasts erotically displayed the Chanel logo embroidered across the skimpy pink tee shirt. Cameras flashed. She pulled an absurd smile and said, 'Not a rôle model, *I am a real model.*'

Bringing order to the cacophony of questions, Leonard assumed the chair and pointed to journalists one at a time. *Are you the Second Coming?* What is your authority? *Show us a sign.*

She smiled.

'Do you want me to turn this dead microphone into a living serpent, or do you want me to turn a reporter into a human being?'

* * *

41.2 On the next day more media and celebrity interviewers arrived. Microphones, cameras, and satellite dishes sprouted everywhere and the Convention Center was inundated by people pushing to kiss the garments of the Daughter of God. (Leonard had persuaded her to dress more decently). Because of death threats the National Guard arrived but someone told her secretary that the Eagles had come to protect her and she should keep the Pigs away in case they had been ordered to kill her.

'The Eagles?' asked Leonard.

Sara explained, 'They're the bikers, friends of mine from Haight-Ashbury. And now they come to save the saviour.'

He let this go on the assumption that it was a joke.

Apparently this network was the organiser of the second publicity conference with some of America's most celebrated TV presenters. In the Lesser Hall of the Dawson Center Leonard was visibly upset when Sara turned the Press interview into her search for Paul. She had leaked the story he was working on into the public domain.

'I have come here to find Paul, my elder brother, whom I have not seen since we were separated by the Catholic Adoption Agency of Paris. Someone saw him two days ago while I was searching for him in the south of France where we grew up. Paul became a Buddhist Priest near St Sulpice and of course I love him very much. I hope that he wants to see me although I realise that he might desire to get on with his own life. But I love him and to me it means everything because we don't have our parents any more. So if anyone knows where Paul is, will they please . . .'

All eyes and cameras turned from Sara to celebrities who eclipsed her. The crowd parted as the Red Sea did for Moses. It was not Moses but someone more important who walked towards her.

'LITTLE DANNY RAYMOND . . .' a voice boomed through the loud-speakers to inform those who were jostling but could not see, '. . . AND THE RAYMONDS.'

Three glamorous girls followed. Slim, long-legged, clad in clinging, glittering, white tops and opalescent stockings. Stylised negrettes of Tinseltown. Leonard saw their skins were lightened and their hair straightened to conform to the American dream, market surveys, or their own self-esteem. They walked with confidence towards Sara. The eldest and tallest one spoke first in a stiff, southern dialect.

'Daughter of God, we're so honoured to meet you, beyond words I'm sure. I am Mary-Anne Raymond. These are my sisters. Anything we can do for you, we would be honoured. If you need somewhere peaceful to crash out, our home is your home. Any donations to your church, or any help whatsoever, I assure you of our love and loyalty forever and ever. Amen. Amen. We are so happy that the Lord chose our day and our country which is so much in need of His Presence. And now we are so proud of our gender that God has chosen to be the sister and partner of Jesus Christ. Amen. Amen.'

A small bespectacled man with light-brown hair and a large forehead which was wrinkled and freckled said, 'Mary-Anne, I always told you that we would live to see the Second Coming.'

Sara announced, 'America is democracy and freedom yet the people are ignored and no-one is free. This isn't a Christian country. It is ruled by a President, by business, by politics, but not by Christ!'

Mary-Anne turned to Sara, 'This is our bishop who wants to meet you to receive your blessings. He is a very good man and has worked very hard to spread the Gospel, but he always told us you was going to come.'

'The bishop' looked like an accountant. Alert blue eyes sparkled behind gold-rimmed glasses. He was demure, reticent, and spoke in a quiet, soft, almost feminine tone.

'I'm Bishop Hugh Brown, Your Divine Holiness, My Lady, I'm Sixth Bishop of the New England Church of Jesus Christ. You sure aren't what we were expecting, but we had no trouble in recognising you as the Divine Daughter . . . You'll have to forgive me . . . for sobbing, it's just coming over me and it takes time to . . . thank the Lord . . . for answering our prayers.'

In front of the cameras he broke down completely and knelt before her. Sara was perfectly composed. She held out her arms then grasped his shoulders as he knelt before her. She gathered the man's head to her bosom. As he was swaying two of the Raymond girls supported him. Sara kissed his forehead and whispered into his ears. She opened her jacket and loosened buttons of her blouse. Very reticently he placed his hands on her breasts which were discreetly bared to him but concealed to others by her jacket. You could hear a pin drop despite the large hall having been in chaos moments before.

Leonard felt a flicker of anger.

Sara rested her hands on Bishop Brown's head in Indian devotional style, palms together, pointing to heaven in prayer. There was continued silence . . . no exception. Not one member of the press broke ranks to ask a question. Even the hostile protesters were silenced. Not a biker whistled but then a woman screamed, 'Whore of Babylon.'

Mary-Anne stepped forward and buttoned Sara's blouse.

Sara released their bishop and two of the Raymond sisters accompanied him as he trembled and wept aloud, stumbling away like a healed cripple. The atmosphere could be cut with a knife. One thousand people had been silenced by her stunt.

Sara turned to the crowds and said with tears cascading down her own cheeks, 'America is a democracy but the citizen does not count. America is free but the citizen is chained. America is Christian but has forsaken the law of God. We have all been alone in dark Hell. Deprived of love for so long that we forget what it is to live in the emotions. You see, this man is not ashamed to show his feelings. He has the wisdom of a seeker and the honesty of a child, just what Jesus told us we must recover. Be wise as serpents, innocent as doves. But you are ashamed and whose fault is it that we are so hard of heart?' And turning to Bishop Brown she called to him.

'Sir, I will come to your church with joy if you will invite me. I fear that many others who call themselves Christians will not welcome the surviving daughter of the Holy Family. They will be wise as serpents and I will hear them say in secret, "She may want to change our rules," – "She may disapprove of our leaders" – "Did she not enter the building of our enemies?" – "Therefore she is no friend of ours," and so on. This is what the world calls wisdom but I tell you, beware, because it is seen otherwise in God's eyes.'

As she launched into her sermon Sara's raised voice became firm and resonant, bouncing around the glass roof and all corners of the Hall.

'The great are poor in spirit if they mislead others. The Daughter of Man will travel wherever She is asked to go and She will spread the Word where She is welcome. The time has come for Satan to be leashed.

Humans can no longer hide their evil under cloak of darkness. The kingdom of heaven is a reality.'

'Oh, yes, do please come to our church,' the Raymonds and their entourage pleaded, hoping she would raise their stock. 'We meet on Sundays at 9:30am and 12:30pm . . . and the children's' groups in the afternoons of Tuesdays and Thursdays. You can stay at our mansion. You know we have eight church houses here in California alone.'

From thirty feet distance Peter Bartlett tried to alert Leonard who was engulfed by the crowd. He had noticed two men who were waiting to see The Daughter. The elder and more formally dressed of the two men handed over his card and Leonard indicated that Sara was available.

> Rabbi Lionel Bleustein,
> Minister,
> San Francisco New Community Synagogue

Here was the company rep from mainstream American Judaism. The religious organisations were divided and ignited in controversy following the Daughter's broadcast on Radio WXQR. Fifty five percent of a polled sample believed that it had been a hoax. Of the sizable minority some thought that Sara had been anointed; while others thought that The Teacher had denounced her.

While Rabbi Bleustein engaged Sara in conversation the second man became agitated and refused to wait. Losing all patience the intruder pushed aside the Rabbi whom he copied by handing Leonard a card; it delayed him from protecting Sara.

She seemed mildly shocked to see him.

Leonard glanced at his card before he too recognised the second man.

> Dr Jeremy Jesus-Leviticus
> WRITER – LECTURER – BROADCASTER
> IN PSYCHOPHARMACOLOGY

41.3 He resembled most people's image of the devil. 'Dr Jesus-Leviticus,' as he now called himself, was tall, slim and dark; but not handsome. He wore black clothes to match a small, tapered, black beard. His cruel and piercing eyes were laser-sharp. Sara continued to react as if she had known him before. Leonard became over-protective and was ignored. The professional broadcaster bellowed towards the cameras and microphones in a clear diction heavily accented like the Film Director known as Woody Allen.

'Hi! I'm Dr. Jeremiah Jesus-Leviticus, the real enemy of Christianity and all scripture-religion. I welcome the opportunity to confront this new fake in a TV encounter. That's how things are settled these days in the USA, on TV. It's to be a duel by media confrontation. As she's a trained actress she has the advantage but I have truth and progress on my side. I am here to save mankind from the abyss of superstition and priesthood.'

Turning to Sara, he declared, 'You will meet opposition from other religions, Daughter of God, but the point is that *religion itself is the conspiracy.*'

He turned to the packed hall. There was a security danger in provoking such an assembly but the atmosphere was receptive and peaceful. People were listening.

'This woman is well-known to me. Her thing is an opiate for the masses,' Jesus-Leviticus bellowed towards the cameras, 'It's a French government-sponsored conspiracy. Some Catholic Priests cooked it up in 1947-48 as they saw the Second War leaving a vacuum of secular values. I can tell you, she is a genuine medium and an actress well-cast.'

He turned to the woman, 'If you can prove you're real, dear girl, you will have upset the progress of the 20th-century. You will have rechained humanity to the jealous old Lawgiver of the Hebrews . . . the successor of his Son, the Baptist's rival, slave to Moses the Lawgiver, reincarnation of Elijah the Prophet.'

Performing to the cameras he waved theatrically.

'Because. *Because* . . . Because, Sélène, you are an epigone and an amusement to all progressives, half-seen, half-imagined. You are the re-appearance of Gaia and Astarte who long preceded the male gods and should not survive in America's Aquarian Age. You are the enemy to all who lead us on the path of the liberation of Man.'

The New Age rebel paused for an audience reaction; there was nothing but at least there was no hostility.

'The great prophet – and I am unfit to untie his sandals – is John. John Allegro, the greatest philosopher of our age, the impious priest, the phenomenal philologist, the peoples' populariser, the only one of the International Committee of the Dead Sea Scrolls who did not report direct to the Sky God. He was the only savant who was free of indoctrination and thus he fought alone to translate the texts and publish them without deviation or delay.

Jesus-Leviticus held a paperback book up to the cameras.

'This is *the real Gospel of John*, liberation from the chains of Mid-East monotheism. Pilate was right: there is no truth, but *there are lies*. Lies and myths cannot be resurrected in the age of decline of the corrupt church. It is a $5.99 bestseller already replicated in millions of time capsules, seeds, a few of which will fall on fertile ground. An open mind. *Gnosis*. Revelation! The book was hated because it reveals exactly how Jesus, Moses, and God were dreamed up under induced trances. Think about that! Starting a Christianity today would be wholly illegal in the USA. And no more real than this woman here, the latest Judaic-Christian counterfeit dreamer acting a part. Yes, the Bible is the product of drug culture. Archetypes dreamed up by Egyptian, Persian, and Hebrew priests under hallucinogenic trance from the holy mushroom, *Amanita Muscaria*. Then in the 13th-century the Cardinals had uniforms, joined Satan and dressed up as bogeymen to frighten the people into submission. The clergy had ceased to ingest mushrooms by the second century. Satan was created in the image of the Catholic priests after they drank too much wine. Truly, the blood of Christ, they said.'

He paused to induce a flicker of laughter then gulped air and flaunted the rapt silence that his performance had achieved. You could hear his chewing gum pass from one molar to another.

'Will someone get me a glass of pure water?'

He was silent. The audience was stirred, exchanging arguments and comments hostile to 'Jeremiah Jesus-Leviticus' but somehow captivated by him.

He turned towards Sara but addressed the crowd.

'So you have been sent to play your part on the Stage of Life. But by whom, sweet Sara? Name your leader! State your substance! This is what we all want to know. Why were you sent? To preach politics? Protestant work ethic? Papist world domination? The West is Best? France is the seat of Christian civilisation? This man beside you, the English newspaperman, has become strangely silent. He knows it all, but will he say? Have you also silenced him with your lovely titties, you sexy Temple Whore? Robert Kohen knows me, but does anyone know *him*? Well, Mr Leonard, I suggest you should expose his media connections, unless you are a part of them.'

41.4 People began to disperse and the TV encounter might have ended thus but while attendants were helping Leonard to move to the microphone, Sara returned to the stage.

'I teach nothing that is new, Jeremy. You rightly say I am the moon and I only *reflect* the light. Wise people do not abandon their powers of thought while they read books like your guru's. You too are a mystery. *Who are you*? What is your real name?'

Her opponent shouted from offstage.

'What is your real name? Sara? Helen? Sélène?'

'I am here to seek the truth, Jeremy, but you are not.'

Waving the book, Jesus-Leviticus roared, 'I challenge anyone who seeks the truth to stay in the Christian mind-set after reading *this*. Allegro *proves* in a six dollar book that the scriptures can be interpreted from the roots of herbal words encoded secretly to survive the censorship of the anti-drug establishment *who have consistently banned and burned books.'*

Sara looked at Michael but he was writing on his reporter's notebook. Jesus-Leviticus observed this failure of contact. He smiled and relaxed his pace.

'Yes, in this matter my colleague, Dr Robert Kohen, is right but he always avoided the conclusion, 'Consciousness is Chemical.' And you know what? Our high priest, Timothy Leary, has preached to you the good news of God's vegetable garden.'

Sara seized the initiative, 'Ah, so like me you are only a biblical character, another figment of Mr Allegro's drug-induced imagination?'

There was laughter and great applause. The audience clutched the relief she threw at them. Leonard looked up in amazement. Now he understood her power, the power of the conspiracy he had to dismantle. She held the masses in her power.

And she was radiant; feeding on the flattery of the people.

Leonard moved to Sara to reclaim his girlfriend. He held her back.

Jesus-Leviticus wasted no time to crush her small victory. In a dramatic display he outstretched his bared arms like Jesus on the cross. He spat upon his palms so the liquid ran. He faced the cameras and he proclaimed in a martyred and pitiful chant, 'It is the dawn of The Piscean Age, and I, Jesus of Nazareth, confess to being a fraud.'

In a demented falsetto voice, he continued, 'The New Age has arrived: first the Psychedelic Sixties, now the twenty-five year approach to the Molecular Millennium, the age of Mary Magdalene and the feminine creator. Now I, Yesa Christée, spelled 'E' acute and 'E', inaugurate the end of Man's suffering – his struggle to rise from the pits of ignorance. *Consciousness is Chemical*. Outside of consciousness, nothing is! Oh, DNA, tree-god upon which thy servant must hang the Chemical Christ. We don't really exist at all. To dream but not arrive. It is Man's affliction. Do I exist? Does Sara exist? Is the sky heavy or light? Matter is energy and what is mass really? Einstein says it is all relative.'

The mood of the crowd was impatient and confrontational. Mary-Anne Raymond ran onto the stage and screamed, '*This* is reality, not dreams, you cloven-hoofed arsehole. This is real suffering on behalf of sinners. *Look*!'

She grasped Sara's hands, turning the woman's palms to the audience. The cameras zoomed in, as the coloured girl forced Sara's shoes off. The crowds went hysterical and the cameras zoomed in on Sara's healed fingers, bent and broken by the American politician, and on partially healed stigmata from her convent years. Miss Raymond tore Sara's blouse to expose ribs beaten and bruised by the Movie Director, and parted Sara's hair claiming to expose dried blood. Pointing to the injuries the pop singer sang, 'This is the lamb of God who suffers for our sins.'

Her sisters joined in.

The power of music prevailed over reason. Emotions ran high. Jesus-Leviticus waited for the singing to cease. Even Leonard was silenced.

He looked at Sara and began to wonder why she attracted attention and injury.

41.5 Jeremy was hissed and hounded out of the hall while others protected and crowded round Sara. She was paraded as triumphant. Her media victory in California was absolute, they claimed, and surely the other States would follow. She and Michael left with an entourage of Eagles and new followers. He was bemused, he just walked with her, holding hands.

Outside Dawson Center there was more action. The cameras following Sara captured some women in the background chanting 'Elvis is alive today.' Leonard turned to them in amazement. He had heard about this thing, but to *see* a messianic movement who really worshipped . . . a dead rock star . . . no more unlikely, he supposed, than a resurrected carpenter; or even a failed actress.

The Elvis freaks had saved Michael Leonard from his very brief encounter with religious faith.

Chapter Forty-Two

Outside the hall Michael became separated from Sara and could not find her in the crowds when one of the Eagles dressed in leather and studs appeared before him with a message from Sara. *Could they escape the Press and crowds by staying at the Raymonds' mansion that night?*

Michael asked him to remind her that they had come here to search for Paul.

'We shall find him,' Sara appeared, exuding a confidence and commanding stance which Michael had to accept.

They were driven to the mansion in a luxurious stretched limo and shown two single bedrooms, three floors and ten minutes apart. Left to his own devices, Leonard toured the stately home. It was like a hotel staffed by friends in permanent residence. The family was outnumbered by the servants who were brothers and sisters – coloured and colourful people from the local congregation of the Church. Cartoon characters. The house was chaotic but clean. All seemed perfectly cast as cook, chauffeur, cleaner, etc. It became apparent that things happened here on the basis of what the Lord intended. And His intentions were mysteriously unfolded in an atmosphere of friendly tolerance to jealousies, feuds, stealing, and scheming to which the Raymonds themselves were apparently blind.

The limo was being polished by the Raymonds' driver, Maurice – a surly, slow-moving, large gentleman whose hair was curling and greying to suit his unshaven dark chocolate complexion.

As this man had taken three hours for a sixty minute journey Leonard booked a taxi to ensure Sara would make an early morning interview with *Time* magazine. They needed to be at the airport by 8:00am. Miss Ruth, the housekeeper, said, 'No problem, sir, I'm sure you don't need *a taxi*,' and she phoned Maurice, the driver.

Leonard couldn't stop himself laughing.

'Maurice can you have the car ready by a quarter to six in the morning? Maurice. Maurice? Oh, I know you can hear me Maurice. I'm real sorry, my darling . . . Well, can't you get an early night? It's real important. Maurice . . . Oh, he hung up on me. Pretends his phone isn't working. Pretends not to hear me. But he'll be ready for you on time, Mr Michael and Miss Sara. I sure do hope he doesn't break anything and hurts himself.'

42.1 After they dined, the family and staff retired to their bedrooms at 9:00pm. Michael found Sara's room and they went clubbing. It was well after 3:00am that Leonard became tired and Sara suggested they should get to their beds. Plural. *Which beds?*

'I'll stay at Kate's,' Sara shouted over 120 decibels of distorted acid rock.

'No, you don't know who she is, and I want you to stay with me. We have the interview and then we fly to New York tomorrow,' he said, 'You'll miss the plane if I don't make love to you tonight.'

'Okay,' she appeared to give in without argument which turned him on. She waved to her friends and, knowing that her older partner had experienced enough of dancing through the night, she allowed him to steer her by her dainty shoulders through the kids, directly to the exit.

In the back of a taxi he wrapped her in his coat. He asked the driver to suggest a hotel. He recognised them but agreed twenty-five dollars for his silence. Leonard booked two rooms at Sara's request.

At his bedroom door she pecked his cheek, snatched her key, and then bolted like a frightened rabbit to the other room.

'Sara!' he yelled like a furious father, threatening to wake the guests. She turned and walked slowly towards his glare.

'Since we got to the States, Sara, you've hardly touched me.'

'Sorry, Mike.'

They embraced passionately.

'Love You too.'

'I could live on your kisses, Sara, but that's not enough for me tonight.'

Again she set off to her room. Again he called her back. But she kept walking, slowly, furtively, so he hoped he could order her back.

He slept alone, disturbed that, thanks to him, she was the Millennial Messiah and he a Mere Mortal. It was all over between them. As he fell asleep he wondered if she had found out about his deal with Bartlett.

42.2 Arriving only ten minutes late for the Press Conference in the airport VIP Lounge she was asked by the *Time* reporter to justify her claim.

Her smile became angelic. She pointed to one of the coffees and asked, 'Is this yours?'

She swallowed the whole cup in one gulp, then she spoke softly but firmly.

'In the Bible there is one event which is prophesised more times than all others, but although you say you read the Bible, I bet you cannot tell me what event it is to that I refer.' She stumbled over the grammatical slip.

There was a long silence. At last she said, 'At least ten of the Prophets received and relayed the message including Isaiah of course, 'That day, the root of Jesse shall stand as a signal to the peoples . . . He will bring back the scattered people of Judah from the four corners of the earth.' And Ezekiel . . .'

The *Time* photographer intervened, 'Did you learn your lines at drama school or the convents?'

There was a nervous laughter which she interrupted.

'I learned a lot of things,' she replied, 'but not much in my Bible class. I learned that all the prophets knew the great intention of the Lord God to gather us back. Ezekiel chapter 37, 'I am going to take the sons of Israel from the nations where they have gone. I shall gather them together from everywhere and bring them home to their own soil."

The reporter held the microphone towards himself and said, 'I meant to ask you to justify your personal claim.'

She looked upwards and around for approval. 'I think you are bored. You are not serious. You are drunk and asleep, and your heart is not open, your ears are stopped. Oh, man you are unfaithful to your Father in Heaven. Listen to Hosea, chapter 3, 'The sons of Israel will be kept for many days without a king . . . Afterwards the sons of Israel will come back; they will seek the Lord their God and David their king; they will come back in those days to come.' And I could quote them all but that is also my right of return to the land. Genesis 49:10, 'The sceptre . . .'

'Yes but I mean, how do you know that *you* are the messiah?' the journalist repeated.

She expelled a sigh of sadness or impatience.

'The man in the street has the skills of survival but no direction.'

'Guide me,' the newsman challenged with his eyes.

Sara nodded and the room went quiet.

'Between David and Y'shua there elapsed less than one thousand years. Before the dispersion, the Temple Priests recorded the Zadokite generations faithfully so they knew the lines of descent from David. The Essenes who left the scrolls were dedicated to restoring the original and authentic Israel, and yet we are told that no genealogy was found among these discoveries. The Romans knew my ancestor was king and a real threat to their false authority. The French monarchs knew it.'

The newspaperman grimaced, looked around, eyes rolling; he explained that he needed to find a story to hand into an editor. She smiled.

'If you want sensation and scoop, write this down. In the Vatican there is a locked drawer with a prophecy from the Virgin Mary. And all Popes from 1950 have read it. John XXIII, Paul VI, and very recently John Paul II have all hinted something important about the year 2002 that neither Satan nor the Pope will reign. It is so curious a thought that no-one has noted this, far less understood even the date. The Gregorian calendar is based on the Julian which failed to calculate the Leap Year or compute the year zero, and it misplaces the birth of Christ in 4BC. You should heed the warnings and read the Scriptures. From the true year 2002 there will be a new age and a new ruler.'

Chapter Forty-Three

Leonard wanted to send a car to collect their belongings from the Raymonds but Sara said they had to return in person to the house. They found Maurice and his shining limousine had been waiting for them since a quarter to six. After the apologies the cook served breakfast to five persons: Mary-Anne, Ruth, and Ray Raymond, plus Sara, Michael and Maurice the driver.

Ray Raymond recited grace before the meal. 'The food we are about to receive was prepared with love to nourish body and soul. May the Lord make us truly grateful. Amen.'

'Amen, the Lord be praised,' his sisters replied.

'The Lord be praised,' Sara agreed after an interval. She was tired.

She fell asleep in the limousine on the way to the airport despite Maurice singing.

Chapter Forty-Four

Michael and Sara spent Christmas 1978 together but in seclusion. Some of the media were supporting her claim and competing for interviews and photographs. He had promised to find the Genealogy, noting that the Christian, and now the Jewish, authorities had failed to deny it.

On 24th December a story broke, allegedly from Robert Kohen's Modern Order of Essenes, that Rome and Jerusalem, in collusion, had 'reburied several parchments with the genealogy of the House of David.'

Leonard fanned the flames of the scandal by agreeing in a radio interview that the first-century Essenes *must* have kept documents recording the generations since David as their objective was the restoration of the sacred nation.

On 25th December, doubtless to diminish its significance, Robert Kohen asked to meet Sara on a public bench in Central Park. The meeting lasted less than five minutes. Michael Leonard agreed to stand out of earshot: *of course she would tell him everything.*

44.1 She looked round at Leonard as she walked alone to the man seated on the bench. It was a cold and frosty morning. Kohen held her hand, 'Blessed One, the Priests have voted in Council to anoint you as the Royal-Messiah.' He waited for her reaction, but she scorned him with, 'Hey, hey, which priests are you talking about?

'Those designated to reconstitute the Sanhedrin.'

'In your new Order of Essenes?'

'Yes, and you must accept my authority as *kohen-mashiach* for I am the descended and anointed High Priest. In spiritual matters pertaining both to this Order and to world Jewry I am your superior. It is your duty to accept that the Christians even more than the Arabs have brought our people close to extinction. Your duty is to your own people. It was the Jewish nation who asked the Lord, and the Lord granted them a monarchy like the other nations. They made you.'

Michael Leonard stood afar, watching them. He saw the frosted breathing but did not hear the words. Sara felt nervous without him. She had to report to both men but deal with one at a time. She knew what Michael would say.

'Central Park is like the eye at the centre of a storm. Listen please, David's throne has been abolished, Robert, and I am not a queen. If Jews were permitted to number people they would not recognise the forced conversions of the past centuries. Religion is for the soul not for the authorities. Besides, despite my heredity, Robert, the Teacher did not proclaim my anointment as royal-messiah, nor yours as priest-messiah. So what does that mean? Some people say it proves that you did not cook up The Teacher.'

'The Law is to anoint a ruler . . .'

'The Essenes were dividers. You are a purist, Robert, but I have come to heal all divisions.'

She shouted, then turned and looked to Leonard but continued to speak to Kohen under her breath.

'Perhaps you think I am an actress? But I am not a channel. I am the goddess, Robert, not merely the channel, not merely the symbol of the goddess. *I am the goddess.* I am not here to teach religion but to teach each man, seek your own soul that you no longer possess. I am here not to divide but to unite; not to splinter but to heal. Robert, this park is like nature in the city.'

Sara called Leonard and asked him to write down in shorthand what she had to say to Robert.

'Truly God is dead, killed by the managers of religion. The messiah does not believe in God. This is what the wise will do. Seek loveliness, not love. Seek godliness, not God. Let go of the past and take no thought for the future. For God everything and nothing; creator and created and without name, gender, direction. Nameless is in an eternal present, but the present is a mere line between the past and future, gone before you can re-enter her womb. Gone yet always here and now. Can you find her? Yes, you have found her. See how Time is God? God is time. Timegod is omnipotent and omniscient. All things come from time and return to her womb. God is pure presence. Do not store up riches nor predict options for the future belongs to God. I am the daughter of time. I come from pure presence and yet I accept the suffering of this world in order to save you. It is *The Gospel According to Sara*.'

Leonard stopped writing and praised the words, 'Wow. Poetry.'

'Gospel is a gentile term,' Kohen let go of her hand, 'and you just told me to let go of the past, by which I assume you mean expendable myths.'

'Robert, you see how I comprehend the darkness but the darkness comprehendeth not me. You once said that love thine enemy was a Christian doctrine. But you forget Leviticus 19:33, "When an alien resides with you in your land you must not oppress him. He is to be treated as a native born among you. Love him as yourself, because you were aliens in Egypt and I am the Lord your God."'

She spoke quietly but with fire in her voice.

'Take heed, Robert, in case people like you think that they made me. Media people. People who put ideas into my head. Yes they did, but I am the goddess, not merely the channel, not merely the symbol of the goddess. I *am* the goddess. What people say about Jesus does not change who Jesus was. And so it is with me. False words bounce off my skin. Talking of false words, Robert, I'm going to the CBS TV studios to do an interview with our friend Jeremy for if you ignore the media, Satan wins.'

She stopped Kohen's response with her hand on his mouth and also asked Leonard to be silent.

'Both of you be quiet.'

44.2 Sara pulled her feet together and sat on the freezing bench cross-legged in an upright position of meditation like the Buddha. Tears streamed down from her closed eyes. Quietly she uttered to Robert, 'We are being watched by hostile agents and by two men who want to guard me as a sovereign, and by the CIA, yes, I kid you not, probably watching you, Robert.'

Kohen and Leonard saw nothing and glanced at each other. She asked them to wait but walked away. After ten minutes she arrived with a pair of binoculars which she offered. Both men were puzzled. Sara smiled.

'I borrowed them from the CIA, so you can watch them looking at you, but I promised to return them, so they have two reasons to watch us now.'

Kohen and Leonard were speechless.

'Yeh, I know,' she explained, 'I am taking the piss of their government.'

44.3 'Three seconds . . . two . . . one . . . we're in their Living Rooms, darling. Good luck.'

The stage director stepped back and the cameras rolled forward.

The audience applauded. The announcer announced dramatically, '*Live* from our New York City Studios, CBS TODAY brings you at 6:00pm everyday a controversial man or woman in the news. Today Dr Jeremy Jesus-Leviticus, writer, lecturer, and broadcaster will interview the woman who claims to be descended from Christ.'

The screens switched to the lectern camera.

Jeremiah Jesus-Leviticus wore a casual shirt of many colours, yellow and lime, green clashing with riotous red and bilious blue. Behind him a poster proclaimed his message for the New Age:

GIVE UP, DROP OUT, COME IN

JJ-L slumps onto the lectern. He groans but does not move for ten seconds. Time in suspension seems longer. It compels attention and heightens audience concentration. The director waves his arms wildly. The cameras zoom in on the motionless body. Breaking his contrived silence, Jeremy swings up his beard with a broad smile.

'You were writing my obituary, weren't you? The sad death today at the early age of forty-two proves dope is bad. *That's what the authorities want you to think*. Why else will you drag your discharged body to work for six days and to church on the seventh? For the measly trickle of money for the groceries you pay them back anyway? The people voted for taxes? *Voted for war?* Voted for their country! That lie was okay for your granddaddy. If you see now that happiness is as easy to achieve as I can show you, you might not want to vote for any son-of-a-bitch that makes you into lots of little donkeys dragging their wheel around a well. Well, would you? Aha, ha! You would not, I'm telling you.'

He went silent. From behind the scenes Sara watched her former friend turned harsh adversary. His acting skills far exceeded her training.

He popped a pill in his mouth.

He smiled and surveyed his audience like a schoolmaster on the first day of a new term.

'*Consciousness is chemical*, my friends, it really is that simple. For three thousand years western philosophers have groped towards all sorts of mind-body philosophies while the enlightened civilisations whose priests were the Magi, the Therapeutae, and Pharmakos, all so-called primitives. So-called pagans who invented alphabet, numbers, and culture. Four and a half thousand years ago they made glass so beautiful but today we don't know how they did it. Built pyramids we don't know how or why. So they weren't stupid but we moderns degenerated these ancient religions to form cultic Judaism which further inbred itself like a monster begetting monsters into the watery milk of moralistic Christianity. The wisdom bred people who thought it all disgusting so they even had to deny *sex*. And now, the modern rediscovery of the sacred mushroom shows us what was there, right at the beginning. *Dreams*.'

Jeremy paused and screwed his eyes in reaction to the theatre lighting. The audience was quiet so he spoke softly.

'Life on earth can be very beautiful again. It can. It's just that they keep your mind dulled. In prison-like conditions. They permit depressant drugs like nicotine, alcohol, and caffeine. They license poisonous medicinal drugs which do all kinds of harm, most of all making the world forget an abundance of readily available and highly effective natural cures, with no cost, *so no profits*. So called primitive techniques. But no, no, no, to the mind-expanding drugs. *They're enlightening*. Food for the brain.'

Jeremy alternately whispered and roared to dramatise his ghoulish performance, tonally riding up and down.

'How sorry, boys and girls, that daddy can't allow you to have the *nice* pills! The ones that make you feel good.'

A few from the audience laughed, as tey were supposed to do, but it was nervous laughter and the good doctor speeded up like a gramophone out of control and croaked in a mock granddad dialect from the southern States.

'Why do you think that is? Eh? Well boy, I'm ninety-nine years old on Tuesday and I've been taking my cortical vitamin pills every day and I'm more alive than the old farts who warn you that *them pills is dangerous*! Who's dangerous? *They are.* They write the laws.

'Religion is dead. God is dead, even Sara says so, and sorry to mention it, but Jesus was a proto-hippie who got nailed to a cross for suggesting that we, and not the state, are our own ultimate authorities. And *he* was on drugs – even on the cross. The cults of Alexandria were yesterday's California and the bit the gospel censors forgot to excise – the raising of Lazarus showed he had overdosed. Yes, Sara, you're right about the contents and not the cup at the Last Supper. The Holy Grail has been concealed. It was *dope*.'

The stage director was waving and frantically pointing to his watch.

Jeremy stormed off stage laughing at his own joke. The host of CBS TODAY ascended the podium but Sara gently dismissed him.

She needed no introduction. She removed the board with 'GIVE UP, DROP OUT, COME IN' and tore it into pieces. She, too, had studied the art of theatre. The spotlight refracted psychedelic patterns from the sheen of her pearlescent dress.

'Dr so-called-Leviticus is a very funny man but he is also a very *dangerous* man and his errors are easily spotted against the purer contrasting truth. His enemies, the old establishment, are bad and outdated, he says, therefore, you can trust *him*. Anyone buy that? Show of hands? Few in this studio, it seems.

'In 381 a law was passed saying that only Rome could define Christianity. Why did they do that? Why was Pope John Paul killed? When will it end? There isn't any reason for suffering. The planet is capable of sustaining all of us in every way. It is for you to decide. Jeremy rightly says, you have the choice.'

While she paused, Jeremy called from his front row seat, 'And your philosophy is free love. You legitimise sex outside marriage. What about relationships like gays and lesbians? What's your view on that? Answer us directly, woman. And are you the messiah? Yes or no?'

It is not unknown on live chat shows for 'spontaneous skirmishes' to be scripted, or at least tolerated, as they boost ratings. Was this planned? The stage director was enraged and twisted Jeremy's arm behind his back. The audience was mesmerised with fear. The director dropped his clipboard and obeyed Sara when she ordered him to let go of Jeremy immediately.

A producer tried to trip up Jesus-Leviticus who stumbled up to the lectern straightening his clothes, preening his hair, and feigning insult and injury. The tension rose. You could hear a chair creak. Jesus-Leviticus stood in front of the lectern and looked up to her, 'Well, *are you* the Daughter of God?'

She smiled and said softly, 'Jesus of Nazareth lived in fear of no man but he knew that if he said he was messiah, the priests would have him stoned or the Romans would have him crucified. You know the outcome. I have only one excuse for silence, which is your wilful ignorance. I am an ordinary human born from an unbroken line of virgins. By the grace of God, Dr Jesus-Leviticus . . .'

'Virgins?' He exclaimed, 'I know all about virgins!'

She ignored the laughter.

'By the grace of God, Dr Jesus-Leviticus, potentially you are not as mean-spirited as you think you are. But at least you know who I am. I knew myself, if not for long enough. I think that my brother is the male first-born in the long lineage which the Bible asserts – more than once – is royal in perpetuity. If you want my opinion, I think that my brother is the modern messiah but we need to find him.'

Jeremy made sweeping gestures with his hands, bowing and scraping before her majesty, but she ignored his sarcasm.

'I have come here to find him. I came before for a part in the movie but now I am the part. In Hollywood I took Sélène thinking that it was only a byname, but then I found it was the Greek moon goddess, and you know she is but a reflector of light from the sun. That is all I am. The Teacher was right. Yes, I see through walls and divisions. Your mushrooms help us to see things both fearful and glorious. There, now, I have spoken, enough for today for everyone to know who I am. But first they must ask of themselves, who they are. Each person is so noble, beautiful, deep, and unique. Like a flower, and we shall all die so soon. Before you die, find out who you are.'

The programme timed itself out and faded into a commercial break.

Chapter Forty-Five

On the third morning of the search for Paul the 1978 Convention of World Faiths was on its final day. The modern messiah and her biographer decided to visit Stand B31, The New England Church. As they strolled down the corridors of the great hall of the Dawson Center Michael asked Sara what she had demanded of Bishop Brown.

The shopping list represented a considerable revision of Christianity: the Trinity had to go along with Apostolic Succession; Childermas must celebrate Herod's slaughter of the innocents on 28 December instead of the winter solstice festival three days earlier; the dethroning of Peter and the demotion of Paul must follow the apology for defaming the Magdalene as a prostitute.

Leonard smiled cynically.

'None of it was based on Scriptural authority or Jesus' teaching,' she countered, talking above the public address system announcing the day's events. Then, she said, there was the restoration of women's worth and their spiritual equality as in days of Ruth and Esther. And free love.

Leonard feigned a choked cough as his eyes widened in disbelief.

'*Free love?* And what did the Bishop say to that, Sara?'

They walked past Baha'is, Scientologists, and Native North Americans.

'I told him that the Bible declared against fornication and perversion, but I went over all the passages with him to show him that Moses, Elijah, Jesus, and Paul had not been inspired by God to condemn anything natural. On the contrary, it is unnatural to suppress the natural, and God knows – but it seems the Church does not know – that both fornication and the suppression of the natural are both perversions that lead to disease. Sex does not have to be within marriage to be free from sin.'

'And where did you learn all of this?' Leonard asked, keeping his voice neutral.

'I lived in Inverness when I became aware of my own sexuality.'

'Ah, at a convent school! The Catholics have a lot to answer for.'

She read out the names of the exhibitors.

'*Transcendental Meditation. Krishna Consciousness. Friends of the Western Buddhist Order.* Michael, the nuns had to do whatever I wanted. I argued against their doctrines in the classes. I freed the other girls. I insisted on free speech. There was nothing they could do about it . . . the arrangement was one of mutual advantage . . . call it blackmail . . . or damage limitation. I offered them a deal. They don't shop me – I don't stop them. I ran their convent. That's why they hated me. For three months I put an end to hitting the girls with belts and rulers. Then they expelled me. The Establishment will always triumph.'

Leonard opened his mouth but was interrupted by Peter Bartlett who ran up to them. He was flushed with excitement. His words tumbled out.

'SARA! FOUND YOU AT LAST! LEVITICUS KNOWS WHERE YOUR BROTHER IS. HE KNOWS *EXACTLY* WHERE YOUR BROTHER IS. That tall, young guy there who's talking to him now on the Buddhists' stand. He talked about your brother Paul; *I heard them.*'

Sara sprang to her feet, ran forward and tried to grasp the tall youth by his shoulder but in her hand she had gripped only his collar. He dropped a music album. He loosened himself free and with the energy inspired by his fear of capture he disappeared rapidly through Door A of the Dawson Center. She gave chase, and a photographer materialised from nowhere; flash, flash, flash! She was hounded by her followers but the young man was propelled by demons. Despite her efforts, he vanished into thin air.

45.1 Sara returned and asked to see the music tape. Leonard told her that Jeremy had also vanished but at least *he* could be traced, that much was obvious.

The cassette was *The Immaculate Deception* by 'Antigens' an artist or band they had only heard about vaguely between them. It was issued by a label called Mushroom Records whose address at LSD was local and familiar. So was the credit to Jeremy Palmer, songwriter and manager.

Peter, Michael, and Sara looked at each other and walked smartly to the door where they took a taxi to *The League for Spiritual Discovery*. Jesus-Leviticus, or Dr Palmer, was due back in half an hour, they said. Five minutes later he drove up in a bright red Corvette.

He protested that he knew nothing. Sara said, 'Michael, Leviticus has always known who I am. Look at the lyrics on these songs. It is a Japanese release.'

Peter Bartlett contributed with his boyish excitement, 'Guys, Antigens is a band which currently is touring Japan.'

Sara was examining the thumbnail photo of the musicians. In a quiet but emotional voice she spoke firmly, 'We must go to Japan. Today.'

45.2 Sara and Michael flew to Tokyo travelling Business Class with assumed names and airline VIP clearance. JAL knew who Sara was and by a small green sticker behind her chair the cabin crew knew that her diet was vegetarian. Leonard's blue sticker meant kosher. He laughed at the idea of his Jewish conversion by Japanese Air Line and asked Sara who had arranged the travel. 'My office.' – 'I did not know you had an office.' – 'Well, I do now, Michael.' – 'Let's hope the JAL pilots are more careful than their catering people.' – 'I think the mistake is all because you're sitting in my seat, Mr Right Man.'

Within an hour of take-off Leonard was impressed by the courtesy and efficiency of JAL. Serving his meal, the attendant smiled and blushed. She said in English that, since he was Jewish, the coffee whitener was non-dairy; she had checked it for him.

'I don't enjoy meat,' he explained. 'I am in love but not carnivorous – I have only one weakness of the flesh.'

The Japanese girl smiled at his joke courteously.

The flight was tedious and four Catholic nuns, returning from a conference, kept Sara busy with questions. They invited her to see their convent in Kyoto, Japan's ancient capital. They asked her about women's' place in the new Kingdom of God, about celibacy, birth control, divorce, and abortion.

Leonard asked them if they accepted Sara's authority or if they were using the opportunity to test her teachings against their Church. He was surprised when Sara answered that 'her organisation' was wise enough to rule against the founding of a new church.

45.3 Foreign celebrities are treated with courtesy in Japan but they are still considered aliens. When Sara arrived in Tokyo, traffic came to a halt. People stopped and workers poured out of their offices. Two Japanese female students, about her size, volunteered to become her translators throughout her stay in Japan. The three girls looked like sisters and they were fascinated that – with her petite build, Mediterranean looks, black hair, and olive complexion – Sara looked like them; and apparently her name was not alien to them in its phonetics.

She turned to Michael. Gripped his arm and said, 'In this world the most unintended thing, the most trivial co-incidence, is in fact a revelation from Heaven. Now I know why we are here.'

'We are here to find Paul,' he replied and denied her the satisfaction of responding to her enigmatic smile.

In the centre of Walkman City Sara was photographed and her words were recorded by many amateurs with tape machines.

'You have an ancient and mighty culture and you have won by your technology and industry. You work hard, you are proud, and you are hungry for tomorrow. You take delight in your teams and pride in your work, and what you make is the best in the world. But what is more precious still, because life depends on it to a greater extent, is your ability to understand nature and harmony. You must pity the foreigners. Understand that they are different from you, but you must not think of them as inferior, even if they insult you in their coarse ignorance. You know that it is a strength to be superior without aggression.

'You must show the west how you blend your ancient religions into each other and into modern life. In Europe, you see, they consider religions as conflicting sects. Your deep philosophy of tolerance and perfectionism is the greatest export you can give to the west. Show them that you can accept your own neighbours here in the east. Be at peace with the Chinese and Korean peoples and share with the western world the knowledge of the religions of the East. Wisdom is your greatest export.

'Believe me, the world is one and I will come back.'

45.4 The stadium was filling up for the last of the three concerts, 'Antigens in Japan'. All shows had been sold out months before. Leonard handed over £100 to the ticket tout.

Sara suddenly said she was feeling unwell. 'I'm sorry Michael, but I'm not going.'

'I think you should, Sara. I just paid two hundred dollars. Is it an aversion to rock music?'

'I love rock but look again at the lyrics. *Why does Antigens hate me?* Why do I need to pay to be insulted by him?'

'I'll look after you, honey. Besides it's great music, a great venue, and it's going to be a great concert. Look at the lighting and effects!'

While Leonard was encouraging her he read the song lyrics on the album for the first time. When she had decided to travel to Japan Sara had correctly chosen to follow intriguing clues.

'You're always looking after me, Michael.'

'I love you too but I see what you mean about these words.'

'I love you, Michael.'

'We must follow this lead and explain how Leviticus, or Palmer, knows about your childhood and see if the 'Antigens' lead singer is involved. According to the credits, he is the co-writer; including these words. *The goddess of the moon, She'll take my place soon* . . . and, look at this, Sara!'

'Yes,' she gave in quietly after she had accepted the challenge of the concert, but a tear fell.

'What is it, Babe?'

'I'm crying in self pity, Michael. Not for having to lose you, but for being separated from humanity in this way. I lost my parents and my brother. I must have a child one day. I shall. That I know. I will love her very much. I want to call her Debora, if she is a girl, but will I have to marry one of my own people?'

Leonard ignored the open question; its shock multiplied by her own denial of barriers and divisions. Was she asking him to convert? *Or dumping him?*

He compared her new attitude toward gentiles to Robert Kohen.

She shook her head and opened her arms as if to embrace the Japanese crowd.

'These are my people,' she whispered almost inaudibly.

45.5 Sara was right about the concert. It was loud, coarse, and rough. Leonard could not hear what she was saying, so she wrote on the cover of the programme, *Antigens. He knows our secrets from France.*

After the song, the applause drowned Leonard's questions, so he wrote. *How do you know?*

Sara wrote, *Words*. She explained she had discerned words that to his ears were distortion.

After the concert he asked her, 'What did he sing?'

They were leaving the stadium before she stated solemnly, *"The severed hand in the haunted house.'* Michael, when we were children, Paul and I, there was an old house near our parents' which had been abandoned for many years. As kids, we thought we saw a hand. It was only a glove hanging inside a window but it was scary. No-one else would know about it, Michael. Such a trivial thing, but it scared us as kids. The severed hand.'

'So you're saying that only Paul is supplying Antigens with information that only Paul would know about?'

Her face drained of blood, then she whispered, 'Dope made him like this.'

Michael the wordsmith, exasperated by her ambiguity, suddenly realised that he had failed to make the connection.

Paul *was* Antigens.

BOOK FOUR

Michael Leonard

MM

Chapter Forty-Six

Michael Leonard was shocked that a double room in a four-star Tokyo hotel cost three hundred US dollars a night. Making the best use of his time he lay on top of the exquisitely draped bed and fired questions to Sara who was preening herself at the Queen Anne style dressing table.

He walked up to her and asked aggressively, 'Sara you're telling me that after your Harvard readings Mr so-called Leviticus had access to the tapes and their transcriptions? Is this so?'

He gripped her wrist tightly. In the mirror reflection, she pretended to give him the evil eye.

'Let go, Michael.'

She explained with agitation undermining her poise.

'Jeremy was a Project Director in the memory regression research. At that time Dr Leary was too busy with the trial . . .'

'At Harvard, Jeremy called himself Dr Palmer?'

'Jeremy Palmer,' prompted Sara, 'and he was Leary's protégé, so close to the master but . . . some people did not like or trust Jeremy.'

Leonard stroked the fresh, silky, lavender-coloured bedsheets which he had disturbed but he kept up the questions.

'What drug was it?'

She wrenched her arm from Leonard's grip.

'What drug was *what*?'

'That they fed you. For the hypnosis sessions?'

She sat at the dressing table and spoke to the mirror.

'Michael, I'm not a pharmacist. But within two minutes my mind was free. I floated in the rainbow and I felt – not just heard – no, I *was* the silent music which harmonises the entire universe. I was the orchestra conducted from within each player. I controlled the world because I *was* the world. I saw through the glass walls of life – don't you see? Divisions are necessary. Divisions are false. The walls that conceal from you the meaning of all creation. It is just like falling in love and you walk hand in hand with the god or goddess. Imagine being all day inside the person you choose to adore. The meaning of life became clear to me.'

Leonard cursed under his breath each time she became poetic and prolix. Normally he would interrupt her flow but he poured himself a gin, half of his mind updating the conspiracy and half listening to her.

'When I asked to see the Lord, I was taken hand in hand by seraphim who knew the avenue for me to enter Heaven was between the walls but not through the Pearly Gates. I approached the inner chambers with the highest order of the angels who said, 'Do not be afraid,' but I said, 'How shall I address Him?' and they said, 'Foolish child, do you really expect an old man with a white beard? Would you prefer if the Lord dresses up with a white beard to meet your expectations? Look there is Louis Beethoven, the composer.' I think I flushed, because seeing this famous man suddenly made me realise the enormity of what was happening. Imagine unwritten music by Beethoven. Well, he's still writing symphonies, Michael. You will think me crazy but heaven is not parallel universes, rather there exists in the eternal present all possible branches stemming from each event and effect of the past. And then I saw the inner chamber lit by celestial lights like heavenly chandeliers formed of galaxies of distant stars.'

Leonard now listened to her carefully. He asked where her science had been learned but she ignored the question and continued uninterrupted.

'Michael, they said to me, 'You were chosen as one of your generation strong enough to suffer. You are a messenger who has descended to a world in error and pain. You can teach but also learn."

Leonard sipped from his drink and retrieved his reporter's notebook.

'Then, Michael, I saw something like a computer screen titled HISTORY OF THE WORLD and I had to press the right button like a game. I was to choose an event of history to learn something they said was missing from the knowledge we have on earth; facts without understanding. I couldn't choose but something prompted my hand then immediately I saw *conflict* . . . an episode of history I had not even imagined but I had to understand. I heard men arguing.'

Michael was agitated. He let his pencil fall, sipped his gin, and looked at her through the mirror on the dressing table.

'Sara, you were tripping and the hand which guided you was reality. People in the room were probably laughing amongst themselves.'

Sara breathed deeply and gasped, 'Michael, laughing is one thing but men arguing in an ancient language with prayer shawls, they were gouging out the eyes of the faces of saintly men, blood trickling through the white beards of Hebrew prophets. It made me afraid, not for myself, but because they were big and – how do you say? – *well-made* men. They were *tzadikim*, righteous souls I perceived. That, I think, is what made me feel such fear. Fear like you cannot imagine, Michael. *Religion made them hate*. The souls of the persecuted are in peace but those of the inquisitors, these are still in limbo, imprisoned in pain. Error ensnared their souls. They are only half-dead, like writhing insects under foot.'

Their eyes met and lingered in the mirror of her dressing table until she spun around on the small stool, looked at Leonard directly, then whispered.

'It was the Sabbath, Michael, and one group was preventing the other from entering the synagogue. I tried to scream, "God, please stop them," but my mouth simply opened and closed. My voice was in our century, not theirs, therefore a soft, invisible hand held me back like a force field or a safety glass behind their time which, of course, we moderns cannot enter or influence. Like a thunderous voice, which I thought was the voice of God, I was commanded "**Be Still**."'

As she paused for air Leonard reflected on the way her voice cycled though many dialects she had collected as baggage on her journey.

'I had to watch the men; I had to understand, but not to interfere. One or two seemed vaguely aware of me but I'm sure they could not see me. The highest of the seraphim squeezed my hand and said, YOU CANNOT PLAY GOD, AND EVEN GOD WILL NOT INTERVENE IN THEIR DEEDS.

'I will never forget this lesson. You see, Michael, we must learn that the world has meaning because humans have the gift of being individuals. You do not follow a star; you make a series of choices. You are not a slave or a puppet. But we cannot interfere in the past nor in any other of the infinite chains of possible worlds.'

'Cosmology from the mouth of a chick simply cannot be argued with.' Leonard gently started to undo her blouse.

Sara ignored his sarcasm and turned away from his sexual advances. The hotel bedroom telephone rang, but she lifted and replaced the handset to continue her recollections. She did not resist as Leonard undressed her. While she spoke caressing him seemed to rekindle the trance state she relived.

'So I watched the struggle from outside the synagogue and outside of their time zone, but I did not participate. Like a motion picture the events unreeled from the vaults of predetermined fate. The House of Prayer was like an inferno. I sensed all kinds of bodily fluids. One man screamed out, "By the authority of Rabbi Akiva you call Simon Ben Kosiba, Bar Kochba the star, our people will be put to death by the armies of Rome who will not permit Judeans to encourage the Alexandrians. It is not the same as in the days of the Hasmoneans." – "Simon Bar Kochba will liberate us, you fool, and certainly not Chrestus who was too cowardly to lead his people to freedom. And you believers in the *mashiach*, practicers of all forms of magic and sorcery, pagan gods, worshippers of the tribesman's idols, blasphemers, and apostates who teach and trade with aliens. You, who lie with gentiles, defiling men and women indiscriminately, you have no place in our community. You say that our priests are liars and *Yesu bar Yoseph* is our king. If he is risen from the dead then perhaps he can come back and tell us himself that he is *mashiach*. Tell us whose side he is on, Roma or *Yerushalayim?*"'

Leonard was not sure why he was allowing her to continue but she was unstoppable. When she finished it was his turn.

She observed that while she sat unclothed on the stool his lust for her diverted his attention from his big story. She asked for her dressing gown and warned.

'Michael, attend well, for they talked about the Davidic genealogy and how it was taken with the treasury scrolls when the Temple was destroyed. Understand, if it was still there at that time, then the line of David through Yeshua and his royalty was known to the Council. Whoever possessed it had the key to heal the split among the Jewish people. But its whereabouts was denied. Do you understand? They shouted, "The Council of Elders at Jamnia have made the decision. It is not for you to argue with." – "Fools, understand this, we are not in dispute with the Christians for they are dreamers whom we merely despise. Either you are with us or you are against the God of Israel. Either way you shall die."'

'"Listen," said one of them, "Peace be upon our divided House. God has made a covenant first with Abram, then Moses, and now on the rooftop with Simeon, whom our enemies call Petrus and the Greeks Cephas. Surely you will listen to him. On the roof of his house the Lord spoke and many witnessed. The Good News is that all nations who will come to the Lord and give up their pagan ways are one with the Lord and all can be saved. You scoffers believe that this thing is not possible for the Almighty but who are you to judge?" – "Ah, you are a damned liar, fool, apostate and traitor. Observe their pagan ways, go and lie with the fair-skinned daughters of the gentiles, lie down with women of all races and languages for they will save us the trouble and they will steal your money and put you to death."'

Sara's face was solemn and she was waving her arms.

'Michael, at this point I became sick and threw up. I felt shrivelled and in pain. The people near me were saying, "Oh, oh, bad trip. Hold her head down the pan. Flush her stomach." You see they are *mere chemists*, but I understood the cause of the pain. It was the psychology of the herd. Mass hysteria by their leaders to train them like sheep into pens of mass control. Group instinct, atavistic fear, feeling of isolation, it compelled each one of these holy individuals to surrender his sense. I saw fields of energy, what people would call auras and things all becoming contaminated with evil, and I screamed out to the men who were fighting, "Get behind me, Satan! The world is bountiful and beautiful. It doesn't need to be this way," but they couldn't hear me. Oh, they couldn't hear me because I wasn't in their time zone. They were on the other side of a wall. I wanted to intervene but the angels denied me the power. In our world, take heed, it is forbidden to cross the stream of time.'

She looked with pleading eyes.

'Oh Michael, *please* try to understand me, and believe that it was so vivid that I can relive my vision and I am there again now as I relate the events to you. *I became angry at God.* I was between our time and His heaven, and I saw the man whose nose was gone, and blood was everywhere and I thought, where are his wife and children? That is when I thought . . . I don't know why. I had a lot of other thoughts, but God said, I HAVE A DISPUTE WITH ALL FLESH, *and then I understood.*'

Leonard asked her to explain *our time and His heaven* but she simply continued the account of her vision.

'In the morning I felt fine and Susan brought me food. I was very hungry. She said she had slept by me all night to make sure no-one touched me. We were all high. I would have let them do it. I know you will be shocked. It was very wild in the sixties, when we were young and stupid, and some of us . . . I guess some of the gang clung onto the ways of lust and addiction for too long.'

Leonard shook his head. 'Jesus, woman, you're confusing me with the time zones. I think your mind was just smashed by drugs.'

'Michael,' she smiled. 'It's just so. It is the time zones that our minds, with the right substance, can walk through at will.'

46.1 Much to Leonard's frustration Sara denied that she was enticing or teasing him.

'Don't you know the difference between lust and love? And love to procreate; love to adore and unite? Love of family? Love of God? Sexuality is all of these and more Michael, I will teach you, but not here in Japan.'

'Why not here and now?' he asked once and then a second time to elicit a reluctant response.

'The Japanese islands are sacred to me. I feel it. Focus your lust on the quest for the genealogy, Michael, for you will find it here.'

He tried in vain to have her explain her prediction.

The bedroom TV was never switched off. Leonard was writing but suddenly called her to see Antigens on Japanese News. After his last concert he was boarding a KLM flight to Amsterdam. The clip lasted a few seconds. She missed it.

They had flown to Japan and her long-lost brother had just flown back to Europe. Leonard buried his head in his hands cursing the loss of time and money.

Sara felt sorry for him and phoned Mushroom Records in California. She refused to give reasons for her inquiries, so the management told her nothing about Antigen's movements except the band was to fly to London to give a concert. Leonard arranged the next return flight and they packed their cases the next morning. Driving to Narita airport he saw disappointment on her face.

'Sara do you want to listen to music? Do you want to stay longer in Japan? Do you want me to sing to you? Do you want some breakfast? What do you want to be happy?'

'You know what I want.'

If only he knew! He had a hired Nissan saloon to drive her to the airport so they could have time to talk but she was locked in her own thoughts. He was cruising along a straight country road with the sun blinding him and illuminating rice fields when she broke the silence.

'It was just like this, Michael. *The car accident.'* Leonard became alert and turned off the car radio. The reporters' notebook in his head was open.

She spoke softly in a French accent but her voice was full of emotion, 'A long quiet road just after a downpour in the bright southern skies of France. The trees were luminescent green, sparkling with fresh raindrops. Paul and I were making mischief in the back of 'Uncle' George's car. I still don't know who he was except that daddy trusted him but we hated him. He had a black Citroën, just like our dark green car which I loved very fondly. Ours had green leather seats and a leather cushion between Paul and me over which we fought pretend battles, distracting my father. And in the front . . . there was the old-fashioned brittle plastic. That day I saw it in pieces just like my radio but . . . there was blood. This man came and I was happy until he forced me to visit the scene of the accident. I still don't know why he did it. Was it because he wanted to show it to me? Rewrite my memory? Do you grasp what I'm saying to you? Years later, I knew it was faked. *It was not an accident.* And we, the victims, were the witnesses for the perpetrators. *Please don't ask me to explain or justify things. It is confused to me too. My memory of it is mixed up and faulty.'*

Leonard calmed her then she continued. 'Paul simply couldn't take it. He cracked up. As we drove towards the place I told him that something dreadful was about to happen. He thought I was playing make believe but I was terrified because I had experienced dreams in which two black aeroplanes were crashing in the sky with an almighty bang and a white flash which always woke me up. I had the dream just before the accident and many times since the day of the accident. Only now do I recall the symbol of a red sun on both of the planes. I told you, one half of me was born on August 1945. I don't blame you if you think I'm quite crazy but I can see through walls so I do get confused, but I'm not lying. Multiple personality is not schizophrenia, Michael. I have one body but two souls. I came to know it was that way since 'the accident.'

'*I have to stay in Japan*, Michael. There is something I'm supposed to do here. These islands are sacred, like Jerusalem. It's exactly the same feeling.'

Suddenly her temper flared.

'Godammit, for all the books you have read, you should be assigned to reporting baseball, not something big like this. YOU AREN'T ANY HELP AT ALL. YOU SIMPLY DON'T UNDERSTAND. Do you know how bad you made me feel last night? You have no feelings.'

Michael was indignant.

'What are you talking about?'

'Don't lie to me, or are you so unfeeling? You are a control freak with one thing on your mind and that is *sex*, and it's not what I'm all about. You think I'm a whore! For your pleasure. Because your newspapers say so. It turns you on. To deflower a virgin, besmirch the daughter of God. *For me, love is spiritually giving myself up*. That's why I can't do it with you any more.'

Consumed with anger, Leonard asked, 'If you fuck other men in your free-love morality, then you *are* nothing more than a whore?'

She went silent and Leonard uttered profanities because she refused to deny it. Then the woman opened her door and leapt out of the moving car. She plunged ten feet into a field.

46.2 *I watched her spin along the ground. I assumed she was dead, I screamed, 'Jesus, God!' Aware of the cars behind me I braked gently, saw* *in the rear mirror that Sara spun, came to rest, then rose to her feet and ran across the field. I drove faster, happy but angry. I decided I should no longer work for this paranoid woman and her crazy friends. I stopped the car in the first possible place, over one hundred yards up the road and two minutes closer to Narita airport. I parked and sat motionless and perspiring at the wheel until she ran up, panting, outside the car. She was only slightly bruised but I had suffered enough of her.*

46.3 Sara sat on the grass. Thirty minutes elapsed before Leonard called the woman back into the passenger seat. Calmly he spoke, 'I think I know your half-life. Thirty minutes. *Half-life?* Every nuclear substance loses 50% of its radio-activity in a specific time. T-point-five of Uranium is about seven hundred million years. That's why we don't fool with it. What is your half-life, sweetheart? How long does it take you to cool down?'

'Many incarnations on this planet, Earthman.'

'Ah, so you are talking to me.'

In his release of tension, he realised that she always talked nonsense about her holy virginity and was entitled to her delusions. She had already launched into another of her stories. Inside the car, he handed her a cigarette. She responded.

'If you really want to write my biography I will talk to you as much as you want. Okay, let's see if you can understand. To enlighten you, it is required you will experience pain. Listen, I was seven or eight years old when the accident happened . . .'

She reverted to her French accent

'. . . but as you know, according to the official records, when my parents died in 1952 I have five years. But, you must see, I had been to school since two years and two more terms had passed . . . and Paul was aged about twelve I would say.'

Sara was sitting on the grass but she rose, preened herself, and climbed over a fence. Leaning on the passenger door of the hired Nissan she looked at Michael and paused for a few seconds before she continued.

'I see myself in the car. I am dead. I have died. When I awake, I am not only myself, I am also *her*. That is why I was afraid to sleep for two months at least. *The two planes,* these I don't understand. She had to die. Part of me had to die. Part of her had to die. We became two sisters in one flesh. Brain implants. Alien abduction. Not exactly modern textbook psychiatric theory, is it? *So you don't believe me, okay?*

'I wasn't afraid of dying because overnight I had become an older girl, someone else fully-aware of the human situation. I became someone else. Do you understand that? Like at the moment of orgasm they say you become one with your partner. My psychiatrist in America, told me . . .'

'. . . *that you were schizophrenic?'* He shook with laughter.

'That I was 'participatory-conscious' whereas most moderns are, like you, Mike, merely 'detached observers.' Survivors. Shallow *morons*, I would say.'

She slammed the door shut but he opened the window. After a few moments she shouted.

'You are a moron. You can see tragedy and yet you do not cry. *If you mock me like that again you may not get a second chance, earthman.* But you see, one day I lived with the most loving parents and with my brother. And things were different in France. I had so much to do, even time was not my own, and then, in Scotland it was so cold and the world cared not a jot about me. They said 'Your parents are dead. Paul will go to a school for naughty children near Paris. You will live with three hundred stupid girls at a school somewhere else.' I said, 'I shan't and I want to see Paul. *Please let me see him.* Why can't we go to the same school?' – 'Boys of his age aren't interested in girls. And we had to give him something. You saw for yourself, he was behaving badly. You know what happens when you behave badly? You are both spoiled children.'

'When we got back to the place of the accident, which looked just like this, when the man took us there, our lovely car was mangled and her smiling face – did you remember the old-fashioned Citroën chevron on the radiator? It was forever crumpled. It made the death of our parents seem even worse. You won't be very surprised to hear that I just cried. After that I had many thoughts that weren't childish but were very formative. The image of our wrecked car with me dead inside – yes, you heard me right, *I was dead for I had to be reborn*. This image has haunted me more than anything else. It recalled the explosion in my dream. And I was told, 'THE LIGHT WAS *GOD*,' and I told this to Paul. I told him that *God* had caused it for a purpose. I really imagined that God had taken our parents to Heaven because they were good and we were naughty.'

Leonard tried to interrupt her and was about to start the car.

'We need to get to the airport. I just realised how late we are.'

'Michael, do shut up, and please, please try to understand what I've just told *you and no-one else*. For the first time I've been able to share my guilt. Just like you asked me, I've given you key to the messianic story. People will say, *How can it be that the natures of Paul and Sara can be so different? One is a singer who snorts and blasts and blasphemes in the world of Heavy Rock while the other is all pureness and light, the Daughter of God?*'

Leonard smiled. It was remarkable how Sélène believed that the public regarded her as pure as the driven snow.

She continued, 'Now, too late, I plead, with my Maker and kind friend above, 'According to the rules of heredity, please God, can't I be the one who is left in peace to have a quiet life? Let it be Paul. We have found Paul. *No, Lord, Thy will be done*. I have taken his birthright but I cannot drink from the poisoned wine that is this world.'

'Well, now you know the answer, Michael. That is the big story. It was really myself. I stole the throne from Paul. I turned him against God. I put Paul down a level. I turned him against God. I blamed God for killing our parents.'

She shouted, *'Do you not understand?'*

'Will you get into the car?' Leonard asked.

She opened the door and stood beside the car.

Leonard extinguished his cigarette in the pristine hired car's ash tray.

'It may not be split personality syndrome. Psychotherapy has a condition called the Family Romance. Freud wrote about the natural feeling that one's family was once grand. It leads to the conviction that destiny will restore glory to a later generation. It explains . . . well, *delusions*, but it is present in us all . . . in varying degrees which . . . influences how we all see things. I learned about it in one of your reports.'

She sat on the passenger seat and closed the car door.

'Psychiatric reports. I'm thinking about it, Michael, honestly! But if you're saying that *I'm mad* then I don't care what you think.'

He tried to start the car but she took the car key.

He tried to reason with her.

'Don't get mad at me, Sara, and try to listen. *I listened to you.* And I am the last one to deny your ancestry and the Holy Family landing in Marseilles and surviving hundreds of years. Maybe even nineteen hundred years. But, and this is a big *But.*'

She waited for his verdict which was not long in coming.

'The king of the Jews, the messiah, etc, are all way past the sell-by date, sweetheart. That is the delusion that your puppet masters are ignoring. You let them feed you drugs because you feel good, and then they can suggest that you are anything they want to suggest.'

She went silent then left the car. She opened the trunk and removed her suitcase. The car keys she threw into the field.

Chapter Forty-Seven

Leonard returned the hired car and learned that she had booked another night at their hotel. They slept in separate rooms but met for breakfast, refreshed the next morning.

The cost of the delay was more than the airfare and another lost day of work. It was Retail Therapy. The Department Stores in Tokyo are amongst the world's most sumptuous and Leonard spent $3,000 on presents for Sara. They avoided buying really expensive things but she admired exquisite jewellery, enamelled furniture, soft rugs, and the Yamaha piano which played itself. These she would not permit him to buy.

'Don't ship the new furniture to Jerusalem. We are going to move, to live in Geneva,' she announced. He was shocked but relieved; at least he figured in the plans.

In the afternoon they took a bus tour round the estates of the fortified Imperial Palace which occupies so many acres of the city of Tokyo. They saw some beautiful Japanese gardens, all accessed by fleets of coaches. The charm of the Japanese gardens had a lot to do with their relaxed feelings this day and they found an intimacy by avoiding any talk of the past or of the future.

Japanese leisure parks cannot be imagined by a western gardener. They are conducers of contemplation and oases of tranquillity in a busy world. Leonard said to Sara, this was genuine religion. Enjoying themselves, time flew and eveing came; the shops of Tokyo became gaily illuminated. When they returned to the hotel she declared she had been disappointed but not angry with Leonard and that she had only acted happy. In his bedroom she wept about her responsibility for Paul's descent to vulgarity and about usurping his 'primogenitive rights.' He tried to apologise for his bad attitude to her 'visions' and soon colour and a smile were restored to her face. She had to stay in Japan one more day. Only under pressure she agreed to share his room.

47.1 In their room he held her and kissed her lips. The Japanese landscapes around the hotel had joined heaven and earth but now he kept his thoughts to himself: he wanted just one more bite at the apple. The gods were most definitely playing with the humans. What was the other thinking? Why was she holding back? She loved sex. Surely she knew that, sooner rather than later, they would go their own ways, journalist escort and actress messiah? Calm, English rationalist and French, crazy romantic. She was not so crazy. *Everything was to suit her agenda.*

The flirtatious actress was bewitched by the magic of Japan. I re-enacted the enticement of her rich American Senator who had turned or on before. When night came we avoided the tourist attractions and chose to walk in the intimacy of a Shinto shrine dedicated to all ancestors. It was a huge park and we could be alone in the crowds, enjoying each other, still holding hands as if time itself had stopped. It was only for one more day. I wanted to have her for myself and let her go before she dumped me. I knew that I would be a footnote in her history; one of her many boyfriends according to the Gospel of Sara.

She was behaving strangely in Japan; merging into the culture where ancestors live on forever. It made me think. In the Shinto garden thousands of suspended paper lanterns cast eternal spells as we walked slowly along the avenues formed by arches and pillars. Huge stone walls devoured millions of tiny folded and crumpled papers. For years Japanese people stuffed messages for their ancestors into the cracks and crevices. I explained to Sara how they sent wishes and messages superstitiously into the past and future in this way.

Her brows furrowed. I had made her think. She bought a parchment, borrowed my pen, and pushed her own inscribed wish into a gnarled pillar.

I demanded to see it. She made a scene to prevent me from interference, and as usual she won. The Japanese expect peace and decorum.

After she won, she relented and disclosed what was in it. I was surprised.

'I want a daughter.'

Then it occurred to me, She did not say, I want **your** *daughter.*

47.2 Leonard was still contriving to seduce her and hoping the last night would be very strong. *Perhaps that was why they were still in Japan*. They ate a late, light supper in their room. Then she – today his lover, tomorrow the World Saviour – drew the curtains, and dimmed the lights. A small TV flickered in the background the lowest denominator of popular entertainment: quiz shows, adverts, and sit-coms. She wanted the lights off but the TV left on. Absurd and incomprehensible adverts about soft drinks and useless home appliances irritated Leonard. He locked the bedroom door took her clothes off but she slowed him down.

'I want you to take half-an-hour until you accept me as I am. I have no big breasts.'

Once, foolishly, he had said that he liked big breasts. The bedroom phone rang and Leonard answered it, which made her angry. It was the front lobby so he hung up and took the phone off the hook. He stroked her small and graceful shoulders and delighted in the perfection of her beauty. She knew how to please men. Now, at last, Michael Leonard could believe that this was God's chosen. He massaged her aching feet as they had been walking too much.

She stared into his eyes with such intense devotion and trust to melt his heart, and she unbuttoned his shirt, getting stuck at one button which she simply tore off – not in a rage or passion, but as if to say, 'it doesn't matter, does it?'

Somebody was knocking at the door vigorously and persistently.

He cursed under his breath, 'For God's sake.'

She recoiled at the phrase.

The intruder simply would not go away. It seemed urgent – like the hotel was on fire. Angrily, Michael snatched his dressing gown and opened the door with the safety chain engaged. Two Japanese male, uniformed, hotel staff communicated in laborious, monosyllabic English, with profound apologies, their incompetent error of double booking their old room and the desire of the management to move them to the Presidential Platform at the penthouse level.

Leonard refused. The men pleaded. Sara intervened. Soon they packed their belongings, and were moved to the hotels' $3000 per night suite.

It was impressive and Michael Leonard normally relished in the trappings of enhanced status. But Sara was cold now and asked if he had condoms. There were too many distractions, even before a maid arrived at the door with flowers and chocolates. Then the manager arrived in person. He spoke in fluent French to Sara.

Leonard's myth of the French as romantics was shattered forever. He sat in a chair waiting for everyone but his woman to leave.

Finally they settled down in separate soft leather recliners to Champagne, fruits, and a forty-two inch high definition television but he was thinking about sex and her reluctance to participate. Although she was full of energy, she would tire and soon they would go to the same luxurious super-king-size bed and fall asleep.

She seemed focussed on the television although unable to understand a word of Japanese. The signs were clear enough. *Not tonight. Not ever again?*

Leonard retreated to the Presidential Suite's writing room to use the opportunity to work on his story. Despite its patriarchal tradition – Leonard had realised while walking in the Shinto Garden of the Ancestors – Jewish status is matrilineal. Even by him Sara would bear a Jewish child. So she would have her wish and her God would win. As his business was with the Davidic Genealogy, Leonard knew the Hebrew law of status: their child would not only be Jewish, *it would be legitimate as the issue of a man and woman free to marry*. In Mosaic Law, it is only adultery or forbidden unions that confer illegitimate status on a child.

In theory, *Michael Leonard could father the kings of Zion*. He was exhausted and the executive chair was too comfortable.

* * *

When Leonard woke up some hours later, Sara had gone to bed in the smaller bedroom. He cursed, then walked into the sumptuous luxury of the main bedroom. The king-sized bed would be his only sensuous pleasure tonight, but even if he never found the Davidic genealogy, he might at least get on to it. The thought kept him awake all night.

Chapter Forty-Eight

Leonard woke up shortly after 1:00pm and stared out of a window twenty floors above ground into the gardens of the Tokyo Palace Hotel. Two workers were energetically tidying the paths. It made him feel keen to get back to work in London. There was no sign of Sara. Not even a note from her.

He reached for the phone. Reception said she had left the previous night and had not returned. Management were politely asking him to vacate the suite. He put down the phone.

In a panic he searched the rooms and found all her belongings.

He decided to wait for her return during which he would contact the band-leader-singer-songwriter.

Eventually the operator responded, 'This is London, Mr Leonard, I'm connecting your call.'

'Thank you. May I speak to Antigens?'

A snooty voice announced, 'This is Miss Hannah.'

'And this is Michael Leonard from the BBC. Antigens agreed to meet me for an interview tomorrow which I must postpone as I have been detained in Tokyo.'

There was a pause. Leonard inspected the luxury he was about to leave.

'It's six in the morning, Mr Leonard.'

'I'm very sorry, Miss Hannah. Please pass on my apologies to your *employer*.'

The journalist, more tired than hungry, planned to skip lunch and keep his appetite for a dinner date. He missed her and vowed to avoid irritating or arguing with her. Around 3:00pm he fell asleep on the chair.

48.1 He was woken by an angel. Sara (No 1 personality) tapped on the door. He kissed her lips but pointed out the time. It was five minutes after five. It tied in with two hours sleep; which seemed about right.

Sara was relaxed and happy but firmly rejected his amorous advances. Leonard spoke like an angry father to his teenage daughter.

'Well, you should not arouse me. If you would wear a bra under that tee shirt, and you might have explained why you left, and where you've been.'

'I've been walking, then I had no money so I went for a drink in the hotel bar and I went more walking and I fell asleep under a pavilion. I dreamed of my prince. Such an erotic dream. He came and took me. It was so beautiful. He looked like you.'

He looked like you. Leonard imagined himself in her dreams. It was a clumsy deception she made and he was angry.

'I know what tired you. Strange coincidence, so was I. They call them comfort girls here. It is hard work, love-making, isn't it, Peach Blossom?'

He observed her carefully to see if she might betray anger or *infidelity*, but she did not answer him directly.

'Peach Blossom, I like that name, Michael. It will always bind us to this sacred land which I love. You are silly to want to rush away. Why leave paradise so soon?'

'Because we were supposed to see Antigens or Paul in London tomorrow, remember? *Well, never mind, I left a message for him to cancel.*'

'Thanks Mike, I can always rely on you.'

'Do I stay in charge of your administration department?'

'At double salary, Mike. Payable in Heaven. In Asian karmas. Redeemable in your next incarnation. When do you want to fly to London?'

'That seems to be up to you . . .'

'Soon. I would like us to go to Hiroshima today. That is the final thing I have left to do in Japan. Can you arrange for me to meet the Mayor of Hiroshima? And I want the world press to be at the commemorative bell there when I shall ring it. First I shall give you the story because you have to earn money as a freelance journalist and you have been using so much of your own time and money.'

48.2 Sara was shown round the Hiroshima city museum and visited a radiation hospice where people die in dignity separated from the cause of their destruction by thirty three cruel years. Then she and Michael were driven to the standing monument by city worthies she hardly spoke to because she was so distressed. The authorities treated western celebrities with courtesy. She could not eat any of the ten course vegetarian kosher lunch including cakes with icing spelling the name S-A-R-A. All the time she hung her head, clung onto Michael, and sobbed from time to time. She uttered not a word, even when she shook hands with the mayor. When she found herself in front of a row of microphones she said just a few strange words, 'Blessed are those who have not seen the horrors of war but know it is evil.'

The trip was over. Her work was done in Japan.

Sara and Michael were driven back to Tokyo in silence in a convoy of official vehicles. They travelled in a black limousine with a small Japanese man and his translator who was never called upon. The silence seemed unreal as did Leonard's role as consort. He lamented that the photos of Sara at Hiroshima would be transmitted to the west before he could return to sell the story. And he had travelled far only to find Paul and Paul had flown back to London.

And he had had no sex.

48.3 Narita Airport is much the same as any other international terminal. Westerners expect it to be bigger, cleaner, newer, more opulent, but it is merely more efficient. Sara and Michael were still silent as they were led down a passageway. Presumably VIP formalities were dealt with by the authorities. They reached the gate where two or three hundred people had gathered to wave her on. Leonard urged her to deliver an official statement to prove she was the messiah.

'Thou shalt not kill, Michael, it's that simple.'

Leonard countered that the war had been ended – not begun – by the A-Bomb, and started – not ended – by the Japs.

'Spoken like a politician but if I am the messiah, Mike, I will impose upon them an Eleventh Commandment, *Thou Shalt not rationalise.*'

He smiled but it was followed by hours of gloomy silence. While she thought about the bomb he admitted he was thinking of his debts and his servile role.

She thought for a moment then said, 'Michael . . . Okay, Mike, will you, please, help me in this work? Or is it not possible for you to work for God? He is a bad employer – no money, just karma and trouble. But is it a problem even if your colleagues will force you to give up your career? You know what Paul has said. So I've got a fortune in an untouched family trust fund in France.

'So,' he replied, 'You are suggesting that, having found the Temple Treasures, I should get some of it myself?'

'Don't trivialise it, Michael? What was the treasure for, if not to restore our rule of the world? So take your insult back. You will get fired if you prove to be insubordinate. Perhaps you're just not up to it?'

'Yes, boss, I take all my insults back.'

'You really are the greatest researcher, Mike. Consider what you have found so far. It eluded all the others. I mean, we are so close to the Temple Treasures, the explanation of the Crusades, and now *to Paul*. I think perhaps you will soon find the Genealogy. *Our careers do not conflict*. We both seek the truth and I need you in so many ways. You can see that and surely I am good for you, just a little? I make you laugh! I make you softer!'

'Sara, I really like the idea that Paul should be messiah if it spares you for reality and for me, but he looks more like *the Antichrist*.'

She ignored or did not accept the insult to her brother:

'That means yes, then? You *will* work with me?'

Michael avoided answering Sara but left her with the hope of his collaboration, 'When we land in London we should wait until ten o'clock and then phone Mushroom Agencies Division. M-A-D, darling, just like us, and see if "Antigens Antichrist" will see us.'

48.4 They landed on time at London Heathrow Airport. Leonard always complained about his financial problems but he had made an investment decision.

'Sara, I bought you a ring, I knew it was right when I saw the rings in Narita Airport and why pay double the prices in the UK? I still love you and you love me. We can work out the problems. We had better make an announcement or else the story of us will give my rivals a boost. Only kidding. The press are after us both now. Or do you want to wait a bit? . . . No? Then where shall we marry?'

'The City of David, *Sancta Civitas*!' declared Sara like a child with a new toy. 'Let us marry at the centre of the world, God's capital which my ancestor founded.'

Leonard nodded and asked sarcastically. 'Just a small ceremony with a few friends and shall we limit it to five hundred journalists?'

After several weeks she denied changing her mind but after an evening out, she prohibited him from parking outside her home with the excuse that it was late and she had to sleep.

He asked her to marry so that they could live together. He agreed; *the modern messiah could hardly live in sin.* He pouted his lips to kiss her, and revved the car with his foot.

She turned away, reminding him that women preferred a romantic proposal rather than a reasoned ultimatum. But she stayed in his car.

He reminded her that she had left him in the early hours of the morning in their hotel bedroom in Tokyo and returned the next day sexually satisfied. An argument was starting.

She exclaimed, 'Oh!' and looked away. He could not see her face. Was it surprise? Disgust? Guilt?

She remained silent but Michael sighed, 'I know that you do not lie, so speak to me, and don't economise on the truth by omitting anything or misleading me. I know that you have been avoiding setting a date to get married and I know it started from the day you wouldn't have sex when you came back to our room, but in a good mood. You were happy but not horny. It isn't normal for one's fiancée to stay out all night, you know.' He revved the car again to show her neighbours the E-type Jaguar is the most masculine car ever built.

'Michael, I did not stay out all night and you will have to wait for fifteen more years if you want a teenage daughter to lecture. As for me, *I am who I am*.'

I am who I am. The Hebrew tetragrammaton. *Was she was saying, I'm a goddess and you're a mere mortal; or was she was saying, I cannot change my nature? Or all these things?*

She left the coupé but closed the door so gently that only on the third attempt it held. Poor build quality.

Chapter Forty-Nine

His group consisted of five musicians: lead and bass guitars, saxophone and percussion. Vocals, keyboards, and chief song writer was thirty-five-year-old Robert Wyseman better known as *Antigens*, born in Boulder, Colorado, USA, according to the official biography.

At ten minutes past three Michael and Sara sat with him at a street table outside a café in London.

Without his warpaint he looked like a normal person; in fact he looked refined, reflective and – like Sara – slim with dark complexion. His hair was black and his face was red-cheeked, gaunt, and weather-beaten. His angular features twitched occasionally. He looked very tired, having just returned from a world trip of eleven energetic open-air gigs.

'He's doped to the eyeballs and close to the edge,' Sara whispered to Leonard but she exuded confidence. Was *she* doped? Like brother, like sister? Perhaps it was her clothes – back to the white tee shirt (but decently attired with bra) and the silly Italian shades. She looked like Sélène again. Celebrities are cliquey: perhaps she was trying to say, *Brother, like you, I am a star.*

Sara kept looking at him. He avoided her gaze but he seemed fascinated by her. He kept twitching. Leonard ordered an Espresso. She had a cappuccino with whipped cream. Antigens *or Paul* kept stirring an aromatic Turkish coffee obsessively until he swallowed it in one. With a grimace, he barked.

'This is neither Greek nor Turkish! Back to British Coffee. What can I do for you, Mr BBC?'

His voice was soft but sophisticated. First hurdle fell: there was a trace of a French accent. He did not disguise his contempt for Leonard. He fidgeted with impatience or nerves. Or was it exhaustion or the need for a fix? He got up, stood behind Sara and placed his hands down her tee shirt, feeling her breasts. Sara was frozen by fear or doubt. Paul was challenging them and pretending that he was not her brother.

Leonard jumped up and as his chair hit the ground, the rock star rushed back to his seat, excessively feigning cowardice. As Leonard began to talk, Antigens swept his cup and saucer off the table onto the pavement.

'Sorry mate,' he called to the waiter, then growled, 'How about getting me a *real* Turkish? And make it *hot* this time.'

Leonard barked aggressively, 'We can do this the hard way, Mr Paul Antigens but I'll give you one more chance for the easy way. The family news first: your sister and I are getting married.'

Leonard placed his hand on Sara's just to make sure that her brother could not be in any doubt. She displayed her Japanese engagement ring. There was no reaction from Antigens.

The Greek café owner, lacking that English tranquillity when all around is in chaos, approached the table to disturb the desired effect of Leonard's timing. He offered to pay for the broken china rather than jeopardise the meeting, but Antigens growled to the waiter in a French-American accent.

'Hey mate, isn't there anything you can do right? Beer? *Tea perhaps?* Just bring me one. My sister's really sorry for knocking over my coffee. We haven't seen each other for twenty years; it's such an emotional thing. You Continentals, you're all close family people. She's French. *I'm American*. So you must forgive my little sister's accident? And can you please bring me a round of meat sandwiches and a proper coffee of any sort? Darlin' give this little man a few bucks to make up for breaking his nice cups. He won't have to wash them now. This is Sélène, the movie star. And I'm Antigens the singer. Give him the money, sweetie.'

He handed Sara a substantial roll of English currency but she hesitated.

'Not for you, dear, give it to the fat little man.'

Sara looked at Leonard as she handed it over to the café owner.

The proprietor took her hand and slowly, gently, kissed the back of it, pronounced 'Mademoiselle Sélène, I am honoured to have you as my guest,' and he wrapped his fingers round the money.

'I shall have this mess cleared up immediately.'

He issued orders in a language Leonard did not recognise.

Sara said to Antigens, 'I just want to be friends, Paul. If you don't want to see me, I'll respect your wishes . . .'

No response. Then she switched to French in the second person familiar, 'You're thinking, *what do I want from you?*'

'Everyone wants something,' he was crunching two sugar cubes but he had replied in French. Sara jumped in to prevent Leonard breaking the spell.

'I want to know what happened to mama and papa? Why are lies told about our family? Who is doing it? According to the French records, *you don't even exist* . . . Paul?'

Leonard was pretending to be detached. The rock star's mouth opened but . . . silence prevailed. A distraction had been delivered to him.

The waiter rapidly and nervously brought a round of meat sandwiches on a cardboard plate. Beer was served in two plastic beakers. Antigens was very hungry and in amazed silence Sara watched him devour the food like an animal.

But he still had the shakes. After he finished chewing a tough piece of cold meat taken from the sandwich and washing it down with beer he burped predictably and loudly. He said, 'I am not what I appear to be because I am a performer with a *persona*. But I am not Paul Plantard. I think you will find that he really died in a car accident.'

Another interruption.

The waiter returned, escorting a well-upholstered young woman with very long earrings and very little skirt. Perhaps she was five feet small and about the same across. She carried a brush with a broken-off short handle. As the waiter guarded the woman, anticipating trouble from Antigens, she bent down and swept the broken dishes with a single and rapid stroke, then withdrew hastily and furtively. It was too late. Having dressed unsuitably for the task she exhibited cleavages at both ends.

Antigens made vulgar whistles and comic gestures. The cleaning woman was young, and she immaturely pouted offence. She wanted to make a scene and Antigens wanted to create a diversion. Saintly Sara rose to soothe her sister, but Leonard made a gesture and she sat down. He ordered the cleaner to leave them and placed his hand protectively and amorously on Sara's shoulder.

'This is your sister, Paul, I don't wish to be impertinent, but I believe that your, eh, real name is, or was, Paul.'

'My real name is Robert Wyseman, Mike. It's not much of a name,' he laughed, 'but I got mine at birth, unlike your fiancée.'

'Where did you grow up, Robert?'

'Mainly *en Paris*.'

'Your parents were from Paris?'

'My foster-parents were from USA, Mr Leonard. My own parents were killed in a car crash.'

'That's what I was told, too, Paul,' interjected Sara. 'Oh, don't you remember your little sister, before your life with your new parents?'

She was at boiling point but he was very cool.

'I don't have a sister, to my knowledge, but if my biological dad also had a bit on the side, and if I have a sis, would I like to meet her? Of course! And if it is you, then, HELLO SIS!'

'This son-of-a-bitch isn't very smart,' Leonard exclaimed, then let brother and sister get on with their exchange.

When Paul was shaking hands with Sara, Leonard's professional interrogation expertise took over. He focussed on an uncharted period of the singer's life.

'You trained as a Buddhist, Paul?'

If Paul hesitated he would lose the advantage. If he answered 'no,' then he was lying. Standard technique of a skilled investigator, but Sara spoiled it by interrupting, 'I'm really your sister.'

Paul or Antigens sneered, 'That's nice to know.' But, irritated by the attempt to catch him out he yelled to Leonard, 'Look I meet a lot of journalists who turn truth upside down. I think Sélène has had some experience of that. But come to the point. Have I inherited a fortune, or have I got laid with one of my sisters by mistake?'

Sara seized the initiative, 'Paul, you know that some people have worked hard to forge papers to conceal our identities. *Why?* Maybe these people killed our parents. Doesn't that trouble you? Maybe you don't want me to disturb your present or reveal your past but you are raking up my past in your songs. How else did you get to know about the flower that spread in Papa's garden? And the way I was taken in the car from my home. And about our real mother? Why do *you* harass *me*?'

Antigens hesitated and said, 'These are just my dreams. Maybe your boyfriend should find out who *you* really are before he gets married or before he writes your story.'

'I heard at least three things in your songs,' Sara protested in a little voice like a mouse trying to frighten a tiger, 'that only you would know, Paul. Look, what does this say? No this?' She showed him his album. 'On the inner sleeve, the lyrics.'

She pointed, and he read out, 'Songs by Antigens. The sporophyte. A plant that generates by asexual reproduction.'

'Such a plant obsessed our father. Read this, Paul.'

Paul or Antigens complied. 'Okay, here it says, The Immaculate Deception . . . published by Mushroom Music. Copyright 1975. Words and Music by Antigens. So what?'

'All songs written by you. That's what it says.'

Paul hesitated and began to speak softly; it was more than calming down but as if he had switched personality.

'I can't remember where I got all the words. It proves someone knows about your childhood, *if you say so*, Sélène. My music saves the masses from the lies of religion and politics. If we're responsible for our actions then Jesus was a bad man. We've had enough of messiahs.'

'You are well placed to sort that one out, Paul,' said Sara but Leonard interrupted her.

He made one more attempt to re-unite the Holy Family. 'Paul, you can choose to preach or to sing to the whole damned world if your mother was in the messianic line.'

Mentioning a mother often ignites a man, but Leonard was taken by surprise by Antigen's explosive reaction.

'Michael, shut the fuck up. Can you really imagine that frail, aristocratic little woman with any man's thing up her? Mathilde wasn't anyone's mum, you stupid man. Not mine, and not yours, darling sis. Still, I suppose an immaculate conception's a possible element of a messianic claim.'

The brother was surprised by the silence and the widening grin Leonard could not resist. In his haste to leave Paul toppled his chair, angry that in this meeting, either doped or down from dope, he had exposed himself. The journalist had trapped his quarry but deepened the mystery of the family.

Chapter Fifty

Rejecting the offers to move in, Sara said she must to stay with her friend in St John's Wood, four miles from Leonard's flat in Kensington. Tamar was a thirty-eight-year-old Jewish divorcée living with her two sons and aging parents. She was a music critic who joked that she needed free tickets to entice eligible men to concerts. During weekdays Leonard had dinner with them then went home. He complained often that they had not slept together since returning from Japan.

On this evening Tamar made some coffee but Leonard had left in a hurry. A pleasant conversation was developing but when Tamar brought in the coffees Leonard was gone and Sara was silent.

The coffees were allowed to go cold, untouched. The hostess tried to encourage her friend. Sara explained only that opposites attract but it makes a very stormy relationship.

'He is a decent ordinary guy; how can he understand my predicament?' she asked Tamar, but she would not discuss the details of the evening's clash.

Leonard had left the house after dinner but thought it a pity to pass by a favourite pub on the way home, knowing that some of his friends would be there.

He arrived at his flat after 1:00am to find seven phone messages had been taped. Six were panic calls from Sara requesting the urgent services of her white knight.

The isolated call was from a certain Jacques Pascal, in St. Germain in

France. In response to enquiries from Leonard's Parisian researcher he wished to speak to the top man. He said he was a retired civil servant who had access to the pre-1945 French records with the authentic families; he knew who had altered them; and why they had remained altered after cessation of hostilities. All information for the bargain price of US$1m.

Leonard categorised people who crawl from the woodwork of the Messianic Conspiracy into cranks, opportunists, and decoys. A crank might ask for an unrealistic sum. An opportunist would be cheaper. And a decoy might do anything as a double-bluff. He wondered if it was too late to telephone France but (he thought) for such a large sum the informant should suit his paymaster. Waking him might catch him off guard. If he were a crank it would punish him.

The response took Leonard by surprise.

After ten minutes of questions, courtesies, and delaying tactics, the Parisian revealed himself as homicide chief inspector Jean-Michel Loisel.

Leonard guarded his words. That people had been killed before in this conspiracy he knew – Sara's parents, a Swiss journalist, and possibly some other people. He placed down the receiver then remembered that something sinister was happening to Sara right now, closer to home.

Immediately his phone rang. After the serial messages she left, Leonard knew it would be Sara as he had been delayed from responding to her cries for help.

50.1 It was approaching 2:00am in the morning of another productive day Michael Leonard was about to lose by lack of sleep.

'Sara, I can't hear a thing over this telephone,' he exclaimed with enough exasperation to upset her more.

Despite his exhaustion he conceded, 'I will be with you soon. I'll leave in fifteen minutes.' He put down the phone and realised that he was tired, irritated, and had too much alcohol in his blood either to drive or to comfort Sara. He felt the danger of being unable to react vigorously to whatever was about to happen.

Something, or someone, was threatening. He had to prepare himself.

Leonard swallowed some dark, black, coffee. He freshened his face and shaved quickly. He chose a fresh white shirt, silk Paisley-pattern cravat, and a blue blazer. It was a dark and damp night and he did not attempt to hide his foul mood. He revved up his XJ6 and sped off much too quickly.

He was still suspicious that Sara had tried to admit that she had sex in Japan and angry that his reaction had stifled her confession. Now he could never drag the truth from her. If she meant that *she* was with child, she might have it aborted. He took comfort in his confusion; at least he was now alerted.

When he arrived at the house he saw Sara and Tamar through her window; it was the only house with all lights on. The door was open. The entire family was assembled in a modern, small room dominated by a large TV. Sara was wrapped in a blanket, whimpering as if she had been injured. The room was excessively warm thanks to a blazing fire. Mugs of tea were scattered everywhere and in all stages of cooling and congealing. Tears had softened her face but now Sara was coherent.

She complained that she had received telephone calls while *he* was enjoying an evening in the pub, 'I'm sorry Michael. Just ignore my moods. That's what I do.'

'Okay, Peach Blossom. What's the problem?'

'The phone calls are from Lenny King at the BBC. Do you know him?'

'He's a staff producer, but I don't know him very well.'

'Is he integrity?'

'Yes I would say so. What does he want?'

She relaxed her grip of Leonard and relaxed into the white leather settee. She looked him straight in the eye.

'The BBC engineers are agitated because they have been getting a broadcast which Jodrell Bank assures them is from outer space. The Righteous Teacher wants to speak to me. I don't know what to do. I believed it before, but deep down, I . . . I sort of trusted Robert, yet . . . *suppose it's a fraud* . . . what might he ask me to do? Or say? Perhaps he is trying to trap me. I go by my feelings but you are rational and worldly. Please, please, Mike, I really want to know the truth. I've spoken to executives in the BBC and they are taking it very seriously. I feel convinced by it myself, yet it is so much like a hoax. It's on Tamar's phone answering machine.'

Leonard felt more awake than ever. Tamar's father seemed to take it seriously. The family had been unable to calm her over several hours and now she clung to Leonard. She was scantily clad. All eyes were on the couple. Leonard decided that he would take her to his bed by getting her away from Tamar's house. And he said they should forget the BBC until the morning.

Tamar took the cassette from the answer phone to the stereo system where it played more clearly. Everyone listened carefully.

'Sara, this is the Teacher. Sara. Do not be afraid. Sara. Sara. It is the Teacher. Come to the BBC. I must speak to Sara. Sara!'

The voice was soft but impassioned. The tape continued with the saintly Priest-Teacher's life story. All of which, as Sara and Leonard both knew, was straight out of the published Dead Sea Scrolls. The Teacher had led a chosen few along the true path from the hypocritical ways of the Temple and the Wicked Priest had even tried to kill him on the Day of Atonement. The Teacher was from the Zadokite family anointed by David, and he had established the true but small community of Israel by the Dead Sea. First the nation was overwhelmed by the Greek-Syrian oppressors, then the Maccabees had turned from liberators to oppressors, then the Roman invaders, and now the Sadducees had exercised power without divine authority over Judea and the other tribes had split. The Holy Land had fallen from divine favour into chaos.

Leonard was absorbed by the story of mankind's downfall when Sara suddenly switched the player off and spoke out.

'The BBC kept on phoning me Michael. But I told them not to call until 2:00am when I knew you'd be here to decide. They want us to come straight to their studio. They will agree to a live broadcast or an edited taped session at my choice. But what should I do? They are afraid 'it' will go away. And I just wish it *would*. No, I don't. Oh, God, I am afraid . . . I don't know. Please help me.'

'Perhaps we should test it by keeping it waiting,' Leonard selfishly suggested. 'After all it, or he, isn't God.'

'But he is God's holy prophet, and very genuine and Michael . . . I love and respect him. He is the voice of the Almighty.'

'Unless he is a hoax.'

'Exactly!' said Sara, smiling because Leonard understood her problem.

Her smile turned to terror when the phone rang again.

It was 2:00am. Her face, drained of blood, and she said, 'You take it.'

Mr King, the BBC producer, was happy to speak to his associate and begged him to come to Bush House *immediately*. Leonard had other plans.

He wasn't listening to King's explanations until he heard that the radio signal really was from outer space. The journalist began to consider the stratospheric fame and fortune the story would bring. Perhaps Sara was also motivated by a similar opportunity – to be propelled in Britain further down her own second career.

For whatever reason, now she smiled. She seemed to be enjoying the drama.

As Tamar's family watched this transformation Leonard held the phone aside and asked her, 'What do you feel?'

'I can't explain it, but I know it's genuine,' she replied. 'And I'd rather behave like a fool than be deaf to God.'

'Then we should go!'

Leonard spoke decisively, knowing that she had always intended to go, but not without him. Then it suddenly occurred to him, 'How did the BBC get this number?'

'The Teacher gave it to them,' said Sara, 'He says it near the beginning of the tape.'

Leonard's face expressed cynical disbelief but after some awkward rewinding of the tape, Tamar found the Teacher's voice '. . . London. British people please telephone Sara at 01-772 . . .' It was a strange mix of two ages, primitive and technological, which made Leonard feel suspicious.

'Don't you feel it's . . . *odd*?'

As he searched for a better word she nodded vigorously and started her silent weeping again. Then Sara said she was very happy that they worked so well together because she was instinctive and he was rational.

'Sara,' the drink in Leonard promised, 'Don't worry, I won't let you down. And I've thought about how we shall test the voice that apparently watches you.'

She cuddled him and needed him. He smiled.

Chapter Fifty-One

In the car Leonard persuaded Sara that no-one could perform well at such an hour. She agreed to keep the Righteous-spy-in-the-sky waiting until after they were refreshed by sleep. And she agreed to sleep at his flat but in her own room.

They were both exhausted.

'I don't care if we are seen to live together,' she said, 'I will not conceal the truth. If I am ashamed of what I am doing then I should not do it. Just because some old monks were driven to deny Jesus his virility and ban sex as sinful but why should I act out their hang-up?'

Leonard began to think that he might like her new religion.

He asked why they should delay marriage.

She smiled, 'Why do you think that my career will be longer than that of Jesus? He had less than three years. *Look out, Michael!'*

He had nearly driven off the road.

'Drive more slowly, darling,' she pleaded, and he slowed down, aware of his deepening brain fatigue and inebriation.

'Sweetheart, he replied, 'I shouldn't be driving, but if the BBC broadcast is a set-up it has to be Robert Kohen and it will be easier to storm Fort Knox than to penetrate that man's activities. He uses US defence technology to manipulate us. And the French side of the conspiracy uses government resources. I can't be sure if I can do anything better or smarter but all I need is one crack in the smooth edifice with which I'll destroy an entire conspiracy of lies.'

'But you will help me, faithfully?'

'Yes, Sara, I will stay by you, *always*. You can rely on me. What is your true feeling about Robert?'

'Robert, he would not impersonate The Teacher of Righteousness.'

Leonard's heart skipped two beats.

Had Sara called him Robert? Perhaps she had altered the offending sentence mid-stream by inserting the word 'he'.

'You see, Robert is my superior, I have to trust him. People think that I am the chief human being on the planet but in our religious protocol I rank below him. He is the messiah-priest and I am the royal messiah . . .'

'Are you sure, or has he told you this?'

'Both, Michael. The Teacher is also the messianic – which just means anointed – prophet or forerunner.'

'Who told you this?'

'The Dead Sea Scrolls are based on the Law of Moses. The Priest-messiah has precedence over the royal messiah. Robert claims to be the priest-messiah who was prophesied to appear at the end of time.'

'At the end of time,' Leonard mimicked sarcastically. 'Gives us plenty time to get on with our lives.'

'Michael,' Sara pleaded. 'Robert is a man demented by his demons but not retarded by stupidity. My point is that he claims to have understood the practical techniques by which man can tamper with time.'

51.1 *We arrived at my home, both of us very tired. Cocooned together in the excessive warmth of winter bedclothes I wrapped her petite olive body in some oversized heavy cotton pyjamas of mine to keep her warm and perhaps prevent her body from arousing mine. I was too tired. Cuddling her very tightly, sheer exhaustion forced my eyelids shut and my brain closed down.*

Then the phone rang.

I was absolutely furious. I watched it ring. I swore ferociously.

'Darling, it will be important,' a groggy sweet voice of Sara assured me, so I decided not to rip the telephone's umbilical cord and splatter the wretched thing over the opposite wall of the bedroom. I cleared my throat and composed myself.

'Good morning. This is Michael Leonard. Who are you?'

(I hoped that it might be the Parisian police.)

It was the BBC World Service.

They had received fresh instructions from the Teacher to phone here to ask Sara to come to the studio.

'Listen,' I said, 'it is ten past four AM. You will phone me here at one PM, and not before.' I saw Sara's face make a reproach, '. . . unless the Teacher, who you say is contacting you by satellite, orders otherwise.'

Sara was listening to the voice on the phone.

'Sir, the Teacher demands her now. He gave us your number.'

I considered that, then uttered, 'Oh, fuck.'

Sara caressed my freshly shaven cheeks with her small hands, took the phone from me and whispered, 'I'll come by a taxi. Give me directions. I have a pencil. Okay, Fleet Street . . . Strand . . . Security Gate, South East Wing.'

She was wasting time. I took the phone.

'Okay, Bush House, at this ungodly hour the traffic will be quiet and it will take me only half-an-hour. Please have someone make me a very strong black coffee.'

I hung up and then my brain started to awaken. I felt happy.

I lifted the phone and dialled Peter from memory. If people were tapping my line I could mislead them. I would then phone my assistant with my real plans from a phone box en route to the BBC.

'Pete, Good morning! Sorry, lad, shop is opening early. Listen carefully . . . I'm on the way to the BBC so you'll have to handle a simultaneous but major development. I'm not going to repeat this.'

51.2 Sara and I arrived at the Bush House by 5:15am. I left the car on a kerb with a parking warden screaming, 'You can't leave it there, sir!'

Grabbing Sara's wrist we ran into the building, past a security guard who hissed, 'You aren't allowed through.'

The 6:00am Breakfast Show had been rescheduled to feature the live broadcast from 'The Teacher.' I made verbal deals by phone on royalties; with the Head of Religious Broadcasts in Manchester and the Controller of Radio One in his bed somewhere in London.

In Bush House the producer, Lenny King, was setting things up. The studio was a small cubicle acoustically damped by suspended curtains.

'Are you nervous, honey?' he asked Sara, forgetting her messianic status.

I probed, 'Lenny! Where is the broadcast really coming from?'

King nodded to permit his engineer to confide in me.

'We've made some progress on that and we're going to discuss it on the programme.'

I reminded the engineer that, although I was not a BBC employee, since 1965 I had been under exclusive contract with them on the Messianic Conspiracy story: 'I'm one of us.'

'Okay, Mike,' King said, 'I hadn't seen it that way. There is an orbiting can out there with a transponder and its nineteenth channel, D-3, is hired out to a global imaging company from Montreal called EyeCan. They are openly sub-leasing time to the Modern Order of Essenes in New York but the circle is closed. It stands up to reason. I've spoken to MOE, and they freely admitted to being asked by 'their founder' to open the channel. I felt pleased until I realised that they meant their *founder of 2000 years ago,* The Teacher of Righteousness!'

'What is global imaging?' I asked.

'Mike, it is a satellite scanning the earth for anything – like geological surveying, weapons espionage, or the commercial equivalents of the military applications of satellites. Private companies, venturer capitalists, investors and speculators buy satellite time to detect resources and information on the planet.'

I still preferred the theory of a simple fraud.

'But surely the Teacher's signal originates from this planet and is merely relayed back to us by the satellite?'

King glanced at the studio clock.

'Well, Mike, unfortunately the answer is negative. In 1976 BBC Special Engineering Projects checked Dr Kohen's American broadcasts in connection with your documentary. We found no explanation then, and today the magic is greatly enhanced. The source is live and interactive. Explain to me how it will interrogate Sara, and I want this explanation a lot. Manchester is going all superstitious on me Michael, and I prefer my Religious Broadcasts Department to be convinced atheists. Seriously, I promise you that on my instructions a thousand communications engineers worldwide will be seeking a terrestrial source. *Count down to a live broadcast, man; we need to leave.*'

When the engineers became busy setting things up Lenny King lured me outside the studio.

'Mike, I will deny this if you betray me, but radio telescopes confirm the source relayed to the satellite is from light years away in outer space. If originating here then it is necessarily bouncing back from the past. *Intellectually challenging*, isn't it? Jodrell Bank confirmed this with the Yanks' NASA SETI . . . Search for Extra Terrestrial Intelligence . . .'

'Americans should try looking in England. For intelligence, I mean.'

I wasn't sure how to deal with the BBC's dilemma of a signal from the past squaring with Sara's observation that Kohen might be manipulating time. Coolly, I felt it was a lead to be followed in my debunking of the fabrication; but I felt disturbed by the possibility, in theory, that the mad scientist had done it. Either way, I decided to keep this line of enquiry to myself for now.

As the studio door was closed and the light indicated 'On Air' I realised that King was talking to me in the corridor.

'Please, Mike, I want to find out how 'our deceased ancestor' can cope with the two-way interactive conversation they have requested with Sara. If it's a miracle, Manchester wants to break the news. If the American military has this technology, they've kept us in the dark. If Kohen has kept the Pentagon in the dark . . . well, let's just say there are people looking over our shoulders right now. Including the Russian military. They are snooping.'

'Understood,' I answered with a smile: 'Well, if it's for King and country, let's get on with it, Lenny.'

Sara came out of the studio, looking for me. She was pale and very disturbed, *and she hadn't heard our conversation!*

'Mike, I've spoken by a link to the Director General of the BBC. The problem is that the BBC is getting several broadcasts from different sources, simultaneously, all from the Teacher, all wanting to speak to me at the same time. All divulging secret information, all betraying knowledge of my whereabouts, all employing radio techniques well beyond human understanding. They are all urging the BBC to let me speak to the Teacher without delay. It's some sort of a time warp. How can I be in more than one place at a time?'

I looked at the BBC Producer.

'Sorry, Mike. I was ordered not to disclose that bit to you,' King apologised. 'But it's true, at least *apparently* so. The radio waves have been bedlam since nine o'clock last night. The Teacher comes through all relay stations, trackers, transmitters, microwave telecoms, diplomatic, military, etc; from Ascension Island to the North Pole. It instructs operators how to network signals to us, little old us, at the BBC. The DG's coming here and will be on a conference with The Defence Department – these boys are worried.'

From the balcony of the mall building everyone saw the BBC's Director General arrival. He appeared with his entourage and staff all over the building. He asked to see Michael Leonard and producer King. He asked for privacy. In a small office he assured us that the signals coinciding on *terra firma* originated from far away, either in time or space.

'You mean that the voices are definitely not from the present?' I asked.

'Correct. If they are not from afar, we can't hear them now, but they were broadcast a long time ago. We can calculate time delay by their distance travelled. Several voices from about 2000 years ago want to talk to Sara. We don't know how to cope. Choose one or more at random, I suppose. I really want to see the broadcast. See for myself how Sara responds to questions and how on earth, or not, the 'Teacher' by interactive replies, proves he is not a fraud.'

We walked down the corridor and pressed our noses against the studio's soundproof double glass.

51.3 Across a large oak table with a forest of microphones and entangled cables Sara faces the Irish disc-jockey on whose live Breakfast Show she is the unscheduled and uninvited guest.

On grey-painted loudspeakers hanging menacingly from ceiling brackets emerged the voices of engineers setting levels, establishing contacts, and patching landlines between studios. The programme was being networked overseas.

'Thirty seconds, Des.'

I am invited to participate but I have only signed a live single-right broadcast contract with the BBC on behalf of Sara. I verbally authorise them to sell to other buyers on the royalty basis of fifty-fifty. I feel really pleased; I know that Sara will not question my decisions. Her money will go to her newly registered charitable foundation.

I knock on the studio door to test my authority. I suggest Sara should try to speak French. If 'the Teacher' could manipulate modern English, why not French? She nods, but without any enthusiasm.

I settle down in the control room. The red lamp lights. The disembodied voice animates the monitor loudspeakers,

!Sara. Sara. Sara. This is the Teacher!

In a childish voice passionately cracking with emotion she replies.

'Speak Master. It is Sara. I am here.'

!Is it really you? You seem so near to me in time, Child of the Third Millennium and Daughter of Zion!

'I am Sara, previously Sarah-Hélène, I was called Sarah Kelly, Your Holiness.'

The broadcast quality from Alpha Centauri is excellent. There is no attempt to dress it with atmospherics to enhance its mystical quality, but I feel uneasy. I can hear the engineers talk about 'multi-lingual' tongues then I hear a subdued medley of foreign languages. It sounds like an international telephone exchange.

'May I ask a question?' the Irish disc-jockey interrupts.

Sara explains but the Teacher says he knows what a disc-jockey is.

The Irishman responds, 'We are broadcasting from London a daily morning programme. Should I call you *Rabbi*? That's what I believe you to be.'

!If you like, but I am a high priest from the dynasty of Zadok. *What you call the rabbis, Irishman, is what we call* perushim. *They reject the false Asmonean priests of Israel, as we do, but from them will come – or to you they have come – your Pharisees, and from these the modern Jewish rabbis which still usurp the authority of the Priests of Zadok, and even the Daughter of David who is with you now. Thanks to God and not to mankind who almost got away with their elimination of the line of David. How fortunate is your generation who live to see Her. Will you reject her too? I do not hear your voice tremble with respect to her. So you do not recognise her, my man, as a swine hesitates over a pearl and crushes it under its feet. You have need of Her. Woe on you, man of darkness!*

'Father, Your Holiness, I hear what you are saying. I am intrigued by what I still understand, that you as a Jewish leader – in the respected sense – accepting Jesus Christ as the first messiah. Am I correct?'

!Ah you test me, mortal man, just as they tested the very one you call your saviour, but in reality you Christians do not know him either. ISRAEL INVENTED THE MASHIAH, SIR. WHO TOLD YOU WE REJECTED HIM??!! WAS IT, PERCHANCE, THE GENTILES??

As the priestly voice shook the loudspeakers, the engineers in the control room denied adding any effects.

'Well the others became Christians . . .'

!Who rejected the Christ, Irishman?? You do not know!!

'The high priests, the Scribes.'

!Yes, exactly the same ones who tried to kill me on the Holy day of Atonement. Much later the rabbis who you say rejected Jesus in fact rejected your pagan idolatry and blasphemy. The true church is the messianic sect which I founded by the Dead Sea, Irishman, long since destroyed by the Sons of Darkness. I have a message for the messiah, blessed above all women, Queen of all Kings, and over all nations, anointed by the Grace of God, God with Us, Blessed be His Name. Acknowledge me, Daughter of Zion!

'Holy Father,' the Radio One disc-jockey interrupted, 'may I humbly ask you on behalf of my listeners and the theologians, why do you refer to God as male. Isn't He . . . ?'

Chapter Fifty-Two

'Ah, Mr Leonard, I've found you.'

I recognised the voice attached to the hand on my shoulder. The voice which had disturbed me on my bedside telephone that had been saved from destruction by Sara's intervention.

I answered thoughtlessly, 'Are you still here? I thought that you worked for the World Service.'

'Yes, we work in Bush House. We are broadcasting Sara live. Don't you want to sit in on it?'

'Yes,' I said, 'I've been listening to it.'

'Well, come with me. Perhaps you should join the panel. You have a great deal to contribute.'

I had no idea what he meant by *the panel* but I was flattered. When he beckoned me further along the corridor into the lobby I asked where we were going. We entered the South East wing and took the C lift to S6 on the lower ground. I had woken up, driven on adrenalin.

I saw Sara sitting with an interviewer at a small table near the control room window. Behind the table, curtains were open to an adjacent sound-proofed room, and there were four experts – hastily-convened talking heads. What she was saying to the Teacher seemed to connect to the Sara of today. She wore the same clothes and She was apologising for being tired.

But how did she get here ahead of me?

While I was waiting in the Control Room for a sign to enter the studio and join the panel I received a note to say that Timothy Colleague wanted to speak to me urgently. Tim was my collaborator on the Messianic Conspiracy programmes we had done for BBC Television. I picked up the Bush House internal phone.

'MIKE! Got you at last! Mark told me you were in the building. You must come here immediately and listen to this. I've never heard anything like it. I thought it was a hoax until right now but the engineers are agog and Mark is dribbling.' (Mark Hay was the head of Religious Broadcasts for BBC-2).

I left Sara and the panel of religion experts on the lower ground floor speaking to The Teacher by landline, and I found her again, the same today-Sara, for the third time. In another studio. Now she was making a recording, not a live broadcast. Bush House is a mall named after its American Architect. But things got worse and I discovered, across the car park in the Centre Block, she was recording for Radio Four a talk with the Teacher hosted by Robert Robinson.

There were four Saras.

I stood motionless. I was glad that I had been drinking, otherwise I would have been afraid. But I felt wretched. The adrenalin expired. I think the blood drained from my face.

Mark was telling me in a state of great excitement, 'A lost Scroll from the Dead Sea Library which was recently confiscated from an Arab antiquities dealer by Professor Yadin in Israel after the Six Day War is the topic of the discussion. The Teacher claims he wrote it and demands none too politely that we open a live broadcast and then he will dictate it to Sara in the public domain free of copyright so that it doesn't get lost or reburied again. Oh, and he can clear up ambiguities and restore the gaps of damaged parts since he condemns our modern scholars.'

It had to be a hoax by Robert Kohen.

I was so irritated that I simply pushed a security guard aside, entered the studio, and intruded on the discussion. Like a doubting Thomas, I touched Sara number four. Robinson was irritated and Sara smiled: they both thought that I was being amorous.

He waved me away. She kissed me.

She saw that I was white, even trembling involuntarily, and she held my hand while she continued the broadcast undisturbed. *Very professional, trained actress.* She stayed calm and put Robinson in his place.

She smiled at me from time to time. In sign language I indicated that I would return in five minutes.

I found Mark Hay and grabbed his shoulder. He protested his need, as the programme producer, to stay in his place.

'Trust me. I have a much bigger story for you,' I insisted as I dragged him to the second floor studio where he saw saw and heard heard a new slant on the idea of simultaneous broadcast broadcast. I wasn't sure if his nerves would take it, but he went white. I then took him to the lower ground floor of the South East Wing. He looked at me in astonishment but worse was to come. I asked if the engineers could patch in live monitors to Broadcasting House. And there she was, again and again.

Mark almost passed out, *'But that's tagged as a live broadcast*!'

I grabbed him by the arm and took him to the World Service shop on the ground floor. I purchased a portable radio, stuffed it with batteries and without replacing the plastic cover I tuned in to The Radio One Breakfast Show with Des Donnelly.

Sara was on the radio.

'. . . I thought that I would get married to Spencer and that we would both be very happy and change the world, but Washington was even more of a bubble dream than Hollywood. I guess it was meant.'

'Okay, we'll play your music now, George Harrison's *Beware of Darkness*.'

'Mike,' said Mark Hay as he recovered. 'You look wretched, man. If it's any consolation, I don't understand it either.'

'Mark, I haven't slept, and last night I had too much to drink. You still haven't seen half of it. Follow me. And if I have to run to the toilet, or when I throw up, dear fellow, wait, I won't be long.'

He looked at me as if I had two heads, as it felt, but I ignored his hesitation and took him to the World Service studios. Through the glass there was Sara talking to the Teacher through headphones. It affected Mark very badly. He laughed ghoulishly, nervously. He went as white as a sheet. He could hardly talk. I think that my inebriated condition had blunted my senses but Mark's reaction restored my equilibrium.

I said, 'Mark, get witnesses. As many as possible, or we will both get ourselves locked up as crazies.'

'That is a damn good idea. Stay there.'

He walked away. I asked myself the crazy question, where do I wait to take my fiancée home? Or do I take them all home? Maybe it is the end of the world? No, I'm drunk. I'm dreaming. I've never felt like this before. I really feel bad. I need to lie down. Get some sleep. It's all a bad dream.

Mark was shaking me. 'No, Mark, I AM NOT ALL RIGHT. She is my fiancée. All of them!' – 'Well just stay there, Mike, I'm going to get some witnesses.' – 'I need a doctor, not witnesses. Please, Mark. I feel bad.'

In the corridor I fell to the floor and lost consciousness.

52.1 At 10:21am according to my watch, I awoke in the Occupational Health Room. Sara (God knows which one) stood by me, kissing my lips. The nightmare, it seemed, was over. Everything seemed normal. We left the second floor clinic, crossed the ornate marble floored balcony from which the ground floor reception area was visible and it gave me a reassuring orientation.

As we crossed the car park, the one and only Sara volunteered to drive me home. Fresh as a daisy she apologised as if it were all her fault. I apologised for being drunk. I looked at my watch, still 10:21. The irony of time stopping was lost on me. I thought my fall had broken my wrist-watch.

Then I realised that I had not collapsed as late as 10:21am.

'Michael, I'm sorry. I'm going to pray that this might never again happen. I don't feel anything, but it must have hurt you badly. The DG has insisted I should not cause alarm. The Prime Minister has asked me to lie to support his official explanation that the World Service and Radio One programmes were taped.'

Tears welled up in her eyes.

'But, Michael, if I now start to tell small lies . . . no-one will trust me.'

I wasn't listening to her. I was staring in disbelief at the clock in the walnut dashboard of my Jaguar.

52.2 As Sara drove we tuned into Radio One on my car radio and I said to her, 'Sara, it must have been taped.' It was the Breakfast Show. I kept looking at the car clock, 10:21am. I asked Sara to consult her precious Swiss jewelled watch. It too had stopped at 10:21. 'But the Breakfast Show ends at 10:00am,' I protested.

The Irish DJ took no notice of that.

'. . . I mean, isn't God above biological gender?'

!You don't need to prompt me, disc-jockey!

The Teacher sounded like the voice of God.

!Of course God is above gender, because 'He' isn't a person, but He includes male personality, like headship and fatherhood. But what higher you can comprehend? If humans you could feel you would need not words. It is only because your powers have degenerated that Blessed be His Holy Name must use words and hire a satellite for communication to His own manifestation. So I please address her in public domain by your radio-phonics concerning her ministry!

'Master . . .' it was the voice of Sara coming from my car radio. But she was in my car, and we exchanged frightened, knowing glances.

Everyday, Des Donnelly is a live show which ends at ten o'clock. I stroked the luxurious burr walnut dash; it was reassuring. Then the voice animated my sports coupé.

!It is within you, Sara. The common man does not believe that I am who I am. So I will not lead you. Tell ME what you must teach the sons of Man!

'And the daughters too, Master. God is Convergence. Man is divergence.'

It was her voice. I asked her, 'Did you say that?'

She nodded but concentrated on her driving and on the radio.

!Yes, yes, yes. God is Convergence. Man is divergence, waste, error, darkness, lost his way. Anything else?

'I cannot love God and hate my fellow man,' Sara spoke along with her own voice on the radio. So, I knew that she had taped it, and she knew her lines.

The Teacher responded vigorously,

!Yes. Yes. Yes. Amen. Hallelujah. Praise be to God! Why do you hate your fellow man, Sara?

'I hate myself and I release the pain. I am cast adrift and lost in evil. *Men have hurt me so much,'* Sara wept.

The Teacher was weeping.

!Yes, yes, I feel the pain of your darkness, isolation, loneliness. You moderns are so alone. Diversion, perversion, inversion. These be your pleasure and your problem. What must you teach the sons and daughters of this generation?

Sara beside me in the car seemed to listen closely to her broadcast.

'Master, the stranger is only oneself whose face is yet unseen. For we are all strangers. But not me, for I am made of nine parts from the House of Light, and I can see, and I can share with the all and I am above all. Truly Master, my mouth cannot utter all that I have seen.'

She parked the car and placed her finger over my lips.

!Daughter, you are ready, so teach!

'Oh man, seek not God, but godliness; if you want love you must pursue loveliness. If you want to find happiness you must be generous. If you want heaven you must find earth.'

I looked at Sara as she listened to her own voice and pride overwhelmed her. She smiled through her tears. I became angry and swopped places. I drove her back to Broadcasting House.

We would soon see if Donnelly's Breakfast Show was being broadcast *live*.

I left the car on a kerb with a parking warden screaming, 'You can't leave it there, sir!'

Grabbing Sara's wrist we ran into the building, past a security guard who hissed, 'You aren't allowed through.'

But I reached the studio still grasping Sara who was out of breath. My nose was pressed on the glass and the security guard was on my tail. The Irish disc-jockey announced technical problems and played another record: John Lennon's *Imagine*.

imagine there's no heaven
it's easy if you try
no hell below us
above us only sky . . .

'See, no Sara,' I said to her as if I had exposed the fraud.

'When that song was playing,' Sara replied to me calmly, 'the engineers told Des that they had lost the Teacher – the broadcast, I mean. The producer said he should continue to interview me. But I was told that you had hurt yourself so by this point I had left the studio to find you. *Remember?'*

I determined to check the facts after I got home and had some sleep.

Chapter Fifty-Three

LONDON, JANUARY 1979

The second hand swept the fourth quadrant of my art deco clock on the wall of my dining room. Ten years ago the thing had cost me £1 at a jumble sale; now it was fashionable. The carpet was dull green, now merging threadbare into its canvas. Once I had been proud of economy. Now I saw my home as tawdry and ill-matched.

At exactly 9:00am my secretary dragged a seventh chair for herself – from my 'sixties style breakfast room into the nineteenth-century style oak-panelled dining room. I sat at the table with my publisher, my agent, my senior research associate, two BBC producers, and Mark Hay who was head of Religious Broadcasts.

They all looked worried. The media were attacking my story. Prices were falling. Moreover, obsessed with finding the two major clues – Paul and the genealogy – I had not delivered anything for some time. With my romantic diversions, and now the broadcasts, I gave them the impression of being compromised; maybe finished.

It was time for me to regain the initiative.

'The flat is for sale because I'm going to live in Switzerland. With my new wife. I'm going to get married!'

'Congratulations.' – 'This calls for a celebration.' – 'Someone we know?'

Struggling to keep my face deadpan I allowed my eyes to wander. I inspected the fading flock wallpaper through the eyes of a prospective house-purchaser and wondered if I was asking an unattainable price.

Then I stated that the purpose of the meeting was to agree with those present where my impending marriage to Sara left me in the Messianic Conspiracy story.

'I've done three films and three books concerning the Lost Templar Treasures, the French Connection, and the Holy Family. Currently I'm under contract to you all on The Messianic Conspiracy, but now I'm too close to it to continue. I need to work for Sara. So I must offer to resign unless we can make an alternative arrangement, and I don't think we should even try. *I can't be impartial.*'

Silence.

'It's a strange outcome, Mike,' declared Harvey Mackenzie, executive producer of the BBC's 'Electronic Eye' series.

I felt very grateful for his breaking of the ice in a friendly manner which was bound to influence the others. Nobody likes to be the first to destroy an old friend, even one who has strayed over to the other side.

I began the defence of my untenable position.

'The Gospels were written by evangelists. Josephus reported history he helped to create as a Roman General. Paul wrote his Letters after converting to Christianity. But I can assure you that I will not be changing my religious beliefs, or lack of them. Opposites attract. We complete each other, Sara and I. Despite our backgrounds we both believe in Truth as the line in the centre of the highway. But we are coming from opposite directions.'

I became aware of the tensions and switched from mouth to mind.

One day Sara had handed me over a suitcase of disordered papers, contracts, bills, and correspondence. Her finances were complex. She had royalties coming in from film performances, land in her family trust in France, an extended law-case concerning the will of Johnny Lord about which she knew nothing and cared even less. There were demands from the US Internal Revenue and European authorities. She was unable to see the difference between postponing and ignoring these things.

Now that we were setting up a home in Switzerland I saw the need to establish a unified and proper professional representation for her. But as her biographer, I was also interested in her past.

The BBC delegation and my publisher had started an animated meeting at the north west corner of the table. Meanwhile Ms Pitman sweetly smiled and used the unofficial adjournment to hand me a synopsis of a book.

'I shouldn't have this in my possession, Mike, dear, but I thought that you might be interested. Read it, then I'll tell you the bad news.'

I was pleased to forget the plotting of the broadcasters and turned to examine the paper. The title and author's name had been blacked out on Petrina's photocopy. Scanning through the synopsis I picked up the themes of the story I once regarded as my own.

> *Part One: THE TEMPLE TREASURES FOUND AFTER 1900 YEARS. The Holy Grail. Bloodline descendants of Jesus secretly survive in the south of France, genealogies kept by anti-orthodox Masonic secret brotherhoods. In modern times the threat to Rome comes from AIFAM, supposedly French communists (Association Independent Français Amis Marxistes) but secretly the M denotes Messianistes hence French Independent Society of Friends of the Messiah.*
>
> *Part Two: MODERN POLITICS AND ARCHAIC MONARCHIES . . .*

'Yet another rival,' I said to my agent. 'Who is the author?'

'A major writer. Can't say more, Michael. Point of honour.'

'Can you say anything? When is the book coming out?'

'Topical fast-seller, so I'll guess very soon. I'm afraid I turned down this publisher's offer for your books and used them to achieve your advances. So they're rivals with a vengeance and they are used to speeding current issue books through marketing and production.'

While the others were talking I had already started to trace in my mind the nature of the people forming AIFAM the backward M-A-F-I-A, people who pretended to be Marxists but were Messianists. A crazy cover. A crude decoy. Vanity crept in: I must be one step ahead of any 'major writer' working my seam. Perhaps I could sabotage his findings even before they were published.

In this way Sara's little baggage carrier kept his eye on the ball.

53.1 **CHAINED TO LOVER'S TOILET**, ran the headline in a London tabloid and by lunchtime the story concocted by my envious colleagues to discredit me had gone global. Sara's PR department decided that we should not dignify such stories with any response.

Truthfully we could not issue a denial. Fearing that I would leave her, she had stood at the door of my toilets when her phobic thinking reached a nadir. She didn't consult a psychiatrist but the headquarters staff included 'a friend' who fulfilled the rôle. This specialist suggested therapeutic creativity.

Sara was unhinged. But I was doing well. From a third floor flat in London I had moved to a palace within a walled estate in Geneva – now headquarters of the Messianic Movement. I had my own bedroom, and Sara was still stalling for time but the delay helped preserve my journalistic impartiality.

One of the Board (the so-called disciples), David Rutt, became emotional in a rebuttal of the opulence. In a Press Conference he explained the Geneva palace in the context of the Messianic Organisation's claims to the poverty of Christ.

'The only exception is the love we feel for Sara. While she teaches the Christian doctrine that the least person is the greatest in the Realm of Heaven, she must be treated with reverence befitting her holiness. We love and cherish her. We will not have her forever. She could live for her own pleasure but she dies for our sins. I do not apologise for lavishing any money on her.'

Freed from repaying a house loan, my own finances improved and money rolled in from all aspects of my work. Sara paid me, broadcasters paid me, publishers paid me, and even the Messianic Organisation paid me. I appointed a guy called Lawrie Whitman as chief of my London research operations to free me to attend to Sara's constant needs. But in the following week I was sitting for the last time in my dining room in Southwell Gardens, SW7, and it was once again a boardroom. Until it was sold, this was the office of my company, Leonard-Whitman Research Ltd.

To close the meeting we joked about the trick of marrying the messiah and my exclusive rights to the authorised gospel. On a more serious note our accountant skilfully steered us through the financial and administrative details of establishing a tax-free offshore corporation because royalties and opportunities were escalating. In two years *The Aquarius Conspiracy* was approaching sales of two million copies. Big budgets and cash-flows made us lose touch with reality and the talk became childish.

The accountant left and the next meeting was a brainstorming session on project 'Fat Boy'. This was our crazy code name for penetrating AIFAM and we memorised several codes, handles, and nicknames. We were getting carried away with the habits of the secret societies which we were increasingly imitating. Lindie, my secretary, started to slow down and asked us to repeat or spell everything: her notes of the meeting became leaden scrawls of gibberish.'How long does this stuff take to kick in?' Judith inquired, and we all laughed, 'One-A has completely gone.'

'But it's supposed to sharpen the wits, I replied.'

53.2 One idea stirred everyone to life. I could ask Sara to submit to drug-induced hypnosis. How would she react?

Later that day I found out. Sara No 1 was on brain duty, her positive biorhythms had converged, the stars were with me, the world had not irritated her for several hours and she was behaving perfectly normally.

But she still refused drug-aided interrogation.

I thought that she wanted me to persist. So I persisted.

I was wrong. She became upset and angry.

'You're a control freak. It's the thing I've had all of my life. And *I* don't take drugs. Not any more.'

I knew better than to contradict her but already she was in a state of spontaneous combustion.

'You never believed in me, did you?'

I apologised that I was a rationalist, reductionist, evolutionist, sceptic, heretic, agnostic, and I wouldn't change for her.

'I just want you to believe in *me*,' she pleaded, 'not in things.'

'I won't believe in any fabrication.'

'You don't know how much punishment I endured to rebel against religion to the Sisters. You never had one hundredth of the strength I displayed to believe what I perceive, not what I was taught. You don't have the right to criticise me. *I think you'd better get out of my life.* You do me more damage than good. Take your ring.'

When I refused it, she threw it across the room and turned to walk away.

I grabbed her wrist and spun her to face me.

'You have been trying to make an argument to break us up. I even know why. In a word, *Japan.*'

She knew that I knew insufficient to accuse her of being pregnant let alone of having sex, but once again she would not deny it.

'I need to be treated well, Mike, to be alert, trusting, open, growing, and receptive to a human sensitivity for which I am a pathfinder. Only my Father in heaven is there. Why won't you help me?'

By summer 1979 I thought I had learned never to confront her tidal moods with mere logic. I would use verbal ju-jitsu to soothe or amuse her or to probe deeply.

'Peach Blossom, I know you are still taking drugs.'

There was no response. No denial.

I persisted, 'Are they medical drugs, or . . . do they dispense them?'

Could she disclose who *they* were? I was probing; I had no idea.

What a story it would become, I could see the headlines. Even without uncovering the conspiracy, I would have the power to dethrone their messiah, or deal with the power behind the throne. I guessed that she was hiding illegal substances in her bedroom. Within a week I had sent off a dozen samples to be analyzed including her dispensed medicines and food supplements, but even cosmetics, bath foams, oils, and fragrant aromas. Just in case.

All proved negative.

Now I was paranoid delusional. The lab was in league with the conspirators. Sara was too smart. I couldn't find the drug but, like the genealogy, it existed.

The crazy headline, Chained to Sara's Toilet, gave me the idea.

I modified our private toilet and installed some creative plumbing. Then I sent her urine for analysis to a pharmacologist who had at his disposal the Swiss laboratories of a major drug company.

There are at least two groups of psychoactive drugs which can go untraced. Some synthetic substances have not been listed. It was the CIA who persuaded governments to classify all hallucinogenics as non-therapeutic, thus obstructing the relief of suffering under the administration of the medical authorities. Second, I was informed that some ancient mineral and herbal extracts would not trigger modern tests – mushrooms vaguely documented by sacred literature. Most churches opposed a sacramental classification of hallucinogenics but elite circles from politicians to creative artists use them, and I was sure that Sara was taking them to elevate her to the gods.

53.3 I hadn't met a pharmacologist before, but I had reserved for one a numbered seat on the train from Geneva to Berne. Nicholas Cadlien was a small blond-haired man in his early thirties, distinguished by distinctive red spectacles.

As soon as I sat beside him he told me that I had been very lucky. The drug would be untraced by most analysts. He had found it but the dosage could not be ascertained. The substance was ZF231, a well-guarded secret because it had been rejected for commercial development. It was mildly toxic.

Cadlien had been employed by the firm who had invented a group of substances one of which had now surfaced like a lost dog coming home. Now he apologised to me, he had been caught and asked to disclose to the police his client. As they would find me soon enough, I consented to my name being put forward in return for further information. I learned that ZF231 was of no medical value but was only listed by the CIA as toxic to discourage its experimentation. Nicholas said it was delightfully euphoric, probably addictive but accumulatively toxic. It would kill her in five to seven years, and the inventors might get the blame.

He became quite forceful. Where was it coming from the lab needed to know in return for my co-operation? They claimed they weren't manufacturing it. I told Nick to promise his firm that soon they would have the answers.

53.4 I considered confronting Sara with my discovery. If she knowingly took this drug, perhaps she wanted messianic martyrdom. She had access to the purest substances and the best experts in California. So why take this junk unless it produced exactly what she desired.

Either she wanted to die for the cause or Sara was fed the drug without her knowledge. The conspirators were willing to sacrifice her life. Another thought. In September the Pope had died, and the Vatican had refused a post-mortem. Suppose someone in our home, the cook, housekeeper, or any one of the staff in Geneva, who opposed the messianic cause – or who supported the cause more than the person – was prepared to administer the substance. I broke out in a cold sweat.

Someone was trying to kill my Sara.

That was a far-fetched idea but my next synaptic connection was not. Why, oh merciful heaven, why does the most obvious explanation elude my genius? I was the one who needed the cortical vitamin pills. QUESTION: Why had I overlooked the obvious connection until this stage? ANSWER: We are all prejudiced. I was pursuing Catholic conspirators, deluded Danes, French fabricators, and an American Defence Scientist. They all had motives. But between drugs and channelling and Dr Kohen and Sara's brother, the common link was surely obvious.

Dr Jeremy Palmer. I called him the sinister minister, but he looked like the devil.

The family doctor I had shared with Sara in London had been dismissed when our $1m Geneva in-house clinic opened. So I went to him to apologise. Of course he could not discuss the details of a patient, but what about a former patient? I explained that I was worried that my wife was taking non-prescribed drugs.

'Doctor, have you heard of ZF231? No? Well, look at the formula.'

'Michael, in answer to your next question, it is not available for prescription, but, yes, it might be effective given certain specific patterns of elation and depression which we can attribute to brain's chemical messengers such as noradrenaline, serotonin and dopamine.'

I topped up the good doctor's cut crystal glass, and he delivered the loquacious effects of Scotch whisky – an interrogation drug that works well without fuss or prescription. I probed deeper.

'In my enquiries, doctor, I obtained from her school in Scotland certain psychiatric reports including drugs prescribed.'

'I have seen them. Faked, dear boy. And incomplete. Any expert can tell even from the records.'

I was astonished but rather than ask how he had seen the records I asked, 'Please go on.' Then I realised it was obvious *how* he had seen her records: *thanks to my introduction he had been her GP.*

53.5 On the following Thursday a source identified as B26 on my wallchart provided me with an early reading copy of a forthcoming rival book. It had been leaked just in time for me to undermine it with exquisite humiliation to its author and yet I must now thank him for the indirect path which resulted in my great discovery.

Bertram Craig was a respected writer, but to write *The Deception of the Devil* he had ventured little from the comfort of his office. I skimmed it in an hour and wrote a book review ending, 'No substance, and much speculation.'

It gave me the opportunity to confront Sara on one of these increasingly rare evenings we spent together. It was a rare occasion when her calm and reasonable personality that I called No 1 was on brain duty. I played the part of a dutiful husband who had just learned that her medication might have unfortunate side effects.

I was nervous about her reaction, but I knew the confrontation had to come. She listened to me silently with big trusting eyes, but it was all an act. Her response was spoken mildly but invoked the ultimate authority.

'Jesus said, 'What goes into your mouth will not defile you, but what comes out of your mouth, that is what will defile you.' You must guard me from bullets, Michael. I've been warned that I'll die from . . .'

She turned to me in panic, 'Michael, are there any molecules of *plomb*, what do you call it, lead in that drug ZF231?'

Chapter Fifty-Four

By this point Dr Jeremy Palmer had come onto my radar. Ten years previously *I am the Daughter of God* were lyrics from Antigen's feminist and flower-power period. I obtained his albums, and in MARY THE PRIEST (1969) I noted *I knew not who I was, yet they knew me . . .* lyrics attributed to Antigens, Martin McDonald, and Jacques Erskine, all titles published by Musical Reality Inc.

I had never heard of this firm but now started to trace the principals. This company, which preceded the foundation of Mushroom Records Group, was formerly owned by none other than Dr Palmer – Jesus-Leviticus – who had a string of directorships and investments in the music business.

My Golden Rule is to look for the money because it leaves a trail. I guessed that his music business would produce a money trail to drugs but some insight told me that while Palmer was implicated, he was not the initiator because he did not have the motive. Then I studied the lyrics of all albums and songs published by Palmer's companies over fifteen years. On the album *Mysterious Messenger* by a Swiss band called Psychic Radio, which clairvoyantly disbanded before its first album flopped, the prime mover was J. Erskine and the psychedelic graphics on the cover had the engraved motto L.A.C.S.

I had discovered the motto of SHIF – the alleged inner circle of anti-Semitic sentiment – was LIGNUM ARBOR CRUCIS SCIENTOR, *the wood of the cross is the tree of knowledge*. It suddenly occurred to me that this indicated hostility by SHIF as a Catholic Order towards the Church of the Fish. The album cover was elaborate yet the artwork was unattributed. If LACS had been drawn by the hand of J. Erskine on a trip it might connect him to the French priests.

I shared these findings with Sara. She became so sweet, so respectful and grateful. If only she would cast out her demons, I thought, we could be so happy.

We met in the middle. 'How good and honourable a thing it is to bring truth to the world, and are we not?' she asked.

It was more than the grammar that disturbed me.

'Truth is mythic,' she said, 'and it nourishes. Facts are ephemeral and merely confuse the soul. Without mystery there is no motivation. If we will one day understand everything, then we will become weak and die. It is the Tree of Knowledge which is the accumulated toxin, dear Michael, not drugs, that is why I fear your pervasive logic.'

I asked her to say directly if she took drugs.

She smiled a little, but it was not a look of smug deceit and she fetched a glass of orange juice into which she dropped four white capsules that effervesced. She swallowed half of the glass and offered me the rest.

After some argument and persuasion I took it.

She asked me how I felt. After half an hour I felt lightened up and inflated. I felt great. I felt very amorous and all barriers between Sara and me, between man and woman, between mind and flesh, between inhibitions and instincts, had dissolved into the orange juice of life.

She curled up and talked about how things grow in the world, especially babies. She pretended to grow inside me. We lit candles, sipped a warm night drink, played music until late, and gradually shed our clothes. We hadn't made love like this for a long time. Instead she had been isolated and frigid like Philippa, my ex-wife, but now the intensity of this night made up for three months of celibacy.

If this was the drug, I admitted to her that I was in favour of it.

Sara was also in ecstasy, and I took her from one orgasm to higher, longer, and deeper orgasms in which she trembled and cried out so much that I really thought she would pass out if not die. The power I had over her turned me on so much that I confused the desire to please her with the desire to kill her. I can't explain it, but I was sufficiently educated in mythology and psychology to know of the ancient fusion of death in love.

To actually experience it was something else.

Sara screamed out, 'Father, no, no more,' but she grasped me tightly. Then I tore away her grip, I had no choice, it had gone too far, and I knelt over her limp body. She caught her breath. My gulping of air soon returned to normal. She smiled as I wiped the perspiration glistening all over her.

I was astounded by the discovery I was making.

I said, cautiously, watching her reaction, 'So, your father . . . *used* you? It was your father. He did a thing he should not do? That explains the whole pattern of why you craved for love. That is why you lost your self-esteem, felt guilt, and also felt nothing.'

In a falsetto voice of a child, she cried, 'No, no, Michael, my beloved papa was the most upright man in this world. Tell me that you believe me.'

She was not lying, and I realised the difference between Papa and Père.

'Oh my God, it was a priest?' I remembered what the nun in Inverness had hinted. This was Margaret's secret. And the secret the convent concealed behind so-called lesser misconduct.

It explained the power she had over the authorities?

She shook her head but admitted everything.

'Papa went away and left me so the priests and nuns used me. I wanted to love them all. I liked it but I hated myself and I washed my sins away with water and then they blessed me. The psychiatrist said I wanted to get into trouble to be punished for what I had done and I knew I would do again. And the pain melted my terror. I can endure pain. It's nothing. The body is nothing. I am not my body. See my hands. It heals. So what. Look, can you see any scars? See, you cannot. Not until I point them out.'

54.1 The white drug had brought us together; I could not argue with that, and its convergence was the point of truth. At last she had shed light on her secret. I expressed my sorrows.

'Sara, now I understand you, but I won't believe in a God who allowed you to suffer like this. If God is good, would he use you like this?'

'You silly but nice man, I have been raised above all others by nothing else other than suffering. No pain, no gain. Just give me love. And I haven't told you everything. I haven't told you about the real scars.'

'I suppose I cannot kill the perpetrator because he is dead?'

'My scars have healed. Perpetrators all suffer the torment of Hell and damnation in eternity for deeds in death's dream kingdom. Life isn't a game, Mike, it's for real. When you understand what the entity called Senator Weidfeld did to the Daughter you will be ready for more than journalistic facts. Don't you see? He destroyed her humanity, but he created the goddess.'

We were both exhausted and soon fell asleep locked in each other's arms. I was reflecting on her words. *Weidfeld had destroyed her humanity and created the goddess.*

54.2 I woke up late in the morning. We were separated by one inch but she was facing away. I lay still and stroked her back tenderly, careful to avoid the painful bruising the good Senator had inflicted while creating his goddess. I was no longer under the influence of the drug, but needed to identify it.

I felt she had been born normal and strong; had she not been kidnapped and manipulated from the age of seven she would be what I called Sara No 1. She was possibly not even the daughter of Pierre of the Languedoc but a spirited child who was grafted into the genealogy to fabricate a modern messiah.

Maybe a girl aged seven had disappeared from somewhere, probably in France. No doubt the conspirators would have concealed police records. Suppose I advertised for witnesses to come forward. After twenty-seven years people would still recall a missing child. Unfortunately, Sara's memory was unreliable. She had been hypnotised. Perhaps she wasn't aged seven.

She had been right about Paul, but we had found no family house and no Golden Henbane in its garden. She said it spread like weeds but all botanists agreed that it was a species restricted to Jerusalem. It grew nowhere else. I said, if Sara's father confused it with another plant then he was making a fantasy of the Jerusalem connection.

I thought to myself, the conspirators are slipping; they should prepare a house for me to discover.

The sleeping beauty awoke and rose. The droplets on her showered body glistened in the laser sharp beams of sun through the vertical window blinds. She went back to bed to dry herself on our silk sheets.

'How are you, Peach Blossom?'

''kay, Mike.' It was almost inaudible.

'What is the substance that merged our souls, sweetie?'

She smiled.

'I'll show you,' she whispered submissively.

I was very curious.

She slowly tilted her sixty-two inches of naked slimness out of bed and walked into our private toilet. I strained to see where it was hidden. Her hand stretched into the medicines cabinet. I wanted to see where she hid her drugs, so she played coy. I backed off.

She cleaned her teeth and returned with a yellow pack of headache pills. She spilled the white tablets onto the table.

With a wide grin she read aloud to me, 'Each tablet contains Aspirin 300mg & Paracetamol 200mg.'

Chapter Fifty-Five

After I gave chase to someone tampering with my yellow BMW within the grounds of our palace I considered that I should inform 'the organisation.'

By now there were several messianic security departments, each one independent and most of them secret. In the 'palace' itself lived **James the Righteous** – Sara's principal bodyguard. Worthington McGrath (his real name) was a big guy, a good-natured Scot and characteristically a heavy drinker. He was rugged, jovial but deeply religious. Traditional, but not stupid. I could get along with him. He hurt no-one who didn't threaten Sara. He knew I was insanely possessive.

'A'm very fond of Sara, and a've sort of chosen ma'self tae look after her, but 'A' swear before the Heavenly Father that 'A' widnae dream that she wid want me in any way you should wirry aboot. A see masel as here tae look after her, and . . .'

'James, you don't need to say anything more to me.'

I have not exaggerated James' speech to indicate a simple and coarse man but there were clear parallels to the disciples of Jesus. Like their earlier prototypes, the new disciples were solid people who dangerously failed to understand the complexities of their leader. In the twentieth-century their characters were a piece of theatre concealing the real power which was vested in a secret committee which I shall describe from my inside view. He had changed his name to Andrew James.

In any case, 'James the Righteous' carried a gun, pointing out that he had a gun licence, training, and no record of violence. He claimed that St. Peter had carried a sword as a bodyguard to Jesus. This was supported by the gospels when the chief disciple cut off the ear of the High Priest on the day the Master was arrested.

I told James all about the toxic drug ZF231. The response amazed me.

'Och, aye, ah've read the books, Craig's and yours too, *The Messianic Conspiracy*, very well-written, and ah've kept mah eyes and ears open. As you know 'Craig is vague,' but his informant was essentially correct about the drug. Nothin's certain in this world, is it? Ah asked her directly if she ever took the drug. She said to me, 'Dear McGrath, we all take drugs of various sorts. Even the fresh air is a drug. I experimented when I came to America when they had this very pure LSD. I left Europe with a head of great pain and I needed a cure. Today the tablets and the atmosphere are both poisoned. In those days we ingested under responsible supervision, not to escape from the world but to find it.' – 'Do you need it?' I asked her. 'It doesn't give me a delusion of grandeur, McGrath, just of adequacy.' Then she told me that Jesus took drugs. This made me very suspicious, Michael, because I thought to masel' *who told her this*? And when? And why? Ah felt like asking her to confirm it, but as never before, ah kent if this woman said it, she spoke the truth.'

I felt angry that she had answered my questions to Mr McGrath. Liberated to pursue my own agenda. She did not trust me, so I did not trust her.

Chapter Fifty-Six

'Antigens still denies being Paul,' Sara told me the next time we met, which was in London, 'and he's right. He is Paul, but he's not Paul. He is not the person I knew. He is aggressive, confused and violent. He says that there are now ten journalists who have been trying to question him about his Holy Family. He was nasty to me. He even said, as if to threaten me, that he gets violent with the journalists and will happily go down for a charge of assault.'

I was in London to meet Sara at the start of her British tour, which exhausted me at the end of ten days. I had to attend to minutiae, explain her worsening moods to people, and indulge her obsessions. Everywhere she went, deeper rows of people lined the streets, even in the rain, to touch her coat or catch a glimpse her. A lot of her British followers asked if they should establish a new church or reform existing churches.

'My hope is that a new organisation will not prove necessary.'

Sara proclaimed that there was to be no new church and that upon her death no new disciples, no organisation, and no body would have messianic authority outside the bloodline. I cringed. As her intended husband, my seed was to be the world leader.

The 'organisation anti-organisation' credo, was announced at this time by her people.

'Messianism is a direct manifestation from God to living rulers in place of democracy or anarchy. God is within each of us. Our hearts and souls must be allowed to grow.'

The slogan *Messianism is not an -ism*, was also coined and proclaimed, advertised, broadcast, repeated, explained, committed to writing, carved in wood, chiselled in stones, and cast in bronze.

The high point of the London tour was Sara's TV debate with leading theologians. My friends at the BBC invited me. This was going to be a turning point in Sara's career because Protestant, Catholic, Jewish and Muslim leaders had accepted the invitation. Presumably they had prepared themselves for the key question, *do you accept this woman as lawful messiah*? The institutions were squabbling internally, each faction afraid of the implications of the other's stance.

The 'messianic organisation' in Geneva was full of Americans, predominantly clean-cut, efficient young men who were quite different from 'The Twelve Disciples.' The latter, as I said, were like cartoon characters representing all the stations and occupations within society. Each Disciple spearheaded a social or national grouping within the cause. There were eight men, three women, and then there was 'Kay' whom I called Fat KD and I despised her. She claimed to be a woman. They all disliked and distrusted me but KD really undermined my relationship with the boss. Between the disciples' groupings and 'the organisation' tensions we were constantly at war and a melt-down was only avoided by the intervention of Sara.

56.1 The British Messianic Media Committee had set up the Magic Kingdom straight from Disneyworld on the Royal Albert Hall stage for their leader. It was a large throne draped in white silk, with small, silver and gold chairs placed around hers in a semi-circle. There were fresh flowers and a single slim white microphone – like a stem emerging from satin ribbon leaves to avoid anything as ugly as clip ties or clusters of microphones. Sara wore blossoms in her hair and henceforth her entourage ensured that the floral kingdom would travel everywhere, even in poor third-world countries.

When I arrived at the hall, the committee members were cautioning the media in a way that began to alarm me.

'She must be addressed as Your Holiness. She is spirit visiting the human realm despite her modesty and you must never forget that she is descended from the most sacred royal blood in our world. Her station is above emperors let alone ambassadors.'

When Her Holiness arrived with her entourage the theatrical suspense was carefully manipulated. The atmosphere was electric. Waiting for her to come on stage many people were weeping. When she appeared it was as if she controlled a magnetic field and the orientation of minds was tangible. I recalled the feeling twice during the 'sixties: when Kennedy was assassinated and when Armstrong walked on the moon.

The powerful atmosphere was discharged by her appearance, radiant and smiling. Dressed in white with embroidered pearl buttons, she was groomed and truly beautiful, not like the artists' depictions of the Nazarene's sartorial modesty. Not only the churches but also the pop idols had better watch out. This was unstoppable. I watched and surrendered in total admiration to 'The Conspiracy.' She was set to become bigger than *either* of her brothers – Antigens or Jesus.

Finally I understood what the conspiracy – divine or human – must have foreseen from the beginning. The loyalty to a Pope or a Dalai Lama creates a political power base within a large section of humanity. But this glamour girl was non-denominational; her appeal was universal. I suddenly felt I was watching Sara – or her controllers – assuming world supremacy. I realised that soon she would do whatever she wanted to do.

Then I shared her precognition of death by a bullet.

Someone would have to do it. Despite the fact that the hall was filled by her own guards. And perhaps by British agents, the Masonic network, Interpol, or all of them. Could I save the saviour?

56.2 'Your Holiness, what is the authority of 'the Disciples'?'

'I will not be here forever. When I go my authority will be vested in them but they will not elect a leader from within their number. *Read the Bible.* Authority in perpetuity is in the royal bloodline of David.'

'Are they going to create a new church?'

'I have the feeling that they will not. I have not been given the authority. God, I think, wants none, but it is my words. Separateness is both real and unreal, like energy of wave . . . or something . . . it's scientific.'

(She seemed to stumble here.) 'Therefore much more so between neighbours, communities, and nations.'

'We must love one another but not become like one another. We must be one another but love our individuality. There is no reason for religions to fight each other. Sometimes they are saying the same thing in different ways, some more advanced, or descriptive, or suited to a past age or a particular people. It is foolish for people to argue that if religion were 'correct' then there would only be one religion. Both A and Z, that is what we must learn to understand.'

'Your Divine Holiness, what is the purpose of your ministry?'

'People cannot believe because it is too simple. I am here to save the world.'

'Your Holiness, is the world going to get better?'

'The world as you see it doesn't exist in reality. 'I am not of this Kingdom,' said Jesus. No, I cannot say that your world will get better and certainly not as a result of me, if this is what you mean. War will not end in my days but I must try. Yes, when people ask who, or what, I am, I shall say in truth, 'I am the moon at night. You only see me because of the dark.' Therefore do not seek God, but godliness; and look not for love but loveliness.'

The hall was warm, full, and absolutely silent. She yawned.

'Enough for now. I am very tired. I will bless you all and set you all to work for goodness and truth in your present occupations. Don't give us money – we don't need it. Just a little of your time. Be blessed, be happy. Blessings to the Yogi Yamakarsi and all shepherds and fishers of men. To the New Age seekers, not LSD, but LDS: Love, Devotion, and Surrender. To artists: express the whole world, good and bad, small and big in your work. To parents and teachers: liberate the heart and mind within each growing small person, and begin again to grow yourself. People, it is more blessed to give than to receive. Couples: it isn't about give and take; it's about give and get the blessing. Be kind to the world and you will be saved. It really is that simple. See, I am so protected beyond death that when I am gathered up to my ancestors I shall not suffer.'

Chapter Fifty-Seven

FORT AUGUSTUS, SCOTLAND, APRIL 1980

It was disturbing that the bodyguard who had learned about the drug had preceded me to the private school which accepted Sarah Kelly after her expulsion from the Convent in Inverness. Whoever McGrath was, or worked for, no doubt the witnesses had been spoiled by his amateur investigation. But I followed after him, like an archaeologist inspecting a pyramid after the grave robbers.

When I met the teacher who had joined the school at the same time as Sarah Kelly, I suspected him as a placed agent of the brotherhood. Colin Gundry was neither gullible nor devious; in no way was he an organisation man, but very much an individualist. Formerly a mathematics master, he had since retired but lived in the staff quarters of the school. He was a ruddy-faced, balding character who had written a humorous book on the Loch Ness Monster.

At his suggestion I met Gundry by the side of the loch itself. It was a crisp, dry day – not what I expected after flying north from a rain-drenched Heathrow. Very likeable and effervescent, CG, as the whole school called him, was the kind of man who waves his hands all the time and touches others without menacing them, and he shouted eccentrically without any trace of loutishness. I could already see how and why such an unorthodox man might have been accused by the grey men of this parochial town of anything from wizardry to paying too much attention to one of his female pupils.

'I never touched the girl, but I agreed to retire. Never had a teaching licence, you see, and never respected people who mask their incompetence with one. But nowadays, you need a formal qualification. I had enemies because I'm too much of an individualist. They offered us a pension and a place to live, and so I accepted their terms of dismissal. Now, you're here to talk about one particular high achiever, your wife, some say the New Messiah.'

Crushing pebbles underfoot we walked along the banks of the Scottish lake on a brigt but cold morning.

'Come, walk with me to the village and I'll show you where the secret society indoctrinated her, because that is what you want to know. True I only joined the school when she came here but I'm not your culprit, sir. Not a believer. Believed in religion even less when I saw Helen MacRae, a lovely child whose spirit they had tried very hard to break before she came here.'

I decided to flatter him.

'I think that you do believe. *In man*, Mr Gundry. You certainly strike me as a humanist.'

'No, sir, we most certainly do not believe in Man. Look, we are born into this world once only and what do we do with the gift of this sojourn? We waste it. Men are blind worms. Women at least are attractive, less logical but nature blinds them lest they see men for what we are. We prefer women and enjoyed teaching a few fine young women here. Glories to their gender. Mostly high-class women and Highlanders – they are a class apart. In London they can hardly breathe for the toxicity of concentrated population.'

While I walked towards the village with CG, I wondered if I would send my daughter to be taught by him. I concluded that he was harmless.

57.1 It was a small and dingy shop whose pre-war green paint blended into weather-beaten dirt but we had arrived at the bookshop. Gundry introduced me to the proprietor, Donald MacDonald, as the local leader of the society of dangerous and forbidden knowledge.

'Don't be reticent. Admit the truth, Donald. You recognise Mr Leonard, don't you? You've made money selling his books. Now he wants to know all about how we indoctrinated young Helen. And how you once sold books to her.'

'No, Colin, I loaned them. She was clever. I always bought the books back from her paying exactly what she paid, so I was her free library service.'

'But allowing books into the hands of young women, Donald, filling their heads with ideas. *Why did you do it?'*

'I had to make up for the incompetence of your profession, Colin. It was the only chance the girls had to get an education in our village.'

I interrupted their banter, 'What kind of books did Sara read, Mr MacDonald?'

'Och, all kinds. No, I won't discuss any of my customers, Mr Leonard. Forgive my conceit if I dignify some professional standards. I'm really only a village bookseller. Look, Mills and Boons my best sellers.'

57.2 In the evening I walked through Fort Augustus and spoke to various people asking them if they had known Sélène as Helen MacRae. 'Och, not another reporter . . .' But I persisted. A few people did remember her coming to the town. Apparently when Helen developed a sweet tooth she spent fortunes in the sweet shop, which was out of bounds to the school. So she purchased sweets for the other girls. Inevitably she got caught and on the third occasion, punished for truancy.

The confectionery store was owned by a man who had bought the business from the estate of a spinster McNiven. Even when Sara was here, Mistress McNiven was a lonely, dishevelled, ill-tempered woman whom the locals only half-jokingly denounced as a witch. Even in the twentieth-century, remote Scottish villages have a traditional respect for the craft – and for heresy.

I saw Donald MacDonald walking along the main road and engaged him in conversation. He stated that Mistress McNiven did not take money from Helen for her sweets. I stared at him, inviting him to be explicit. He invited me to his shop. Despite the hour and the closed sign on the door it was unlocked and we entered. He handed me a second-hand book priced at forty-five pounds. I wasn't sure what he wanted me to look for.

'In 1589, Mr Leonard, Scotland's King James VI, son of Mary Queen of Scots, visited Denmark and brought back the strange combination of a beautiful Queen and a fear of witches. In the following year he outlawed demonic witchcraft as heresy, and at his initiative the terrible trials and burnings of Europe began in Scotland, to our nation's shame. In 1603 he united the kingdom of England and was titled James VI & I. A few years later he introduced the Authorised Version of the Bible. Until then, it was not that other translations of the Bible were unauthorised, but the Church forbade translation into any modern language. In this first authorised version, witchcraft acquired its Scriptural condemnation because the word poisoner was rendered as witch. The church equated anything female – from visions to midwifery – as the work of the devil.'

The bookseller banged the book on his counter and the dust flew in all directions.

'Forty pounds to you, sir. The king would be called a control freak today. He showed little interest in his queen but lived in fear of witches. Two years after William Shakespeare became the subject of His Majesty, the Scottish monarch, the bard wrote *Macbeth*. Was it not to engage the interest of the king that this play dramatised the murder of a Scottish king under the malevolent influence of witches?'

The bookseller slowly cleared his throat, 'Now, you sell your stories so presumably you will make me an offer for what I can tell you? After you buy this book.'

'Where can I find Father Maxwell?'

'Perhaps you would like to buy that book?'

I examined and put *The North Berwick Trials: the History of Scottish Witchcraft in the Reign of James VI* back on the shelves.

The merchant glared at me as I slammed his door and left him alone with his friend, the retired schoolteacher.

Chapter Fifty-Eight

'Here Sara would be burned as a witch, even today,' I chuckled to myself as I sped along the country road from Inverness.

I roared out loud, 'I can sense the claws of evil here, but the details are incomplete.'

As a lorry appeared out of the rainstorm I drove off the road into the long grass that concealed a ditch and thus the car toppled over into gravel. No worry. It was a lovely day and I felt great. Was it I, or was it chemical consciousness?

I had enjoyed a confrontation with the editor of the *East Highlands Gazette*. Unfortunately he was too busy with, Hold The Front Page, TIBBY THE CAT RESCUED BY EMERGENCY SERVICES FROM LOCAL ROOF. Where were they now that I needed them? I managed to open the undamaged driver's car door by the roadside and climbed out into the pouring rain. I felt at one with the rain, the trees, the soil, and the forest. Or he did. Michael Leonard, the Son of God. He felt very close to God, the heavenly Father of my wife. He had a real presence here. No wonder the people of the Languedoc had no need for the priests of the Roman Church.

I had shown the editor the front page of 25 June 1959.

'Before my time,' he said (no cat rescue story here).

But the coolest cat was walking on local waters. Or rather, she wasn't. Don't you see? The perception is to explain the deception.

'We don't keep records that far back,' he claimed.

Huh! I designed my own information retrieval system for Leonard-Whitman Research Ltd, fully documented and cross-referenced. A filing clerk of mine was fired for carelessness. That's how I operate. That's why ML became the most famous investigative journalist in the world.

I feel euphoric; I can see 'myself' from outside my body.

He strips off his clothes, at first the coat, then everything else. He admires his body, caresses it against a tree-being and mingles soil into his body which is sweating profusely. But the soil washes off with the sky rain.

Sara is everywhere, in the sky, in the rain, like a bird of the heavens. She is Astarte, the goddess of fertility, the mother of the earth. Her firm young breasts are round and her nipples dark and oozing milk. He handles his penis roughly and ejaculates. The sexual pleasure is more than a minor sensation, because he wanted to mingle his seed with the good earth. And the Demiurge saw that it was good. He and I knew it. I mean, I know that He approved because it rains more fiercely and thunder roars. Modern man has lost the ability to control the climate, but Michael Leonard has regained it. I cause more rain.

He climbs to the top of the wooded hill and looks down upon creation.

I will give you the world, Michael Leonard, if you will poison the Daughter of Israel.

'She is being poisoned slowly in any case, as well you know,' I replied. 'I will not take the blame.'

Name your price. Women are creatures of base instinct, poor logic and sexually depraved.

'She enjoys it, she even said so. She is a danger to men. Here she would be burned as a witch.'

She is a Jezebel. She has no fidelity. You know that in Japan she lay with another? She left many men before you and she will leave you for the American Jew. When she is away from you she is still depraved and she leads men into indecency. She lies naked with women to recruit them to her cult. She takes drugs to elevate herself to My divine level. She mouths my words, scatters my truths, disburses my buried treasure, and preaches free love. You know that she is dangerous. I will make you rich beyond your wildest dreams if you will stop her in any way. Expose the sinister brotherhood; it is a coven of male witches.

* * *

I try to concentrate on my work. I must pursue the investigation. I am climbing the grass bank looking down at my car through a torrent of rain I have caused.

I curse the editor. A local paper would have carried stories about newcomers; that's what I said to him. Surely a new priest who came into the region at the same time as Sara came in order to watch her at the new school.

Some reporter must remember some details. They must be in on it.

Surely I am dreaming? I became aware that I am breathing heavily. Panic. Fear! I was not myself. I was outside myself. I found a sharp stone and tore a small abrasion into my left lower thumb. Blood. So, I am not dreaming. The rain washes it away. I put some soil onto the wound, but the rain washes it away. Who was tempting me?

I shout at the top of my voice, 'Get thee hence Satan, for is it not written, *Man shall not live by bread alone but. . .*'

His voice sounded pretty good.

I am confused. I must make plans. He will stay here for some time and eat only honey and wild locusts to purify him. The rain was an adequate baptism of water. His wild curly hair was washed into his face.

'I love you Sara. I love you. I will not kill you. I will purify you.'

I saw the rainbow, which connected Heaven, to Earth and the dove of peace descended. 'I love you, Sara. You are good. I am not fit to tie your sandals. I will find out who did this to you, Peach Blossom. If it is money or the share of a story, I'm your man. I didn't break your glass door on purpose, Mr small-time Editor, but I find your journalistic standards as far from mine as London is from this stupid little town. And it explains our relative positions, fellow wordsmith, on the journalistic hierarchy.'

It was too late. The Temple Guards overpowered him. He tried to fight them off, hoping Peter would use the sword or Andrew James would use his gun, but the guards lifted him. His nakedness was covered with a gown. He was folded into a car which had appeared behind his own crashed vehicle. Oh dear, it was not his, but a hired car and badly damaged.

The prisoner was taken to the dungeons and examined by a doctor. We were given dry prison clothes and began the rest of our days in this cell with lepers, thieves, and outcasts. But we were not afraid of crucifixion. They spoke in tongues and languages from all over the empire. *Och Aye The Noo!* In my cell there was John the Baptist who laid hands on me and took away my pain. Told me I would die on the cross, as I was the consort of the messiah. I saw the dove descending and the ladder to the heavens. There was a radiance of light and harmony becoming a tone.

They spiked my drink, Jesus! They followed me here, or they were here already. I'm drifting.

Perhaps I was already dead, for now I ascended and was carried through the splendid golden gates, like a temple or a palace with a dozen walls, a giant maze, but even from the outside somehow I could see God on His throne. It seemed that the walls were transparent and the Gates were all in a line, and with my escort I was approaching Him. Seeing Him all the time yet never getting any closer. *I do not believe. I do not believe.* Through an infinite number of outer chambers I sensed that I would never arrive but I heard Sara prompt me, 'Michael! Speak to the Father.'

'We all travel to God but we shall never arrive, dearest Sara, oh, my darling, I am so very sorry. Like the horizon, you see it but He does not exist.'

There were tears in my eyes (or was it rain?) and I humbly walked towards His throne but the more I walked, I never got there. The angels dried me and clothed me. Words were exchanged. None were necessary. It could not be spoken.

I cannot describe the place. Any attempt would make it sound like a Spanish hacienda or a Gaudi cathedral. I kept pleading in my defence how hard I had tried to expose Sélène's conspirators.

Chapter Fifty-Nine

I woke up early the next morning but I had no watch. I saw the interior of a brick-built police cell. Architecture: Earth, late 20th-century. Plain prison pyjamas, no convict arrows, but I was myself again and I knew what had happened. Under my breath I cursed, 'Bastards! They nearly killed me.'

My own clothes had been cleaned and were hanging inside the door. There was a surgical dressing over my left thumb where I had cut it. I gave them Sara's phone number.

At 10:30am the police surgeon arrived to sign me out. A softly-spoken Highland gentleman, he told me that my drink must have been spiked.

'At first I tested for alcohol, but you were not drunk, sir. The landlord said that you had apparently imbibed nothing before you entered his premises and you consumed only two pints of beer. I have sent your samples to the lab in Glasgow. Do you have any idea what caused you to behave in this way?'

I shook my head in order to give me time to think: if the secret drug was relatively undetectable or unknown, the Glasgow laboratory might not trace it. I also reminded myself that the police were controlled by the conspirators through their Masonic links.

After I protested my innocence and ignorance, Sara was admitted. She kissed and hugged me, asked me a thousand times if I was all right. I showed her my left thumb.

'That is the full extent of my injuries. I went off the road,' and I said within the hearing of the police, 'It seems someone may have spiked my drink. It's an occupational hazard, asking too many questions. People get irritated and worried.'

Sara had hired a large Mercedes Benz.

'I thought that you would be afraid of cars after your accident, with no desire to drive home, so I got this carved-from-solid piece of German engineering. It's so beautiful to drive, *I love it*. I stayed in the hotel. They said that you were fine but they gave you something to sleep long and deep, then they wanted to ask you a few questions. So what happened to you?'

I paused to consider how much to tell them.

'I came to see your old school and someone taught me a lesson. Gave me more than an aspirin, this time. I may find out when the police laboratory checks out my sample.'

'But what were you doing here?' Sara asked.

'Same as the other researchers. Same as you when you were speaking to Antigens. We are all obsessed with the past. To bring the truth before the world – *is that not a good and honourable career?*'

She was not amused by the resurfacing of her own words.

I told Sara many times that I wasn't hungry but eventually I thought it best to agree that I was hungry. We stopped at a roadside café and ate a light lunch.

'Sara, I don't want to go home right now. We deserve a few days' holiday.'

She called it our second honeymoon.

She said to me, 'Michael, you know how you explained my delusion of grandeur by Freud's psychology of the replacement of the parents by grander people? Well, I looked it up. See, I've got my notes.'

She showed me the page in her journal. I read, in her delicate handwriting,

FREUD, COLLECTED WORKS Vol IX, page 241

'He is turning away from the father he knows today to the father in whom he believed in the earlier years of his childhood . . .'

'Michael! This never applied to me. After my father was . . . *after he died*. I mean, the opposite would be more likely, don't you think? Are you really trying to find the truth?'

Chapter Sixty

Sara and I returned to Geneva after six days touring Scotland's north west coast in the hired Mercedes. We stayed in small Bed & Breakfast houses and crofts. If the natives recognised us they made no fuss. The Highlanders are tranquil and practical people. I overheard a counter waitress in a harbour cafeteria, 'Jimmy, that's the Daughter of God' – 'Aye, lassie, that's as maybe, but they've ordered haddock and chips and a pot of tea and they're waiting to be served like anyone else.'

We travelled as far as the island of Harris where Sara found peace and anonymity. None of the sheep had heard of her. It appeared as though our landlady did not recognise us but the islanders are withdrawn, strict Calvinists. Any careless breach of the Sabbath attracts silent contempt. I believe that Mrs MacDonald knew exactly who we were and deeply disapproved of both investigator and modern messiah.

Away from the pressures of the world, Sara was at peace and free from her mood swings. She was great fun.

On the return journey we parked the car at the Kyle of Lochalsh. At its fishing harbour the metal-corroding salt water was swept into every nook and cranny of cars and men by the fierce wind. We boarded a ferry to the island of Mull and travelled onwards by boat to the Christian Community on Iona. I'm not sure why Sara wanted to visit the sacred island but I found it warm and hospitable. I joyfully recall these two days. Like a planetary eclipse, the civilised pace and the peat fires briefly refreshed our lives. We should have stayed there forever. Sara said that *I* was free of mood swings during our holiday!

Unfortunately we both had fish to fry in the so-called real world, and Iona seemed to focus our minds to our need to drive south. The Church Community received daily newspapers, albeit the next day, but we read that the Court in Jerusalem had ruled for Sara's 'Right of Return' as a Jewess. The newspaper article explained that the judicial decision was completely separate from any rabbinic ruling, 'If Sara and her fiancé desire, they could convert together.'

I was not keen to yield to the rabbis, and Sara never suggested that we should. I think that Robert Kohen had lowered her esteem of rabbis.

60.1 True to form, just as Sara became an Israeli citizen she had already moved on. Geneva was now our home. For her, moving into 'the palace' was like the start of her new job, saving the world. For me it was a time for decisions about my own priorities. One morning I sat down in my new study and cleared space on my desk.

Sara had challenged me about my desire to uncover the truth. Was I afraid of finding solid evidence – like the documented genealogy? Had I become a well-remunerated hack, an unpaid mouthpiece of the conspiracy, or both? Suppose Sara was deluded and descended? That made her famous, but careless with her claims as to her authority.

One, the delusions, why is she so intense? How can she swing between the polar extremes of innocence and intelligence, purity and promiscuity? Secondly, those who supported her delusions – when and why? And which came first, the delusions or the supporters?

I knew that I too was living a delusion. Sara and I were leaning on each other but not as soulmates as she claimed; maybe even she believed it. I believed that she was pregnant and that her Swiss team would make her self-sufficient and probably even an eligible young man.

60.2 And then my mother died. I returned to London and broke down when I saw the squalor and pain of her last years. I had neglected her and she had dedicated her life to my welfare. My guilt was softened by defence mechanisms. Paradoxically she had been visited by nuns and was buried by the Catholic Church.

Canon Conlan gave me much support. I respected him so much, I felt like saying, 'You're a good man, Father, and well-read, so how can you preach all these lies to your congregation?'

By accident I met Canon Conlan in the street and asked him to join me for a cup of tea. In a café I suggested he might persuade the Vatican to surrender the genealogy on their terms rather than let me storm their gates. He did not refuse, but he said, 'Michael, some people live for the day; you think in terms of tomorrow; but The Holy See has a much longer term to consider.'

News was thin and the media launched Sara's career into the charismatic cult I believe she had craved since her Hollywood days. The 'Messianic Organisation' grew so fast that it appeared like a sleeping global network which had been woken.

The established churches perceived this to be menacing but on 15th May 1980 'the organisation' calmed them by announcing that no new church was to be formed. Orientation was to be achieved by the doctrine of Dual Allegiance (also called Parallel Membership): 'the kingdom to come' comprised people who remained in their work places but focusing their lives. Satan, Sara declared, was obscured in the very same bodies as her followers, disguised as the other side of good intentions. Apparently not even Satan was past his sell-by date. He was no one person or group: he was a herd instinct, she said, the group mind of death's dream kingdom.

'Sara,' I pleaded, 'aren't you playing medieval demonology in the twentieth-century with the words of a poet?'

'Mike, don't you see what I see? You meet a sad guy in a pub and he's a pusher. You meet another. He talks about his mum. Tomorrow, on the streets he'll knife an innocent as part of a gang. You meet a Business Executive in a wine bar and he's human. He talks about his wife and kids. Yesterday as part of a corporate he sold two thousand pins for anti-personnel landmines.'

Soon after we returned from Scotland, Sara spent time on judicial disputes and appeals which poured in from all over the world. I have figures showing the trend. In the week before the Messianic 'Department of Justice' was created (in August, I think, because it gave us another week's holiday) we received over two hundred cases! From peasants of Pondicherry to a personal friend, Padrique 'the poseur' – a yuppie living in London. He had crashed his Porsche and faxed me the details to see if my wife would prevail upon his insurance company to offer a better settlement. It was the beginning of Thatcher's decade of individualism and assertion: the dissolution of Society. Of this Sara said, 'We will be here to catch the pieces when their plastic balloons burst'.

The Gospel According to Sara.

In contrast to my young wife's hectic pace I enjoyed leisurely weekends befitting an aging royal consort. My work was in the gym and I developed muscles and masculinity. I realised that I was narrow and selfish and I felt empty and depressed. I wasn't exposing the conspiracy, but supporting it. I had a sense of overwhelming defeat despite the earnings. I gave little thought to working until 10:00am, when, according to my new routine, I shut myself in my study with two mugs of coffee, one warm, the other five degrees too hot to drink until after the first. I had no sense of urgency. I had no energy.

I began to wonder if I might be drugged.

I felt that if the Vatican had a Genealogy, they would not announce it during my lifetime. My gloom lifted very briefly late in October when I realised that I had other work to do.

Now she was pregnant my priority was to ensure that Sara wasn't being doped by the delusion drug. She sustained long hours at peak energy and in Hollywood the stars were run on expensive substances. Since my discovery of ZF231 her food and medication was carefully screened by her own organisation. But there was one source of stimulation we could not control: acclaim. Love was her drug, and now everyone loved her. Except me.

And I couldn't believe in her as the modern messiah. However either drugs or events had gripped her so pervasively that I feared the outcome. She had yielded to the suggestion that she was divine. The conspirators would have planned a spectacular self-sacrifice. Death. Martyrdom. She would not choose to age gracefully but rather die tragically, young and beautiful.

A lover is at a privileged point of perception. He can damage a woman more than an assailant. Who was Sara's true companion? She was a beautiful woman fatally attracted to wolves, Johnny Lord, Hero of Hollywood, and to the political power of a Spencer Weidfeld. And Me? I simply carried her bags for a time and I wasn't waiting to get humiliated by her next lover. If she did this to me I was determined be in a position of power.

60.3 She was touring Germany. I had no right to do so, but in this mind the journalist in me entered our bedroom with a bag of tools, carefully prised open the back of her locked wooden wardrobe. I retrieved and photocopied her diaries.

It made me angry. She had dedicated pages of soppy love poems to a lover who had planned each step of dominating her and breaking her spirit. Her diaries and his pillow talk disclosed unbelievable revelations which tested my ability to absorb incredible horrors. The scale of his schemes to break her self-esteem and reduce her to – what? He wanted simply to pick petals from the daisy. She noted but did not absorb the facts; that he never promised to marry her; that he never even said that he loved her. Never sent her a birthday card. Then pages of plans, politics and priorities when he made it to the White House and she would be the First Lady.

That was the dream. The reality was she only saw him for sex for one hour each weekday when he was in Washington. A male minder was employed to stop her from socialising and bought her clothes, food and probably mind-numbing drugs. Presumably her time was spent planning her view of Utopia, the Green America as conceived by the flower people. Free love and legalised drugs to be introduced by a Republican President! Kept as a subdued plaything in an opulent cage, she was forced to account for the last penny of her allowance.

Control freaks are careful with their cash, I should know, but I am shocked at the entries, income on the left pages, expenditure on the right. A little food, but many slimming tablets. Paperback books, cosmetics, fake tan, and contraceptives.

I walk into my private study and I hide my photocopies. I didn't think I had any feelings left, but I am close to tears. I cannot contemplate selling this story. But I think that now I understand everything. I want to weep for the way I treated my mother and now I understand that Sara also was neglected and abused. It is not too late for me to care for her.

Agapean rather than erotic love, I say to myself, always needing to rationalise things when the messianic parallel struck me. Like Joseph, I am betrothed to a woman carrying the child of another man.

I badly need to share the absurd coincidence with someone, but McGrath has turned against me and Bartlett might go solo one day soon. I am just sitting down, head in my hands, elbows on my bedroom table. Not even the maid will disturb me. I shall replace Sara's diaries, back under her clothes in the bedroom wardrobe as if undisturbed and later I shall replace the back panel. But I am disturbed. I contrast the strong Sara in Germany today to what she survived in USA and now I think I understand everything. Or, at least, enough for now.

I sit in my study and I recall her brother's assertion that Mathilde was not his biological mother. And Sara's crazy claim that she was born from an unbroken line of virgins. Not even Canon Conlan could persuade me of the Immaculate Conception but now I feel convinced there is something behind the doctrine that neither he nor I suspected.

I read about the beatings and violence the politician inflicted on her. She told me it made her strong. It suggests an inversion of my messianic conspiracy; that Sara's mindset was created – as she once said to me – by the anti-Christ. When she spoke of ethical government, she wrote that Weidfeld skilfully asserted its futility to her.

Strength is being shallow. If you submit to fine feelings, little woman, you submit to slavery. It's best to be shallow. I'm making you strong by breaking your spirit of Christian charity. It's an invention. The milk of human kindness does not run tanks or fuel 'planes. I'm trying to show you strength as it really is. Might is right. Would you have believed that you would do all these depraved perversions to turn me on? Yet you do, and I still haven't found where you will stop. You'll do more. You're strong, but you're the most submissive woman I've ever had. You're classy. I'm from nothing. You're an intelligent, woman. What is your weakness? I'll tell you. It's all this conscience and depth. I'm telling you this for your own good, it's better to be shallow. I'll break you unless you fight me back. I want you to fight back. One day, you will fight, then I'll have done you good. I'll make you strong. That's what I'm doing. I'm breaking you in like a mare. I want you to rebel against me.'

60.4 After fighting this monster, Sara had learned to challenge Satan and his perversion of the churches. However, revising the Lord's Prayer was provocative. Shortly before Christmas 1980 'The Lady's Prayer' came forth from my sweet little wife's lips; 'like an ICBM aimed at Rome,' as one of my newspaper colleagues put it, 'and we all thought that she was against nuclear missiles!'

In her International Christmas Broadcast, she was asked (probably a planted question), *how should we pray?*

She answered, 'As the Lord Jesus commanded, but I have updated for the Aquarian Age. In the twenty-first-century world citizens shall pray as follows:

> 'Ruler of the higher realm,
> God of universal acclaim,
> We do our best to live
> according to your vision.
> May we take only what we need,
> not strive to store up more.
> Put us not in debt for all that we receive
> and thus freed, let us give more generously.
> Make us feel happy and fulfilled
> by harvesting the seeds of kindness we have sown
> and always save us from the dangers of desire.

Chapter Sixty-One

GENEVA, JULY 1980

One evening I woke up in my armchair, squeezed into my slippers and switched off the television. I heard Sara's voice and went to greet her, 'Hi, darling. A hard day at work?'

Aware of my sarcasm she smiled, but I was determined to exaggerate my reduced rôle of house-husband, 'Have you eaten?'

We shared a midnight snack. Sara approved of my British habit of taking breakfast cereals with milk at any time of the day. We crunched the little morsels of food and I told her that I really wanted to help her, that my investigation was jointly motivated for her career as well as for mine. If I wanted to pursue journalism for its own sake I would pursue a fresh field of enquiry.

Sara was delighted. She hugged me. I told her that if she had the time we should become a happy family. I told her that she had to make the time.

'A modern messiah,' I said, 'must learn to delegate.'

She spoke equal nonsense. Or so I thought, at the time.

'But I am born from an unbroken line of virgins.'

In plain words, the child was not mine.

I told her that the drug could be very hard to identify if it was from the ancient world, or (curiously) the opposite, if it were a modern unregistered variant.

'The opposite of hate is not love, but fear. You know, when I was fourteen, a priest of the church made love to me and I enjoyed it because the love he gave me was so spiritual that it was not physical and I think love is not the sin of the flesh because love is of the psyche not of the soma . . . but you know, sex is also used in religion and that is quite different. He used to tell me that the Egyptian Priests knew the formula, dosage, chants, and constellations for the act of coitus with the temple prostitutes to heighten their ecstasy and propitiate the gods.'

'Sounds like fun to me,' I quipped, hopefully. 'I'll join your cult.'

'Robert Kohen said to me, that the Essenes learned such things from the Therapeutae, and this was excised early from the Gospel account of the initiation of Lazarus. Some people say that I entice men with drugged orgies. Do you believe that?'

'Do you entice young men?' I asked, 'I mean, you never regarded the flesh as sinful despite your PR people gagging you today?'

Once again the pattern of our relationship was the pendulum between dependency and irritiation. Still unsure of my facts, I suggested that the drug was running her down like a clock and I begged her to allow me to discover it. 'Are you really happy, Sara? Do you understand the rubbish you talk? Do you want to lose your mind completely? Is it necessary for you to die to begin a new religion?'

Her silence betrayed contempt for my question. I walked away to my own room but she pleaded that I must not leave her.

61.1 When I woke up I found a letter profusely decorated with floral patterns.

> *Had to catch the flight at 8am. Back home tomorrow around 10pm. How petty is my career, you'll be thinking. A jet-setting executive wife. Love you. Your Peach Blossom.*

I had coffee in the 'domestic wing' kitchen with Karen, Sara's personal secretary, and asked her why she didn't travel with Sara. Apparently it was the function of an Official Secretary called Gabriella Muschio who compiled most of the material for *Sermons, Speeches, and Sayings: a Fifth Gospel*. Karen worked wherever Sara was living; Gaby worked wherever Sara was travelling.

'Are the disciples going to be based at our headquarters?' I inquired.

No, next year each disciple would be sent away to arrange his or her own supporting staff outside 'the organisation.' And scattered worldwide. They were to be. . . She stopped. I prompted her.

'Karen, Sara has already told me that she thinks that they will inherit her task very soon.'

'Yes, sir, that is what we are all being told to expect.'

'Don't call me sir for Heaven's sake. At least Mr Leonard, or better, Michael. If you're the home girl and I am the house-husband we'd better be friends! Tell me, do you believe that her consciousness is altered by a drug which gives her energy but will burn her out?'

Karen hesitated.

I changed the question, 'Will you allow these people to drug her?'

Karen was struck by the dilemma I posed.

I sat at the kitchen table and allowed her to buy time by making us a cup of tea. After a few moments she spoke softly.

'You knw that Sara talks about Golden Henbane which grew in her father's house. And you identify the plant as evidence which contradicts the story of her alleged childhood in the house in the Languedoc. But, come here.'

She took me into Sara's study and retrieved a facsimile of a nineteenth century book, *Materia Medicina: Hyoscyamus Niger, Albus, Muticus, et Aureus.*

'Unlike you, I don't read Latin,' said Karen, 'but it's all about hundreds of preparations. And I looked at it very recently, because it's a paperback printed in France. The spine is broken here so perhaps Sara has read this page.'

It is not only Catholic priests who once used Latin to conceal forbidden knowledge. I assimilated what was written but divulged none of it to Karen.

At my suggestion, she telephoned 'the General.'

Wendell Reichardt lived in New York with a wife 26 years his younger and two infant children. It seemed that he was CIA (retired), now appointed as co-ordinator of messianic security, the one man who was most aware of the security cells of the organisation, the international governments and the M-bodyguard. He invited me to see him any time I could fly to New York.

* * *

I enjoy even the airport and flight parts of overseas travel but my first taste of Business Class created an instant addiction. Reclining with eyes closed after the cabin Dinner I thought about the ancient book of herbs; it occurred to me that perhaps, like Karen, Sara was aware of the page but not the contents; or the contents but not the meaning. Either way, if Reichardt was responsible for keeping her alive then he should be informed.

61.2 Wendell Reichardt lived in a small but fashionable Manhattan loft which, he explained, belonged to his daughter. He had, only six months ago, lost his life-partner to cancer and He had been 'a company man' until his retirement two years back. Now he saw the futility of the Russian and American people threatening each other because of their ideologies. That meant that he saw the futility of his life's work and as an empty gesture he gave the pension to a charity.

I asked which charity.

'One that I chose and Jesus advises us not to boast openly.'

It was the most friendly refusal to answer I put up with in twenty years of interrogation. He continued.

'I had to take care that, in my commitment to Christ, I didn't repeat my mistake. The churches make that very hard. At fifty-seven I don't expect a third chance. I spent weeks making tables of which organisation believes which doctrine until I realised that it wasn't like choosing a make of car.'

Reichardt didn't spell it out, but apparently after finding Jesus he found Sara. I discussed the purpose of my visit. I didn't tell him that I strongly suspected she was carrying a child that wasn't mine. His response took me by surprise.

'As you were the first to reveal, Michael, your Sara is of the royal bloodline and preparation for the rôle hardly invalidates the legitimacy. As for the drug, well this is what we are here to discuss. Sara has consulted with an organisation doctor, not your family doctor. She teaches against the misuse of all substances – gunpowder, pesticide, and uranium – by individuals. Governments and professions are group covers for individual irresponsibility. That's what she said. Think about it, Michael. It's what Sara teaches us.'

When I started to protest, his massive frame over six feet high, wrenched itself from his chair and he came back with a photograph of his late wife, Doris.

'Sara will become your wife, Michael, but she is dedicated to Almighty God and to repair the world. You will make a faultline in your marriage if you persist in questioning her about her medication or whatever. You have travelled a long way, and I know that is not what you have come to hear.'

What I did hear for the rest of the day was a great help for me in understanding Sara and the big picture. What distinguishes journalists and investigators is that they build stories from a string of facts in two dimensions but we impart understanding based on nine tenths of the undisclosed facts.

Reichardt told me that the CIA *was* the drug problem. Like the Cold War, they didn't actually invent drugs; they just escalated it by knee-jerk reactions instead of high-level policies. Right from the start the military saw psycho-active drugs, not as therapeutic or sacramental, but as a useful instrument against the Communists.

On the plane I read his words from my notebook although I had promised Reichardt it was off the record.

'We fought hard during the 'sixties before we got the government to make the CIA, and not the FDA, as the regulators. History would have been better if the healing and nutritional agencies took control. Because when we won, we abused the substances in every way: we traded it; we experimented on black prisoners without their consent; we used it as date-rape drugs. The we busted people like John Lennon and Mick Jagger for doing much less. What kinda message did that send to the kids?'

On my return to Geneva I felt very angry that Sara no longer shared or entrusted the drug investigation with me, however the most severe shock possible jolted my professional pride. I had been bluffing about my knowledge of the family Genealogy in an attempt to smoke it out. Now I stood in the newsagent and bookshop in the airport having been attracted by a newspaper with a photo of Sara.

The headline will remain etched on my brain until I depart from this world. It was in a French newspaper, a language that was not my first, but the message was clear enough.

MESSIANIC GENEALOGY EXISTS
SARA IS DESCENDED FROM DAVID AND JESUS
VATICAN TO DISCUSS PUBLICATION

Within two days, worse jump out of newspapers to bite me.

The obituary of Canon Conlan.

He had done so much to help me accept my mother's death. Perhaps, like her, his virtue was enough reward and a good passport into the realm into which we pass after this world of 'death's dream kingdom.' He was killed under the weight of books when a cabinet, or some shelves, collapsed. The timing and the tragedy carried a powerful message with my name on it. I had asked him to speak to higher authorities in The Church. Had he done it? Or was his death an accident or an act of God? *Did I believe in God?*

After a few days, I calmed down and came to the conclusion that it was a message; it was a message to me from corrupt men within the Church. I could not attribute blame, because in reality I was to blame.

I was not merely reporting a story after the event. I was making it happen.

Chapter Sixty-Two

'MT SINAI', AUGUST 1980

A off-track jeep – a fashion accessory in London – is essential to negotiate the track which degenerates into the terrain of the Judean Wilderness.

This desert is unworldly in two senses. It is a non-life supporting region of the so-called water planet; and it has been the refuge of holy men branded throughout the ages either as mad or inspired. The Baptist and the Christ were two figures in a long line of holy men who reached or proclaimed their insights from this place. After my meeting in New York I had read the Gospels more carefully and taken Reichardt's point that these holy men were skilled pharmacologists.

About two hundred years before them, the community Scrolls re-established its fortified settlement on the north west bank of the Dead Sea. Archaeologists found the water cistern and the baptismal baths from which John would derive his name. We do not know the name of the place in the days of the community we call the Essenes, but in later times the nomadic Arabs called it Qumran. And despite their having scrolls, we do not know how the first-century villagers styled themselves nor even what they were called by their rivals – the Pharisees and Sadducees – but our historians call them Essenes.

Leading from the track a beaten path at this place leads to a misleadingly named settlement: Mt Sinai is neither a hill nor is it the place at which Moses received the tablets of the Law. The buildings belong to the Modern Order of Essenes, registered as a kibbutz in Israel and a charity in the USA. Like their predecessors MOE used place names to mislead outsiders and codes to inform insiders.

Sara told me the commune was called Damascus in the Essene Scrolls. St Paul was travelling not to Syria when he experienced his conversion.

When we arrived, we met about one hundred Jews, mainly Americans who had reached various levels of spiritual attainment in the rigorous ascetic community which R.F. Kohen had reinvented after 2000 years.

Unlike the original Essene community (itself reconstituted after at least one break) Kohen's *Berith Hadashah* (New Covenant) did not attract the weak, nor those weary of the world of affairs. Today's candidates mostly came from positions of influence and comfort; and all their wealth was given either to the common pool or to other causes or charities. In exchange they received only the necessities of life and a highly regulated existence.

Their community regarded itself as the pure and priestly summit of Israel, governed by the Law of Moses. It would be going too far to call it a state within a state, but its citizens were governed by rigorous codes. The Rule of the Community, The Rule for All the Congregation of Israel in the Last Days, and The Benedictions; all modified from writings of the Dead Sea Scrolls.

The Megillot ha-yahad (Scrolls of the Community) and Procedures of the Assembly were thoroughly modern statutes – documents of great length which precisely regulated the constitution, purpose, and methods of the community. Written in Modern Hebrew and English although both languages were regarded as secular.

Sara pointed to a cuddly toy sitting on top of the stone wall. As I admired the masonry a slim bearded Brooklyn recruit introduced himself as Boruch Mendelsohn.

'Limestones. I helped build this part with my own hands. Gives me a great feeling of destiny.'

I smiled. 'I confess that it looks so . . . I mean I thought it was repaired.'

'The original settlement is five kilometres from here. It's an archaeological site but ours is built for the future.'

* * *

Two thousand years ago, the Essenes had impressed historians as diverse as Philo of Alexandria and Pliny the Elder. Flavius Josephus, a Jewish General who had sided with the Romans wrote:

> They are Jews by birth and are peculiarly attached to each other. They eschew pleasure-seeking as a vice and regard temperance and mastery of the passions as a virtue. Scorning wedlock, they select other men's children while still pliable and teachable . . . Contemptuous of wealth they are communists to perfection, and none of them will be found to be better off than the rest . . . They possess no one city but everywhere have large colonies . . . When they travel they carry no baggage at all, but only weapons to keep off bandits.

Two thousand years later the chronicler Flavius M. Leonardus now pens something along these lines:

> The evil and shallow nature of the modern world – destroying itself and leering everywhere to mock the God of all creation and invite certain destruction – appeared central to the new Essenes. That the Five Books of Moses, the cornerstone of the Hebrew and Christian Bibles, was the divine word loomed equally large in the daily lives of both ancient and modern sectarians. They saw themselves as the blueprint of the true Israel in contrast with the modern secular state and the rituals and customs of modern Judaism.
>
> Kohen had gathered and certified the hereditary priesthood, described as an eternal planting, the true Israel, an Assembly of Supreme Holiness for Aaron and Zadok. They followed their predecessors and dressed in simple and seemly white garments, took their meals communally and sang their praises of God together.
>
> The society was egalitarian and democratic in joint session but rigorously structured in both houses and ranks of membership. In all matters the priests had precedence according to those celebrated Scriptures miraculously rediscovered by the shores of the Dead Sea.
>
> According to the Scrolls, supreme authority was jointly vested in two persons. The Anointed Priest (Kohen-mashiah) was the

> founder of the New Order. Dr Robert F. Kohen was responsible for religious direction. And the Anointed Ruler (Royal Mashiah) from the tribe of Judah and the House of David – was about to be installed.
>
> I travelled as her consort to attend the Messianic Banquet with all its powerful ceremonial resonances of the Last Supper and the communal meals described in the Dead Sea Scrolls. I was full of curiosity and flattered by a personal invitation.

Expecting an exclusive story, I was disappointed to discover before long that there were no satellite dishes but the media had arrived in numbers. The long-term significance and purpose of the Dinner would emerge before too long. The organisers had set me up for a fall.

Chapter Sixty-Three

JUDEAN DESERT, AUGUST 1980

The Collegiate Dining Chamber of the Modern Order of Essenes was a grey stone temple of unlined walls; the floorplan was shaped as the six-pointed Star of David. The vaulted roof was hexagonal. This provided six groups of tables some intimacy but a full view of the high-ranking Brothers seated at a centre table.

The pillars were roughly hewn stone. A few arched beams of undressed timber and crude black ironwork gave a sparse and ancient appearance in contrast to the ornamentation of the Cathedrals of Christendom. Doubtless the architecture of 'Mt Sinai' also expressed the original Essene sect's contempt for the pagan grandeur of Herod's Temple. The design was unique: the outer wall of the four-storey main building was the inner wall of the Assembly Hall and the two were joined by windows and walkways.

Food was blessed before, during and after its preparation then brought along a walkway before, of course, a Grace before meals was recited.

The ritual of The Messianic Banquet was prescribed in detail and accorded great significance in the Dead Sea Scrolls. Apparently the Last Supper of Christ was modelled on this ritual.

When I discussed this with Mr Mendelsohn he dissolved the discrepancy of two Gospels concerning the timing of Passover in relation to the trial and execution of Jesus. Cynics and scholars say that one Evangelist contradicts the other; but it may be resolved by the different calendars of the Temple Priests and the Essenes. The latter party rejected as erroneous – and sacerdotally ineffective – the lunar calendar and thus the festival dates later observed by Rabbinic Judaism. This was based on the Book of Jubilees 2:9, which my new friend quoted from memory.

'And God appointed *the sun* to be a great sign on the earth for days and for Sabbaths and for months and for feasts and for years . . . and for all seasons of the year.'

The Essenes had always set themselves apart from the rest of Judaism by their non-synchronous festivals. And today was not a Jewish festival in New York.

63.1 While most Judaeo-Christian sects might derive benefit from Sara's support, her presence was essential here this evening. She would fulfil time-hallowed prophecies to validate the Essene Scriptures: the restored nation of Israel and the significance of the millennium to the Jewish people.

In the hour before the banquet, Dr Kohen came to my room to apologise in person for having *cancel* a meeting with me. I thought that it had been postponed. I assumed that he had come now to be interviewed but when he walked away I knew that he was planning something I would not like.

I joined my wife in her tour of the settlement. It gave me a reason to snoop around with my eyes and ears open and aware of something awaiting my discovery.

MOE members and candidates came from many corners of the globe but they all spoke Modern Hebrew among themselves. (Biblical Hebrew, in which they worshipped, is different).

We saw the usual kibbutz goats, irrigated fields and workshops, but this was a dedicated community. The Essene tour guide gave us detailed explanations of their goals of purity and self-sufficiency. We were told about the organisation of the qahal (assembly) into the camps of the nomadic days preceding the Promised Land. These were the twelve tribes, organised into the hundreds, fifties, and tens according to the Book of Numbers. But our guide was curiously reticent to disclose numbers.

'We have a flow of candidates at varying stages and ranks, and not all are living with the edah (congregation).'

I was impressed by the relaxed but purposeful demeanour of all persons. They constituted a community whose purpose was unworldly – to praise the Lord constantly in three watches throughout the 24-hour cycle. What also took me by surprise was the sincerity with which many people – astute elders and naive youth alike – revered the presence of Sara.

It seemed as simulated as any film setting from Sara's Hollywood days for soon the cameras from the world news followed us everywhere. She was taken to the preparations being made in the Dining Chamber by way of a rehearsal.

I was introduced to Barbra Streisand who exuded her amazing personality and sexuality, and I was shown where the two of us would please sit together. She smiled at me. After a slight pause, I said of course I would be delighted but I realised that I had been parted and safely removed from Sara. And that it was not Barbra Streisand; she just looked and spoke like the star. In America, you can rent almost anything.

The reason became clear as Sara was snatched from my arm to sit by Robert Kohen at the centre table. My companion lacked the wit and conversation I imagine the real Streisand possessed, but it was too late. The ceremony began even before we were all seated with a speaker reading solemnly from *The Messianic Rule* – one of the Scrolls discovered in the first cave by the Dead Sea.

> 'This shall be the assembly of the men of renown called to the meeting of the council of the community when the priest-messiah shall summon them . . .'

Robert Kohen gulped air and Sara steadied him. His eyes were moist and his face swollen with pride in contrast to his plain white robes as the words were read aloud in four languages – Biblical and Modern Hebrew, then English and French.

> '. . . He shall sit at the head of the whole congregation of Israel with all his brethren, the sons of Aaron, the priests, and those called to the assembly. And they shall sit before him in order of precedence. And the messiah of Israel shall come and the chiefs of

the tribes of Israel shall sit in the order of their precedence. And they shall gather at the common table to eat and drink new wine. When the common table shall be set for eating and the new wine poured for drinking. Let no man extend his hand over the first fruits of bread and wine before the priest, for it is he who shall bless the first fruits of bread and wine and he shall be the first to extend his hand over the bread. And all the congregation of the community shall pronounce a blessing, each in order of precedence.'

63.2 While modern Judaism interprets the Ceremony of Ordination of priests in the Books of Exodus and Leviticus as an historical event, the Essenes practiced it as an annual festival. This evening was not Sara's coronation (as the Press stated) for no-one could do anything to deny her hereditary right. The Ceremony of Ordination was like a seminary's graduation, a formal conferring of rank and rights already earned.

After the meal Robert devoted his time not to his protégée Sara but to me. I was worried and not flattered; I knew that everything had been prepared and I would serve his purpose.

He took me from the dining hall to a long curved room without windows. It led to a low-ceilinged tunnel that contrasted greatly with the spacious banqueting hall. The inner chamber of the building was a secret control room or laboratory hidden from the world. It suggested everything about the true and sinister megalomaniac seeking world domination. It was a James Bond film set of a launch centre.

The function of what he called the 'Hall of Universal Time' became increasingly puzzling to me. It was a combination of ancient stone inlaid with brass and framed with silver designs of planetary paths, logarithmic curves, equations, and cosmic clocks. Each semi-circle had four iron gates leading to eight named chambers.

Kohen proudly claimed that some of the sect's two-thousand-year-old astrological documents had been unearthed by his own monks. As we stood at the centre of the brown marble floor he reminded me that Herod had tolerated the Essenes because of their skills including prophecy based on their understanding of predestination.

Kohen glowed with pride: 'Oh yes, they gave him a reading and many years later he was impressed. We moderns have lost the knowledge until by science of the Swiss Jew, Albert Einstein's equation of the time-space continuum suggests again the reality of fantasy.'

His explanation of the physics and psychology of time was very impressive so far as I, a mere gentile and history graduate, could tell. He launched into a lecture which justified the solar calendar in terms of therapeutic biological rhythms, natural historical cycles and the millennium. He approached precariously close to claiming Jerusalem to be at the centre of the world and of all time. In view of the shortage of time at our disposal (and I had to smile) he invited me to enter the last of 'the rooms that orbit the Hall of Universal Time.'

The eighth room was called 'Micrometrics,' he explained, and was closely related to his own previous defence research. This was the world's most subtle application of periodic interval. He explained a rubidium clock mechanism which extrapolated to sub-atomic time whose function was communication and information retrieval. Its mechanism was fibre-optics and information storage beyond my imagination was by glass discs read by lasers.

As I wondered about the cost to build the laboratory Kohen quoted me state-of-the-art speeds of communication and capacities of data which were impressive; then he boasted that his personal knowledge had developed ten to twenty years ahead of that level, 'too dangerous to fall into the hands of primitives. You know. The Americans. The British.'

He didn't allow me to write any details, nor did he want to divulge these things to scientific journalists. He told me that his so-called Organic Technology simply combined biological function with electronics by converting brain and radio waves.

'Radio Archaeology,' he assured me like mad scientist with a slight accent from central Europe, 'will render the burrowing rabbits as archaic as chip computers.'

I asked if he meant that earth-sifting was obsolete, but he continued.

'Unable to cope with too many projects I have hived off one important branch of my work, a personal gift to humanity: it is the medicine of the twenty-first-century – nanotechnology, even more advanced than organic technology, it will be exploited in my lifetime in this community. We will soon have here the most advanced hospital in the world. While Hadassah prolongs survival, we can raise from the dead. I am talking resurrection and reincarnation with the inventor himself as the first potential client. The ethical considerations defy . . .'

'What is nanotechnology?' I interrupted, avoiding the question of his immortality.

'It will supersede all surgery and drugs. We will make little bugs of molecular dimensions to go into the body and do what is needed. In the wrong hands it has frightening implications. I realise you think that I am a lunatic playing a game, but I am very serious, and there is no game. I see the soul as indestructible, lasting for eternity. You need to have meaning made material as if the fifth dimension does not exist because it cannot be measured otherwise in your scheme of things. Well that is exactly what we do here. We synchronise heaven and earth and soon the planets will be in harmony. Using your own phrase, Michael, you write history, but I make it.'

63.3 Television monitors come to life and I peer to see if Sara is in the banquet hall. Kohen smiles.

'I will restore God's order despite any arrogant individual who thinks that the Covenant is well past the sell-by date. We Jews are the most arrogant sons-of-bitches on God's earth, and yet we are his beloved and chosen people.

'I know you better than yo know yourself because I know your future; it is because of time, Michael. The light from the furthest stars hasn't reached us yet. But it is there. Think about it. I don't think you can.'

It is a speech rather than a conversation. The man is obsessed with his own genius and the fact that I have the woman. He can only play with her mind.

'People dismiss this as 'modern physics,' Michael, but it is timeless physics. Hendrik Lorentz, who wrote the equations for relativistic time and space, passed from this life in 1928 – two years after I was born. But the so-called scientists still live in the days of steam engines and cannot imagine anything else. Their minds are in the nineteenth century through intellectual laziness. Maybe you are right, Michael, there is no shame in being a man of the world, one of the boys. You are simple, shallow and selfish as getting on in the world requires, but I do beg of you one timeless thing beyond your faith. You wrongly think that I care about what you write about me. I make history despite anything or anyone. What I require of you is altogether different. It is for you to love, cherish, and BELIEVE in Sara. You take her for granted and you act like a tired lover, ready to betray her. *And betray her you will.*'

Now we have it. He fancies Sara. I smile. 'As you know the future and everything, you will know that I am taking notes in a pocket memo?'

I pull from my pocket a primitive technology Philips micro cassette. He does not refuse permission but he is angry:

'I find it curious that you have done so much to establish her genealogy. But the steam engine cannot reach the moon and so you have not the means to your destination. You will not reach heaven. You are only a physical lover, and lover is a euphemism, Michael, because you aren't capable of love. You don't fool her; she fools herself. She thinks you love her because she thinks everyone loves her. She is the one so full of love, reflecting enough love for the whole world it makes the miracle of the loaves seem a picnic . . . She is a woman, seductive, unclean and unchaste, hardly a fine judge of men.'

I want to strike him but in anger only my Cockney accent lashes out at him.

'Robert, enough is enough. The woman is a deluded, disturbed, deranged, drugged, and damaged as a result of people like you and she attempts to free herself of the confusion which was hypnotised into her young mind. Sara herself simply waits for the day of the bullet of the last lunatic who will liberate her from the pain which is her mind.'

'Sara chose to accept the ministry,' Kohen bellows, 'And I promise you it was offered by God not imposed by . . .'

'You aren't even who you claim to be. You admit that your American identity was fabricated by the US government to keep East European scientists out of Russia. Did you get to choose all your own details?'

'Michael, I don't even care enough to respond to your article about my immigration records which do not correspond to those of the Horthy regime – the Hungarian equivalent of the Third Reich. Forgotten by all but those of us who lived through it. But out of courtesy, I will enlighten you now if you can suspend your hostilities. I have already decided to pass to you during your visit the details of what you call the conspiracy

– how people came from many parts of the world to meet Sarah-Hélène knowing who she was.'

A journalist should not allow his ego to impede the flow of information, so I apologise with an air of anticipation.

'Perhaps I am a primitive male guarding my woman, so I apologise to you, Robert.'

Kohen nods slightly, hesitates, and then he speaks softly but his words pierce me.

'I escaped from Hungary with forged papers provided by the Swedish government. Oh, this surprises you. As a scientist I became part of "Paperclip," a top secret programme to absorb Nazi researchers in USA rather than let USSR get them all. No doubt it increases your suspicion of me but I have nothing to hide. The source of my information about your woman was – wait for it – the CIA, and they got it from their allies. After the War, you see, the British continued to monitor the French Committees for Public Safety. Churchill was a believer in omens. He even had a Black Magic committee – ostensibly to manipulate Nazi High Command which believed in occult historical destinies and so on. All of this Churchill publicly dismissed as mumbo-jumbo and so he justified it to his colleagues as effective psychological warfare.'

I nod and we sit down on comfortable black leather settees.

'This you do not know, Michael. The child was initiated by an Alexandrian cult and taken into the world of spirit-beings by exquisitely subtle use of herbal drugs of antiquity. Her astral body was expanded and almost certainly she is unaware of the proceedings. Her self-consciousness, her ego, would have been extinguished by hypnosis. The girl absorbed the soul of another girl. Thus, in part, she was not born of the flesh. She is in the perpetual line of virgins. That is how it was done in the ancient near east. The ancient Egyptians called it the Temple Sleep. But she would be in a deep trance before the spiritual immersion into the eternal ribbon of time and cosmos.'

Kohen spun his chair round and typed some commands on a keyboard. The monitor showed me a series of photos of a young woman on a couch, attached to instruments probing her bio-activity.

'We started with fairly crude physical stimuli. Done with full immersion it is a dangerous condition, and highly delicate. The traditional way involves skilled knowledge of the candidate's metabolism, psyche, state of health, and in the past was interpreted as an astrological branch of knowledge. Many modern western women have been damaged by such far-reaching psychic surgery, unknown to the authorities as the culprit practitioner always escapes detection; the police don't believe what they find. In Eastern Europe they just don't report it.

'One of the recovered Dead Sea Scrolls is an encrypted chart, supposedly fragmentary and mumbo-jumbo, yet if only the public realised how advanced and central was the Essenes' knowledge of the mind, human health, and the cosmos, they would understand the need for the encryption. It is similar to the magic of the Egyptian Therapeutae, the Persian Magi, and the Babylonians.

'Sara is not a separate ego-entity as moderns are. When she has sex with you, it is only your pleasure she experiences, Michael. In that sense she remains a virgin. Like a battery torch shining into the sun, you do not give her pleasure. She shares yours. She does not give you sexual pleasure any more; she has expired and thus you will leave her. You will never be married to her, you are just one of her many men.'

63.4 I held my tongue hoping that he might disclose something serious to fortify this nonsense and smoke screen. He did not stop talking.

'We have resumed water-immersion here, not as mere symbolism but as a momentary drowning in which the initiate senses the eternal ribbon of past and future. He sees his past lives and his place in the creation. And the Robert Kohen who came to USA was indeed a different man from the one who lived in Hungary. You see, dear boy, the modern age of reason was ushered in by the war of Hitler. Its organised depravity was denied and concealed by the shocked victors. The Concentration Camps were the end of conscience and compassion.'

The monitor showed images I had not imagined. Involuntarily, I broke down, my spasmodic breathing showing Kohen that he had succeeded.

'Elements Mr Churchill called evil, you would call mumbo-jumbo, and I would call occult. Elements 20th-century man denies but which he cannot expel. But, Michael, I have seen it for I was born in Hell: it was Hungary in 1944, part of the Third Reich. Eichmann was in charge of the Final Solution and the local fascists were getting on with it. Shall I describe it? Losing my parents, aunts, and uncles was the least of it. Losing civilisation and happiness was a greater shock. I cannot explain it. You see, to be dead wasn't that bad in the circumstances.'

I yelled out when I saw the image of a Jewish child lying dead on the pavement with other children walking past her; modern European children to judge by the shops in the background.

'But to see what happened,' he juddered an intake of breath and his eyes moistened, 'to my two cousins. . . And as a young male, to agree – yes to agree happily – to be used as a woman, night after night, because I was young, or . . . in any way, to kill or be killed . . . two German officers were temporarily stopped from raping local girls . . . to see what people, my own people, would do to others to survive.'

He recovered from his shock. I wanted to speak. To silence me, he placed his hand over my lips and he recovered with a smile on his. In fact he was beaming joy. I was all ears.

'Listen to me! I do not despise you because you are a gentile. Amongst this furnace of hell, one day I actually met the famous gentile who was called The Swedish Saviour. A legend. Handsome, elegant, tall, he swept into our sewer of a war-torn city to save us . . . three dirty Jews, my two sisters and me. Oh Michael, we were the rats. By leaving the others behind we escaped. By Raoul's quick wit, and unbelievable risks, total daring and dedication . . . the numbers he saved . . . some people say one hundred thousand Jews but we do not count humans in our religion, Michael, a superstition that considers each person as an infinite universe and now my science confirms it . . . only God knows the statistics . . . they say six million . . . but I was not to be one of them. I wish I was. Guilt is unbearable until you block it out. Truly I wish I died and in my place someone more superficial than me was saved.'

Kohen was overcome with grief. I felt my eyes moisten and a lump in my own throat. I held back from touching him because of his comment about being used by a Nazi officer. We both cried then I waited in silent respect until he had composed himself. Then he smiled.

'I will return us to the dining hall after an hour but to them it will be ten minutes.'

I shook my head in disbelief and glanced at my wristwatch. To confirm that it had stopped I placed it to my ear.

Kohen laughed when he saw my face.

'I learned from Raoul Wallenberg my life's value; I learned that the power of a man is limited only by his desire for good. The Robert Kohen who arrived in USA was indeed a different man. No longer selfish. No longer truly alive. And he was, of course, officially a Swedish citizen, ha-ha. By September 1944 the Americans were also saving European Jews, but only the useful ones, so I was invited in through the back door.

'Mr Wallenberg was also treated illegally – but that was according to the Law of USSR. He was "interviewed" when the Soviets "liberated" Hungary. Raoul was expected home by his family in Sweden as soon as the war ended. But you see, the Soviets could not believe his story. "You are a blue-eyed, blonde boy from wealth and privilege, who once enjoyed a playboy life in neutral Sweden. You then went to live in squalor and danger to save some lousy Jews? What was your real mission? You are a spy! Who put you up to it? The Americans? You must be an American agent!"

'They took him to Russia, Michael, to extract a confession from him. Who was he spying for? What was he really doing? Presumably they found it frustrating that they could never draw their lower truth from him, as he existed on a higher plane they could not see up to. But, my friend, you too are looking for your lower truth in Sara. Yes, she is human, so human!'

Suddenly Kohen shifted into another gear. He spoke to me in another accent, higher pitched, and more urgent.

'What time did we leave the main company, Michael? You can see from any of the unedited broadcasts of this Dinner, I didn't hurry away from it because in a synchronous parallel universe I, as host, am also greeting my guests and mixing in the hall. I don't need to hurry back. I can operate in the solar calendar, the lunar calendar and anything in between and beyond. Hey, you don't disbelieve me? It's only because you can't understand me. I'll show you. I can hear my own recitation on the monitor. Look. It is from Isaiah, Ch 2. Look at me, there I am, in the closed circuit TV. You've seen my magic before, I don't wish to bore you with it. Look on the screen, then go into the hall and see with your own eyes.

On the TV screen I saw Kohen was delivering his speech to the assembly:

'"In days to come
the mountain of the Lord's house
will be set over the other mountains,
raised high above the hills.
All nations will stream towards it,
and many peoples will go and say,
Let us go up to the mountain of the Lord,
to the house of the God of Jacob,
that he may teach us his ways
and that we may walk in his paths.
For instruction comes from Zion,
and the word of the Lord from Jerusalem.
He will judge between the nations
as arbiter among many peoples.
They will beat their swords into mattocks
and their spears into pruning-knives;
nation will not lift sword against nation
nor ever again be trained for war.
Come, people of Jacob,
let us walk in the light of the Lord."'

I looked away from the doppelganger.

'You're doing another BBC trick, Dr Kohen. If I go back to the dining hall, I suppose you will be there in the flesh?'

'You make it sound easy, Michael, and it is. I'm bending radio waves in time. I'm close to bending thought waves in time. Simple memory is not chemical but dimensional. Even without the genealogy that you strive to find, Sara and others with or without mind-expanding drugs can bend time. And I can identify the process. I will join any two points through the fifth dimension at will. Do you know what that means? I'm writing history. But not like you. What I am doing makes your investigative journalism look like a dog finding buried bones. It's a time machine. Perpetual motion is against the law of nature, but a time machine is predicted by the laws of science.'

'If I go outside will I see you there?'

'You'll stay in this room because you are very anxious for me to tell you about SHIF and the soul in your girlfriend, Helen Capulé. They killed their own candidate, the Aryan girl, by overdose and orgy. By accident. The year, you know was?'

'1952.'

'Correct. SHIF – a secret fascist fringe of embarrassment to the Vatican – wanted the Jews to apologise for killing Christ and accept the blame for our own genocide and acknowledge the Christians as the new chosen people. In this climate of lunacy Sara was registered as dead and taken into hiding for preparation in safety. Her identity was changed to Helen MacRae, a name she was hypnotised to adopt. Her paternal grandmother was a Jewish scientist but he converted for his career. By Mosaic Law Sara is not Jewish because she will never persuade the rabbinical court to accept her emotional argument about forced conversions being invalid. The Essenes do not agree with this racial stand, but we agree with the state's Law of Return (Amendment No 2) 5730-1970, section 4A(a) which is, by anomaly, a secular law. It vests the right of citizenship in Sara and therefore she won her case against the Minister of the Interior. Those to whom evil is done do evil in return. The holocaust of Europe defiled the MidEast. The war is in their heads.'

My mind was elsewhere, 'Robert, if I go back to the hall I'll see you? Yes! Well let's go together, hand in hand.'

'You'll get a surprise, Michael.'

We returned to the hall and no-one was giving any speech. How could he? He was with me. He could not 'dissolve' as he entered the large chamber. I held on to him firmly. Kohen was approached by other people and I, too, mingled. Sara, who I saw was cheerful, sensed immediately that I was disturbed. I did not tell her why. It seemed so stupid. Maybe half an hour passed and then Kohen rose to give a speech.

'In days to come the mountain of the Lord's house
will be set over the other mountains . . .'

During this recitation I fell silent in shock. I think I was very white; I certainly felt the blood drain from my face. I studied Kohen. Every small inflection and mannerism I had seen on the TV monitor.

'All nations will stream towards it,
and many peoples will go and say,
Let us go up to the mountain of the Lord,
to the house of the God of Jacob. . .'

Looking across the walkway through two windows I watched Sara singing Jewish folksongs and dancing in her short black dress. Her smile was infectious but I was shivering in fear. In the banquet room I carefully observed the scientist-priest delivering his talk, hoping to fault his conjuring but it continued as a scary déjà vu.

'They will beat their swords into mattocks
and their spears into pruning-knives;
nation will not lift sword against nation
nor ever again be trained for war.
Come, people of Jacob,
let us walk in the light of the Lord.'

63.5 The diners applauded Kohen. He was a very fine actor and recitor. He left the lectern. After his reading I followed him out of the hall across the walkway to the dancing. We watched Sara for a few moments and she smiled.

He beckoned me with the words, 'Press Conference' and I followed his entourage to another building where the press had assembled. It is a lecture hall with a hundred seats; perhaps twenty or thirty are filled.

I felt at home with the journalists although I recognised none of them. I stood at the back of the room, hiding my face, but my mini-recorder held high. I recorded some words.

'They think the story is about a new religious cult; but I know the real story is about timeshifting. I am more afraid of this than excited to be, once again, ahead of the pack. Losing a grip on time is like the ground part beneath your feet, not that I have experienced an earth tremor.'

Then on my tape Kohen announces his countdown for a forthcoming world conference. Its purpose is to lay down plans for 'the Second Council of Jamnia.'

Talk about long-term planning – it is scheduled for over one hundred years into the future, 2090! As Nicaea had largely defined Christianity in the Council of 325AD, so Jamnia had defined Rabbinic Judaism and codified the Bible in 90AD.

The world's news agencies were being given the footage of Kohen's world Diaspora plan. As I listened to him, I thought to myself, the deranged scientist has plotted everything.

Kohen had missed his true vocation as an actor, and Robert Hardy was obviously his role model. As he spoke – Kohen, I presume, but was no longer certain – became the English actor. In any case Hardy, or Kohen, addressed the journalists with a tone of solemnity, and they seemed to understand him.

'In the beginning was time and time was God. It is implicit in the final things Einstein wrote. When primitive man divided the days, he confused event intervals and measurements for time itself. Einstein could not gaze into the sun. But I have done so. What did I see? The Mosaic tetragrammaton, which no Jew can utter, says that the future has come from the past, thus the eternal is cyclic, the beginning is the end, the soul of man returns to its source. Like a moebic loop, God is always on the other side, man is always alone. Nietzsche was wrong, God is not merely Dead. God is Death. Life was given to us. *Some kind of punishment*.'

63.6 After the Press Conference I return to the banquet hall. Sara's face is panic-stricken and white. She asks me to find Robert but I already know where he is. I take her to the lecture theatre where he is sitting on a table.

She shouts that he must abandon the Press Conference.

'Too late,' I say, 'It has finished.'

Kohen laughs like a maniac, 'It hasn't even started.'

She pushes his sleeve and holds his fat and furry arm and he flirts and flatters her in front of me and for the cameras. He thought he had won. But her delicate finger displays my ring, not his. She silences Kohen. Looking into his eyes, her own eyes shed tears and you can hear a pin drop in anticipation of her words.

'Robert, I love you and God loves you . . . but you will be punished for using the truth drug on me. God says that you stormed the Gates of Heaven and you should have used the genealogy, not the chemical, as the key to regression. But I want it to be known that it happened with my consent, except only that I am not sure what information I was able to disclose, or retrieve, and for all I know, some of it may be false. It was my sight and I, too, must deserve a punishment and perhaps I will be judged harshly.'

She wipes the tears from her eyes, but cries out to the astonished journalists, 'By the Law of Moses Robert precedes me as has been confirmed this very day and Robert still works as the servant of the Almighty, as I do, and it is my obligation as God's messenger to deliver this message. As with all punishments, it should serve as a warning to us all concerning obedience and duty, and I shall be more careful. Thank you for your attention.'

Robert is visibly shaken and dismisses the journalists with a wave of his hand and they all pack up without another word. According to his plan his colleagues still hand out freshly printed copies of the Prospectus of the new Sanhedrin's Constitution in four languages but Robert is much more concerned to secure private reassurance from Sara.

I am the only one watching them.

'Please be kind, Redeemer. What will happen to me?' he asks.

She smiles.

Chapter Sixty-Four

GENEVA, AUGUST 1980

The Y2K was distanced from TTM – The True Millennial which was proclaimed as 1991. Messianic International University pointed out that the Julian calendar had calculated the birth of Jesus 400 years after the event and got it wrong. Then came the emblem – a circle enclosing four arcs – which threatened a schism within the messianic movement. One faction feared that a 'new church' had taken a step towards a further division of humanity. But the brooches, badges and tee-shirts went on sale on Sunday 5th October 1980. In all five continents two badges were manufactured for each man, woman, and child of the population. In total, some nine billion, self-financed by royalties.

The circle with four arcs formed an interior square supposedly representing 'interiorisation and squaring of the circle,' or the four points of the globe, and various other suggestions. The Conservative Christian, Catholic, or High Church chapels of the messianic movement proclaimed four as representing the points of the cross; a radical wing spoke about the newly enlarged Holy Family, 'Father, Son, Daughter, and Holy Spirit.' This provoked a new wave of aggressive questions to Sara. As I was pursuing the drug explanation she seemed to be tripping out on deification to judge by her unhinged 'poetic' responses.

From our living room, I watched her on TV one night.

Who are you?

Some say She is a love child, running mild. Daily She is crucified by controllers and critics. In the Messianic Age all stand equal before God.

Thus She is no-one special and everyone unique. She is the great soul.

Are you the Messiah?

I am not the Son so perhaps I am the Moon. They call me Sélène because I merely reflect the light.

But you accept all of the appellation, adoration, and affirmation?

God promised eternal sovereignty to the House of David from whom I have come. You know how keenly I sought to find the male first-born of our line for I desire to relinquish power. Their evil is good because it suits God's purpose.

You teach by example. Do you deny your past?

A church which equates sex with sin denies not only love but life itself.

64.1 A prophetess is sometimes honoured in her own town. From the south of France a copyright fashion-badge stemmed: a *fleur-de-lys* with four daisy petals, those at three-o-clock and six-o-clock emboldened to form the letter 'L' designating *L'amour,* or *Elle*, or Love. Cynics suggested 'L' for Libido!

A desecration of the logo took place in March 1981 when it was reproduced with symbols of black magic on the sleeve of the Antigens recording. The lyrics of *The Immaculate Deception* purported to debunk the Messianic Conspiracy. It attacked Sara with unprecedented ferocity and vulgarity. The liner quoted Sara, 'I actively and fervently seek the male first-born of our line.'

It had been hard for me to understand Paul's negative response to an invitation and opportunity to unlimited power. I began to wonder if he had been written into the conspiracy from the start. Perhaps to represent the Anti-Christ and focus support for his sister.

'The conspirators,' I wrote for *The New Yorker*, 'understand the techniques of rabble-rousing. They create and control their own opposition. Even this they did not entrust to the Church. Nothing creates more unity than the existence of an external and powerful enemy. Sara has been cast for the part of the modern messiah. Paul has been cast as Satan.'

64.2 In the spring of 1981 Paul predictably entered the drama. As Antigens, he supposedly had a breakdown and 'confessed' from hospital to the media that he was a fallen angel. In his plunge into the darkness of spirit aged fifteen he had 'renounced God, superseded superstition, gotten away from moral things.'

Now, in a new song titled *The Final Solution* he promised that within 666 hours of the single's release the identity of 'the beast' would be revealed in an acoustic recording made outdoors, sung live on the eleventh hour of the Satanic constellation. Then the Messianic Conspiracy would be fully exposed along with 'the deceptions and disinformation of the consort.'

I recoiled in anticipation of a personal attack. On its release the name of the song was highly significant, *Golden Henbane*, and I had the feeling that the entire hoax was about to unravel.

Publicity rather than quality ensured that it reached the charts. Parish priests and theologians formed lines outside record stores with acid rockers. To me it confirmed Antigens' part in the conspiracy. Some suggested that Antigens himself might be the great deceiver. But at the inception of the plot he was a boy aged nine!

64.3 As an investigator my Rule of Thumb is follow the money. Everything costs money, and society imposes clerical trails of all expenses. Paul's royalties could finance the Messianic Conspiracy so I traced his earnings through a network of offshore companies and charitable trusts most of which belonged to . . . Jeremy Palmer! The name kept appearing. Like many rockstars Paul was actually left with very little money and I discovered that he generously supported Buddhist and Third World causes. Apparently he had insignificant capital and he lived modestly. His ethic emerged as minimalist and cynical rather than malevolent. My trusted technique of tracing treasures had once more taken me from a wilderness of confusion to a clear result. Antigens was not the unintelligent monster he seemed to be. He began to interest me.

Sara tried to dissuade me that her brother could be a part of any conspiracy but of course she did not accept the existence of any plot.

64.4 The latest research pointed to his manager, Dr Jeremy Jesus-Leviticus, or Mr Palmer, once the friend of Timothy Leary and the colleague of Robert Kohen. They were joint heads of the LSD (League for Spiritual Discovery) – the instigators of Sara's drug-induced memory regression séances. I drew a wall chart in which the French Fascists and the Catholic Masons groom rivals, the dominant one gives trouble and is sent away to Scotland. She is so wild she attracts dangerous attention. In the attempt to dope her she is dependent when she takes off to America in 1971 and almost burns out by the summer of 1977. I fleshed out the timeline with details.

A circle of vipers was closing. I envisaged a ring of pincer-to-tail scheming little monsters, in league, but pursuing selfish fantasies.

My associate flew to the USA with Peter Bartlett and flushed out Jeremy's dark background. He had been a member of a secret circle of frenzied adepts, black magicians, ritual devil-worshippers and suspected child molesters: people who were capable of manipulating the brother and sister, arranging a car accident, taking them from their village in the south of France and setting them up – one to believe she was a Christ, the other an anti-Christ. It seemed so contrived that I withheld the lurid story in case I was being fed a new deception either by the French Fascists, or even by Palmer himself, to discredit me.

As we speculated and I hesitated, Antigens seized the initiative in March 1982 and proclaimed that, 'A further announcement will come soon through the mouth of the one closest to the Daughter herself.'

This caused me great alarm. Who could he mean? Robert Kohen? Or me? Or one of Sara's Disciples? Not one of them had been appointed leader. Surely I was the one closest to the Modern Messiah? I refused to believe that she was having an affair with the good doctor who dressed like the Klu Klux Klan to cover his portly belly, who was old enough to be her father, and who had founded a rigorous, pious, and celibate Order condemning the promiscuous principles she preached.

Meanwhile my research company signed an exclusive agreement with 'Sara's Secret Service' and the Swiss police to investigate a ring of drug dealers I had connected to Palmer. A French-owned pharmaceutical company supplied recreational substances to a circle of his friends who had corrupted the very top levels of the French government. We used our connections to secure police warrants to enter and search various premises in a series of dawn raids, one of which – Sacramental Biochem Societé Anonyme, Genève – was conveniently close to my home.

I rose at 4:00AM, telling no-one, not even Sara, where I was going. At 4:30AM I entered the premises with the Swiss police but I kept to myself whose desk I intended to inspect. In the excitement and confusion of the raid I broke away from the main group. I headed down the corridor to the door which actually bore the name of my quarry. I filmed it with a mini-camcorder. To my surprise, the door was not locked. My surprise was short-lived. I was expected. I saw nothing but I felt the blow to the back of my head.

64.5 When my eyes opened they opened wide. Despite the pungent fumes I felt powerfully alive and aware. I felt omnipotent and all-seeing, like the master of the world. But I had no idea where I was, the time of day, or (suddenly) even who I was.

I felt good, in shock, but if drugged, something calming not delusional. I definitely sat on warm sand but I was in darkness except for a single beautiful shaft of light from the skies which indicated the depth of the subterranean cave. I then realised the proximity to midday. My nose was overwhelmed by the noxious bouquet. I could hardly breathe. I recognised potash – a smell wafting from the sea, apparently from a circle of light – it was a cave entrance. But from the silence of the dark recesses there emerged noises and a slight movement.

Someone was trying to scare me, unsuccessfully thanks to the sweet indifference induced by the ingested substance. Then I observed something menacing like a row of toy soldiers. The noises became realistic and even frightening. A small winged (rubber?) reptile flew to me. A bat? Its snout actually pierced me. A fall of dust. A vague sound of chants.

Then I saw that the 'toy soldiers' were ceramic pitchers, and parchments were spilling out of them.

It was supposed to be the Dead Sea Scrolls. I laughed out loud. I called out, 'Robert Kohen,' and slow hand-clapped to indicate my contempt.

The scene became more absurd when a man dressed as a film director handed me a camera and clapper board. He suggested that I might like to film what was about to follow as I had wasted twenty years of my life peddling disinformation while trying to discover what I would learn in the next twenty minutes, if I paid attention to the teacher. I heard myself laughing but I knew that it was convulsive and highly pitched.

A theatrical spotlight illuminated a man dressed as a schoolmaster with traditional black gown and mortar-board. I pointed my camcorder and decided to film the action rather than concentrate on it.

'The school-master' was Jeremy Jesus-Leviticus, and he spoke in a high pitch to mock the Righteous Teacher from the satellite:

'I am the fallen angel of the Lord, the agent of the Demiurge, the jealous God. I am responsible for the great deception. The leading lady seeks to convince the sleepwalkers that humanity is reality. That the undead are alive. That the unminded can think. That the unwashed are clean. As such I must stop her but you must learn that consciousness is chemical and truth is illusion. Psychic lights and mirrors which we adepts can manipulate at will. So, you are on to me, Michael, and Antigens is revolting, more revolting than I intended.

'The people drink from his poison. But I tell you that one hundred years of your penlight of reason has failed even to crack the hypocrisy which calls itself religion. You seek the drug, but lust is the drug, dear boy.'

I began to wonder where this film set might be. Even allowing for my state of mind the cave seemed very real; I was sitting on sand and rocks; I could see, hear, and smell the tropical ocean from an opening perhaps twenty metres away. Jeremy was mid-way through his act.

'I taught her the intensity of desire, of attraction and repulsion, of unleashing the consummation and the inversion of perversion. Humans in ecstasy. The creative life-force which your puny religion denies and fulminates against as fornication that they themselves subdue into the hell of their own torture. The primal energy they depict as the essence of sin. Woman despised as witch and siren as seducer. Writing and scriptures banned and burned. Darkness fell, and God said, This was good. Huh? So what does that tell you about God? So the serpent, wisest of all the beasts said, We shall make woman to reawaken the libido of all earthlings.'

Jeremy finished his theatrical ravings and came over to me. He stood beside me and I was afraid that he would kill me, but he spoke softly.

'In the beginning was not the Word, oh no! In the beginning was carnal desire – lust which the serpent conceived even after God made man and said, 'It is not good that Man should be alone.' Take the true message to the world, Michael Leonard; see if there is anyone out there who is listening.'

Chapter Sixty-Five

I woke up warm but wet which was hardly surprising, as I had been dumped and left floating in the Dead Sea. I was momentarily engulfed by panic which rekindled my strength to full measure. Despite the painful irritation of the salty water in my cuts and bruises I reached dry land. There were no signs of my kidnappers but I still had the camcorder. The cassette inside seemed dry but I wondered if it was the one I had exposed.

After a short walk through the Judean desert I telephoned Sara from a hotel in a modern town called Arad. Her secretary, Karen, took the call and arranged for me to fly from Tel Aviv to Geneva. She said that I had been missing for three days and Sara had gone to Athens where she had been informed (wrongly) that I was being held by the police. Karen gave me Sara's hotel number and I soon was reunited with my wife in Geneva. I never traced the person who sent Sara to Greece. The conspirator had set up the tip by word of mouth.

'It seems that the organisation needs to look after us both,' she told me between our kisses, trying to elevate my stock to her level, 'but tell me what happened.'

'I can do better, darling, I can show you the video.'

I told her about my raid on the Swiss drugs factory, then played the videotape, and watched her face.

'Presumably we're supposed to show Palmer's nonsense to the world but I think that we should ignore it,' she said.

* * *

65.2 I told Sara's bodyguard-disciple, Andrew James, about the 4:00AM police raid on Sacramental Biochem and I showed him the video.

'You see, it's all fabrication,' I said, hoping to shake him from believing in the Second Coming. Then I told him about my latest progress in my drug theory: how, I believed, Sara was manipulated and animated by Palmer.

'Women are secretive,' he replied, 'But ah canna lie to you, Michael. Sara admitted to me that she had tae conceal it because . . . it was a sort of professional secret.'

'Who administered the drug, Andrew? *Who gave her the drug, please?'*

'Ah'd rather Sara told you. I think she will. But you'll see for yourself, it doesn't support your puppet theory. You say she was addicted when she arrived in USA. I've seen in Hollywood how they work under stress from 6:00AM 'til 2:00PM. Actors have to be at their peaks from early morning to whenever it takes because every take might be the cut and celluloid is the modern immortality. In Hollywood drugs are almost tax-deductible. In Haight-Ashbury it is in the air. It is hard for her to admit it to a provincial Englishman having a metabolism and mindset which are used to the bad press.'

65.3 'Okay, you write a list of the drugs you take, and I'll do the same,' Sara protested. 'Last night you had alcohol, this morning, coffee. Painkillers for headaches, Michael? And you play pretty loose with your truth drugs. I take things to calm my nerves, so what? And sometimes to speed me up and sharpen my senses. Sometimes to chill out and sleep well. A prophet is not honoured in her own town.'

She explained her use of drugs by saying that according to her reading of the Gospels, Jesus not only had doubts about who he was but that his disciples also had doubts and dissensions. We argued. We slept. Apart.

By the morning her drug confession had become my denial of her authenticity, as she saw it. Although Jesus had answered most questions concerning his identity indirectly, if at all, only towards the end did his claims became firm, I said.

'Is that what you call rewriting history?' she asked playing the little girl lost but it was pointless and tragic. It was dishonest. Sara looked at me. I looked at her.

There was a gulf between us. She spoke no more. I wanted to know and she wanted to conceal facts. Who fed her theology? Who fed her drugs? Who made her pregnant?

'Because I take drugs I am false? Michael, it isn't what enters the mouth that defiles the body, but the bad words and the impure thoughts.'

'It is because you act a part; that's what makes you false.'

'But you don't understand why I have to act it. Why it is my part in . . .'

I walked out of the door.

Chapter Sixty-Six

For the messianic cult, 1981 was an eventful year. Ten years to their Millennium.

I suggested that as man's calendar is astronomical we should count from our best estimate of the time the slow-spinning dwarf star became the centre of our swirling orbits of planetary rocks and gases. Reckoned by my calendar, the Messianic International University was established in the year 5,000,001,981 at a dilapidated sprawling second-hand campus leased for four years until the property developers levelled the site.

Campuses of MIU opened in London and Paris by the end of the following year. They began with degree courses in subjects academic and vocational, religious and secular, and they absorbed the pre-existing Messianic Seminaries. Although Sara disapproved of jargon I heard mumbo-jumbo from her pretty lips. Presumably the dose was being further escalated.

'Any attempts by the University to teach philosophies,' she said, 'would reverse the evolution towards super-consciousness. A balanced masculine-feminine university must educate hearts and heads. It must not orientate students to worldly success but elevate their unworldly aims: unless they fail to calculate, manipulate, and achieve gold coins they would not open their hearts, love this world, nor aspire to learn the principles of the realm which lies beyond.'

For some reason MIU courses were not very popular.

Chapter Sixty-Seven

Soon the 'Messianic Organisation' worked so well by itself to permit Sara to be a good housewife to me and an attentive mother to Debora.

The child was now approaching three and forming her own remarkable personality. This inclined me to a belief in Kohen's time warps and in the imperishable soul. I could not accept that a brain could form in thirty-five months to learn all that my little girl was saying. I loved her and I just accepted her mother's mythic truth-avoidance responses. We were a family.

'Her little grey cells act as a radio receiver,' said the proud mother, 'not a record player. Her mind isn't in her head, nor is it in any place, nor in any time. She taps into the over-mind, that's why she understands the deepest things. We must not uneducate her.'

'Who told you this?' I asked her, still trying to name names.

'Don't use me,' Sara joked, but there was always something menacing in our confrontations.

'It is Bergsen, apparently,' she said, 'but I can come up with my own theories . . .'

'No doubt Robert suggests plenty of these,' I interjected.

'Yes, yes, Robert always tells me, 'Oh your theory was invented by Bergsen, or Hegel, or Russell,' and he gives me a book I can't read and I give up.'

'As long as he only gives you books.'

67.1 MIU published a lot of books.

I was intrigued by a quotation I had seen in the MIU compendium of *The Full Sayings of Jesus: A Scholars' Edition*, a fast-seller which was described as 'a new attempt to extract and compile the words of the first Messiah at the date of his death, without any later Christian editing and explanations.'

It was interpreted as an attack on the churches. I read out loud a saying from *The Gospel of Thomas* discovered contemporaneously with the Dead Sea Scrolls.

"If the flesh has come into existence because of the spirit, it is a marvel; but if the spirit has come into existence because of the body, it is a marvel of marvels. . .' So, Jesus anticipated the MIU theory of evolution. What do you say?'

I expected her to babble about Kohen's non-directional time.

'Do you know, Michael,' she replied softly, 'how our baby was Made in Japan? I did not know what I had to do in Japan. Even when I offer you the gift of the spirit, Michael, you cling to the flesh. But I am born from a perpetual line of virgins and Debora came into existence because of the spirit.'

'Yeh, and if I understood then I could be a good Catholic,' I replied.

Other examples of Sara's new feminism emerged with her arguments that Jesus had lovers and women were diminished by the legend of the twelve male disciples.

And then there were her 'kind weapons' and the feminine space vehicles being invented for the US government, supposedly to continue Robert's work 'for which he was once persecuted.' Instead of bombs, America should win hearts and minds. And instead of rockets, she told a handful of MIU recruits working for NASA to design dishes or saucers for the future as they saved fuel and did not penetrate the heavens by 'phallic force.'

NASA fired the first people who proposed the Messianic dishes or saucers; and a committee of the ex-employees retaliated. They 'proved' that NASA was controlled by right-wing Christians who secured its future from right-wing funding committees.

Messianic Intelligence had penetrated the CIA so successfully, that Sara was called to a briefing. She was informed that NASA's true problem was a turf war, which USAF won. In the palatial Drawing Room in Geneva, she grasped the meaning before I did; but then she had known

Senator Weidfeld and had set out conscientiously to be the First Lady. She knew American government from the inside view.

Now she was World Teacher she summoned a handful of western Intelligence agents whose identities were known but not publicly. Around a table in what we called the anti-war room, the story unfolded.

'Supersonic flying discs, invisible to radar and deflecting light, were a Top Secret project of the AirForce. Had been since the end of World War II. And just like rocket science, the foundation work had been done in Germany. By 1944, America and Russia were recruiting Hitler's top scientists according to their capitalist or communist inclinations. By 1947, the Cold War began, and billions of dollars financed the compartment-alised stealth jet projects in total secrecy. Project Y developed a weapon code-named 606A.'

After the meeting I wrote down as much as I could recall. What a story! I just kept my mouth shut. I thought about a certain mad scien-tist, a former defence chief, a man brought to USA under Paperclip. I think he said 1944? I thought about the beans I could earn and I laughed.

67.2 Kohen smiled. He lay down on top of his new water bed. I told him politely that I had come to trade information but was not interested to learn about his latest hydrotherapy and relaxation.

'You don't know what you're missing, Michael.'

'Do you know anything about these projects of the 1940s and '50s?'

Kohen shook his head in a theatrical display of 'Who me?' then burst out into a very exaggerated laughter, obviously intended to insult me and answer in the assured affirmative.

I burst his bubble with inside information about how the Priory of Sion was nothing but a joke and a decoy, five rings removed from The Church of the Fish which set up Sara-Hélène against Helena Capulé.

He topped that by telling me his story.

For three years he headed the Pentagon program to conceal the flying lawnmowers.

'I headed it, Michael. I reported directly to the President and the Chief of Staff. I ordered the Air Force, and told NASA and the CIA to keep off the turf; my turf. The problem was that the manoeverable, invis-ible, supersonic kites were not manoeverable, not invisible, and not supersonic. At the height of the madness, I employed sixty agents to cultivate a 'mass diversion' for or against UFOs. Michael, about one third of sightings were our wretched flying lawn mowers that were seen, off course, burned out, crashed, or whatever; the other two thirds were our agents' decoy jobs, delusions, or maybe a few aliens really did come to USA to see what was happening; who knows? So long as the Soviets bought it we had done it right.

One day, I turned to Almighty God and I realised how wrong it all was, and I did a trade with The Boss. I had seen how they let John Frost get out their hair. They let him retire gracefully to New Zealand and start a new life. The Soviets would lock their failures in mental wards. In that respect, we are superior. West is Best. The President appreciated my insight.'

'Who was John Frost, Robert?'

Kohen slid off his waterbed and robed himself in a white gown with his initials embroidered in gold thread. I followed him through the ornate doorway into the drawing room where he poured us drinks and sat down.

'Frost was the guy who invented the world's most expensive flying lawn mower.'

'You mean it didn't work?'

'John was a brilliant man, but he didn't work well with the aircraft corporations. The point is, Michael, the madness must end.'

And he whispered, to me, 'Massiach has come. The land is restored. Israel must become a land of peace and a microcosm of sensitivity and obedience to Almighty God, as it was in the Beginning and now and ever will be. We can only change the world by one Teacher, and then a pure community of around six hundred souls, then a priestly nation, and finally the world will be redeemed and worthy of its Creator. That is not a new idea, Michael.'

'It is not a new idea, Robert,' I replied, 'and I hope they will send you to New Zealand when it too will crash and burn.'

67.3 I had enough of the manipulators and I purchased a cottage for myself in a wooded area about two hours drive from our home in Geneva. I told Sara that I needed a retreat in order to write but she sensed the independence I craved. I did not tell her that I was preparing a wholly new field of investigative journalism. It would be my Top Secret until I was ready.

One day the bodyguard McGrath – renamed James – appeared at my cottage (where I had no telephone to interrupt my writing) to tell me that Sara was asking after my well-being and wondered if I had seen *The London Times*.

At the door I hesitated to let him in and he pointed to his newspaper. Under **PERSONAL ANNOUNCEMENTS**, he read aloud:

> To Joseph the Carpenter from Z. It is preserved in the way of the ancestors. A written copy was dispersed in two parts raised to the sixth power. Metal corrodes, paper withers, but the word sent forth can never be recalled. RSVP BOX No 4516.

I thanked him and took the newspaper.

I could identify with Joseph, the husband of the mother of Christ who was ignored by posterity, and already I felt that after giving Sara a daughter (if I did) I was thought to have defiled the modern messiah or at least to have served my purpose.

In the beginning I had searched for a treasure, and two raised to the sixth power (or sixty-four) parts referred to the hiding places of the Copper (or Treasure) Scroll from the Dead Sea. Its metal had corroded. But perhaps the real treasure was a code – a message preserved 'in the way of the ancestors.' Passed down through generations. Mr Z had already indicated that the Davidic Genealogy was something powerful and it was hidden somewhere special to Sara and me.

I thought about Japan and in the Shinto gardens, the Avenue of Ancestors. It was preserved in the way of the ancestors! This was the park we had visited. Its thick stone walls had crevices into which millions of prayers and messages to the deceased on paper, rolled miniature between the fingers, and for hundreds of years deposited in the apertures.

To think about emptying and inspecting them would be as sensible as an Israeli plan to demolish the Al-Aqsa Mosque.

In the evening I felt oppressed by years of futile investigation, then my instincts told me that the advert was placed by the people in, or associated to, SHIF to help us remove Jeremy Jesus-Leviticus. Success depended on my being able to identify, play off, and balance the players. In this way I could assume a central role. It is said that history is written by the victors. I could write the victors into history. My explanation would become the truth.

I began to realise that the perception of deception is the truth! Always has been. In a sense, Sara was saying this. Mere facts, which as a journalist I had worshipped, are an unconnected chain of human urges. Sara had perceived this ahead of me. To make sense of history or destiny is the job of the writers: most are craftsmen, those with vision become artists.

And I was the official chronicler of the Messianic Conspiracy.

Although my troubles did not end on this day I felt liberated. Jesus had rightly said, the truth shall set you free. Pilate had said, what is truth?

I had the answer to Pilate's paradox. As he knew well, truth was political expediency. Truth was the prevailing way of seeing things.

67.4 As I worked it out in my little forest lodge I became aware that I was being watched. Carefully. Even in Japan, in the Avenue of the Ancestors, it seems we had been watched.

No need to puzzle or search for what she had asked the gods. Sara's maternal instincts would surely have been expressed in the wish she had placed, and it was also the safety of the dynasty if her brother did not produce an heir.

As the cottage was not very secure I moved my files elsewhere and rejoiced that at least I had no phone to tap. I sharpened my pencil, tidied papers, and made tea. Still awaiting a surge of inspiration I heard a noise, went outside, and captured a watcher just to prove that I was no mere armchair journalist.

The first job upon capturing a tail is to secure him; then identify his associates; identify for whom he works before interrogation and misleading.

This man could be working for the MMI (Messianic Military Intelligence), or perhaps an agent of the FISH, SHIF, Vatican, Essenes, Grail Committee, Templars, Masons, International Police, CIA, Mossad, or Mushroom Records. I had a lot of enemies. And the fear made me very handy with my fists. I soon realised that he knew too little to be any use to me. He claimed he was of the lowly housebreaking ranks of humanity who could not take me to any leader.

Having doped him with goofballs to his eyeballs I knew I had to keep the man for forty-eight hours to let him dry out, for his own good. Unfortunately he went blue. Lost consciousness. Now I really needed a telephone to get help.

Anyone but a fool would have installed an ex-directory telephone.

I was a fool.

Feeling reluctant to accept this insult even from myself I suddenly realised that if this man wasn't an agent, one might be lurking nearby and he would have a radio. So I tied the poor fellow to a chair and prodded him until he screamed. At this sound I was proved right. Two of the Messianic organisation's men demolished my front door within ten seconds. Like stormtroopers their boots led them into my room, and astonished by what they saw they asked me, 'Who is this guy?'

'I was hoping you would tell me,' I replied very calmly, my heartbeat beginning to settle. 'But he needs medical help. Have you a radio?'

'Never seen him, Mr Leonard. But he's coming to life.'

I wanted to terrify the wretched man. I shouted to the agents.

'I have already started to question the villain. Do you have any more of that drug that releases the tongue until the victim chokes on his vomit? Or must I heat up a poker?'

'Oh, we have access to a newer truth drug than that, Mr Leonard. It's fatal but effective. You have to work very quickly before he snuffs it.'

'Ah, yes,' I said casually 'I suppose we could test it out on him.'

My captive went very white and struggled to loosen his cords. One of Sara's men said to me, 'We've stopped several housebreaking attempts here, you know.

'Yes, I'm just a housebreaker, Monsieur, I swear on my children,' he uttered in what even I identified as French slang.

The messianics pretended to request delivery of the drug over their radios while I watched the expanding patch on the interviewee's pants and I knew what he said now would be truthful.

'I had to report back when they should break in and help them steal some papers they wanted from you.'

'Who?'

'Claus, a tall, heavy . . .'

'Either you take me to him or you'll die in agony.'

The messianics began to realise that I was out of control.

'A medic will come with the substance, Michael,' and his colleague volunteered, 'He won't be long . . . we'll wait until . . .'

'SHUT UP,' I yelled, 'I have a problem. There's no pulse.'

I wasn't really going to assault him. I knew I was playing a dangerous game with truth drugs and threats. But I felt guilty. Capturing him had started out almost as a game. Now he was dead.

We called a Swiss para-medic but all he could do was call for a doctor to issue a Certificate of Cause of Death. Heart Failure. He asked, what would I do if they found my truth drugs in him? I would be in trouble. I suggested I should call the police immediately; tell them the truth. I had no telephone so we used the agents' radio. I began to relax; the police would see that the victim was an intruder and with my connections they would not wish to judge my use of violence as excessive.

At Geneva Palace Headquarters there was consternation at the news, and they issued commands over the radio, including the order to their own men to stay at the cottage.

Within thirty minutes the head of security made an impressive arrival in a helicopter landing in a field. He was accompanied by Sara's personal physician. The Chief asked me to leave the room. I protested that it was my house and I had accidentally been involved in killing a man. I had asked them to report the matter to the police.

'Yes, they know about it, but do you see any police here?' the Chief of Messianic Security asked me with sarcasm.

I decided I should co-operate with the organisation rather than the police, but the doctor was not in agreement.

'Whoever he is, I'm afraid he has expired Mr Leonard. Just because I follow The Way, I can't regard myself above the Law of the Land. I'll have to report and certify cause of death.'

I was accompanied to the helicopter feeling that I was being taken to Sara like the day I was marched to the office of the Headmaster.

After moving to my cottage, 'the palace staff' held me in contempt. I would not get a good deal. Only she could save me. That's what I was thinking as the helicopter pilot pointed out Geneva from the sky and prepared for landing on our back lawn.

At the Messianic Palace the word was that Sara was flying back for some sort of crisis. They were confused. What crisis? I told them what had happened. I was the crisis. *The small matter of my killing someone.*

After waiting for Sara for four hours I walked from the palace and decided never again to co-operate with her 'organisation.' How dare they attempt to hold me as virtual prisoner or even restrict my movements.

I decided that I didn't need Sara and I didn't need her organisation. I drove back to my cottage. Not in any desire to return to the scene, but because it was my home.

I had planned to tidy things and lock up after the Swiss authorities removed the criminal's body, but I saw company cars parked outside.

Sara was indoors.

And beside her 'the dead man' was drinking a cup of my tea.

Chapter Sixty-Eight

I walked up to my wife, French-kissed her, and played with her emotions. She believed that I longed for her, convinced as always that everyone loved her. She seemed to have aged prematurely, probably drugs, but now that she was famous I should have realised that any word of criticism from me was out of the question.

'Sara, I love you very much, even if you have become a part of the conspiracy I don't understand. The world works by deception but please don't expect me to write up this crazy stunt as a miracle.'

Her reaction of shock was followed by ferocious anger. Her brows raised and her face reddened by a rush of blood. She let go of me. In a deep and hurt voice, she said, 'Blessed are those who have not seen and yet believe.'

'Did you encourage the intruder to speak the truth or do you wish him to remain silent?' I inquired.

'Maybe you think that this is a publicity stunt? Well, who started it, Michael? Perhaps *you* are in on it?'

We were about to row in front of a housebreaker which I considered undignified but apparently she didn't mind.

'Sara, why did you fly here to raise one man from the dead when millions are dying in wars, famines, on the roads, factories, smoking . . . and even drug abuse?'

The small audience of a housebreaker and two police officers was augmented by members of her organisation who entered the room. Sara was an expert at dodging questions using what I called the Jesus Formula.

She became very intense, 'Michael, the poor will always be with us but I shall soon be gone. I cannot make the world to stop the killing and the leaders to stop uncaring. I ask others to change from within, then to do what little they can. As the Chinese say, rather light a candle than complain about the darkness. It is my job to light candles.'

I may be of hard heart but the doctor, the police, and her heavies were wide eyed, even close to tears by the end of her speech.

One of the Swiss police uttered, 'I will give up my life for you, Sara.'

'It is for the Lord and *tikkun olam*,' Hebrew for the repair of the world), she corrected. 'If you give up your life you will have it back tenfold like the best investment. *Do* your job with intensity and purpose, but do not *be* your job. You are not the policeman just as the policemen is not the uniform.'

The intruder then proclaimed *his* lifelong faith in her, and that for her he had risen from the dead.

I couldn't believe my eyes as the scene unfolded. The police just accepted it when she told the criminal to go away and work honestly as best as he could to bring peace and happiness into the lives of others.

'In that way I can be sure that happiness will be visited upon you. Your life will be better. You will not commit any more crimes.'

'You can't just let him go.' I said, looking to the Swiss police for support. 'We still don't even know his name. And he admitted he was going to burgle me.'

'I'm a housebreaker. My name . . .'

Sara saved him again, 'I think it would help your new life if you seize your opportunity and leave us now. Freedom is greatly undervalued by society.'

As the man seized the opportunity, the police just watched him go and my wife turned to the rest of us and continued, 'This man, you see, has admitted his guilt and I have found in him the will to reform. What more can a legal ritual do? No-one is guilty of any burglary . . . or of a killing.'

Sara looked to me, 'You want a trial. Jesus got a trial. Every day there are trials. Does it help? They seek truth. What is truth, Michael? You will never find the truth because it doesn't exist. Can you even explain this man? No. But I have *cured* him.'

'Find me a space ship to a universe with Sélène. At least I understood her.'

'In this world, as you say, Michael, the old Sara is transforming all the time. Love flows like a river. The water is never the same, yet we identify the river as the same river, even over many centuries. Do you flow or are you still?'

68.1 Sara had arrived at my forest cottage by helicopter but we departed in the company grey Volvo estate I had borrowed it from the Palace. My expensive sports car had vanished. I suggested that Sara's 'reformed' criminal might have stolen it.

'You are driving a car,' she said.

'Yes, but with the owner's permission.'

I knew what she was driving at. The latest messianic economics programme had claimed that nine tenths of cars were made due to the concept of ownership rather than transport. I tried very hard to get the new Law into my head. The housebreaker had a greater need of 'my' car at the time for his future.

'So the Swiss police should be reassigned to hired car retrieval,' I suggested. Then I changed the subject.

'Debbie will be asleep now. I've missed her. Has she said anything about me?' I asked nervously. 'Will we have breakfast together?' I asked and she said, 'Yes.'

I didn't want to save our relationship. It was sex I contemplated, not love. But I was being manipulative. Sara thought that any man who slept with her loved her. She said she had wanted me to phone her. She could take torture, but not rejection.

She talked dirty and got me very aroused.

Volvo estates are spacious. They are not designed for off road driving, but I knew we were close to a secluded patch of moss ground shaded by trees.

When we arrived home she straightened her clothes for the staff, but they were soiled and torn so she blushed. It gave me a perverse pleasure to make it obvious that she was human, oh so human!

On the following days most of her entourage sneered at me, and I challenged Karen. I got on well with her. She was respectful but direct.

'It's not that you are Sara's little problem,' she said to me. 'The demon lies buried in her past.'

'We shouldn't talk about it in the hall,' I pointed out.

When we reached my study with properly prepared ground bean coffees, we sat down, and I asked if she had meant that the priest lies buried, he had died?

'We both know about the priest, Karen.'

'Then you should understand her problem. Because a man continuously raped her under age she is emotionally damaged and disqualified from anointment despite being the first modern in the messianic bloodline. It is highly symbolic, because sexual problems are the imbalance and disease of the modern age; and the modern messiah is a victim.'

I hadn't thought of it like that. Nor even that I was taking advantage of Sara.

'I shall say only that I have reason to understand her . . .'

Karen paused for air, and added, 'I think maybe in His wisdom, God positioned Sara here and now to focus on this issue. You are in a unique position to help her; or help yourself, Mr Leonard.'

I nodded my comprehension, 'Thank you Karen.'

She left behind her full cup of coffee in my study.

68.2 In the evening Sara and I retreated to her private living quarters. I kissed the sleeping Debora.

Sara cooked dinner, poured drinks, and made me a nightcap. In her private study we argued through the night although she faced an early morning start.

'It is because of my career. You are really just an old-fashioned male chauvinist pig. Man on top. You don't see how much I need you. I think that is the tragedy.'

'I think that we should talk to a marriage counsellor,' I said.

This angered her more because we both knew that she was unwilling to get married, discuss her past, or trust 'social workers and atheists.'

She kissed my forehead, 'I know that in your heart you have left me forever, Michael. In Japan it began and it ended for us because you can never understand, nor forgive. You are so old-fashioned. It makes me love you but I just cannot be what you want.'

She went to her room and I locked myself in my study. I could not sleep. I wept because I was a hard bastard and being alone I could weep all night. I knew how much I had hurt this woman, my woman. Something she had said: property attracts theft, but in this way her sexiness attracted addiction. Handle the goods but on her terms only. I think I understood why men in her past fought her. I wanted to provoke her to send me away. And yet I loved her. She would be weeping, I knew it. I had to go to see if she was all right. But I knew that I needed freedom. I needed to be myself, not a baggage carrier of a monarch, not a duped component of an elaborate deception. Maybe, like her, I needed to sleep around a bit. But right now I had to see her.

I left my room on tiptoes and crept upstairs to her bedroom. Her door was locked so she was inside. I tapped. I knocked. I spoke. I shouted. I took scissors and started to cut a hole through the door before she opened it.

I squeezed her tightly. I said, 'Please, help me.'

She cried, 'I can't, Michael. You'll have to get help. You're sexually repressed by your culture.'

I said, 'You're sexually repressed by the abuse you accepted as a child.'

68.3 She pushed me away with these words. I shook my head in disbelief. The drugs had eaten her brain. The one thing we had left between us was good sex. I tried to make it happen. She pushed me away and shut the door with a peephole I had made with the scissors.

I went to see Debbie. Sara followed behind me. Debbie was asleep.

'I love Debbie as if she were my own child,' I said to test Sara.

No response. Just a stupid grin.

I returned to my room and started a bottle of whisky. I certainly wasn't going to sleep. I couldn't read. I couldn't think straight.

Perhaps it was my fault. I was modern man with all his stressful and emotional problems, struggling for goals, disorientated by rationalisation, and alienated, not from God, but from his fellow beings. And the Modern Messiah couldn't save her own relationship.

I thought of Jesus. Was he really married to Mary from Magdala (a watchtower according to some scholars). In the Talmud she is megaddela (of braided hair). But she was condemned by the Vatican as a woman of easy virtue. *Were they good in bed?* We don't know, because the Gospels merely acknowledge the kindness she gave to Him. Then the historians denounced her.

Same with Joseph the carpenter. He supports his wife and child and then he is written down as a minor character. That, I thought, is what will happen to Sara's consort unless he writes his own story. The truth, the whole truth, and nothing but the truth. The devil may care.

Unable to sleep that night I began to consider everything that had happened to this schoolboy from North London. It was a full moon. Seemed most appropriate to start writing this book.

Chapter Sixty-Nine

GENEVA, APRIL 1985

Debora was six when she came home from school and pleaded, could she join her Jewish friends in the Lubavitch Weekend Children's Camp? Then came her torrent of disapproving questions. Were jelly biscuits kosher? Why did we not go to synagogue on Shabbat? And we should have a miniature prayer scroll on the doorpost of every room in our house, as *the Un-nameable One* commanded?

Sara and I exchanged glances which launched my long-awaited I-told-you-so and my continuing disapproval of all child mind-benders.

We had discussed this six years ago but I had given in to Sara's wishes. I wanted Debora to be taught to think for herself.

The Rabbi fixed an evil eye on the child's wicked gentile stepfather and watched for signs of the child breaking my will. The myopic epigone stared through greasy bottles of pebble lenses. God forgive an atheist for offering up an apology – but I felt nothing but contempt for this medieval survivor of diabolic superstition. If these are Jews, I thought, then what the hell am I doing by allowing another innocent child to be brainwashed?

Debbie and I both saw that while I was struggling with shame her mum was apparently unaware of the man's unkempt appearance.

'Please, mummy, let me go to Sabbath Camp. I'll be good. I'll pay you back with all my pocket money next Sunday. May I not go, mummy? Lilith is going.'

'Yes, you can go, sweetheart, but you must be good. And be careful. And do everything your elders tell you.'

'I promise. I promise.'

The Rabbi's wife, a small fat woman stood with her painted saintly smile which widened. *Or was it a satanic grin?* I gave her the child's subscription money. And then I gave her the child.

'Thank you for having our Debbie,' I lied as they walked out of the back door of the Palace.

The woman turned back, 'You're very welcome, Leonard, it's our pleasure. And I don't like asking for myself, but do you think that you might be generous enough to sponsor a new minibus for the Lubavitch? Our old Renault goes well enough, but it's rusty, only has eight seats, and it's done 280,000km. I fear that one day we might risk children's' lives. We would paint your newspapers' names on the doors.'

That is how I paid for their bus.

When they had driven away with our child in their original dark blue Renault dog-catcher, Sara said to me, 'They preserve a tradition which is very precious.'

I said to her, 'Well if you think so, then since you are the Daughter of God, and I a mere newspaper reporter, I can't argue with you. So why don't you humiliate me further with prayer scrolls on our front door? Light candles. And go to synagogue on Saturdays.'

Sara tried to explain why she had shut me out of her life.

'The Lord's work is a burden to me. If I had my own way, darling, I would choose to live with you and Debora in your little cottage away from everything, just an ordinary family away from the horrid ways of the world. The holidays we had together were the happiest days in my life.'

I said, 'I simply cannot encourage my daughter in this time-warped anachronism of medieval European culture, which is not even authentic according to most Jews but something which mocks human progress. We'll just have to differ on this, Sara.'

She cut to the bottom line, 'You aren't happy with me, are you?'

'Not really.'

'You really want to leave here and live with someone else, don't you?'

'Yes. But there is no-one else.'

Although I had almost whispered it, my response was so spontaneous that it was joyous to unburden myself. It relieved me. It pierced her like a bullet.

It was like one of the dirty ones that splinter into a multiple injury. In shock her body recoiled but I thought, it is high time I did it finally; be cruel to be kind.

Sara walked away weeping. Rejection the one thing she could not take. She locked herself in the bathroom and slept alone. No-one phoned or called us the next day because it was Saturday – which she had restored as the Christian Sabbath and neither Karen nor the housekeeper worked for us on this day. Debbie was away being brainwashed. Sara ate nothing but she cooked elaborate meals for me. All I did was eat and sulk and watch her in silence.

Then I said, 'It's no good. I must ask you to have the courage. I'm sorry, but it isn't all my fault. I'll leave on Monday. It must be final. It will be interesting if you sue me for paternity pay.'

I must confess that my leaving did change her. Until then she had been human pretending to be a little aloof, as one of the gods. Now humanity had rejected her and she rejected us. She was vain as is any woman who knows that she is beautiful and accomplished, yet no man worthy of her love had wanted her. Robert Kohen was distinguished, but older than me and physically unattractive.

This weekend Sara ascended to heaven after her crucifixion at my hand. On behalf of the human race I had said, 'I find no wrong in her,' but I had washed my hands, I had said, 'Scourge her. Crucify her.'

Sex was the last thread of her anchor to the real world.

Chapter Seventy

On Sunday evening Debora returned and shared the gloom of her family disintegrating. On Monday morning Karen arrived for work. Seeing that my bags were packed she left Sara and me alone in the kitchen over breakfast.

Sara, pathetically, asked me to confirm if it was really over. I said that we had better face up to it. She wanted to tell Debora who was a daddy's girl and might choose to live with me. It was partly the strict religious instruction, but also the relative neglect from her mother. I tried to soften the blow.

'You have been forced to sacrifice your life for God's work, but I have been living at home as a house-husband, idle and spoiling the child.'

The newspapers reported that she attacked me or I attacked her. This is totally untrue. As tears squeezed out of Sara's eyes I felt such pity that I reached out to hold her. As she recoiled, her chair crashed to the ground. She tore off her rings and threw them at me. In a chilling squeal she uttered, 'Take everything and go.'

Karen rushed into the room, then retreated and repulsed a small army of bodyguards. Their radios crackled, 'It's a domestic.'

I moved to London and was sustained neither by Debbie's company over the weekend nor by my work over the five days: I felt defeated by the Conspiracy and despised by my daughter. Aged six coming on sixteen, she was unsettled.

I had a new girlfriend and received the trouble and unhappiness I deserved. I heard that Sara had taken my rejection very badly. Her friends published their bitter hatred of me. The media continued to attack me, especially after my unwise affair with a new woman.

My supporters blamed these stories on the messianics. I had lost the love of my life and an exquisite lover so I craved excessive and perverted sex. Perhaps they were right, but I drifted promiscuously until the day I was informed that it had probably cost me my health. Unless they found a cure it was downhill all the way.

That's what it took to make me see sense. But truth was the first casualty of my own predicament; I couldn't face up to it.

After two more years my face was gaunt, my complexion unnatural, my stare vacant, and I had lost weight.

Then I found new energy and a reason to live, the struggle to survive my illness. By the age of fifteen Debora became a feminist, having chastised me many times and constantly belittled me as her stepfather – a punishment which I fully deserved.

Chapter Seventy-One

Sara and I had parted in the spring of 1985 after seven years but twelve months later our paths crossed again. My health had run down and I was staying with my Italian publisher and friend Roberto Coioa. His summer home is in Campobasso – a mountain village located to the south east of Rome and so small that it has mirrors at each end of its winding mountain road to make it look important. Before my marriage to Sara I had enjoyed many holiday weeks there in return for which Roberto secured favourable terms from my literary agent and early publication dates in Italy.

In May 1986 the Italian newspapers were carrying the story of the proposed visit by Sara to the town of Issernia. There was much discussion about whether or not it was a provocation to come so near to the pope (never mind near me?). Then the audience with the pope was announced. Sara had returned to Italy for the first time since her convent school days but now she was causing tensions in the Roman Church and recruiting many Italians 'of the badge.'

I was not a fly on the wall of the local chief Prosecutor's office but I imagine the telephone on the desk of the Chief District Prosecutor rang so loudly it began to melt.

'Mr District Prosecutor, it is the President of the Italian State.'

The youngest Chief Prosecutor ever to be appointed to the District of Issernia stands to attention while speaking to the President even on the phone. The stretched wire almost hauls the red-hot instrument off the cluttered desk and pushes some files over the edge. The President says,

I am leaving Rome to see you in two hours on a matter of great delicacy, can you be available?

The helicopter arrives one hour late. One hundred and eighty minutes have passed in a flash, so much cleaning and tidying up of the office is required. You can get some quick drying paint for the door. No, never mind. Best we appear economic with public funds. Got it! *Wallpaper, get some fast*. Fresh flowers. Soon they think they can hear the helicopter. Get ready for formalities. In Italy formalities equal substance; façade is reality.

The President is in no mood for formalities, not even greetings, nor does he notice the state of decoration of the office of the Chief Prosecutor in the Town Hall.

'I have dropped all my business for this morning to speak to you, Mr District Prosecutor. You have a reputation for scrupulous attention to your duties. Please understand that I would not wish to impose any wrongful influence on you in case you decide to proceed with these charges against *La Figlia* but you should know about the consequences. I am going to tell you something in great confidence. As you know I am a son of the church, and I consider one's religious feelings to be one's own concern. But I will not hide from you . . .' Under his lapel was *the badge*, the version with the cross and the alpha-omega symbolising his belief in Jesus *and* Sara, the First and Second Coming.

'And His Holiness, *Il Papa*, would be greatly relieved if you dropped the charges against her. Please appreciate the terrible appearance of our country putting her on trial for the rather minor offence of unlawful assembly you have quite correctly filed. You see that there is no announcement of any assembly and apparently no intention to deliver a public speech, so you might even lose a case against her.'

It is all in my mind but we do know that the meeting between the two men degenerated rapidly for the simple reason that it lasted less than ten minutes without achieving the wishes of the elected head of the nation and, supposedly, the wishes of the Holy Father.

'I am aware, sir, that you are the President of the State but are you saying that some people who are not even citizens of Italy are above the law for the purposes of expediency?'

'Look boy, you've had your moment of glory in the sunshine. I've come down to tell you to cool off. It's madness. Do you realise what is happening? *Golgotha in your town?* Do you want to be fucking Pontius Pilate? I do not want to be Herod. Do I have to spell it out? The Holy Father wishes to come to terms with the woman. *Not fucking arrest her for holding an illegal fucking assembly. Gettit??'*

71.1 Sara arrived on Thursday morning and attracted crowds variously underestimated at one hundred thousand. It was hard to tell because her organisation kept the crowds circulating through the square, never assembling, but entering by the streets on the south and west and leaving on the northbound streets. Moreover the people were not allowed to linger nor encircle Sara so that she could touch and talk to hundreds of people per hour. By all accounts Sara possessed a heightened mesmeric ability to make infirm people faint, or recover temporarily, and to induce young people to feel that they were in a divine presence. Badges were sold and many peoples' faiths were strengthened.

She spoke endlessly in Italian.

'God Bless you all. Have faith in Jesus. Read the Scriptures. May your leg be restored to health, I pray for you in the name of Our Lord and my forefather Jesu the Christos.'

All day and night people recirculated by using the roads closed to cars to see *The Daughter* once every three to four hours. However the crowd circulation exposed Sara to access by the police. Apparently this constabulary had no connections to the Conspiracy. The men were taken by surprise to receive orders to detain *The Daughter* for questioning at the local station.

Most refused to follow orders and even restrained their colleagues. This was relayed by radio to the police headquarters who sent the reinforcements which were repelled by the crowds. Within one hour anti-riot armoured vehicles and helicopters were called in and *The Daughter* restored calm by offering to go down to the station provided a small entourage could accompany her.

The footage shows the crowd gives way, but they taunt and wail disapproval as Sara is escorted by uniformed police as if being led to her crucifixion. She is taken down from the platform in the city square by more than a dozen men, probably for no more sinister reason other than all wanting to be in on the act. The crowd disperses to make way, like the parting of the Red Sea, and perhaps they deliberately allow the authorities the rope to hang themselves.

Within minutes a man approaches with a wooden beam taken from the stage which is tied to her outstretched arms and she falls, or is pushed, to the ground. *The culprit is arrested but who has organised this outdoor theatre?*

At the headquarters of police she was charged with minor offences against public order. In the morning she appeared before a local magistrate who openly declared himself to be a 'man of the badge.' He kissed her hand, and declared that the state had no authority over her. He received her blessing and severely reprimanded the prosecutor and the police. Sara returned to her tour of Italy and after two days the magistrate was dismissed for failure to discharge his duties according to the law.

71.2 As Sara left Rome Airport she would say nothing to reporters about her meeting with the pope which had been extended from one to three hours. Privately I asked her a key question.

'Did you disclose to him the great secret that Saunière and others have used to protect themselves and gain power?'

'I cannot say what was discussed with the Holy Father but blessed are those who will not touch me in the flesh yet will commit to my work.'

Having attended a convent school in Italy, Sara had spoken to the Polish Pope in private, in Italian, and without an interpreter. Thus until the next day no-one knew what passed between the rivals to the leadership of Christianity. She told me a little in very general terms. But then I asked her if she challenged the Pope about the Genealogy.

'He has it,' she whispered, and my heart jumped. 'But he will *never* publish it, so you best give up any hope, Michael.'

The way she said it. I was looking into her eyes, and although she was vague and diplomatic on all other issues, about the genealogy of the Holy Family she was certain.

71.3 It is remarkable how the world united on 22 November 1963; most people recall the moment they were stunned by hearing the news of the assassination of John F. Kennedy.

On Thursday 28 August 1986 I read the morning newspaper. In South Africa, police had opened fire on black demonstrators, killing eleven and wounding sixty-two. In America the trade deficit is expected to exceed $18bn. In Russia, the Chernobyl disaster is expected to kill 24,000 by the years of cancer cases. But events in Italy were closer to home in more ways than one.

Chapter Seventy-Two

POPE ACKNOWLEDGES SARA AS MESSIAH

Invoking the doctrine of infallibility, and without any council, the Pope made a personal announcement at midnight committing the Holy See to a recognition of the Daughter of God taking Her place with the Son of God. His Holiness Pope John Paul II has ruled that the doctrine of the Trinity remains intact as the Son and the Daughter appeared as male and female, children incarnate of God the Father, just as man and wife are in the eyes of God a single body, separate in time for all time, but of one flesh. The third part of the Trinity, namely the Holy Ghost or Spirit completes the fullness of the Godhead.

Roberto and I switched on the television and we were bombarded with reports and reactions from every channel. Predictably, some were very stupid.

The Holy Father will deliver an address in St Peter's Square on Sunday . . . this is a calculated snub to the Jews and one up on the Protestants . . . this was a panic political decision . . . this was blasphemy . . . this was the beginning of the Kingdom of Heaven . . . this was the end of the world. Over to our studio in Rome.

'Everyone here has been taken by total surprise. The Cardinals closest to the Holy Father have admitted that they were unaware of the announcement. Apparently the question was being debated and considered, but until now The Holy See has accepted warnings of caution. Now the Holy Father has issued this personal revelation. A careful reading of the text indicates that His Holiness has in effect exercised the infallibility acquired by the Holy Office in the nineteenth century but has carefully denied any legal authority or de facto power to The Daughter. Thus he is acknowledging her lineal status, like a figurehead monarchy, but not necessarily her authority. One thing he does accept is Sara's statement that she is not here to found a new church.'

I turned off the television set. I was stunned. I kept saying under my breath 'Sara, you've really done it, girl. I don't believe it. I just don't believe it.'

I was sweating and shivering. I felt myself caught up in the universal invisible excitement. Roberto just shrugged and went out for a walk. He seemed annoyed by my reaction and left me by myself, until Debbie, who was staying with us, would return.

What was I going to say to Debbie? What was going to happen to Debbie?

I found out soon enough. Now, she wanted to go to her mother. I felt a little angry. I felt that at such a tender age female infidelity was prematurely rearing her ugly head.

As I had expected, her mind was made up and even delay was unthinkable. I asked 'the organisation' in Switzerland to meet her at the airport. I wanted to go there myself. I felt that I wanted to share the joy of Sara's success. To my shame, it even strengthened my belief in her.

The faith of a man is the reaction of the crowd.

I returned to Switzerland accompanying Debora as my excuse but inwardly hoping for a miraculous cure to my health and her mother's forgiveness.

Debora was received but I was snubbed. They knew already there was something wrong with me. Sara was 'expected back very shortly' and I was invited to submit to a full examination by one of their doctors. I suggested they should examine every member of the crowd including the sick who touched her every day to obtain cures but there was a nurse and two bodyguards. I thought I would not be permitted to see Sara but while I was in the clinic she appeared, tears pouring from her eyes. As I burst into tears she dismissed the staff with a slight flick of her hand.

Hand in hand Sara led me to her room and I tried to apologise. She changed the subject to Debbie. She wanted us to be happy and for Debbie to see that we were a couple. She said Debbie had apologised for leaving and ignoring her.

I waved my hand, asking her to be quiet.

'Sara, I cannot soften this blow,' I was unable to be coherent but I stuttered, 'I . . . will be dead . . . in two years. . . . Now I need you . . . so sorry . . . I don't want to die. Must I die for my sins? I want to repent.'

'No, it is I who needs you, much more, I always told you, Michael,' Sara sobbed. 'I have always told you the truth, and we shall have to treasure any time we have left together. Now we must think of Debbie and do the best we can for her. You know that she is very unhappy and confused.'

I supposed that this meant that she couldn't, or wouldn't, raise Lazarus but on the following day she handed me a gift, an eighteenth-century ornate French silver watch – an heirloom or a talisman. I pondered upon the significance: it was, after all, a timepiece.

'God is not time,' she whispered. 'But it is all that we can measure.'

Back in 'the palace' what amazed me was how very petty the messianic organisation all seemed now. It was falling apart and people resigning every day because the media were finding new stories of the behaviour of Sélène the wild child, publicity whose timing was calculated to counter the papal blessing.

Even Sara herself was so small. It reminded me of some of the films about Jesus in which Pilate or Herod sees the troublemaker for the first time and comments 'My goodness, I hadn't imagined that you were so small.' And so it was with the Messianic Organisation, essentially the creation of an American business consultant.

72.1 Suddenly Robert Kohen's radio station in America was made insolvent by defending an extended lawsuit. The regulatory authorities – which Kohen alleged were manipulated by the Christian Right – had alleged that he was infringing telecommunication practices, contaminating airwaves, and interfering with local broadcasts.

Sara sent her people to buy it. *As a present for me.*

'Michael, I want you to find out about the 'Faraday cage.' Were we deceived? You are the best one to find out.'

I was in my element. I still wondered how close Kohen was to the messianic conspiracy. Until now I had nothing except my suspicions. Now 'the Boss' desired to know the truth and I was sent as head of the delegation to buy Radio Qumran, Connecticut, USA.

I felt pleased, very pleased. So pleased that . . . although I could not fly, I could not heal the sick, and I may not cheat death. BUT THE RESEARCH WAS ON AGAIN. And with full co-operation from Sara.

Chapter Seventy-Three

I flew to Connecticut with two accountants. At the hotel we received a message that 'Radio Qumran' had been acquired by an anonymous donor to Messianic International University to defeat a competitive bid and our accountants would arrive from New York later in the day; deal done. We were asked to check an inventory of eighteen pages.

The Faraday Cage had not been listed as an asset of the station and I arrived at the premises to find that the mesh had been stripped and the studio had been redecorated. During the day, MIU men and women arrived to take over. Their business team communicated openly with Geneva's treasury office but I had to contact the intelligence service as discreetly as possible.

Radio Archaeology was a secret of great sensitivity because of its military applications of remote viewing; also it was arguably stolen from the US Defence budget. I think that negotiations were proceeding above my head between MIU and USA. Remote viewing was legally a secret process rather than a published patent. A secret process (such as a military application) affords protection only when there is no apparatus that can be examined by the other side. I wanted to pursue the peaceful but deceptive application.

The science journalist John Legion, who wrote a biography of Kohen, told me about a PhD thesis on extra-terrestrial broadcasts and Einstein's postulated gravity waves. To cover my tracks I hired an impoverished student, Leah Levy, to find it for me.

I read my unauthorised Xerox in the limo of the Messianic Organisation which drove me back to the airport with my colleagues. One chapter analyzed the content which WXQR alleged originated from its infamous 'Studio 1C' – which had earned the station its nickname of *Radio Qumran*.

Most of the paper was technical and the author's fantastic explanation of the Faraday cage was 'a resonance rather than a contact with the fifth dimension' and 'a collective prescience from the before-life of sensitive humans subliminally accessing the past thus connecting the future at the intersection of the beginning and end of the circle of time.'

The dissertation explained how the US Defense Department had voted massive funding to eccentric research after the publication in 1970 of a book called *Psychic Discoveries Behind the Iron Curtain*. This had created a shock wave, disclosing, like Sputnik in 1958, that the Soviets might be leading in an area of strategic significance. Anything Kohen learned with Uncle Sam was, of course, beyond his exploitation, and this may explain why his wave trap was not specified for a patent nor used openly. The Faraday Cage was supposedly the para-psychological application of the electrical device, a shield from external electrical fields or to collect streams of charged particles such as electrons or gaseous ions.

I was sceptical. The young Michael Leonard coursed through my blood and animated my bones again. Once more I read the university dissertation from cover to cover and suspected that Robert Kohen might have planted it. From UFOs to Radio Telescopes, it was a mixture of fantasy and practical matters concerning 'remote viewing' and telepathic activation of enemy agents who had 'slept' behind American borders for up to thirty years. Kohen's published works were acknowledged along with many others.

To explain the broadcasts from space-time the paper invoked the relevance of telepathy to extra-terrestrial intelligence. Although I had no evidence for either, the PhD candidate alerted me to a point. By the time any waveform communication arrived on Earth the senders' civilisation might have perished. Unless he lived astronomically a few blocks away, ET's best hope of making contact was ESP or 'the fourth dimension' which is instantaneous.

My impoverished student (Leah Levy with the sallow complexion, slim build and dark-rimmed glasses) rang me to say that her rented apartment had been broken into and searched, so I returned to NY with some money in cash. Cheque book journalism is a misnomer.

She took me to the university building where I was introduced to the post-graduate student who had written the thesis.

'You think I'm crazy, Mr Leonard, because I don't respect or live on the beaten path, but that doesn't invalidate my discoveries. Sara is from a different planet. You didn't know that, did you?'

I should have guessed.

73.1 I returned to Radio Qumran where our accountants were at work. I inquired about the control electronics for 'the cage.' There were elements in Studio 1C of perforated copper capacitive plates behind the timber but elsewhere more signs of recent wall covering.

John Legion warned me that Kohen went to great lengths to mislead prying investigators. The metal, according to a studio engineer's estimate had been about eight miles of ultra high purity Italian silver ribbon – not copper plates. Kohen bought it from the Italian Treasury because they identify and date silver bars. The invention required silver to have sat for at least twenty years to form a fine crystal structure.

It might have been removed for its value.

73.2 I hadn't informed anyone of my visits to the medical specialists in New York until the third prognosis confirmed the first two. I was never too good at accepting defeat. Alas, my biggest enemy was now my own body.

I set myself a goal: to work until my sixtieth birthday. This would give me another fourteen months. I was in a race with the conspirators. I was in a race with myself.

I kept thinking about the author of the thesis. His partner kept saying that Sara was literally the saviour of the world. It disturbed me very much that, although he was deranged, he probably knew things from Kohen's boasting to him. I went home and spent the night revising my memorised wall chart of the conspiracy. I divided the Church of the Fish plot, which began with the car accident and culminated in the girl walking on water; that was them going public. I tried to draft a timeline differentiating the aftermath of the Christian Schism – the point at which the Priory of Sion lost its battle to put forward the pure Aryan candidate. And I tried to identify the next parting of the ways in which I was convinced of Kohen's Jewish hi-jacking of the thing. All three parties were actively misleading me, a fact that had probably made me useful. It gave me the will to conquer my illness by whatever alternative means I could find. The doctors had no cure but this actually gave me a plan of action.

Chapter Seventy-Four

True to Essene practice Kohen had not married, but my press cuttings reminded me of the existence in America of his two sisters. As they would rebuff journalists each would require my own very personal enticement of the women.

Caroline, aged forty-eight, was unmarried (not that she was an Essene) and Anna, aged fifty-two, lived with her husband and three children by the Massachusetts Bay a short drive from Boston.

Anna replied to my letter and reluctantly agreed to see me at her home. I saw her first. It was a great home and aspacious hall, but I didn't get beyond it. We never sat down.

'You were very insistent, Mr Leonard,' said Anna with great feminine charm and refinement, 'but I do promise you that neither Caroline nor I know much about Robert's affairs. We are a close family but we only see him when his work allows. We are all remarkably different from one another. I am very conventional and completely fulfilled as an American Jewish housewife and mother. My interests are my home and my husband, and with our children grown-up I'm doing the old charity and socialising routine. Caroline is very liberal and against all religion, ashamed of her roots. And Robert, well, you know my brother, I hardly see him. He is too busy. Please don't harass Caroline. She knows less than I do. I know you wrote to her.'

'So she received my letter?' I asked rather impulsively. I pursued Anna's second slip, *she knows less than I do,* with its suggestion that they both knew something.

'I really know only as much as the outside world. His radio business left some unpaid debts and before that he was accused of misappropriating US military funds and secrets. His communication device must be extremely valuable to military and commercial users. I think that this forced him to go into hiding. But even this I learn from the newspapers and they contradict each other.'

I asked her to continue speculations for me but she declined.

'I don't want to be rude but I don't wish to help you to find Robert; if he is alive; if he is hiding. Has anyone tried the obvious places? Maybe he isn't hiding. I tell you and I tell everybody else, I really don't know.'

I drove off and went to visit Caroline hoping that I might reach her before the reports of my visit to her sister hardened their resolve against me. The janitor of her fashionable New York apartment said that she was out buying food so I walked around the block hoping that I might bump into her 'by chance.' Armed with the janitor's description, I managed to meet her 'accidentally' and get off to a good start. She was laden with groceries. One bag had torn and so the white knight in shining armour won her heart. She invited me in.

Caroline was a small honey-blonde woman, exquisitely groomed and dressed. She spoke in a refined voice but she talked ceaselessly about trivial things. I think that she was nervous. She was well educated and cultured, but affected. No doubt she saw me as a bit of rough. Only when she spoke of the operas of 'Motzart,' she spoke with passion. She was intelligent but shallow; snobbish but very lovely. Her elevated comments about the arts and politics were quite unconnected to life but rather, I felt, an escape from it.

Over coffee she mentioned Robert.

'My sister thinks he's gone into hiding. He's always able to outsmart his enemies by one means or another,' said Caroline, 'but this time I fear the worst. He has powerful enemies. We're always so poles apart, Anna and I. Robert's nature is somewhere in between, but if you imagine my IQ is 'x' and Anna's '2x' then Robert's is '5x' and don't imagine that I'm being either modest about myself or starry-eyed about Robert. He is the cleverest man I've ever known. He is a gifted scientist, of course, but you know he plays games to conceal his true intelligence.'

'What sort of intelligence?'

'Almost every kind. He is a consummate games player. And can memorise music and poetry. He has a photographic memory. He commits engineering diagrams to memory and avoids charts. The Americans accepted him straight into their Intelligence Service before he was naturalised. Forty years on I think they would now regard that as a mistake. In Hungary he could manipulate theories and – what's the word for it – get machines to work without vital parts.'

Caroline stirred my loins. Not a honey-blonde hair of her head was out of place. Her hero-worship of her brother was delightful and she observed me with more than a passing interest. Her home was immaculate, not a speck of dust could be found on her glass and steel shelves displaying a collection of fine porcelain – fabulous figures of mythology. Seeing that I was admiring some pieces, she smiled and began to talk endlessly about china and ceramics. I tried to feign enthusiasm.

She offered to send out for food. *Would I like to have a kosher delicatessen, salt-beef with sweet-and-sour rye bread, or BLT?*

When in New York . . .

'*Salt beef or bacon?*' I smiled. The wine may have loosened my tongue, but I heard myself say, 'Would you forgive me for being so indelicate to express some surprise that someone so beautiful and accomplished as you is flying solo?'

She avoided my eyes but only by a few inches, and demurely downward. Smiling sweetly and reddening, she spoke ceaselessly about all my favourite subjects.

'Robert purifies himself, intensifies his life, channels his sexual energies, and dedicates his all to God. If he had found a good woman who would assist him I think that he might be happy married. At least for a short time. He might be too difficult to live with. He is obsessive and a non-sleeper. Many of the Essenes are, or were, married as you will know, but for him, as for the rest of us selfish people, the novelty wears too thin to support the obligations. As for myself, I'm just a realist. With the one most wonderful exception of Anna and Ricardo I don't know many marriages that work and I prefer to avoid the unhappiness and disappointment. Time-hallowed it is, but primitive. So you see that we three are so different. But Robert is the one with extraordinary intelligence. I am the most superficial of us three, but the happiest . . . and I talk too much . . . even without wine.'

She laughed. She was nervous, tidying crumbs I had dropped onto her lacquered table, 'Mr Leonard, would you like some more coffee?' I stroked her back with my fingers, and asked her to call me Michael. She sat still, wanting me to take off her clothes, but I would get around to that, only after using the charged interval to elicit information about her brother.

74.1 We went for a walk in the park and were overcome by the aroma of delicious hot-dogs with onions from a street vendor. So much for her kosher delicatessen!

'Some rules are made to be broken. Just don't tell Robert, although I think he knows I don't keep kosher! Buy me two.'

When we returned to her apartment I said, 'Caroline, I think we were being followed. I bet we'll see that the man standing around on the pavement.'

We pulled the curtain aside, and there he was.

It broke the spell and she asked me to leave.

I hadn't learned much about Robert on this trip. When I returned to my hotel I booked a flight to London. I looked forward to seeing my English team. On the telephone my secretary added, 'Oh, and there's an Air-Mail letter post-marked Jerusalem. It's hand-addressed to you. It's from Robert Kohen.'

I asked her to open it and read the contents. Sure enough it was from RFK. He was in retreat, not hiding, he said, and preferred not to be harassed by me, or by anyone else from the corrupt world, but he agreed to help me with what I needed rather than what I wanted.

The offer was health rather than information.

He agreed to restore my body's natural defences. The Essene method, he claimed, had lain dormant for more than two thousand years until 1947. The conditions were that I must make peace with Sara and inform her of everything. I must then purchase a one-way ticket to Tel Aviv from which airport I would be met – with a single suitcase containing my needs for up to twenty-four months – to a secluded retreat with very basic comforts. I would not be able to leave this place until I was well. And I must cease to womanise.

74.2 When I phoned and told the truth to Sara she cried about the prognosis of my disease. She was non-judgemental; even blamed herself for my problems. She made me promise to take the first flight to Geneva then fly to Tel Aviv. I said to her, 'My home is where you are.'

Sara met me at the airport. Although Geneva is a sophisticated and civilised city, she was swarmed by masses of curious people. But we were in our own little world of renewed love. On borrowed time. Set apart from her admirers and the celebrity hangers.

Debbie angrily demanded to know everything about my condition. She did not accept my confession of guilt, atonement, and regret. She denounced me as one of 'the weak men who plant their seed irresponsibly.'

'A Conscience is a benefit of a good Religious Instruction,' I told her sarcastically and I also said that that her mother had admitted that a wife should satisfy her man in all ways.

'You're full of shit and I hate you. You even lied to mum about it being cancer. The MI knew from the start that you visited the Zurich genital-urinary clinic.'

'I hope Messianic Intelligence do not betray your mother's intimate privacies.'

Sara, once the priestess of psychedelic free love, now turned against me; she remained silent and thus defended her daughter's aggressive feminism.

In an awkward silence we were driven back to the palace by a driver and a bodyguard. Wife and daughter continued to attack me. Perhaps they won the battle of the sexes, but they lost the war. I felt so angry with them I knew it had to be the shocking awareness of my own guilt. But my reaction was even less defensible. I wanted just one more dance.

74.3 I flew to New York and took Caroline to the opera. We had dinner together, and then some drinks in New York's most sophisticated wine bars. We got back to her apartment just before 4:AM. She had a gift for me. She smiled as I tore away the wrapping. She had presented me with an antique silver pocket watch on a chain.

I took a second look at it. Did not Sara give me an identical silver watch? My heart skipped a beat and I sweated. Some sort of a mental break explains the sensation of déjà vu, but I had complex feelings about my sexual guilt. Debbie was like a teenager when she scolded me, like a girl who had become a woman.

'Are you all right, darling?' Caroline mopped my brow. Even in her act of kindness I despised her. 'I'm okay,' I said impatiently. I despised her for making it so easy for me. She slipped out of the room.

People were watching me and sold or gave her my gift. I had to stop the events I had set in motion. I had to find an excuse.

There was a card with the watch. I read the message. I was captivated by her poesy. She was a work of art. A goddess. Not a goddess or Madonna, but a romantic and a real woman. Just like the real world, Caroline was exquisitely artificial. For her, like me life was not about God and Jesus, just a delightful diversion. There was no agonized philosophising or moralising. Just pleasure. At this very late stage I had met my perfect partner.

She had slipped into something more comfortable – and very scantily clad she sat beside me on the settee. She was so slim and refined. The comfort and opulence of her house contributed to the inevitable outcome of events. The brass uplighters bathed the walls in a warm glow, and shone through her negligee.

She pulled both of her legs onto the settee. Her delicate fingers caressed her left knee so that the silk material no longer veiled it. She was so slim and golden.

'I'm not on the pill. Do you have any protection?'

I wanted the fullest pleasure of sex with her, so at first I denied having condoms. I broke out in a cold sweat with guilt and recalled Debora's rebuke. It pleased me to think that my stepdaughter would be smarter than a very sophisticated woman like Caroline. I felt driven by anger and revenge to use a sophisticated woman like Caroline. I had heard enough moralising for a lifetime from the various religions, and I felt that life was really a struggle of individuals.

I had been struck down by a condemned woman – not Sara as her doctors would know to check her twice a week – but Caroline might be called upon to pay the price of the lust of women. If there's a God, let him solve His own problem of evil. Devil may care, God evidently doesn't. I was dead or dying, so I felt that nothing must diminish this enchanted night, neither condoms nor conscience.

Perhaps she thought that I was nervous because she held me still for a few minutes until her own breathing was in gulps. Her golden body was incandescent and the soft tungsten lights cast reflections from her finger rings and ear pendants. Her hands wriggled out of the bracelets on each of her delicate wrists. Soon, in complete surrender, she wore nothing, not even jewellery. As if to demonstrate my domination I still wore my unbuttoned shirt. I pushed her so that I lay on her delicate frame, hardly supporting myself and deliberately hurting her, squeezing her onto the very expensive soft leather settee.

I made it clear it was a one night stand by pushing her to the edge of pain, biting her nipples, forcing her arms almost to the risk of breaking her shoulders. She didn't like it. I had exquisitely judged and timed her threshold of acquiescence to pain as I took her from one orgasm to another and planted the venom in her body. The ultimate revenge of the male who made the woman suffer because she chose to become man's tormentor rather than his companion.

74.4 I felt a mixture of fulfilment, pleasure, regret, and guilt. How had Caroline Kohen overpowered me? Why had I felt so angry with women, and classy women especially? I would never know. God's little virus had struck me down, not long to go, and I would be dead before I would be traced let alone punished. Was it fair? If you answer yes, go read Nietszche, and learn how Moses and Jesus were no more genuine than Sara: morality is fear of living.

I felt detached as I watched little tears squeeze from her eyes, tears from her silent bearing of pain. Morality, I reasoned, was invented by Moses for a stiff-necked tribe and refined by Jesus for a gullible world. So why should I feel guilt?

Chapter Seventy-Five

I returned to stay for a week with Debbie and Sara in Geneva. I was sullen and silent. We only broached the subject once.

Sara said, 'You did not pass it on to me.' I think she was justifying sleeping by herself. I think that she had decided to cease to love me.

I said, 'If you're the messiah, can't you heal me?'

She looked at me with shock. 'You were the first to tell me that my descent from David and Jesus, even if true, doesn't make me the messiah.'

'I thought you hated rationalisation. It's crazy; we seem to have switched roles.'

I hated religion. I hated her. One thought gave me perverted pleasure; or was it consolation? The failure of my miracle cure would be a public humiliation for both Robert and Sara. What my living brain had failed to expose my dead body would finally accomplish.

On the seventh day I packed one suitcase including the tools of my trade. I planned to use my final weeks or months to complete this book. I would learn about Robert Kohen and the Essenes from within their hospice. Perhaps he knew that was what I would do, but I would still be better in their captivity. But I was depressed because once again the truth had found the seeker, the quarry its hunter. I could not contact 'Them.' I simply had to trust that in Tel Aviv airport I would be collected. I hated to surrender control of my own life but without a miracle from the Essenes my life would soon start to ebb away.

I made a photocopy of my incomplete manuscript and sent it to a friend with instructions that only my agent or my daughter should have it in the event of my disappearance or demise.

I always avoid tearful partings so I didn't talk to Sara or Debora about my flight.

I got up, dressed, kissed them goodbye, and waited for my taxi to Geneva's International Airport.

As I sat in the car I opened the little gift Sara handed me.

It was a wooden box which made my heart jump.

I felt in my pocket the silver watch that Caroline gave me, just like . . .

Inside the empty jewel box a folded paper; six words in Sara's handwriting.

My time has not yet come.

I lost control and wept like a child, as never before. I think that it was fear. Given the choice I would have spent my last month with my wife and daughter instead of travelling into the trap of Kohen's healers who attributed their arts to astrology, alchemy and herbs.

When we parted Sara was crying but would not show me her fear. I did not fear dying. I didn't care about my life. I told her so. Debbie was so choked by tears that she fled to her room. I felt that they both worried that I was going to die very soon.

As I reached the gatehouse I halted the driver and opened my window. I looked round and bore the punishment of Lot's wife. I turned to salt. Terrifying physical pain coursed through my bones as I placed Sara's silver watch back in my waistcoat pocket. Through my salty tears I stared back at my girls. Their noses were pressed by grief onto glass which was steamed-up.

Sara, disrobed and distraught, stood at the window of the Drawing Room.

Debbie was in her bedroom, upstairs.

Too late, I had discovered family life and real love. I broke down; I wept. Like Jesus my time had not yet come. But I understood his suffering and I felt the pain of another. I was about to die and yet reborn.

BOOK FIVE

Melini

MM

Chapter Seventy-Six

MT SINAI, AUGUST 21, 1991

I feel discomfort about adopting my father's name. And Debora Leonard sounds so western, conventional, and archaic. It is flowering of Anglo-Jewish roots – none of which I am becoming. My father was English, but did not know who he was. My mother was French and he did not know who she was.

Their libidos were explosive but not in front of the children. As is well known, mum thought she was the Daughter of God and dad was an atheist. And he was not my dad. Confused? Well I was, until I grabbed my independence. Freed from such pressures, I had no problem in finding myself, unlike most kids who drift while some tide or another catches their lightweight rafts.

In my 14th year, when I went through turmoil and troubles, the western name was a real burden, so I changed it. I felt I had been tagged and labelled as a slave of a narrow, bourgeois, antiquated, western world. I grew up in Geneva and then I was educated in England where I lived with my father. I had taken Jewish instruction to please my mother and logical materialism to please my father. It made me different from my friends and from society. I was neither one thing nor another. My life was defined as the daughter of a famous mother who believed that the world was full of hired assassins and she was its saviour.

I rejected Judaism and atheism. I found my spirit blossom in the enlightenment of Buddhism. This was fortunate, as most probably I would have gone wild in the sort of lifestyle that destroyed one of my best friends and damaged several others.

On the second visit I made to my father at the Hospice of the Essenes near Jerusalem I appreciated something I had been too angry to notice before. I saw that here, pious Jews were closer to my Buddhist brothers than to the 'Brooklyn-beigels-and-barmitzvah' brigade rightly repudiated by my father . . . and by Robert Kohen! (Michael made a special exception for its queen, Barbra Streisand, maybe because of her voice and looks).

At Mt Sinai (actually neither a mount nor Sinai) I saw that the followers of 'The Jealous God' need not be narrow, selfish, materialistic, shallow, loud, and all the things that make them avoid looking into their own souls and discovering ignorance. The shell of arrogance, which had formed by excretion to protect my prejudices, was subsiding. In Jerusalem, thanks to the Essenes, an entire chunk of my emotional baggage labelled anti-Semitism thawed into dirty slush and broke off.

Best thing, I thought, to avoid judging people by labels. I learned from Buddhism that I was not a Buddhist. I learned more about where I was coming from because I could relate to my ancestors. For, whatever remains controversial about my mother's career, her line of descent now seems incontestable. The Holy See, in possessing the Genealogy, as my father proved, was the first of the authorities to concede, despite having the inclination to defend its base of power.

Buddhism is sometimes thought to teach the rejection of the ego, but it is (or should be) a rejection of the *illusion* of separateness. An individual is just that, but he or she is a part of creation, which includes both good and bad. The love emanating from the Essene family brought me back full circle to the Lubavitch Foundation.

In this way it became possible for me to return to the Judaism of Sara, my mother, whom I had rejected by choosing to live in England with my father. Then I left him too and lived in Japan with Paul my uncle (and that is where I became a Buddhist attaining the rank of priestess in western terminology. Michael Leonard, in reality my step-father, stated that I became a feminist but he was wrong; I simply grew up and saw how he treated women. Finally, Sara, my mother, became my best friend and my guru until the end of time. Literally. But that is a long story.

I tried to express, and then deny in my unpublished poems that a small element of love between a mother and daughter is erotic, lesbian, and incestuous, because forces hostile to my mum were already viciously and variously attacking her as sexually inverted, perverted, frigid and promiscuous. You name it, she had been accused of it. Like my father I am not prone to emotions but I shed enormous tears when I read such articles. I weep for the evil world in which diabolical men trample over women who are gentle and beautiful. Even when I was still convinced Sara suffered delusions, and for her reasons acted out a rôle on the stage of life, I knew that she was a pure soul who (alone in the world) had let her enticing body be used, first in childish innocence, then to give joy and wholeness to sad people, then to express the innocence of an open heart. For some time I hated her because of the mask of messianism, but I knew even then that her soul was beautiful. And I knew her well. The more I hated her the more my love grew for her, and when I came back to her our love for each other was so intense that our metals fused by the heat of libido. Descended from a line of perpetual virgins, it was super-sex; instantly we were aware that we were bonded *until the end of time*. There was no separateness between us. (She said, 'forever', but her scientific thinking is poor.)

As I said, I chose the Buddhist path, progressively surrendering emotional baggage for logic. When my father died, however, I left Mt Sinai carrying his heavy suitcase. The contents, which weighed me down, were dedicated to me. Two boxes of A4 papers. The manuscript from which his book has been reconstructed.

Although I am the daughter of both author and subject, I did not tamper with the writing. I may be influenced by his style. I have left untouched step-father's little hang-ups including his male chauvinism; let it serve as a case study. But the story was unfinished – *is a story ever complete?*

He finished his own final and painful year with his professional honesty. He thought he had a grasp of the messianic conspiracy but no proof, so he could not have anticipated the outcome of events, not in his wildest imagination. He thought that he could have sex with my mum, and he thought he could discover the Genealogy; but he could not get onto it by mere copulation. Mum's boast that we are born from an unbroken line of virgins attracted the ridicule it deserved and Michael laughed; he was a reporter of facts, but unable to perceive their meaning and truth.

He was aware that something untoward had happened that night in Tokyo when Sara herself did not know what was about to transpire. In my father's journals, he compared himself to Joseph, and yet still he did not grasp his own point. Perhaps he was pretending to others that he was my father, and on that occasion the newspaperman had certainly moved far from gathering facts when he wrote, *I began to realise that the perception of deception is the truth . . . and I was the official Chronicler of the Messianic conspiracy.* Wrong on both counts, stepdad.

He lied about their romantic night in Tokyo. He could not admit that she had evaded him, but when he wrote about 'his' baby she said it – that is Debora – was 'Made in Japan – but by whom? I would soon discover.

However much mum and dad needed each other, and Sara's career might not have been possible without his early support and the persistence by which he compelled others to pursue the Genealogy from the 1st-century settlers in Marseilles, through the Grail Society, and the gospel Scroll. These exist as incontrovertible evidence amongst the confusion and speculation which liars introduced to cloud the issue.

Much of the fraud was a device to persuade people that the real thing was contrived: the so-called Aquarius or Messianic Conspiracy as father called it. His work persuaded 20th-century man that, despite the mumbo-jumbo, Sara was genuine. They say that love is blind, but did not the journalist fall in love with the subject of his enquiries?

Alas, compelled by the Anglo-Judaic anachronism of having to marry they quickly found themselves incompatible in the deeply flawed domesticity to which they were quite unsuited. In which turbulence and insecurity I grew up. Mum, who could not take rejection, rejected Michael.

Eventually I ran away from them both.

Chapter Seventy-Seven

'The Medium is the Message,' or *what the Press says hangs around for a long time.*

Most people recognise my uncle Paul as 'Antigens,' the furious rock star of the early 'seventies. But 'Antigens' was his mask and a phase of despair. *Did I mention that my family was dysfunctional?* I myself wasn't too far from going off the rails but I was lucky because he was there for me.

Paul had been desensitised and dehumanised as only the evil in this world can do to people. The French are capable of sustained deception and cruelty. Who else would kill two parents in their car and separate a small boy from his sister? By the time he left Paris, he was living and thinking rough. No-one befriended him but the rejects and exiles from polite society. I wasn't nearly so damaged so he knew exactly how to treat a kid niece who was so like him.

Sara always remembered what we call the soul-essence of her brother, whom she knew until 1952 as gentle and intelligent; like herself. What happened to him after the deaths of my grandparents – 'Pierre et Madame – may perhaps be better understood one day by psychological or supernatural methods. Paul told me only that he had unhappy and vague memories of his adolescence.

'Were *you* drugged?' I asked Paul, implying that the guilty ones had manipulated Sara. Paul shrugged his shoulders.

He loved deafening noise and deep silence but nothing in between.

I have been taught that everything is meant or meaningful in this world and we find truth by a natural and inevitable process. Consider the awful crime of killing my grandparents, Pierre and Lisa – people of great refinement. Consider how the evil plotters unintentionally set Paul on the Noble Path to enlightenment, and his sister, my mother, to messianic glory. Both came from greatness and they accomplished greatness despite the illusory world whose images Sara always calls 'death's dream world.' Like most people, stepfather called it reality; I think not.

My deeper understanding of the world without co-ordinates of myth separates me from my mother and even more from my father. She calls it heaven and clings to the absolute myths. Father was a man conventional in his views at the close of the 20th-century. For him, mind-powers beyond computer logic did not exist except in witchcraft. As a western man he lived at the lowest point of civilization – at the decline and rebirth of the natural powers of western human beings.

He reported the facts but missed the great truth emerging from the struggle of Robert and Sara, the Scientist-Priest and the Moon-Goddess. It was about Man's first steps of recovery – through drugs and hypnosis – of the atavistic powers of perception. Kohen discovered it scientifically and called it Radio Archaeology. Sara was his radio antenna. That's all, but through that they tried to restore the values, harmony, and happiness the world had lost. They tried to stop wars and planetary destruction. Kohen through his device and mum through her clairvoyance. Did they foresee the future? George Bush and Saddam Hussein, the hollow men, the stuffed men, Commanders of the Death Kingdoms' first and fifth largest armies?

I write on the day that diplomacy has failed and ultimata have expired. Another war has started. Gloom, or maybe it is fear, overcomes me. God knows if and who will survive WMD.

If you are there, I learned about the higher powers of the universe by training as a Buddhist. I took the name *Melini* and I chose to follow Paul's wisdom and enlightenment. For two years he taught me. I stayed at the retreat near Paris, and then I left for Japan.

These sacred islands are as central to the world as Jerusalem.

When the Panchen Lama died in 1989, Mother sent a message to the Dalai Lama in which she told him of her memory regression, *'the successor will prove to be a predecessor,'* and she hoped that this would *help* us find the new Panchen Lama! It made us confused.

Chapter Seventy-Eight

I returned from Japan when I heard that my father was departing this life.

I flew to Paris then to Ben-Gurion International Airport from where I was driven to the Essene Kibbutz (misleadingly called Mt. Sinai unless you appreciate that it was named after the giving of the Law, not the place! They also use their own calendar – a solar year – as imposed by the Book of Jubilees).

There I met Sara. She seemed to be smaller and older than I recalled, and she was fiddling nervously with her hands; classic withdrawal symptoms. Gone was her confidence. No wonder she had retreated. I burst into tears. Father and I had done this to her. With us she could have sustained the contempt of the world Press. She asked how her brother Paul was keeping, and we both smiled when I replied that he was enjoying great health and happiness. She still struck me as so Jewish, London, and conventional in this reaction. I thought that if she was really 'Her Divine Grace' (as she was addressed) then she would be happy that Paul – as I told her arrogantly – was spiritually very accomplished, and arguably he had attained well above her level.

I was still criticising her.

Then I felt a little sorry that so many people rejected her.

Because she supported me, her wild child of a pregnant teenager, her own wild years had been dragged up again by the media. And in that wild life: three schools, two parents, three partners, one brother, one daughter and 50% of the world. Although (I thought) she was foolishly misguided in her career, she was only trying to do good.

And now I write about my reunion with Sara. The Daughter was kissed by her homecoming daughter. My hatred completely dissolved. She was human, small, pathetic, and had aged ten years. Mt. Sinai healed my hatred. I just looked at her.

She looked very worried.

When I asked for reassurance if father was all right, she said, 'I don't think so.'

We had both received cryptic – almost sinister – messages saying that father was ready to *leave* the Hospice on this day. When I saw Robert Kohen, he was so insincere that all my hatred transferred to him.

He seemed physically and morally repugnant to me.

While my own preferences inclined to orange, he was dressed in white with a silly hat which reminded me of the high priests in the stupid film which Sara loved so much, *Jesus Christ, Superstar*.

And here he was; Caiaphas in the very backdrop in which the film was made! Even the cameras were there because, typically, the rodent was somehow using the story of Sara and Michael to manipulate the media with practised skill. In the scorching sunshine in front of his 'hospital' – a celebrity clinic complex at $500 a night plus extras – he had lured us into a stage set, his eye on the ball of the legend he was creating for posterity. I began to work out his motives.

'My darlings,' he said for the cameras, 'you must know that Michael has been ill. We have the British medical records all agreeing the terminal prognosis. In fact, here he has been clinically dead and spiritually asleep. This is a post-mortem cure that 20th-century medicine cannot conceive. For mankind it is the dawn of the 21st-century. This will be for Michael also a rebirth both spiritual and physical. He will be as a newborn babe, and his mind . . . what we have tried to do for him is medical history. He has been suspended in a state of low consciousness for ten weeks while we have asked the Almighty to spare him and the community to accept him, and we pray that his psyche and soma have turned from the errors which his mind allowed to ente . . .'

Then Sara and I were distracted by a doctor and two nurses who were standing in a shaded corner of the cliff face which looked like a cave entrance. The patient was wheeled out of the cave. He was shrouded in heavy bandages. The TV cameras turned from us to the new activity, which made me feel extremely nervous.

Kohen walked mother to the patient, asked her to recite a blessing and unwrap the bandages. Some of the Essenes chanted prayers in the background and incense began to rise. There was a funnel effect in the sky: the smoke concentrated instead of dissipated as it rose speedily to the highest heavens but in a slight eastern direction. There was a putrid smell. Down here, many of the commune had gathered and one of the crowd said to me that it was human flesh of the *shoa* (meaning the holocaust) whose spirits had been resurrected in these last days and were drawn to the site of the Temple to the east.

I knew this man and reflected upon his comment, *in these last days.*

Mother was the prophetess and the one who had read Hollywood screenplays, but I was the one who knew what was going to happen.

You saw it on television.

You saw Sara's shock. But – because he was standing behind all the cameras – you did not see that Robert Kohen could not suppress his grin. He thought that all eyes would be glued to his horrid spectacle, but I was watching him. The loathsome toad feigned sympathy as he took Sara's arm to lead her away from the stench of her lover's decomposed corpse.

I was also capable of symbolism, so I toppled a camera, pushed Kohen away, and put myself in his place. I led Sara indoors and demanded that our car must be called to take us away immediately or I would summon the police in front of the cameras of the world Press. I forgot that Sara already had an entourage. On the first sign of commotion her bodyguards had closed in and on my instructions they escorted us to a white Mercedes car. Sara was passively going along with my barked orders and we set off in convoy.

My poise, presence and authority even surprised me.

In the back of the stretched, white, bullet-proof, Messianic Merc, a gift from the Daimler-Benz auto company, I said, 'Sara, he's set you up, honey. Probably from the beginning. He himself wants to be the Messiah. We must find out if he killed daddy. Would you put it past him?'

'He was our last hope, my child. Your daddy was far too ill. I'll show you the papers if you will come home with me. . .'

'OH MY GOD! MUM, THE PAPERS, THE PAPERS,' I panicked, 'Mum. Trust me. There is something I must do.' I asked the driver to allow me to speak to the bodyguard. He stopped the cars. I ran up to the security men and pleaded, 'My father has written a book about these events. He told me to safeguard it if anything happens to him. The papers were kept in his leather suitcase in his private ward. That's where I last saw it. Do you trust Kohen? Neither do I, and he *knows* about the manuscript. We must retrieve the suitcase NOW if it is still possible.'

A hunk of a guard called Marc said to me, 'If your mother will allow me, I'll speed you back to Mt. Sinai in the Audi and let the others get home safely.' They all shared mum's fear that she would be assassinated and none of them wanted the blame. 'Besides it would be better just the two of us going back to claim Mr Leonard's possessions,' he reassured Sara.

Mum agreed. I smiled to him. We drove back to Mt. Sinai where Marc warned the Press, 'Follow me if you want the real story.'

We were taken to the room that had been my father's.

The bed was freshly made, but thank God (to coin a phrase) the brown suitcase was still at the bottom of the wardrobe. But my heart sank. The two boxes of papers were not inside it. There were some essays, notes, sketches, letters, and unused pads of paper. Tears fell. I wanted to scream the place down and challenge the hospice staff in front of the reporters.

Marc said, 'Trust me, Debora, you're untrained in this. Ask calmly and officially if the ward Sister knows where the rest of the papers are. Tell her simply that they are very valuable. And tell her that your father said that you were to safeguard them. *Do it now.*'

It was no use. The woman said that she knew of no more papers but promised that she would make enquiries of the Hospice Administrator. I demanded that she do it immediately. She telephoned the Bursar of the Community and arranged for us to see him there and then. I knew it was a waste of time. Kohen had my father's book.

Marc took me away. I was burning with rage. I carried away Michael's suitcase with the remaining papers and a few personal belongings. I demanded to see Robert.

He told me that my father would be buried at 11am the following morning. It is the practice for Jewish burials to be the next day, given the heat of the Mid East long before refrigerated city morgues. I stated angrily that I would insist on an autopsy to be done by the state authorities on behalf of the family. I would make trouble.

I told reporters that I would have something of my father back if only I had his memoirs; it made a good story. By now, of course Kohen would know what was in the manuscript but I fed the Press the human-interest story to place it in the high headlines.

Marc dragged me away, 'Your business is finished here for now. You must ask your mother to make arrangements for the funeral and she and I'll work with you to recover the book, if you'll let me.'

'Gladly, Marc. After all, I'm not trained in these things!'

'You take one hell of a lot of protecting. Your sweet mum's a pussy cat compared to you.'

'In some ways I'm afraid I take after my step-daddy, Marc!'

Marc drove me back to Sara's house, a Spanish style hacienda belonging to a Jewish businessman who had walled it in and kept it for her rare visits to the Holy Land. (She had long since sold her terrace house in Jerusalem).

After Sara and I arranged for a burial in London – to respect dad's wishes and annoy Kohen – there was an autopsy in Tel Aviv because of the suspicious circumstances. The police department were playing politics with the Department of Religious Affairs. (But because my father was neither Jewish nor Israeli they had no jurisdiction.)

When things settled I mentioned the book.

Sara was fussing about the air tickets to London although she didn't have to get involved in such matters. As was normal, others were making the arrangements. She wasn't concerned about Father's memoirs. Maybe, I thought, she didn't want them to be read.

I examined the contents of the brown suitcase. Again I wept in rage. All the manuscripts I had seen were missing. If only he had let me take them away before. It wasn't like him to be so careless: it is clear that he increasingly mistrusted Kohen. Perhaps Kohen had outwitted him by having his medical staff gain my father's confidence. I was furious, but had not given up.

I travelled to Geneva with Sara after the funeral in a Golders Green cemetery. She demanded that he was buried in a Jewish cemetery so that she could be beside him one day. It appalled me that she still thought in terms of sectarian cemeteries and physical remains. However, in a remarkable show of strength, she won the power struggle against the London rabbis.

Excited by my new plans, I wanted to make my bid for freedom as soon as possible but she badly needed my support so I stayed with her for a few days. She was playing the part of the little lady messiah, which irritated me; but she had been there for me when I had Yashi and needed her.

When we arrived at the Palace of Geneva I got my reward.

One of her staff handed me a package which had arrived by the Swiss Post. From the size and weight – which was in my mind – I guessed the contents. Mailed from Jerusalem almost three month previously. Addressed to Debora Leonard c/o Messianic HQ in Geneva. Hastily but carefully, I removed the string and wax, peeled the brown paper apart, and found an envelope on top of the papers. The note was informal, undated, and anonymous.

Dear Debora,
Your step-father was anxious for you to have the manuscript he jokingly called The New Gospel. Facing death he still had his sense of humour and he considered 'The Moonlit Messiah' as the name of the book which I have scribbled on the title page. I considered mail was the safest route. I will destroy the safety copy when I hear through the media that you are in receipt. I am happy where I work. I respect and revere Your Highness, and I wish you a long life and God's Blessings, dear Debora.

After fighting a bit with Sara, I packed my dad's brown suitcase with his book and my belongings, then I set off in a taxi for 'my new home' which I had promised faithfully never to disclose to her.

Paul's cottage by the sea was situated only about 25km from Marseilles.

Chapter Seventy-Nine

KYOTO, AUGUST 1995

Aged sixteen I left school. Paul got some money for songs he had written so he paid for me to fly to Osaka. He spent his summer at Dharmasala, a monastery near Basle amused that mother had no idea he was so close to her.

For six weeks at a Japanese Temple I sat at the feet of a handsome young Perfect Master and learned more about the Inner Path than I assimilated in three years with the European teachers of Buddhism. The girls (all aged 16) giggled as we agreed that he was indeed a perfect master.

We pretended that we laughed because he spoke imperfect French. The sponsors were *Les Amis*, the French Order of Buddhists. He tried to teach us some Japanese words and calligraphy but our heads were much too stupid and we just giggled more. The formal classes were held in the temple, and meditations, chants and prayers were in the gardens of the Nara Park.

We were taken to the Todaiji Temple with the colossal statue of Buddha completed in 752AD from 452 tons of bronze and erected inside the oldest and largest wooden building. This was destroyed by fire on several occasions and the present reconstruction was finished around the late 17th and early 18th-centuries. I cannot describe the feeling of awe inspired in us, except to point out that each week one or two visiting Europeans are converted by the experience.

I don't think that it is a form of idolatry. Nobody prays to the thing, although it may seem like that to outsiders. While the architects of western churches design in stones, their Japanese counterparts conceive in a domain of high consciousness.

The Enlightened Masters teach us right words and thoughts, mainly about aims and means of living, appearance and reality, meditation and breathing, exercise and discipline. 'Suffering stands out in human life as clearly as the snow peaks of Mt Fuji against the cloudless blue summer sky. Only our infatuation with transitory pleasures prevents us from seeing the fact in its fullness. Even when we ignore the existence of pain we tacitly admit that it is there; and the more we are determined to deny it, the more damning does the admission become until the day we are violently torn from whatever pleasure we are clinging to, and confronted with the fearful visage which we had avoided for so long.'

We were taught that mankind progresses for the same reason that the amoeba evolves: from irritation. To avoid throwing Pearls before Swine I cannot disclose any more than this. Buddhism must seem foolish in the way I try to explain it, but we were given practical experiences and practical answers. Not dogma and doctrine. I marvelled at how the solution to modern problems is really the ancient, eastern, Buddhist philosophy. I might have become a disturbed teenager but thanks to Paul I was grounded by this enlightenment and discipline.

The food was a meatless cuisine that made Paul's vegetarian cooking in France pale into inadequacy. When I arrived back at his cottage in Marseilles I joked that, despite my Feminist views, I was going to do the cooking or leave him.

It was two months after I got home that I became ill. Paul took me to the doctor three times, and on the third time, 'Well what is wrong with me?' I asked.

'There is nothing wrong with you, little niece. You will be okay. Just take care of yourself. You should have learned in Japan that, Healthy body, healthy mind, and *vice versa*.'

He returned to his writing, and I returned to whatever was my diversion at the time, but I was still concerned about my health.

One warm evening, a few days later, Paul and his friends were rehearsing their music. The sun set and the tide went in, or went out – I can't remember – but we were all happy. Then he refused to let me smoke with the rest. I protested too much but he held his ground. After our friends left for their houses or the commune, Paul and I walked barefoot on the wet sand. We sat in the dry sand against a mound of tall grass, but I felt unwell, and I knew that Paul was going to talk to me.

At last Paul said to me, 'Debbie, as the doctor said, there is nothing wrong with you. You will feel okay again after you have had your baby.'

'After I have had my baby!!??'

I held my hands over my womb and I looked at Paul in horror. I was echoing his words, but not alarmed by them as he had broken the news to me alone when I was calm. But I had not turned seventeen. Perhaps the drugs had blown his mind.

'I don't even have a boyfriend!'

'Listen to me,' said Paul, 'In the garden of Kamakura, the home of the Great Buddha, where we went from Tokyo, you were with my brother Dhammarati, the one named Jean-Luc before his admittance to the Order, the one you saw this evening. I was in the Japanese garden, the exquisite perfection of heavenly nature and earthly craft. You two walked together as an item, the two of you entranced and unaware, into the water, and you undressed each other like a divine ballet until you were both naked, and then it happened.'

I looked at Paul in astonishment but not (I think) in horror or shame. I pulled him down and we sat on the wet sand. The wind swept through us and I felt that in the scheme of things we were as a pair of insignificant ants.

He continued, 'Cast your mind back to Japan, Melini. At first I ran to stop you, as your chaperon, but the Master held me back saying *'It is not against her will,'* and I agreed, it seemed so natural and free from guilt.

'I did not know if the Master realised what was happening, and at first I thought that you were both fully conscious but I realised later that you were both quite unaware of what had transpired. The Master assured me that everything was okay, and that it was with your higher Will and Purpose than mere erotic intercourse which takes place at base consciousness within a legal marriage of ordinary people. You had chosen him as the father of your child.'

I looked at Paul in astonishment but he just continued.

'The Master explained to me, *"You see, 5,000 years ago it was like this, but in these days the female gender has evolved, no it has degenerated, into the modern lustful flesh-and-pain consciousness. Immaculate conception was quite normal in the aristocratic nobility descended from the gods. It was only around two thousand years ago that it disappeared. I think that your niece will conceive because her higher Self wants this child so fiercely."'*

'Jean-Luc has tried to forget the thing. He just hopes that his seed was not fertile and that his friends will not tease him in your presence.'

I was silent for a bit, then blurted out, 'Then I, who conceived in Japan, was myself conceived in Japan? But it was not by Michael, my adoptive father. I knew that. Did *you* know that? And Paul, I think that my mother was a virgin. I mean, her marriage to her first husband was not consummated; the film director was turned on by boys, and she became the mistress of a vicious pervert turned on by violent abuse which Mother had learned to blank out in her mind. She sort of goes to heaven when it happens. My father, in his memoirs, contradicts himself and acknowledges me as a step-daughter . . . I have a strange suspicion.'

Paul laughed cruelly.

'Debbie, or Melini, I've never heard of brain rot as a symptom of pregnancy. Your mum was a very lecherous lady, and you weren't no miracle, kid . . .'

I gasped at Paul's impertinence but he was unrepentant, 'Before opening mouth, girl, put brain into gear.'

I stopped talking about mum and started thinking about my own predicament. My father had been obsessed by research into the messianic genealogy.

'The Gospel genealogies declare every generation down to Joseph and then they make him irrelevant by saying that Mary conceived by the Holy Spirit. Paul? Paul? Why are we both so angry with Sara? Why do we hate her so? What is wrong with us? Why do you deny her a miracle?'

'*Helena Capulé* was my sister. Now she is dead. SARA-IS-IN-HER-PLACE.'

'Brain rot! Sara is your sister, Paul, admit it to yourself. A lover clings to a body, but a brother to the essence-soul. Say it, Paul, *Sara is my sister.*'

'*Helena Capulé* is my sister.

'Sara is your sister, Paul. All separation is illusory. You told me so. Feel it, don't think it.'

He pronounced the words for the first time and he trembled. With a superhuman effort he tried not to cry before me. He failed. His pain had built up over many years. His weeping was convulsive. *Sara is my sister. Sara is my sister.* Like the crying of a man who had never cried before. He was so explosive that I was afraid to touch him. I just watched him, waiting for him to become violent, ready to run fast, and then he stopped, almost choking in catarrh, blood spurting from his nose (he suffered from hypertension and did drugs). *Sara is my sister, I played with her when we were children.*

He was sweating, and I'm afraid he shit in his jeans. I was so scared I did the same. I thought he might die.

But he recovered, blew his nose, saw the blood, wiped his face in his shirt, then stripped it and buried it in the sand. He ran down to the sea, immersed himself – clad in his pants – and he returned cleansed and dripping water. He said, with perfect composure, 'I'm sorry. I'm all right now. I'm trained to be cured of the sin of pride. I realise now that I am ignorant. I love Sara. She is my sister.'

'*Then who is Helena Capulé?* And why did you hate your sister? Paul, please tell me.'

'She broke my toy soldier.'

Okay, so he wouldn't tell me. I had done enough to him already, and I felt guilty, 'You are a purer man now that such a big piece of baggage has dropped off you. Am I not like a Perfect Master? Don't you feel lighter and leaner?' I smiled.

'Yes,' he laughed. He laughed as convulsively as he had cried, 'I feel . . . I feel . . . But I still can't meet her. Too emotional. Far too emotional. God in heaven, please help me, I cannot meet Sarah-Hélène!'

He covered his tears, but I removed his delicate fingers.

I looked into his face: it was the same smooth olive skin as my mother's, same nose, except manly and starting to age; and he had the same shiny jet-black hair. But his face was angular and severe, full of pain, and he wore the type of glasses without rims on the bottom of the lenses that many of the Buddhist monks wear.

'Paul, I managed to face up to Sara after what *I* had done. She's quite forgiving, you know. Who was my grandmother, Paul?'

He stared into the void.

'Who gives a fuck? You haven't learned a fucking thing, and neither have I. We're not real Buddhists, Debora. Bits of your grandmother are pushing up the daisies, other bits are exhaled oxygen, now inhaled and becoming many people you have met; and her soul is now the overmind and more dispersed than her body which itself changed and renewed each day. You are your own grandmother, Melini, and everyone else is also your grandmother, Debora. Your infant will even be your grandmother, the poor little mite.'

I understood. I had to laugh at my uncle. A man of such fine feeling and vulgar language – designed to shock and repel people.

Man and pregnant niece walked back to his cottage along the beach.

We tried to unwind, drank a hot chocolate. I asked if he thought about 1952. About Pierre. I wondered how much he really knew. I did not dare to ask him directly but I knew that I had opened the box with seven seals. He sat staring at the wall. Time stood still.

Although it was late at night his intelligent face was still but full of energy. He was too disturbed to sleep. He would take a substance only after I turned in.

I cried a lot that night but I didn't think only about my baby.

I thought about my biological father in Japan. *Who was he?*

Michael had just laughed when a stranger said I looked like a Chink, meaning Asian. Sara had black hair and sallow complexion, so my eastern looks did not ignite his fierce male paranoia. I felt so much love and understanding for Mother. Nobody else save perhaps the Grail Committee could understand her, nobody but me. I knew that I would have to leave my uncle in the morning. I knew that he would miss me.

As I couldn't sleep I got up and went to the refrigerator, washed away the tears and saliva with a chilled Coca-Cola. Paul was still sitting at the kitchen table but we ignored each other; it was weird. I returned to my room and packed my father's brown suitcase with some books and some clothes. I could not lower the Buddhists' reputation by returning to the messianic headquarters with too much baggage. I had intended to leave a note on my bed and exit by the window in the dead of night.

I must have fallen asleep, but here we always wake up early to the sounds of the ocean and we share orange juice, coffee, warm croissants and our plans for the day.

'You used to take drugs, too.' I said to Paul.

'Yes.' he said, and added nothing more.

'You can't condemn Sara. I've decided that, and also,' I said, 'Paul, I don't want you to tell your friend, the flasher with the big cock. Okay? The Master was right: I want the child with all my heart. I don't know why I'm angry with Dhammarati. I'm not saying that he did anything wrong. I'm not moralising at all. I just don't want any man in my life. Tell him that I went to live with Sara. More servants there, and cool fashion stores in Geneva. After the birth I've decided I'm going to college. I'll pay my own way, okay? Please. Please-please? Promise me?'

'I got this needle of wood in my finger, from the damn floor' he replied.

'Men!!?? Let's see, ooh, stay still, Paul, I'll fetch tweezers from my vanity box.'

I had not packed my make-up things so I was back from my bedroom after a few seconds and removed the thing without difficulty. Was he indicating that he needed me?

Tough luck. Men are so weak.

Soon he saw the back of 'girl with a brown suitcase'.

He did not see the tears streaming down the girl's face. She never looked back. When far enough away, she started to wail. It was the pain of tender love. It said thank you for everything, Paul. For being there. For bringing me up. Most of all, for teaching me the Inner Path.

IP said to my self, 'You Fool, remember we Buddhists must not become attached.' It's time for me to go! But out of his earshot I screamed and wept, as thankfully we Buddhists have no gods looking down on us. I crossed the beach to the road where I stopped and composed myself.

I blubbered a little more on the busy train from Lyons to Genève.

Chapter Eighty

Yashi was born in the private clinic of the Messianic Palace in Geneva. I was well aware of it combining a Japanese name and the intimate Aramaic nickname of 'our famous ancestor.'

Yashi Junior, Yashi II, was circumcised – whether or not I was anti-Semitic. The Mosaic line of descent is matrimonial. Hopefully he was duly entered in the Genealogy by the Grail Society and by the Vatican. I added it to my copy with the date of birth (21-05-1996) and the father, Dhammarati, aka Jean-Luc Espion.

In the Swiss birth certificate I entered the father as 'unknown' for I did not plan for my son to be a messiah. People said that, aware of the lineage and the name, I must have made preparations. Well, if that is so then I accept it. At the time I was satisfied by the love of my child, the safety of the beautiful house and the domestic chores that filled each day.

Sara was very happy in our household, isolated from the madding crowd. It was as if her work in the world had been done. But She denied being reclusive or afraid of the assassin. We both despised the brutal world outside. The organisation and the disciples got on with assuaging it. For four months it managed without her. My mother was yesterday's news. The newspapers, having dredged up her past, ran out of stories until my teenage promiscuity story broke. I was held not to blame, as The World Teacher had obviously corrupted her daughter and all the world's young females. They printed all sorts of explanations about my secret lover and it was called the 20th-century Immaculate Conception.

The journalists, Michael's former friends and rivals, were either unaware of my mother's infidelity or allowed his wishful thinking; or confusion. I confused things by foolishly publishing my sentimental poetry which suggested to our enemies that mum and I were a pair of dykes. Some lurid stories were supplied by hippies who needed the money; mainly concerning Sara's abuse of drugs from the days in America leaked out, but of course, my illegitimate love child or Immaculate Conception was *the* cause célèbre because I had registered the father as 'unknown'.

Sara's stock fell low. Kohen's contrived cinematography of my mother failing to raise my father from the dead, which just happened to take place in front of the world's cameras, also condemned her in the eyes of those for whom the messiah had to be a miracle-worker. The outbreak of the Gulf War condemned her as a harbinger of peace. And to cap it all, the Lubavitch sect's New York Rabbi, Mendel Schneersen, declared himself to be the messiah. All the other Jewish sects rejected the claim. It was a farce.

In our walled and guarded palace we were protected from this cruel world. After four months Mother even started travelling a little. Some devotees still cherished her dearly, still called her 'Your Divine Grace', and they reminded her that Jesus was rejected. When she travelled she was still surrounded by white flowers and dressed in fairy silk. She did not mind that the numbers within her organisation were shrinking fast. In fact she thought that it would prove to be far more effective in the long-run.

She shared everything with me and I cannot divulge certain secrets. My spiritual training had enabled me to square the two irreconcilable Judaeo-Christian aspects that cause the eternal strife: cosmic Christianity and church Christianity. The C-word really means messianism, and begs the question, who was Jesus? He was a Jew. Why did the Jews reject Him? Did they all reject him? Did the Christians not reject him by redefining him as a Roman-type god? Who was Sara? Why did God send Her? And why did the Christians reject Her? So I asked her. And I was shocked. I really thought – and I still believe – that she was the first feminist messiah.

'This is a task for a man, Debbie, but it was not for Paul,' Sara said, smiling at Yashi, 'We must teach the little one what we can, and when he is ready he will assume the task, and I think that the world by then will be ready to understand.'

'If we survive.' I replied.

Sara was silent. Then she said, with a nervous grin, 'What do you mean?'

'One man is ready to destroy the planet. And not by an atom bomb.'

There was something I had not spoken about, something scary.

We sat on the balcony of the palatial mansion in Geneva. It gave us privacy and she said she had plenty of time. *Well, it was time to talk about time.*

'Mum, I've read Kohen's scientific books. Robert Kohen's megalomania forces him to tell the world what he can do. To sup with the gods he must tamper with time. It's scary. Don't you get the spooky feeling that something is wrong, even *now*? Whatever *now* means, now that it might have happened? What if Yashi isn't born yet in the universe of the Common Delusion? Kohen is like Herod, trying to seek and obliterate our bloodline by shifting time. And Common Man is trying to find the messianic kingdom. Isn't that wild? Am I crazy?'

'Darling, it is probably because you feel that he might have killed father. But Michael was terminally ill.'

'Mother, why did he use you to gain credibility for himself, then destroy your credibility? Once he loved you, besides, if his plan was preconceived . . .'

'Then it changed . . . or *he* changed?'

'EXACTLY,' I replied.

'I refused to believe the Righteous Teacher,' Sara said, 'But now I recall, in 1977 or '78 he said that I could not trust the scientist-priest. If that meant a power-struggle then I didn't care about it, but I'm not very good at science. . . I must pray for guidance. You are my daughter and you understand more than I do. Robert and I know about seeing into the past but he has told us very little about seeing the future. He explained his paradox that the future is capable of being foretold although it is not predestined. Yet the Essenes believed in both. He said the future belongs to God and must not be stolen. Is Robert not stating the truth?'

'I told you, Mother,' I repeated, 'it's all there, in his books and lectures. I don't know why people don't understand what they read. They believe what they grasp. Kohen reminds us that Einstein's maths is solidly proven, understood, and used everyday, but it has failed to change our concept of time only because Man doesn't *want* to be disturbed by the truth. And it was only theory, so it didn't matter *until now*.'

'And now?' Sara enquired.

'Now he wants to play God. Not chief messiah, but God! *Timegod*.'

Sara laughed, 'And only my daughter can see the truth?'

"Man is divergence. God is convergence.' Remember these words, Momma?'

'I remember, but I still don't understand.'

'You do not *grasp*. Kohen was a very brilliant man. Now he is a loathsome toad, squirming in his own venom, consumed by the . . . I can tell you about his *principia scientia,* but not his years of work because that, presumably, is his secret, with the Pentagon, or the Pentangle. Kohen knows that he will die unless . . . I think he must have set himself a timetable because until he gets to a stage in his plan he has to work like the rest of us in classical, linear, irreversible time. Until he masters it. Which he knows he will. What age would he set?'

'Debbie, what did you mean when you quoted the MIU Motto?'

'Mum, your people teach the greatness of convergence not the poverty of division and multiplicity. The world outside is in turmoil. Perhaps the world doesn't exist. Yet it blows like the desert storm. Is it real? In one of his printed Lectures, Kohen explains the God of Isaac and of Ishmael and of Jesus. Abraham is the father of the three religions in all their branches. But Abraham's father worshipped idols. Only with great struggle did the Hebrew deity evolve through El Shaddai into Elohim – the people always regressing, causing divine vengeance, prophets rending their clothes, kingdoms lost – and eventually the single, invisible God which the Christians go and split back into three, or now with the Daughter-of-God making four! Only kidding. But even the Hebrews call God 'Elohim' which is a plural noun. This is Kohen's explanation, not mine, and I'm coming to his conclusion. Slowly and irreverently, but I promise, mum, it's worth the wait, I'm coming to the point.'

Sara stopped me until she could write down the gist of what I was revealing so she could try to understand me.

'Mum, the Book of Genesis, the first scientific textbook, says God created this, then God created that, but when it comes to creating man, the text has God saying, "Let *us* make man in our own image." To whom was he, *or they*, talking? A few verses later, Genesis says that *the sons of God* looked at the daughters of man, saw they were pleasing, and married as many as they chose. The Dead Sea Scrolls disclose an earlier Genesis with even more of what was censored.

'The unspeakable Tetragrammaton – by which the gentiles betray themselves by uttering Yahweh and Jehovah and such pathetic pronunciations – was revealed to Moses as EHYE ASHER EHYE which seemed incomprehensible in the interval between ancient wisdom and modern science. But it means "I am what I am (or I shall be what I was)". Momma, it means time has no direction. God *is* dead. Because *now* is dead. The Buddhists are right. Nietzsche is right. As soon as it comes it has gone. Like the seed which dies into nothing; to become a plant it must die. The Hindus say that God is at the beginning and end of the world, but the interval is dark without God. They too, are right. We are in the god-forsaken middle, and when the cat's away the mouse can play. I always said Kohen was a rodent. Now you have to save the world. It is the end of time. You disagree?

'Momma. Steven Hawking shows that when the universe stops expanding, time MUST reverse. Where does this leave cause-and-effect? Where does this leave evolution? Backwards is equally valid. Even dad perceived that history was 'cyclic' but he failed to consider an explanation. History can be read backwards. *God was made in Man's image.* There I've said it! Blasphemy! Every megalomaniac wants to be God. Like Kohen. But reversing time, it's so fundamentally easy but so insanely dangerous; it makes the atom bomb and genetic engineering into safe toys by comparison. God is time. Time is the template of creation. Control time and you dethrone God.

'Do you think that because I'm only Debbie, your daughter, that this has to be rubbish? In your position, can you let the deranged toad storm the gates of heaven? I'm telling you, *you really are here to save the world.'*

Sara was seeing the point but not how I reached it. She was in a time-precedence trap: she saw the theory but clouded by the mists of her mindset, so I drove it all home with a hammer blow. 'Momma, listen! Genesis says Kohen is God. He's eaten the fruit of the Tree at the Centre of the Garden. To the scientist-priest you are an obstacle and he's going to erase you and me from history . . . and Yashi. You feel this awful weirdness? As if he's already done it, as if Common Man will remember another world from the infinite universe. In the new reality we were never born. He's writing the ending to our story, but you can stop it, Daughter of God, because He promised our line would be everlasting. I don't know why he chose our line as the bottom line, I guess it had to be someone.'

Chapter Eighty-One

JERUSALEM, AUGUST 21, 1991

Today the Allies' ultimatum has expired. I have a strong feeling of *déja vu;* I have been here before and I expected this unavoidable war to happen. I tell myself that it is the effect of fear and anticipation of human suffering, but it is a feeling of reliving the experience. When the scaffolding of time is removed, it is like everything you assumed real is melting against which even my Buddhist training in mental detachment and the unreality of the world does not help me.

Messiahs are employed to stop wars and our Messianic Intelligence has informed Sara of the weapons of mass destruction supplied by the west to Saddam Hussein. The public do not know his reasons for ignoring the ultimatum. The American people think that the Iraqi dictator is deranged; that he must know his army will be brushed aside like toy soldiers poised against their high-tech arsenal. The Iraqi Dictator thinks the Iranians are common foes, and the Americans are his friends and his suppliers.

With this information we know why the Americans have shipped in massive resources and I fear for a Chemical Armageddon. It feels like the end of time. I know that the people in Israel are ready for war and I know that the former Pentagon Defence Scientist has the ultimate weapon: the manipulation of time; the super eraser of historical mistakes. I haven't slept for three nights nor eaten all day, I just write down my thoughts quickly, as if it will be my last day. Perhaps nobody will survive to read them but thoughts do not perish.

I see myself as a child in a dim and distant past that might have been cancelled. My absurd behaviour hardly merited permanence: I denounce my own stupidity but put in writing the memories of my childhood in case I survived but they dissolved. I had been full of contempt for my mother's religion. I had whined about why a boy, but not a girl, should have a barmitzvah. It wasn't fair. And why did my mum support everything the rebbe said? In 1992 the Lubavitch rebbe had put himself up as the messiah. So now he was her rival. Wasn't it loopy?

I will never forget the day we cried for my dad. My nose pressed against the steamy window of the house in Geneva. I didn't know that Sara was also watching you go, with your courage and guilt, to the Hospice of the Essenes, to die. You died bravely but you had to die. You were bad.

The former CIA Chief Wendell Reichardt had resigned from our organisation but agreed to Sara's request to meet her in Geneva without any delay. By helicopter, jet, and helicopter he lands on the grass and rushes into the drawing room. Nobody stops me as I walk in to hear the conversation.

In the First Gulf War armaments supplied by western industry to both sides killed a million Iranians and Iraqis, a figure that hides uncounted injured and unmeasured suffering. In that war which ended in 1988, we deny arming Iraq but Reichardt shows us satellite photos of ships unloading chemicals, machines, and parts allowing Iraq to manufacture the weapons of mass destruction. Officially the fifth biggest army in the world, it was funded by oil revenues; it was beyond the scale needed for any local war and perhaps they had even reinstated the Israeli destruction of their nuclear facility. Messianic Intelligence believes by its measure that Iraq has the world's *third* largest army, possessing mountains of chemicals more toxic than radiation.

Reichardt is visibly shaken; close to tears he hugs Sara, 'My Lady, and my saviour, I was blinded by patriotism to what my country overlooked, but I am at your command if you will trust me with whatever can be done now.'

I don't understand my own feelings, I am the last to believe, and yet *my mother really is the world saviour.* The whole world is a deadly mix of destructive weapons and peaceful toxins; the women are like men, and the men are losing fertility. Genes are mutilated. Boys born without penises. Children lose limbs. Let women rule the world, their psyche-somas may yet save the 21st-century, or it is too late, the planet is poisoned; ready to be abandoned as our home. Sara claims that Yashi is the messiah? *Is he?* I try to persuade her to believe in *herself.*

'Mother-God, She has sent *You,* Momma, I played my part in undermining your belief in yourself, so now I tell you to believe that you are my saviour and the saviour of the world. I also plead with you to accept my sorrow and guilt for being so dangerously wrong.'

I tried to undo so much error but she would not *Believe in Herself.* The stupid people try to make her contradict herself, diminish herself, endanger herself and deny her authority. Recently nationalist Jews and Moslems asked her to judge on Palestine and the division of the City of David. She promised that she would search for the answer and proclaim it unequivocally without fear or favour. But not now, *not until after the war.*

The private phone rang. The voice on the telephone belonged to Robert Kohen. He demanded that Sara must come to Mt Sinai. I was shocked. I took the telephone and demanded to know what he wanted.

'Debora I want you both to come out here, if you want to see your father alive and rise from the dead. If not, he will have to travel back to Switzerland alone because you rejected him. It would be best if you were seen to come here to get him. You know, an act of love for your dear father in front of the cameras. He's not yet well enough to talk on the phone or I'd let him ask you himself.'

I hung up in anger. We held each other, my momma and I, and we trembled. We didn't have to express our thoughts in spoken words. We were thinking, if father is really alive we must go, but it is a frightening thought supposing . . . already . . . *time is being reversed.* We stared at each other thinking all of these things and looked at a calendar and then the clock. How could we forget the day the war began?

Sara began to speak to Reichardt, but she hesitated and stumbled.

We jumped out of our skins when the telephone rang. It was Kohen again. Sara called him Michael more than once. I think She was confused because he was trying to confuse Her. I was furious. I took the telephone. I heard a voice that might have been my father, or Robert's imitation of father. Remember, in Hungary he was a trained actor and director.

He said to me, 'If you don't believe me, Debora, watch the news on television. We're all going in different directions, now. The future is easier for me to remember than the past. If you want your daddy, come and get him. If not, let him rot in your contempt for what he did to my sister.'

I slammed down the telephone. I thought to myself, mum doesn't know what he did to Caroline and *the loathsome swine doesn't know that Michael isn't my real dad.*

'Momma, maybe he is going to pretend that he is reversing time and use you as the hook for international publicity . . . mum he is using our love for father as the hook . . . con-artists know that to hold out an enormous prize makes us all gullible . . . Mum, please, you must trust me. *Don't go*.'

She looked at Reichardt, and then agreed that it was a trick and we tried to talk about other things until we were informed by our own staff that Michael was cured and was on his way back to Geneva.

'No,' Sara said, 'it is not true. He died last year.'

'No,' they argued, 'We are watching the pictures on the news. We saw you raise him from the dead in the Essene Community. You can't deny it. We saw it on TV, a miracle, just like the raising of Lazarus. Now you are to go to meet him at the airport.'

Andrew James – who had become a salaried and a full-time 'disciple' – knew the flight number. He had confirmed its arrival on time and had come to accompany us to the airport.

Sara and I looked at each other in horror. I uttered a profanity, '*Jesus,*' and wondered if I was swearing or calling upon my ancestor.

'Small wonder, we cling so tenaciously to the safe old mindset, daughter.'

Thank God, now she understood.

James ignored what he could not grasp, worried about lesser dangers, yet perhaps they too were real, 'Others will drive before and behind your car, dearest Sara. You'll be safe, lassie. I promise. You have nothing to fear.'

Sara and I looked at each other in horror. I uttered a profanity, 'Jesus,' and wondered if I was swearing or calling my ancestor.

'See why people cling so tenaciously to the safe old mindset, daughter?'

Thank God, now she understood.

James ignored what he could not grasp, worried about lesser dangers, yet perhaps they too were real, 'Others will drive before and behind your car, dearest Sara. You'll be safe, lassie. I promise. You have nothing to fear.'

We switched on the television in the limo and saw the bulletins about the Gulf War, then came the day's minor stories to which The Essenes' spectacular miracle had been reduced.

Bad media manipulation, Kohen is slipping, I thought.

On TV we watched momma loosen the bandages and raise Michael from the dead. He stood up. She kissed him.

> 'Robert F. Kohen the American scientist, who resigned from a top defence project in 1974 to re-establish the peaceful Jewish sect of the Dead Sea Scrolls, is seen here with the husband of messianic claimant Sara, known as the Daughter of God. In 1988 Michael Leonard was diagnosed with an unnamed illness too advanced to hope for any recovery. With a revolutionary deep treatment combining ancient Egyptian techniques Kohen's medics have perfected a holistic technique to regenerate the body from the deepest diseases from which humanity can suffer.'

In this way, Sara and I were persuaded to meet father at the airport. Like me, Sara must be remembering the day Michael died?

'Hurry, ladies,' shouted Andrew, 'or we'll be late.'

I couldn't stop laughing because the I saw comment was so ludicrous, but it was panic. I went into convulsions of fear and weeping as I saw the absurd nature of being late for Robert. Sara had to calm me.

She understood so she shook me, and then slapped my face to stop me from laughing until I hurt myself. It worked, and we held each other so tight. I said to her, 'Mum, just think that he's playing tricks on us, *and pretend it's not for real.*'

Sara held me tight and said, 'I know you're only saying that, my sweetness. But it *is* for real, my darling, and you know it. He is changing reality. You were the one who explained it to me.'

I had explained the scientific theory to Sara, but She had been able to grasp the predicament. I was unable to do anything but run frequently to the toilet in my animal fear of insuperable forces.

I didn't like the car; there was no toilet.

As we approached the airport I ran over my memories of *how it felt* when I was trained to transcend the limitations of western science. To regain a calm mind I repeated and absorbed the Master's slogan several times. So well etched on my brain, yet now that I needed it, the wisdom seemed only to sit on the surface like oil on water. Now its meaning was sinking in. Finally I understood,

Above, not a tile to cover the head;

Below, not an inch of ground for the foot.

So it was *for real*, and the world was in Kohenfusion.

At least I could really look forward to seeing my dad again.

Like a zombie on autopilot I was led though Geneva International Airport. At a bookstore I suddenly saw Myron Grombacher's biography of R.F. Kohen, *Science not Fiction*. On my instruction an agent paid for it, then I found what I wanted. A quote of a quote of a quote. Words thrice encased. A biographer quoting his subject who quotes his friend, Timothy Leary.

I read it aloud to my mother.

'Now dig. The atomic fission in December 1942 changed the whole system of energy in this solar system. The higher intelligence decides to make a few simple changes in the electronic structure of some atoms, and zap! We have LSD, an incredibly powerful substance that is the exact antidote to atomic energy. People take LSD, and flash! They get the message and start putting things back in harmony with the great design. Stop war! Wear flowers! Conservation!'

Robert Kohen emerged from the airport lounge, dressed like my father. He walked up to embrace Sara. The media were massed in strength, creating more footage for the story of R.F. Kohen, as if he was a rising World Dictator.

In order to feel better and remind Sara of the artificial illusion, I exclaimed under my breath but quite audibly, 'Fucking lying bastard, *he isn't father.*'

Then Andrew informed us, 'Someone travelled Swissair under Michael's name.'

The cameras were all around us. When we emerged from the VIP lounge, Sara embraced him before she recoiled. She said to me defensively, 'I thought he was your father.' Now She was really upset.

Kohen tried to embrace me. He had acquired some of Michael's mannerisms, especially the voice. He turned to Sara and said, 'You will come to love me, and you will come to understand.'

'Understand?'

'That our child will be the modern Messiah as he combines the line and legitimacy of Aaron *and* of David of Judah.'

I think that mother was going to speak about Yashi, but (thinking of Herod's slaughter of the Innocents) I tugged her arm in time.

On the airport's television monitors the miracle of Sara raising 'her husband' from the dead was being broadcast as the second story after the War. Her stock had shot up. Or had it never really gone down?

As the bandages were unwrapped, the face she embraced was that of Robert, not of Michael. I wondered why the public was not confused, but the people in the airport were saying, '*Gee, Michael Leonard is alive, it's a miracle.*'

Kohen was explaining to Sara, 'Two thousand years ago Jesus cast out demons, but we chose not to believe it. Truly our age is the end of time, because now we can scientifically choose a future, determine our own fate, make our own Divine Destiny. But to you, ignorance is bliss. You are still afraid. You want to keep people in the old mythic traditions, return to the evil secrecy of the medieval church. Let people choose to do evil. No, we the people are forced to leave paradise. You must accept it. I see that your daughter is very afraid. But her father's soul is safe in my body. Like the Aryan Davidic girl is safe in you. I did nothing to harm Michael despite the evil he did to my flesh and blood. Like his ego, his body went bad and has gone the way of all flesh. He was neither your husband nor your consort nor the father of your child. You chose him wrongly, by carnal desire, a sin is a historical error which I have corrected. I have re-written time to correct wrong – if we can talk any more of precedence as unique, I am legally your husband.'

Sara is listening but whether she accepts or rejects his words, she betrays no reaction. Kohen tries to turn his back to me but I follow them. Behind us the busy airport functions normally. People buy newspapers, catch flights, wait for announcements; but we are in a new world that Kohen is in some way fabricating.

'Michael married Helena Capulé, the Aryan messiah, he believed in, but only her body. As is written in the Book of Genesis, *The sons of God, looking at the daughters of men, saw they were pleasing, so they married as many as they chose.* The sons of men had no right to take you to wife, Sara. Or he will not, or he is not doing so in the eternal present, which is the accurate way of looking at this dimension. That is why your liaisons with the filmmaker and the politician were equally illegitimate. You allowed your body to be defiled, and whatever your error in logic it was an abomination of nature and God's Law.'

Kohen is still smiling when he sees my gun.

I take it from Andrew James and I immediately pull the trigger. The body of Dr Kohen with the soul of my father falls to the ground.

I hear myself say, 'Father, I'm sorry, but I had to do this.'

Someone takes the gun from me. It is Sara but she says to me, 'What have you done, daughter, for it is written, *Thou shalt not kill*?'

Now, everyday I see and hear these sins of my past on television. A smoking gun is soon surrounded by crowds. Time slows down. Is it shock, or has the Time-god beaten me?

Everything is in my head. Everything is closing in. What have I done? The time warp. My intense fear of killing. The hybrid soul with his hand on the button of Time. My blind rage. His fraud confused me and my mind went blank. Mum takes the gun and confesses in order to save me. Despite Andrew's protests the Swiss police put her in handcuffs.

Chapter Eighty-Two

Maybe I have died and gone to heaven. On the kibbutz it is so peaceful. A quiet summer morning and volunteers are preparing for the picking and canning season. It is 21 August 1991, but according to the letters I was the one charged with killing Robert Kohen on 26 April 1995, at 18:06PM in the Geneva International Airport terminal of arrivals and departures.

Something has gone wrong. I keep thinking that absurd quote of Lewis Carroll, *it is a poor sort of memory that only works backwards.* I felt like Alice, but I had hoped that my criminal act, such a positive legal event, must synchronize the world's seasonal, orbital, atomic, or *any* natural chronology. What was time now? Would 'he' come back alive and earlier – as in a monster of science fantasy – and kill *me*? It would be a good legal defence? I wish he would. I felt sick.

Maybe my bullet missed. Maybe he did not die. How could he allow himself to die if he had mastered the future? The police did not charge me with murder. No human relies on rational thought under the intensity of crisis. He looked dead. Blood trickled. His mouth did not move, but his eyes pierced me even from across the abyss whether it was oblivion or heavenly immortality. Am I dreaming? His face was smashed to the ground. I heard with my mind's ear the unutterable words of his anguish, no longer able to force his breath and form his tongue. This convinced me that he was on the other side. He was dead and I had won, otherwise, he would have predicted these events and stopped me in his alternative future.

It was a comfort to find myself in a predictable world of being in trouble with the police, and gradually I felt much better despite the custody and interrogation. I confessed to the crime. I just wanted to see Sara. They said I would see her if I co-operated.

I had to run through my confession again. I told them whatever they wanted to hear. I confessed, yes, we had gone to Mt Sinai, Sara and I, and, yes, Sara had 'raised my father from the dead,' technically, that is. He was clinically suspended while the healers removed terminal cancer and the body healed during a suspension which medically was an extended death. I told them whatever they wanted.

'But your father died in 1992.'

'Yes, clinically,' I added helpfully, 'but he was . . . not really dead.'

'He was buried, Miss Leonard. Dead and buried in London. See, we have the certificate.'

I laughed. I heard myself laugh. It echoed in the unfurnished Interview Room Number 1. Although it didn't look good I couldn't help laughing then I cried.

I said, 'I really want to confess. Please write down what I must say formally. I'm too confused to think. Help me to write my statement, *Robert Kohen killed my father in 1992 and humiliated my mum in public. I killed him for that reason in a moment of blind fury.*'

I signed their paper without reading it and then I asked to see my mother. They said that a psychiatrist would come to see me in the morning. They said I would have to stay until a senior judge saw me.

I said, 'I really want to confess. Write down what I must say formally. I'm too upset and confused to think. Help me write my statement, *Robert Kohen killed my father in 1992 and humiliated my mum and me in public. I killed him for that reason in a moment of blind fury.*'

I signed their paper without reading it and then I asked to see my mother. They said that a psychiatrist would come to see me in the morning. They said that I would have to stay until a senior judge saw me.

Chapter Eighty-Three

Forgive the expression, but it was a long night. In the morning I was placed in the dock.

'Why did you kill him, Debora Leonard?' the female Judge asked with deep compassion.

'Kill whom?' I wanted to check whom they thought I had killed.

'Robert Kohen.'

'Because he killed my father. He loved my mother. He wanted her. He tried to kiss her. But I regret killing him.'

The Judge stared at me, blinking her heavy eyelashes more than once. She was so slow. Wrote everything down. I was bored so I entertained myself and I imagined myself blurting out, *Well, LadyJudge, I really killed him for the safety of mankind because he invented a time machine and . . . took over the soul of Michael Leonard 'cause he wanted to screw my mum . . . and also to play God . . .*

'Did you plan to kill him when you went to the airport?'

'Only when he tried to kiss my mum and I saw the gun of her bodyguard.'

I had spent the night working out what the world and the police wanted to hear and I stayed with that story. I was found to be of diminished mental responsibility and I had committed a crime of passion in a moment of irrational impulse.

The law appeared to take its course but my freedom was restored with the minimum of fuss. My confession and guilt was recorded and I was told that nothing else would happen. I was released on my signed agreement to attend therapy for two years.

Of course the footage was shown repeatedly on television. After the Jack Ruby murder of Oswald, sadly, my televised murder was not the first committed live before cameras but it was still sensational. The explanation that I had fabricated was uncritically accepted by the media, but not by Sara.

She said, 'You did it for me!'

She was right, but I would not burden her with it.

'Yes, momma, you had to save the world but you would, could, never kill. I hated him. So I killed him. Best leave it like that or your soul will get into trouble. Let's not talk about it.'

I did it for her. I did her job. I had saved the world.

We settled back to normality in the comfort of the palace in Geneva's international sector. After six weeks a letter arrived from Israel. I ripped open the envelope with horror and disbelief, having recognised the handwriting of my father. My legs gave way so I sat down.

Mt Sinai, 27th Day of Month 5, 5751

Dear Debora,

At six o'clock on Thursday evening, I will take the Therapeutae's substance and fall into a deep sleep. Thus I cannot tell the next part of the story first-hand, but my own council now want rid of their chief priest and mad scientist. 'Project Frankenstein' is their opportunity.

Whether or not the medical procedure will work at the first attempt I cannot tell. Either scientifically or by a messianic miracle. But we wanted Sara to participate for a number of reasons including the fact that it seemed right to show to the world a Lazarus miracle that would cause people to believe in her.

I will regain consciousness in the body of another, my own being hopelessly destroyed by a disease I recklessly risked passing to another body. His sister. Do I feel remorse? Define guilt. I did not create disease. But you killed me by your own hand. I know you are not my natural daughter but a miracle child. You are of my nurture.

I look forward so much to the gentle hands of my darling wife and to seeing your joyful smile.

I love you.

Michael.

I re-read the letter in a state of panic before being properly confused by the dual authorship. I was familiar with the handwriting of my step-father, though anything can be forged. And then I checked the date and told myself that Michael was confused . . . or the letter had been delayed. Or I was receiving my punishment as a criminal. Or, having advanced in the Inner Path to perfection, now I was suffering in agony at having taken a human life. In cold blood. Melini, Debora, the vegetarian, the one who signed petitions and went on demonstrations against cruelty to animals.

I double-checked the date from an entry in my diary. It was definitely written after my father's death. I couldn't phone anyone. Let me explain the confusion. The Essenes scrupulously use a solar calendar of 364 days as the decreed division of God's year; this is in accordance with the Book of Jubilees and the First book of Enoch, which were found within the Dead Sea Scrolls but were not accepted into our canon. Many people judge this use of the solar calendar to conveniently distance the sect from the outside misguided world including mainstream Jews whose calendar is lunar. The celebration of festivals is thus unsynchronised. For this reason, the creation, possession or use of a calendar of equivalents in the Modern Order of Essenes was a transgression in the category below raping a woman.

After a few days, I produced the accursed letter. It worried Sara. She informed me that she felt the guilt of both crimes. Father's crime was her fault for being a bad partner, in conventional terms, how shall she put it? Unfaithful?

As for my crime, She felt that I had been compelled to do it, therefore I, Debora, was not 'guilty,' having no freewill, and yet . . . (her eyes moistened but I forced it out of her mouth),

'You will not be anointed, Debora. The Lord is angry with you, too, and yet it had to be done. I asked Him to explain how He could be so unreasonable and the Teacher spoke. He said, *You regress to your human mind as a mother.* It is because you are in precedence time trap. No grasp. Not elevated. When you are gathered to your ancestors it will be Yashi – not Debora – who is anointed. Take him to Mt Sinai with Debora!'

I told Sara that I never had any wish to be the ruler-messiah after her but I felt that Yashi should have the chance to accept if the Lord chose to anoint him. And I agreed that for this reason we should live with the Essenes. They were dedicated people and I loved them very much.

They knew, every one of them, that I had been God's chosen instrument to kill their evil founder.

Chapter Eighty-Four

In September Sara and her convict-daughter left Geneva and went to live at Mt Sinai. This surprised people but the Essenes published a statement in three parts. First, condemning Robert F. Kohen as having stepped over the boundary of genius into madness. Second, although Kohen's surname indicated his priesthood by heredity, his election to chief was democratic, thus he had no automatic claim to be the priest-messiah. Third, the Community recognised Sara's status as ruler-messiah and also Yashi's succession. The Community needed her blessing and assistance to re-establish itself after the crisis.

Unlike its founder the Community just wanted to live in peace and be of service to humanity, thus, all ethical questions raised by Kohen's scientific inventions and unpublished papers would be safeguarded until consideration. The diplomatic, military and commercial value could be beyond imagination. This was a secret which gave MOE protection and power.

So, as I said, in September Yashi and I went to live with Sara in the Essene Community. By the Law of Israel, Yashi and I had automatic rights to claim full citizenship.

I soon realised why God had directed us there. The Community was happy. I received good therapy and recuperated from the past. Yashi learned to become a spiritual entity clothed in the human adventure.

Sara also began to feel better although maybe that was because, freed from control or supervision, she took drugs again. She had some visions and she gave dramatised readings from the Dead Sea Scrolls. She became the unchallenged informal leader of the small Community just as her rôle on the world stage had declined.

In this Garden of Eden, or Nirvana, my son grew strong. Time was in perfect harmony with the universe. The Essene's belief in the solar calendar and the regularity of the holy days seemed perfectly right. I began to feel the desire to ask to join the Community, to assist them in their goal of restoring Judaism to its pure Buddhist origins! As the daughter of a Jewess, I was Jewish in their eyes. Even though I had renounced my religion and embraced another, there is no excommunication procedure in Judaism – no way to get thrown out!

The only problem Sara and I could see on the horizon, now the war in Kuwait was over, was the renewed and increasing demand for her messianic pronouncement on the sovereignty between Arabs and Jews.

Chapter Eighty-Five

Late in the ninth month of the year, that is Kislev 5758, I was asked to assist the Messianic Intelligence Service to defeat an attempt by two Japanese men in Jerusalem who were trying to learn about Robert Kohen's secret technology. As the legatees of all his intellectual property, MOE had concealed them lawfully. We were very concerned about the dangers of these secrets falling into the wrong hands.

We discovered that one man, Mr Watanabe – who called himself 'Tommy' – had lived in Geneva with his wife since 1949 and their child had been born there in 1956. He ran a one-man business, an independent importer of electronic components. He settled in a small house in Switzerland (he said) so that his large overdraft was at Europe's lowest bank rate. Now he was a naturalised Swiss citizen speaking several languages. He appeared to be the link to a man he telephoned regularly in Tokyo – Mr Yamamuri.

Soon after the death of Robert Kohen – or rather after the murder – a certain Mr Ongaku had arrived in Jerusalem and had spent several weeks as a guest at Mt Sinai, researching the Dead Sea Scrolls, not normally a subject of prime concern to Japanese institutions of learning. Significantly, Ongaku was the youngest appointed Professor of Electronics at Kyoto, and like two of his brothers he was a Buddhist priest of high attainment.

MI felt certain that I could test the authenticity of Ongaku, although the security men were convinced that agents (especially Japanese) prepared themselves too well to be exposed by any westerner.

Messianic Intelligence admitted that they knew nothing about Buddhist priests and so I was asked to meet Mr Ongaku and discuss Semitic and Buddhist scriptures. The encounter took place in a small library, the Adi Levinson Room, on the second day of Av, the day before the Festival of the First Fruits of Wine (which mainstream Jews no longer observe).

Ongaku-san introduced himself with his spiritually-acquired name (which means joyful harmony). I realised at once that he was a high-born Buddhist priest – a Lama in the Tibetan and Mongolian tradition influenced heavily by Tantrism and Shamanism; to put it crudely, by sexual energy and by ancestor awareness. In 1949 he had been smuggled in great secrecy to Japan as a young boy escaping from the Chinese Communist occupation. Now in his early fifties, he was very handsome and I greatly esteemed him.

It transpired that his two friends were Mr Watanabe of Geneva (a thoroughly westernised and cheerful little man who kept talking about having just played golf at the Old Course at St. Andrews in Scotland), and 'the Tokyo agent,' Mr Yamamuri.

They were amazed that I spoke some Japanese and I performed their rituals for welcoming guests. Before too long, the barriers were completely dropped.

They were shocked by our fears.

'Oh no, Debora, we not spies in Dr Kohen's electronic sciences. We seek Yashi. Yashi Japanese name, you know – why else you call him? We know your mother care a lot about Japanese people. She very good person. Came to our land to understand and respect us. Her words are well known in our country.'

I looked at them and I smiled. Ongaku-san smiled to me.

'We come not for western technology. We three foolish men come to see Yashi, the new lama.'

Chapter Eighty-Six

MT SINAI, AUGUST 21, 1991

Yashi, my son, the next Lama, was brought from the nursery. He was in good humour despite being awakened by three men. Gifts were handed over. Japanese people never arrive empty-handed so, despite the cynics, I would say there was nothing sinister – no intended parody of the gospels. Tears fell from Ongaku. The hall was soon filled with curious people from the kibbutz.

Ongaku was now weeping violently. Hiding himself in the corner, comforted by his two companions, he could not hold his glance at my son for long. I was afraid to let him near Yashi.

Momma arrived with some leaders of our Community.

Ongaku, the most vital and uninhibited of the three men, and Sara were humans of divine radiance. They immediately gravitated together and paired off. Their charismatic auras had joined and their spontaneous joy was felt by everyone present. Like intense electricity in the air, it was something portentous. The auric energy was so intense that at the moment the two leaders embraced, we felt something like a mild electric shock and Yashi cried. This was really spooky. I took the infant to sleep in my own room in the single mothers' suite that was nearby. Sara had a palatial suite of rooms in the main building, which, of course, I unofficially lived in – rank has its privileges! When Yashi settled I returned to the meeting.

Momma was in the arms of Ongaku, and her face was flushed with tears.

I ran to her. Ongaku grabbed my arm forcefully to lock the three of us in embrace.

He was grasping a photo of Yashi.

Sara found gaps in her wailing to explain to me, 'It is . . . his grandson, my darling Debora, your little prince is his grandson.'

Chapter Eighty-Seven

Sara suggested that Yashi should live in Japan when he was aged sixteen. *Was that okay with me?*

I did not hear her. I was in a state of shock:

'Momma, talk about *me*. Who am *I*? This man is my biological father?'

'Debora, it is not from shame that our secret should be concealed. I myself said, long before I understood the meaning, *'We are born from an unbroken line of virgins.'* You conceived by the Holy Spirit, and you were conceived thus, and yet even you don't understand. Perhaps even you called me promiscuous?'

I looked in the mirror and realised that perhaps my slight oriental features were not Jewish but . . . *Tibetan*? Mr Ongaku did not look very Asian and I could not believe he was my father.

'But what about Michael? I thought that the one thing the two of you had was amazing chemistry?'

'Debora, I don't know what led me to Japan in November 1978. I went with Michael to find Paul, but Paul was going to return soon to London. I was totally unaware of the shopping list. As soon as I fulfilled one destiny, I tore up another set of air tickets knowing there was something else. Fate beckoned, I obeyed. Michael freaked out. Mr Ongaku was near Hiroshima and he still thinks of the corpses when he sees black charred dust.'

Ongaku whined with tears in his eyes, which in turn made Sara talk about God still seeing the Great Light in the Sky of the Mushroom Cloud. Most of the time it was in Japanese, hushed tones between interpreters, and as there was no record the exchange was lost to me. But we knew that they talked about weapons and the evil forces already unleashed by a criminal humanity.

My true father gently gripped my arm and said to me that the world could no longer be left to a destiny of dictators and nominal-democracies. Then he asked to speak to Sara alone, 'about the meeting of east and west in supreme authority.' She agreed and asked everyone but me to leave but to pray for them. It was to be some sort of spiritual world summit.

I stayed with Yashi in Sara's room where I retrieved Michael's journal. November 1978 in the Tokyo Palace Hotel. I thumb through the pages where, once again, mother declines to leave Japan.

Sara threw on a white tee shirt and denims. No bra. She never travelled so casually dressed. 'Aren't you going to pack your things?' I asked. She had paid for the replacement tickets. They were full-priced and transferable, but I had things to do in London. 'I'm going out for a walk on my own. Please, Michael. I want to stay in Japan. There's something I have to do. Something undone. I don't even know what it is yet.'

I turn to my mother's diaries – keeping notes was something they had in common. In fact I know that Michael spied on hers, so had he missed her quote, or its meaning? When she quoted from the Bible he skipped it as meaningless.

'22nd November 1978. It's in English. Oh my God, she was so honest and insightful.' I utter the profanity under my breath to myself as I read out loud Sara's floral scrawl, spidery yet so clear.

On my bed, at night, I sought him whom my heart loves.
I sought him but did not find him.
So I will rise and go through the City:
'Have you seen him whom my heart loves?'

Yashi whimpers a little but he is not hungry. I take from the bookcase a Bible Concordance and her well-thumbed *La Bible de Jérusalem*. I find what I am looking for.

Had she written Chapter 3 Verses 1-4 of *The Song of Songs* from memory or copied it down? I know it was copied, because it was letter-perfect from The Jerusalem Bible (1966) – I checked it first – a part of her was always a good Catholic, and a French Catholic at that! I look again at the words in Sara's journal.

Scarcely had I passed them when I found him whom my heart loves.
I held him fast, nor would I let him go till I had brought him
Into my mother's house, into the room of her who conceived me.

I put back the Bible and thought about its chief editor, the astonishing man who headed the International Dead Sea Scroll translation project for so many years. What had the imperious Père Roland de Vaux – a Domican monk – made of the sexually-charged *Song of Solomon*? In the above text, he had only 'edited' the true meaning of innocent intercourse that his church confused with celibacy and virginity.

And here I was as living proof. Born of a line of *broken* virgins, a dynastic alliance, or something like that.

I was called into the conference on account of my linguistic skills. Eifat Cina took care of Yashi.

The two mahatmas and I spoke together for an hour. Mostly French and English were used as we were alone and Momma speak no Jap beyond half a dozen words that I taught her. Then she asked me to bring Yashi.

In the plain hall food and drink was served. It was excessively hot and humid but the Essenes were becoming very friendly with Watanabe and Yamamuri – two cheerful characters who laughed a lot about being taken for spies. Holding Sara's hand Ongaku emerged from the summit talk. His face – once flushed with tears – was now radiant. Sara approached me slowly but I ran up to hug her. I reassured her.

'Momma, just allow me a little time to adjust and I'll love Ongaku, but my mindset is so bourgeois and conventional. I still haven't learned to open my mind.'

The Japanese asked to stay to observe the Essene celebration of the festival which would commence that evening. While their guest rooms were prepared, I'm sure they were unaware of the consternation behind the scenes: the Constitution of the Order strictly excluded gentiles or even ritually unobservant Jews. To westerners, including American Jews, the sharing of religions – beyond mere tolerance – is abnormal. I explained to the Essenes that in the east, religions are not understood as excluding other truths or systems. The Japanese were seen as very intrusive in their request to attend the meal, but Sara told them angrily that this was a Spiritual Summit – reconciliation between east and west.

At first I had no reason to believe that anything would come of the Summit Meeting. I began to feel the cynics' charge, that Momma was a false messiah because their criticism – that she would fail to leave peace on earth – might be validated. Then I began to see a new wave: the meeting of saintly minds, east and west, might conceivably influence people in a way that eluded their political leaders. It was happening here. The most narrow minds and fundamentalist Brooklyn black-hats listened to Sara and understood.

The talk turned to the threat from the Arabs. I broke out in a cold sweat. The worst test was yet to come. With the Gulf War over, I knew She had to proclaim unequivocally over the sovereignty of Jerusalem or forfeit all credibility as modern *messiah* – a title acknowledged by Tanakh, Bible, and Koran (although interpreted very differently, of course).

Pressures were mounting on all sides. I was convinced we were going to have to flee from this place before an assassin would be given hashish and gun. Even the western newspapers had printed that Sara had agreed to make judgement on the Arab-Israeli conflict. Hopefully not today.

At the communal meal in the evening (which marks the start of a new day) we broke bread and I asked what had passed between the two world pilots, because they were both apparently elated. Sara said that I must wait until the end of the meal and then ask her publicly before the whole assembly.

'We are,' she announced, 'now under a bridge across the Holy Land joining Europe to Asia. It is the obligation of all advanced nations and enlightened individuals to bring joy to all mankind and to develop a permanent peace plan. As an innocent boy Ongaku-san thought the Great Light in the Sky was a miracle, then He discovered that it was the Angel of Death inflicting the punishment for the Japanese militarism.'

At this point my true father emitted a most chilling whine.

She continued, 'It was the beginning of the decline of imperial authority. Then He saw the west as the source of discipline and peace. But the west itself is lost in chaos.'

I asked her in public, 'Are you also saying we will soon recover our powers of extra-sensory perception?'

'*Yes*,' she said, 'But that is only the moralistic way of seeing the beginning of a reverse of evolution. Mankind is still degenerating, gradually losing all powers of perception and life energy, including the discernment of good and evil. By halting time, the disgraced High priest of this sacred community has interfered with the whole progress of divine evolution.'

After the meal she said she had to mingle with the others, and she left me.

The celebrants left the tables and dispersed to the dormitories. There was no dancing or socialising in order to prepare the festivities starting early the following morning. We all felt quite elated by the holiday and by the east-west summit.

Momma knew I needed to cling to her, and she came back. I asked her, 'Did you know the cameras would be here?'

'I didn't invite them. And this isn't a special festival; it may be synchronicity not conspiracy. But I thank God for assembling them here in this very significant summit at Sinai.'

'What are you going to do, now? About the judgement of Solomon?'

'Nothing.' said Sara, and she was quite positive.

I had to think about her response but I laughed as I knew exactly what she meant and she rose even higher in my estimation of her authenticity.

Only a true Buddhist knows that in a crisis it is best to do nothing.

Chapter Eighty-Eight

The Israeli Defence Forces were demobilising after their inaction in the Gulf War. We had suffered only very minor casualties from some Scud missiles. I was grateful that Sara was going to do nothing. I needed some tranquillity. I had suffered enough shocks. Then I met Ari. Formerly a Colonel in the Army, his left leg and self-esteem had been shattered by a land-mine in the South Lebanon where he tracked down some of the most fanatical terrorists, those who trained in the camps of Hisb'allah, *the Party of God*.

Ari helped me take care of Yashi who really loved his new dad.

I warned him about falling in love with a member of the Davidic Family but he said he was wounded below the belt, not in his brain.

'Debora, my darling, I fear Sara will need more than divine guidance to manage the little problem of allocating the Holy Land. But we are Israelis, and we do not run away from our land.'

Chapter Eighty-Nine

I found comfort in conforming and felt settled in the spiritual retreat that was Mt Sinai. With Ari, I had returned full circle to my Jewish upbringing. I was putting down roots in part because I anticipated that Sara would not grow old gracefully here – if anywhere.

My wild spirit liked Israel's non-European lifestyle and the Essene's pure and joyful brand of Judaism. I took the classes and desired to attain their higher levels of spiritual accomplishment. But nobody was admitted to membership of the Order until the age of thirty, and women were suppressed. Nobody except Sara was above the limitations of rank attained within the sect. She encouraged me to hang my hat here, partly because Yashi required intensive religious instruction.

One day Sara said, 'Debora, listen, The Messiah belongs to the world, not to this Commune nor to any other spiritual hothouse; nor even to you, his mum. When he attains sixteen Yashi will not be yours as you wee no longer mine; you will be free. Now I am free; my work here is finished.'

'And then what?'

'We shall see. You must make peace in your head before preaching it to your village, and in your nation before preaching to the world. I must attain purity before I proclaim on the land problem that is Palestine.'

'Momma. I love you, very much,' and we hugged. *What was she telling me?*

At the Festival of Passover she made a speech to the community banquet. No-one took her seriously. At least no-one discussed her words.

All I did was write them down. She asked everyone to be silent and stop eating and drinking and listen.

'As the war of smart missiles rages, we live at the eye of the storm, the City of Peace, and I have undertaken the burden to deliver judgement between the children of Abraham without fear or favour. Is it not written, *Writhe, cry out Daughter of Zion like a woman in labour, for now you must leave the city and camp in the open country?*'

So I know that Sara wants me to stay here but she must leave Yashi and me. What I don't know is when . . . and why.

Chapter Ninety

MT SINAI, AUGUST 21, 1991

I awake in the morning with a menacing precognition.

You can't escape news in this land. In Israel the radios blare out in every public place: in the Kibbutz common rooms, the buses, and the market places. In the streets your neighbours' transistors force-feed news, music, and more news. It is hardly surprising in a small nation continuously at war.

Today, according to my radio, the IDF are pulling out of Ramala, leaving security to Arafat's Palestinians under the first phase of the Peace Agreement. *What Peace Agreement?* Is this a sick joke? The radio says it is December 1995. My heart pounds. I look out to the fields, it is the Passover and the crop is unharvested.

Outside my room I meet people talking about the ultimatum to Saddam expiring today. '21st August, Debora, how could you forget?'

The calendar in the office is August 1991.

I recognise once again the feelings of deep terror I had experienced with Kohen's tampering with time. I feel his presence. I am waiting to perceive the time warp like he felt my bullet. I stir myself. The sun is in the sky. Yashi is happy. I will go and see if Sara is okay, but what I find instead is the end of an era. It is the end of the Second Coming.

I find Ari in the corridor and he sees immediately that I am white and trembling. It troubles him because I am carrying his child. At present only he and Sara know this.

I ring Sara's room.

A woman answers and rants like a lunatic.

'She's gone. Do you know that last night Mr Epstein was playing *Wagner,* at 2am in the morning on his broken down piano? He said it was transcribed by Liszt who was ordained as a priest . . . so does that make it okay?'

'Oh, please shut up! What do you mean, *She's gone?*'

I feel my face drain of blood. My stomach turns, and my throat smells vomit. I am barely able to avoid screaming which would have scared Yashi.

'I mean she had her coffee at 5am and left with Sam Levi to collect the provisions. She left a letter here for you.'

I replace the phone and forget about Ari and Yashi. I am running faster than my legs want to carry me.

My eyes skim over the letter faster than they want to; I am concerned only to learn where she is going.

27th Day of Fifth Month of 5751 from Creation
(Calendar of the Book of Jubilees)

To My Darling Daughter,
I do not belong to this community of essenouai now that my task is finished and the sins of their founder are over the horizon. Must go where no-one can follow. Be happy. Kiss Yashi for me every day, and as for that lovely man Ari, kiss him for yourself. I love you. I think you are the best friend I ever had, and you will understand more than anyone else what must be done . . .

I read no more. I run outside looking for her. Ari cannot give chase, thanks to his injury, but he can shout very loudly, 'You'll have a miscarriage, woman.' I am extremely vulgar to him; I almost tell him that he means nothing to me.

Dropping his crutch, he shakes his fist, 'You Israeli women are like these Cacti, the Sabra, hard and prickly on the outside, but soft inside. You are now a true Israeli woman.'

But I am not listening. I am running.

I love you, momma, I love you so much. I see, I see – Messiah was a man's job. It broke you. To hell with my Zen mental discipline – I go to pieces.

So, my Buddhism is skin deep. I can't control my grief. I say nothing. I just want her back. I take the Egged bus to Jerusalem following the route of Sam's lorry.

I wonder what can she proclaim? Three thousand years ago the city was founded by David, revered by the Jews; it is central to our government and we never accepted expulsion by the Romans. Repeatedly our enemies captured the city in envy and caused damage and desecration. *We* never damaged our brothers' religious sites that offended *us*. *We* never denied access to Moslem or Christian worshippers or tourists.

On the bus I concentrate on Israel Radio hoping I might learn the correct date and the movements of my celebrity mother. Outside the kibbutz it is 1995 and by nine o'clock Sara had arrived at the Territories. (In Israel we don't use the word 'Occupied'). She is interrogated by Israeli border guards who, like me, have guessed her motives and they question her loyalties. She argues in Hebrew to the microphone and to the officer in charge.

'I came on *aliyah*,' that is *I arose*, meaning that as a Jewess she came home, 'but now I must rise up *again*. You are a soldier of Abraham's people but you forget that the sons of Ishmael are your cousins.'

The Israeli officer turns and orders the female soldiers to escort Sara back. He is a border controller, not a politician.

TV cameras and reporters join Israel Radio and the confrontation is menacing. Instructions to detain her arrive from the Defence Forces. Suddenly Sara wriggles loose and, still grasping her suitcase, she turns round and shouts to the Israelis, 'Father forgive them; they know not what they do.'

Then she runs across the border, hoping that she will not be shot except by cameras. She runs as fast as her burden of a suitcase permits. The camera crews are ordered to remain on this side and we lose sight of her. I have arrived just too late. It takes the six soldiers to restrain me, the seventh screams abuse against the camera crew. I find myself locked up in a small room belonging to the military border patrol.

* * *

Sara ceases running as she sees the first Palestinian settlement. The dwellings are broken-down and dirty. She is a fish out of water, dressed in the high style of the fashionable west: white tee shirt, Levi denims, Cartier shades, and Chanel leather bag. She looks so young and stunning. The villagers see another charity do-gooder but Sara has no food parcels, no medicines, just a suitcase which is searched by an armed welcoming committee.

The unkempt and unshaven men had initially been curious, but now they are brandishing weapons and grouping to block her way. Perhaps they know who she is. If she feels unsafe she shows no fear of them. She shouts beyond them into the village.

'We are the cousins of Ibrahim. We are not your enemies. It is the politicians and kings who lie to us. DO YOURS COME HERE? I have authority over all these leaders. I have sovereignty over the City of David. If you will let me stay as your friend we will make peace. I have American dollars to pay if any family has a little space and I can buy food for myself.'

There is no response although She is offering them Jerusalem and American dollars. She keeps repeating her message. She will not go away. No-one knows what to do until three women arrive and order the men to leave the stranger. The Palestinians discuss the matter and eventually tell Sara to wait.

By the time the Jordanian film crew arrives to film the events, Sara has gone.

'She is staying at another village with some women until the men make up their minds.' But the crews also have ten-dollar bills and they find her quickly enough. Before long she has delegations of Palestinians who want to speak to her: from groups of curious children, to representatives of the indigenous and international organisations, PLO, Red Crescent, militias, the local mayor's office, reporters, and suspicious women from the In'ash al-'Usra Society. They all want to talk.

Representatives of her own Messianic Organisation arriving in panic, are relegated to the end of the line so they will never reach her.

Perhaps it was to God, Allah, the Global Media, or to the sky that she mutters.

'In a few days, or weeks, you will all go away and leave me here. I shall not leave this run-down place until there is peace with dignity. If this town is good enough for our cousins then it is good enough for me. Yes, I am made of the stuff of dreams and that makes me of the spirit of Allah and of the Prophets and I shall never die. But are these people different? I think not. If you do not respect human dignity, then I tell you, you are in a worse prison than them because your own mind is the smallest prison. It is suffering that has hardened your hearts, and made walls out of time and space. Thus you cannot see the walls are built of political bricks and politics are lies.'

Over the next few days Sara walks through villages, stopping, healing, and talking.

'Those to whom evil is done do evil in return. The children of Ibrahim are all blind for we believe in an eye for an eye; and we are condemned to the eternal cycle of ten thousand years until the first one stands up and sees the light, and then his comrades will shoot him dead. And the second will stand and be shot, and then more and more until – at last – that will be the end of the dying. People will say, *'This is enough. I have found peace.'* Does anyone understand what I am saying? I am the second. I am the second.'

After these words, which are captured by film crews, Sara remains silent for several days. She speaks to nobody from the west but learns the language of the Palestinians. Of course she gets by because she is gentle despite her power and poses no threat. While the PLO men hold meetings about her, the women protect her and the children play with her. She walks though the villages, talks with the women, and kisses their children.

The cameras love it.

In Amman it is rumoured that she was granted a royal audience with King Hussein. I am not aware of what was discussed but I imagine it was an attempt to achieve peace by diplomacy. I can reveal one secret thanks to a letter sent to me at UNWRA in Geneva. It was from Sara, the student of archaeology. In Amman, she had been introduced to a local archaeologist and become the first Jewish scholar to see the Copper Scroll.

In her letter Sara told me that the Copper Scroll was corroding and yet it was the enduring treasure. She said that it repeatedly expressed, 'Here is the key,' which she believed meant a code, or inner meaning of the message. She wrote to me.

While men are divided crime exists and their treasure is lost. The scrolls return to the earth. The Copper Scroll is crumbling to dust, Debora, already beyond any hope of salvation. I feel now that the Essene Scrolls were a time capsule whose wisdom could be recovered only through a narrow window, but, alas, humanity has missed it.

She also mentioned some Dead Sea Scrolls that Arabs had withheld, not to punish the Jews, but to gain by speculation in prices. But for sentimental reasons I cherish the letters Sara sent me every day, post-marked from the refugee villages and camps of Bethlehem, Beit-Jala, Beit Sahur, Jericho, Ramala, al-Birah, Birzeit, Nablus, Jenin, Tulkarm, Hebron, Halhul, and Dura.

Day after day, she led the world's cameras through the misery of 'Palestine's political pawns, disowned by both sides of the Semitic fault-line,' but publicly she would not discuss politics or attribute blame. That was the source of the saying, *'Politics can't even fix a drain, here.'*

There are several filmed versions of Sara preaching to men and women in terrorist training camps on the West Bank and in Lebanon. She won over a few 'hearts and minds' to non-violence.

'Learning to hurt the enemy is the betrayal of your own leaders' fear and error. Setting out to defend is noble. In America we possessed the most powerful weapons in quantities beyond dreams, yet our leaders and people, having learned that they did not make them secure, built more and more of the useless things. Their future president would never believe that Love, hearts and minds, is the most powerful military weapon, so no-one will, and that is why I, sovereign of Jerusalem, must now demonstrate. Words will not suffice. Alas for me, it is too late. I must die. I have to teach by example. I will never ask people to do what they do not wish to do.'

The health experts, knowing that she was used to Swiss levels of hygiene predicted that she would catch something, and soon she was standing outside a clinic. Her infection stopped her from kissing the children. Her complexion was dirty and ruined with lumps and boils that were broadcast worldwide by satellite.

She was committing suicide.

Those who said it was deicide were right. They saw what I could see.

She was winning peace for the Middle East in the only way possible in this land: *another sacrifice.*

And yet her opponents still mocked her, describing it as her greatest acting rôle. The Israeli right wing was venomous. Described her as a European liberal, a religious fraud, an enemy of Israel, deceiver, manipulator, legal immigrant, and whore.

Admittedly here was something tragic but ridiculous. The fading European designer clothes and the conditions of decay. More films being made with more crews and more cameras than in her Hollywood days. But which actress would agree to die in front of cameras? Even for love? It was not love of a man, but love of humanity, a super-Wagnerian death-in-love ending.

Mine was the second murder seen live on a newsreel – Jack Ruby had beaten me – but this was the first crucifixion on film; live from Golgotha.

Oh yes, *She* – and in my writing I now awarded Her the capital letter – sweated to death more slowly than the agony of the cross. She was scorched in the sun, confused by fever. Not talking about, not even portraying, but *becoming* the victims of man's inhumanities across eternity.

As her fever gripped, She was babbling religiose, grotesque things – accusing, confusing, and mixing episodes of history.

Holding Ari's hand four days after I lost his child, I watched Sara on satellite TV, from the foot of the cross so to speak. As a daughter, I still wanted to run and grab her back. As a believer, I just had to weep. I could not interfere. Did she know that I suffered more than she did? She was going delirious, but I was still sane. I prayed only that She had drugs to soften her pain. For most of the time she spoke but could not be understood.

'Her best part, yet,' declared many cynics. 'She is acting consummately, using her artistry to express to gaping soulless humans the truth, performing to the cameras, conscious of the global media.'

Her tongue formed some of her last breath into the most grotesque utterances. Capitalised names indicting humanity, some names unrecognisable, many all too unutterable: Masada, Montségur, Inquisition, Crusades,Pogroms, Holocaust, Hiroshima, Jihad, Nagasaki; and she spoke some lines from the religious films she had played and seen. She sang her favourite, *I Don't Know How to Love Him*, from *Superstar*, smiling serenely.

She quoted her most famous line when she played the nun, *'Compassion is a strength, not a weakness.'*

'The present,' Robert Kohen wrote, 'is where time touches eternity.'

Sara was touching eternity.

Like a rose that was fading, She was between life and death.

The Dead Sea is the lowest point on this planet, the final destination of the River Jordan, which name actually means going down. Under this sun our forefather Jesus surrenders himself to the authorities only a few miles to the west of this place!

This is also the wilderness that the ghost of Elijah still haunts, and where the Baptiser John will still be arrested each moment and put to death for inventing repentance and announcing the One who is about to come.

Here too, the Teacher of Righteousness, harbinger of two Messianic Ages, was expelled by corrupt Temple Priests from the Jewish capital. He still leads the elect of the Chosen, the saintly people we call the Essenes. We are the only people remaining true to Abraham and Moses, an Israel in miniature, a seed group protected. Womb of the world to come, nurturer of a small man of great light.

Right outside the commune, at earth's most arid, dark hovel, the religious and cartological centre of the world, is a place hidden and neglected.

A spiritual black hole. It is the place of three skulls, the greatest secret in the world.

In Ramala, angry people are tearing down posters of Arafat, denouncing him as a traitor to the Palestinian people – instigator of a so-called peace without any justice.

Inside the hospital a stranger incongruously dressed in a white raincoat wanders into Sara's private ward. He sits by her bed and whispers, now she has won, he begs her, 'Go home of your own free will.'

Because of her, he pleads, the Israeli government has recognised the PLO, and they have signed the Peace Process granting Palestinian autonomy in the west bank, Jericho, and Gaza.

She tries to compose a reply to 'Michael.' But for most of the time she just stares with hollow eyes into infinity.

A Druse doctor begs the stranger to leave his patient.

'Mr Michael, she is much too ill to hear you, or understand what is happening in politics. We have sedated her. She doesn't even know where she is, sir, or who you are. She imagines herself entirely in the past.'

The doctor, still calling him Michael, offers him coffee. He sees that his patient knows the stranger and agrees that perhaps he can help her. The doctor relaxes and kindlysuggests, 'Mr Michael, you tell her that we have heard that Yasser Arafat was at Norway. Tell her there is peace coming here. She talks all the time about peace.'

The intruder turns to Sara, kneels by her bed, and whispers.

'Tell Debora, *the one she loathed was the one who saved Israel*. Saddam had his finger on the button, he used the war to destroy Tel Aviv, and he became the leader of the Islamic world. But I intervened, I changed history, I communicated back ten years and on June 24, 1981 the CIA had our boys take out Baghdad's uranium generator. You won't remember the IDF Phantom F-4's armed with America's first Smart Missiles. Sure, I left a time-crease at August 21, 1991, but I saved the world, all except you.

'You still believe in the brotherhood of our jealous cousins. Look at their primitive medicine, and it's all western. You're already dead and forgotten, Sara. I will write you out of history.'

He begins to laugh. Doctors and nurses are assembling to persuade this crank to leave. They tug at his arms and shoulders. He screams.

'You could lift humanity to its next plateau but you persist with the moralisation. Listen Sara, primitive man perceived nature gods, then the Greeks their anthropomorphic muses, then the Hebrew's Lord of Hosts, then the Christian Father in Heaven. The Tetragrammaton implies the ultimate. The Mohammedans will set us back if they kill and maim in the name of Allah the Merciful.'

The doctor cannot remove the intruder and sends for help.

The intruder shouts.

'Don't you understand me, woman? Substitute the word Time for God, and then you can understand how God is seeing but invisible, passive but powerful, not living and yet eternal. *In the beginning was Time.*'

It is impossible to shout and to hear at the same time.

'Robert,' she had said, 'My work is done. May God have mercy on your soul.'

Epilogue

Before we laid my mother to rest in London I flew to Paris with Paul.

It was his idea. He hired a yellow Citröen and drove me in total silence to find the childhood home he had shared with Sarah-Hélène. I braced myself for something significant but knew better than to ask. When we reached the village he took a small road which led to the overgrown ruins of a long-abandoned stone farmhouse. It was not located near Marseilles, as Michael had said, but 20km to the south west of Carcassonne.

Paul wept when he saw its dilapidation. Nature reclaiming its wilderness from the domestication of man. I could not drag him out of the car; nor a word of explanation from his mouth. I realised that it was more than the state of the house that distressed my uncle so I left him alone.

I got out of the car and found behind the house a terraced rockery cascading from a massive stonewall. What the experts declared impossible was here to be seen. All around were the little blue Jerusalem cliff-plants – Golden Henbane – which the books and botanists told Sara could not grow in Europe.

She had told me of the complex pharmaceutical cocktails which different species of Henbane yield: how great is expertise to separate them and even distinguish between many species of Henbane. *The ancients knew much more than us,* she said, *unless, maybe the knowledge was still preserved in secret.*

I returned to the car, and before I could close the door, I had told Paul about the Golden Henbane and its significance.

He talked over me.

'The active ingredient,' he said calmly, 'is scopolamine. It causes delirium. It is used medically to counteract the effect of acetylcholine, a neural transmitter.'

'And,' I said, trying to emulate his genius, 'it grows at the foot of the Tree of Knowledge at the centre of the Garden of Eden. Ingest and, zap! You are Time. You are God. You are each other. All is one.'

I savoured this strange feeling of dignity of my family; my Buddhist training had left a little splinter of pride which had expanded into a beam. I felt so close to Paul, and I said, 'Funny how the male has such a protruding Adam's Apple.'

Thinking that he was French-born I explained the expression.

'Your thyroid cartilage is protruding too much, *mon oncle*.'

Paul smiled at me, but in his moist eyes I saw sadness and suffering. And guilt and enlightenment.

'She died in my place. She had the courage.'

I hesitated and then said unhelpfully, 'Maybe she wanted to.'

He closed the car door and as we set off I heard him reply.

'No, it was her destiny.

The Holy Bloodline Novels
INVESTIGATIVE FICTION

Moonlit Messiah (1997)

The forerunner of today's bestselling genre of Grail thrillers.
Depicts the unknown wife of Jesus and the prominence of women in the early Church.

An English journalist deciphering the clues in the Church of Rennes-le-Château discovers Sara, a survivor in the Davidic line, known to a secret society.

The Joseph Secret (2007)
GENERATION TWO

Debora, the daughter of Sara, has four days to find the Templars' secret: the true identity of the man who died on the cross.

Set against a number of archaeological discoveries in 2002 including the translation of the gospel of Judas, condemned by history because he alone knew the secret of the man who died on the cross.

Einstein's Violin (scheduled for 2009/10)
MAN PEERING INTO THE MIND OF GOD

The sacred and sexual teachings of Jesus implicit in the lost gospels.
THE GREATEST SECRET THE CHURCH SUPPRESSED.

The grandson of Sara reaches maturity in a dark, concrete cell in Beirut, bound by an iron mask and chains.

Experiencing the reality of the space-time continuum, he learns about the complicity of the western Establishment and of a secret teaching of Jesus: sacred sexuality in the ancient world torn between depravity and discipline.

For the full story visit the author website:
www.jacklawson.com